MUSICAL RESOURCES FOR THE REVISED COMMON LECTIONARY

compiled by
ARTHUR WENK

The Scarecrow Press, Inc.
Metuchen, N.J., & London
1994

British Library Cataloguing-in-Publication data available

Library of Congress Cataloging-in-Publication Data

Wenk, Arthur, 1943-
    Musical resources for the Revised common lectionary /
compiled by Arthur Wenk
        p.   cm.
    ISBN 0-8108-2909-6
    1. Organ music--Bibliography. 2. Hymns--Bibliography.
3. Anthems--Bibliography. 4. Revised common lectionary
(1992) I. Title.
ML 128.P7W46 1994
264' .2--dc20   94-11481

For Adriana

Table of Contents

Acknowledgements

I should like to thank Dr. Giles Bryant, Director of Music at St. James Anglican Cathedral in Toronto and Past President of the Royal Canadian College of Organists, and Dr. Fred Graham, Worship Consultant for the United Church of Canada, for their suggestions in establishing the format of this work. I am grateful to Lydia Pederson, Music Director at Royal York United Church, and Catherine Palmer, Music Director at Yorkminster Park Baptist Church, for furnishing me with copies of their choral library lists. I especially appreciate the efforts of Giles Bryant, Fred Graham and Vernon Gotwals, who read different parts of the manuscript and made suggestions for its improvement.

I would welcome any comments from those using this work on ways to make it more useful.

Preface

One can imagine an ideal worship service whose individual elements fit together in such a way that the whole is greater than the sum of the parts. The musical elements (organ music, choral music, and hymns) as well as the sermon and prayers would harmonize with the scriptural lessons to form a cohesive worship experience. The adoption of a lectionary not only permits the advance planning necessary to achieve such an integration of worship elements but makes possible two additional unifying aspects: the relationships among the lessons for a given day and the ordering of individual days within the cycles of the liturgical year.

Musical Resources for the Revised Common Lectionary offers assistance to ministers, organists and choirmasters interested in selecting hymns, organ music and choral music appropriate to the lessons appointed for worship. This handbook has been conceived in terms of a specific calendar of readings but may be usefully employed wherever musical choices are to be based on scriptural references.

In contrast with other published handbooks which freely associate anthems with scriptural readings, *Musical Resources for the Revised Common Lectionary* connects anthems with biblical citations only when the anthem is an actual musical setting of the scriptural text. All other anthems are listed either by season or for general use.

The book comprises five main sections:

I. Music for the Church Year: suggested hymns, organ music and anthems for each Sunday and major feast in the three-year cycle.

II. A Scriptural Index of Hymn Texts: a compilation, drawn from a number of hymnals in current use in North American churches, arranged in biblical order.

III. An Index of Hymn Preludes: a compilation of chorale and hymn preludes, published individually or in series, arranged by hymn tune.

IV. A Scriptural Index of Anthems: a selection of choral music, listing composer, distribution of voices, and publisher, arranged in biblical order.

V. Appendices: organ works cited, choral works cited.

A detailed introduction appears at the beginning of each section.

Abbreviations

45	Choralvorspiele alter Meister (C.F.Peters)
80	Eighty Chorale Preludes (C.F.Peters)
AC1	Anthems for Choirs 1 (Oxford University Press)
AC4	Anthems for Choirs 4 (Oxford University Press)
ADW	Alte Deutsche Weihnachtsmusik (Nagels Verlag)
AGCS	All God's Children Sing (Wood Lake Books)
AI	Alleluia, I Will Sing (Augsburg Publishing House 11-5115)
AM2	Anthems for Men's Voices, Vol.2 (Oxford University Press)
AT1	Beck, Seven Anthems for Treble Voices (Concordia 97-5218)
AT2	Beck, Seven Anthems for Treble Choirs, Set 2 (Concordia 97-5163)
AWK	Alte Weihnachtsmusik für Klavier (Bärenreiter)
B18	Bach, Die Orgelchoräle aus der Leipziger Originalhandschrift NBA IV/2 (Bärenreiter)
BC	Buxtehude, Sämtliche Orgelwerke, Choralbearbeitungen (Breitkopf & Härtel)
BC1	Anniversary Collection of Bach Chorales (Schmitt, Hall and McCreary)
BC2	A Second Book of Bach Chorales (Schmitt, Hall and McCreary)
BCL	Bach, Dritter Teil der Klavierübung, NBA IV/4 (Bärenreiter)
BE	Brahms, Eleven Chorale Preludes (C.F.Peters)
BK	Bender, Kleine Choralvorspiele, 3 vols. (Bärenreiter)
BN	Bach, Organ Chorales from the Neumeister Collection (Bärenreiter)
BO	Bach, Orgelbüchlein, NBA IV/1 (Bärenreiter)

FVW	Festal Voluntaries: Ascension, Whitsun and Trinity (Novello)
GB	The SAB Choir Goes for Baroque (Concordia 97-5232)
GG	Choralvorspiele für den Gottesdienstlichen Gebrauch, 4 vols.
GH	The Green Hill Junior Choir and Duet Book (E.C.Schirmer 1546)
GRV	Graveyard Gems (St. Mary's Press)
GT	Church Organist's Golden Treasury, 3 vols. (Theodore Presser)
HB	The Hymn Book of the Anglican Church of Canada and the United Church of Canada, 1971
HC	Handel, Collection of Anthems arr. by Hal Hopson (Choristers Guild GCC-10)
HE	Held, Six Preludes on Easter Hymns (Concordia)
HOR	Historic Organ Recitals (G.Schirmer)
HP	Hymn Prelude Series, 42 vols. (Concordia)
HPC	Hymn Preludes for Holy Communion (Concordia)
HPP	Held, Hymn Preludes for the Pentecost Season (Concordia)
HS	Hanff, Sieben Choralbearbeitungen (Breitkopf & Härtel)
HT	Hymns for Today's Church; Toronto: Hodder and Stoughton, 1982.
HU	The Hymnal of the United Church of Christ; Philadelphia: United Church Press, 1974
HV	A Book of Hymn Tunes Voluntaries (Oxford University Press)
JF	Jackson, Five Preludes on English Hymn Tunes (Banks Music Publications)
JS	Joyful Sounds (Concordia)
K	Kloppers, 3 Plainsong Settings (Concordia)
LA	Langlais, Three Short Anthems (Hinshaw Music HMC-423)
LC	Lebegue, Complete Organ Works, Vol.3 (Belwin Mills)
LF	Lenel, Four Organ Chorales (Concordia)
LH	Leighton, Six Fantasies on Hymn Tunes for Organ
LO	Langlais, American Folk-Hymn Settings for Organ (H.T. FitzSimons)
LP	Living Praise, London: Marshall, Morgan & Scott, 1983
LS	Lübeck, Sämtliche Orgelwerke (Breitkopf & Härtel)

LW	Lutheran Worship (Concordia)
MA1	Mozart Anthem Book I (Concordia 97-5230)
MA2	Mozart Anthem Book II (Concordia 97-5275)
MC	Marpurg, Twenty-One Chorale Preludes (Augsburg)
MH	The Methodist Hymnal, Nashville, Tennessee: The Methodist Publishing House, 1964.
MJ	Make a Joyful Noise (Concordia 97-4684)
MS1	The Morning Star Choir Book (Concordia 97-4702)
MS2	A Second Morning Star Choir Book (Concordia 97-4703)
MS3	A Third Morning Star Choir Book (Concordia 97-4972)
NT	Now Thank We All Our God (Oxford University Press)
OB	Orgelbuch zum Evangelischen Kirchengesangbuch (Bärenreiter)
OC	Bissell, O Come Let Us Sing (Waterloo)
OEA	Oxford Easy Anthem Book (Oxford University Press)
PA	Pachelbel, Ausgewählten Orgelwerke (Bärenreiter)
PC	Peeters, 30 Chorale Preludes for Organ (C.F. Peters)
PCB	The Parish Choir Book (Concordia 97-7574)
PF	Purvis, Four Prayers in Tone (W. Mitmark & Sons)
PG	Peeters, 30 Chorale Preludes on Gregorian Hymns (C.F. Peters)
PH	The Presbyterian Hymnal. Louisville, Kentucky: Westminster/John Knox Press, 1990.
PHP	Peeters, Hymn Preludes for the Liturgical Year (C.F.Peters)
PK	Pepping, Kleines Orgelbuch (B.Schott's Söhne 3735)
PL	Purvis, Leeds' Organ Selections (Leeds)
PM	Purvis, An American Organ Mass (Harold Flammer)
PO	The Parish Organist, 12 vols. (Concordia)
PP	Schütz, Five Psalms of Praise (GIA G-1790)
PPS	Preludes and Postludes (Augsburg)
PRC	Praetorius, Choralbearbeitungen für Orgel (Bärenreiter)
PS	Parry, Seven Chorale Preludes, 2 sets (Novello)
PT	Purvis, Seven Chorale Preludes on Tunes Found in American Hymnals (Carl Fischer)
RC	Reger, Choralvorspiele für Orgel, Opus 67 (Bote & Bock)
RM	Rejoice and Be Merry (Concordia 97-5901)
RS	The Renaissance Singer (E.C.Schirmer 2974)

RSCM	Royal School of Church Music, Addington Palace, Croydon
RT	Ridout, Three Preludes on Scottish Tunes (Gordon V. Thompson)
SA	Sweelinck, Ausgewählte Werke, Vol.2 (C.F. Peters)
SC	Sursum Corda, A Book of Organ Voluntaries in Memory of Charles Peaker (G.V.Thompson)
SFGP	Songs for a Gospel People (Wood Lake Books)
SG	Sing Gloria (Concordia 97-5029)
SJ	Sing for Joy (Concordia 97-5046)
SMB	A Second Motet Book (Concordia 97-5205)
SN	Sing Noel (G.Schirmer 48724c)
SO	Schroeder, 12 Organ Carols for Christmas (Concordia)
SP	Schütz, Seven Penitential Psalms from the "Becker Psalter" (GIA G-912)
SP1	Speller, 3 Preludes Based on Hymn Tunes (Concordia)
SP2	Speller, Three Organ Settings for Advent (Concordia)
SS	Songs for Saints (Concordia)
ST	Schack, Preludes on Ten Hymn Tunes (Augsburg)
SV	Schroeder, Sechs Orgelchoräle über altdeutsche geistliche Volkslieder (B.Schott's Söhne 2265)
SW	Sowerby, Advent to Whitsuntide (Hinrichsen 743b)
TB	Thalben-Ball, 113 Variations on Hymn Tunes for Organ (Novello)
TH	The Hymnal 1982, New York, The Church Hymnal Corporation, 1985
TP	LeJeune, Three-Part Psalms (Mercury Music 352-00056)
UM	The United Methodist Hymnal. Nashville, Tennessee: The United Methodist Publishing House, 1989
VW	Vaughan Williams, Three Preludes Founded on Welsh Hymn Tunes (Stainer & Bell)
WB	The Worshipbook, Services and Hymns, Philadelphia, The Westminster Press, 1970.
WBM	Weihnachtliche Barockmusik (C.F.Peters)
WC	Willan, Six Chorale Preludes, 2 Sets (Concordia)
WF	Willan, Five Preludes on Plainchant Melodies (Oxford University Press)
WH	Willan, Ten Hymn Preludes, 3 Sets (C.F.Peters)
WHD	With High Delight (Concordia 97-5047)
WO	Walther, Orgelchoräle (Bärenreiter)

WP	Willan, 36 Short Preludes and Postludes (C.F.Peters)
WP1	We Praise Thee, Part I (Concordia 97-7564)
WP2	We Praise Thee, Part II (Concordia 97-7610)
WS	Preludes for the Hymns in Worship Supplement, 3 vols. (Concordia)
WT	Whitlock, Six Hymn Preludes, 2 volumes (Oxford University Press)

xvi

I. MUSIC FOR THE CHURCH YEAR

Introduction

Sections II, III, and IV of this handbook offer numerous suggestions to those selecting hymns, organ music and choral music for a given worship service. Once the scripture lessons have been assigned, one can choose from an often vast number of hymns appropriate to the lessons, an even vaster number of preludes based on those hymns, and choral music appropriate either to the specific lesson or to the liturgical season or occasion.

Many of those who plan music for the entire three-year cycle of the Revised Common Lectionary wish to address other issues as well: variety of musical styles and historical periods, avoidance of excessive repetition, difficulty of works for a given occasion relative to those performed in weeks preceding and weeks to follow.

Music for the Church Year presents suggestions of hymns, choral music and organ music for the three-year cycle of the Revised Common Lectionary. It recommends hymns commonly found in the hymnals of the major denominations and offers selections of choral music, in English, for a variety of church choirs. Unless otherwise noted, works are for four voice parts, SATB, but wherever possible, anthems for unison voices and works for junior choir have been included as well.

Those wishing to link organ music directly with hymn selections may do so with the aid of Sections II and III. The organ music listed in Music for the Church Year offers an alternative approach based on the overall repertoire for the instrument. It includes virtually the complete works of Bach, Buxtehude and Walther, along with representative works by some ninety other composers drawn in part from the syllabus of the Royal Conservatory of Music in Toronto. German chorales with specific scriptural associations have been assigned to Sundays for which those readings are appointed in the Revised Common Lectionary.

Other chorale preludes by Bach have been distributed according to season.

Each entry begins with the scriptures appointed for the day, followed by suggestions of organ music, choral music and hymns.

● Organ music is divided into Prelude, Offertory and Postlude. Sources for the organ selections found in collections are given in brackets, followed by approximate timings. Publication details of other works may be found in the Index of Organ Works Cited on page 538.

● Choral music: Scriptural references in brackets following the name of the anthem indicate that the music is an actual setting of the words of that text. Otherwise, the anthem is chosen for the appropriate season or festival, or for general use. The distribution of voices uses the standard abbreviations: SATB for Soprano, Alto, Tenor, Bass. "SB" indicates a two-part anthem set for women and men; "U w/d" refers to an anthem for unison voices with a descant. Publication details are given in the Index of Choral Works Cited on page 567. No publisher is given for Handel's *Messiah*, which appears in various editions in most church music libraries. Sources of Junior Choir selections, when drawn from hymnals or collections, are indicated in parentheses after the title.

● Hymn selections are followed by scriptural allusions, in brackets, and sources, in parentheses.

Music for the Church Year follows the calendar of the Revised Common Lectionary:

Season of Advent
First Sunday of Advent
Second Sunday of Advent
Third Sunday of Advent
Fourth Sunday of Advent

Season of Christmas
Christmas Eve
Christmas Day

First Sunday after Christmas
Second Sunday after Christmas

Season of Epiphany
Epiphany of the Lord
Baptism of the Lord (First Sunday after the Epiphany)
Second Sunday after the Epiphany
Third Sunday after the Epiphany
Fourth Sunday after the Epiphany
Fifth Sunday after the Epiphany
Sixth Sunday after the Epiphany
Seventh Sunday after the Epiphany
Eighth Sunday after the Epiphany
Ninth Sunday after the Epiphany
Last Sunday after the Epiphany (Transfiguration Sunday)

Season of Lent
First Sunday in Lent
Second Sunday in Lent
Third Sunday in Lent
Fourth Sunday in Lent
Fifth Sunday in Lent
Sixth Sunday in Lent (Passion Sunday or Palm Sunday)
Holy Thursday
Good Friday

Season of Easter
Easter Day
Second Sunday of Easter
Third Sunday of Easter
Fourth Sunday of Easter
Fifth Sunday of Easter
Sixth Sunday of Easter
Seventh Sunday of Easter (Sunday after Ascension Day)
Day of Pentecost

Season after Pentecost
Trinity Sunday (First Sunday after Pentecost)
Sundays between May 29 and November 19

4

Last Sunday after Pentecost (Christ the King) (the Sunday between
    November 20 and November 26)

Special Days
All Saints (November 1 or the First Sunday in November)
Thanksgiving (Fourth Thursday in November [US] or Second Monday
    in October [Canada])

Principal Dates

Year	Ash Wednesday	Easter Day	Pentecost	Advent 1
1994	February 16	April 3	May 22	November 27
1995	March 1	April 16	June 4	December 3
1996	February 21	April 7	May 26	December 1
1997	February 12	March 30	May 18	November 30
1998	February 25	April 12	May 31	November 29
1999	February 17	April 4	May 23	November 28
2000	March 8	April 23	June 11	December 3

YEAR A

Begins on the First Sunday of Advent in 1995, 1998, 2001, 2004

DATE: First Sunday of Advent

READINGS:
Isaiah 2:1-5
Psalm 122
Romans 13:11-14
Matthew 24:36-44

ORGAN MUSIC:

Prelude	Suite of Noels	C. Balbastre [17:00]
	Prélude	
	A la Venue de Noel	
	Joseph est bien Marié	
	Où s'en vont ces gais bergers	
Offertory	Prelude on "Veni Emmanuel"	J. Bender [HP 3:19]
Postlude	A Cei-ci le moître de tô l'univar!	Balbastre [p.46]

SENIOR CHOIR:
Rejoice, O Jerusalem, Behold,   H. Willan
Thy King Cometh [Rom.13:12]
Come, Thou Long-Expected Jesus [Advent] [U]   D. Busarow

JUNIOR CHOIR:
A Journey Just Begun (AGCS 51)

HYMNS:
Thy Kingdom Come, O God [Is.2:4] (276HB)
"Sleepers, Wake!" the Watch Are Calling [Rom.13:11-12] (394HB)

6

DATE: Second Sunday of Advent

READINGS:
Isaiah 11:1-10
Psalm 72:1-7,18-19
Romans 15:4-13
Matthew 3:1-12

ORGAN MUSIC:

First Book of Noels		N. LeBègue
Prelude	Symphony in D Major	
	A la venue de Noël	
	Une vierge pucelle	
	Noël pour l'amour de Marie	
	Noël, cette journée	
	Or nous ditte Marie	
	Puer nobis nascitur	
	Où s'en vont ces gays Bergers	
Offertory	Les bourgeoises de Chatre	
Postlude	Laissez paistre vos bestes	

SENIOR CHOIR:

Lo! How a Rose E'er Blooming [Advent]	arr. H. Distler
Arise, Sons of the Kingdom [Advent] [U]	D. Buxtehude

JUNIOR CHOIR:
Light One Candle (AGCS 13)

HYMNS:
How Bright Appears the Morning Star [Isaiah 11:1-10] (117HB)
O Come, O Come, Emmanuel [Isaiah 11:1] (390HB)
Hail to the Lord's Anointed [Ps.72] (154HB)
O Christ, the Word Incarnate [Romans 15:4] (22SFGP)
Herald, Sound the Note of Judgment [Matthew 3:1-12] (103HB)
On Jordan's Bank the Baptist's Cry [Matthew 3:1-12] (391HB)
There's a Voice in the Wilderness Crying [Matthew 3:1-3] (153HB)

DATE: Third Sunday of Advent

READINGS:
Isaiah 35:1-10
Psalm 146:5-10 or Luke 1:47-55
James 5:7-10
Matthew 11:2-11

ORGAN MUSIC:

Prelude	Noels 2, 3, 4	C. Daquin [15:30]
Offertory	Lo, How a Rose E'er Blooming	F. Peeters [PH 1:4]
Postlude	Noel 1	C. Daquin [4:00]

SENIOR CHOIR:

Behold, I Sent My Messenger [Matthew 11:10]	H. Willan
Magnificat [Luke 1:46-55] [U]	J. Duke

JUNIOR CHOIR:
Joy Shall Come [Isaiah 35] (SFGP 65)

HYMNS:
Lo, How a Rose E'er Blooming [Isaiah 35:1-2] (216UM)
She Flies On (St.2) [Isaiah 35:1-2] (126SFGP)
O Jesus, King Most Wonderful [Ps.146:10] (121HB)
Herald, Sound the Note of Judgment [Matthew 11:7-10] (103HB)
Prepare the Way, O Zion [Matthew 11:7-10] (65TH)

DATE: Fourth Sunday of Advent

READINGS:
Isaiah 7:10-16
Psalm 80:1-7
Romans 1:1-7
Matthew 1:18-25

ORGAN MUSIC:
Prelude   Nun komm' der Heiden Heiland [Matthew 1:18-25]
               (Saviour of the Nations, Come)
                                        J.S.Bach [B18:55;4:00]
                                                 [B18:59;4:00]
                                                 [BU 73;1:00]
                                                 [BO 3;100]
                                   J. Walther [WO 98;5:00]
                                   J. Pachelbel [PA 2:4;3:00]
Offertory   Nun komm' der Heiden Heiland
                                   D. Buxtehude [BC 105;1:30]
Postlude   Nun komm' der Heiden Heiland
                                        J.S.Bach [B18:62;3:00]

SENIOR CHOIR:
Behold, A Virgin Shall Conceive [Advent]   J. Sweelinck
A Ship With Cargo Precious [Advent] [U]   M. Drischner

JUNIOR CHOIR:
Go, Tell It On the Mountain (HB 404)

HYMNS:
Hark! the Herald Angels Sing (St.2) [Isaiah 7:14] (407HB)
O Come, O Come, Emmanuel [Isaiah 7:14] (390HB)
Saviour of the Nations, Come [Matthew 1:18-25] (54TH)
Lo, How a Rose E'er Blooming [Matthew 1:18-25] (81TH)

DATE: Christmas Eve

READINGS:

ORGAN MUSIC:
Prelude   Vom Himmel hoch [Luke 2:1-20]
               (From Heaven Above to Earth I Come)
                                        J.S. Bach [B18:98;15:00]
Offertory   Vom Himmel hoch   J. Walther [WO 125; 3:00]
Postlude   Vom Himmel hoch   J. Pachelbel [PA 2:18;4:30]

SENIOR CHOIR:
At the Cradle [Christmas] [SA]   C. Franck
My Dancing Day [Christmas]   Parker & Shaw
Christ the Lord to Us Is Born [Christmas] [U]   M. Drischner

JUNIOR CHOIR:
Rocking Carol (AGCS 87)

HYMNS:
Carols

DATE: Christmas Day - Proper I

READINGS:
Isaiah 9:2-7
Psalm 96
Titus 2:11-14
Luke 2:1-14, (15-20)

ORGAN MUSIC:
                                                    C. Franck [5:00]
Prelude   Five Noels
             In dulci jubilo [Luke 2:1-20]
             (In Sweet Jubilation)

                                        J.S. Bach [B0 16;1:30]
                                            [GG2:152;1:30]
                                        J. Walther [WO 67;2:00]
                                        D. Buxtehude [BC 52;2:00]
                                        V. Lübeck [HP 4:20;1:00]
                                        F.W. Zachau [80:44;1:30]
Offertory   In dulci jubilo   Bach [BU 52;2:00]
Postlude   Magnificat   M. Dupré [2:00]

SENIOR CHOIR:
Glory to God [Luke 2:14]   G.F. Handel

JUNIOR CHOIR:
Rise Up, Shepherd, and Follow   D. Walker

HYMNS:
Break Forth, O Beauteous Heavenly Light [Isaiah 9:2-7] (402HB)
Christ, Whose Glory Fills the Skies [Isaiah 9:2] (362HB)
Come, O Long Expected Jesus [Isaiah 9:6] (389HB)
Carols (see Luke 2:1-20)

DATE: First Sunday After Christmas

READINGS:
Isaiah 63:7-9
Psalm 148
Hebrews 2:10-18
Matthew 2:13-23

ORGAN MUSIC:
Prelude Noels
A. Raison [9:00]
        A la venue de Noel
        Voici le jour solennel de Noel
        Joseph est bien marié
        Or nous dites marie
        Une jeune pucelle
        Der Tag, der ist so freudenreich [Christmas]
        (The Day of Gladness Now Appears)
D.Buxtehude [BC 10;2:30]
J.S. Bach [BO 11;2:30]
[BN 2;1:30]
Offertory Der Tag, der ist so freudenreich

J.C.F. Fischer [1:30]
Postlude Der Tag, der ist so freudenreich

J. Pachelbel [4:00]

SENIOR CHOIR:
Psalm 148
G. Holst
From Heaven Above, Ye Angels All [U] [Christmas] M. Drischner

JUNIOR CHOIR:
Away in a Manger
H. Willan

HYMNS:
All Creatures of Our God and King [Ps.148] (1HB)
Ye Watchers and Ye Holy Ones [Ps.148] (7HB)
Unto Us a Boy Is Born (St.3) [Matthew 2:13-18] (HB423)
Lully, Lullay, Thou Little Tiny Child [Matthew 2:16-18] (247TH)

DATE: Second Sunday after Christmas Day

[For use when Epiphany (January 6) is celebrated on a weekday following the Second Sunday after Christmas Day]

READINGS:
Jeremiah 31:7-14 or Sirach 24:1-12
Psalm 147:12-20 or Wisdom of Solomon 10:15-21
Ephesians 1:3-14
John 1:(1-9), 10-18

ORGAN MUSIC:

Prelude	Gelobet seist du, Jesu Christ [John 1:14]	
	(Now Blessed Be Thou, Christ Jesu)	
		J.S. Bach [BO 10;1:00]
		G. Böhm [BS 69;2:30]
		D. Buxtehude [BC 23;7:00]
		[BC 31;1:30]
		J. Pachelbel [PA 2:12;1:30]
		J. Walther [GG2:112;1:30]
		J. Bender [BK 1:12]
Offertory	Gelobet seist du, Jesu Christ	Bach [BU 31,32;2:00]
Postlude	Gelobet seist du, Jesu Christ	Böhm [BS 72;4:00]

SENIOR CHOIR:

The Word Was Made Flesh [John 1:1-14]	M. Reger
To God the Anthem Raising [New Years] [U]	D. Buxtehude

JUNIOR CHOIR:

O How Beautiful the Sky	H. Willan

HYMNS:
Rejoice, Ye Pure in Heart [Ps.147:1] (160UM)
Walls That Divide (St.4) [Eph.1:12-14] (32SFGP)
Amazing Grace! How Sweet the Sound [Eph.1:5-8] (49SFGP)
There's a Wideness in God's Mercy [Eph.1:7-8] (76HB)
Of the Father's Love Begotten [John 1:14] (429HB)
I Heard the Voice of Jesus Say (St.3) [John 1:9] (115HB)

DATE: Epiphany of the Lord

READINGS:
Isaiah 60:1-6
Psalm 72:1-7, 10-14
Ephesians 3:1-12
Matthew 2:1-12

ORGAN MUSIC:
Prelude   Wir Christenleut' [Christmas]
                 (Come, Christian Folk)

                                    J.S. Bach [BO 22;1:00]
                                              [BU 100;2:00]
                                              [BN 4;2:00]
                 Christum, wir sollen loben schon [Christmas]
                 (Now Praise We Christ the Holy One)
                                    Bach [BU 23;1:00]
                                    J. Walther [WO 18;6:00]
                                    G. Böhm [BS 54;1:30]
Offertory   Christum, wir sollen loben schon   Bach [BO 20;2:00]
Postlude   Christum, wir sollen loben schon
                                    J. Praetorius [PRC 1;3:00]

SENIOR CHOIR:
The Three Kings [Matthew 2]   P. Cornelius
How Lovely Shines the Morning Star [Epiphany] [U]   M. Drischner

JUNIOR CHOIR:
Many Are the Light Beams (SFGP 104)

HYMNS:
Arise, Your Light Is Come [Is.60:1] (19SFGP)
Hail to the Lord's Anointed [Ps.72] (154HB)
Jesus Shall Reign Where'er the Sun [Ps.72] (164HB)
Brightest and Best of the Sons of the Morning [Matthew 2:1-11]
(432HB)
Earth Has Many a Noble City [Matthew 2:1-11] (431HB)
We Three Kings [Matthew 2:1-11] (254UM)
What Star Is This, With Beams So Bright [Matthew 2:1-12] (124TH)

DATE: Baptism of the Lord
(First Sunday after the Epiphany)

READINGS:
Isaiah 42:1-9
Psalm 29
Acts 10:34-43
Matthew 3:13-17

ORGAN MUSIC:
[See Epiphany]

SENIOR CHOIR:
Out of the East Came Magi [Epiphany]   J. Handl
Mary Rocks the Holy Child [Christmas] [U]   R. J. Powell

JUNIOR CHOIR:
What Star Is This, With Beams So Bright (CS 33)   H. Willan

HYMNS:
All Glory Be to God on High [Acts 10:42] (421TH)
"Welcome, Happy Morning!" Age to Age Shall Say [Acts 10:39-40]
(462HB)
Songs of Thankfulness and Praise (St.2) [Matthew 3:13-17] (433HB)
Come, Gracious Spirit, Heavenly Dove [Matthew 3:16] (265HB)
Come, Holy Spirit, Heavenly Dove [Matthew 3:16] (244HB)

DATE: Second Sunday after the Epiphany

READINGS:
Isaiah 49:1-7
Psalm 40:1-11
1 Corinthians 1:1-9
John 1:29-42

ORGAN MUSIC:
Prelude   O Lamm Gottes unschuldig [John 1:29,35-36]
               (O Lamb of God, Pure, Spotless)
                                            J.S. Bach [BO 34;3:30]
                                                     [B18:38;6:30]
                                                     [BU 74;2:30]
                                                     [BU 76;1:30]
Offertory   O Lamm Gottes unschuldig   Bach [BN 14;2:00]
Postlude   O Lamm Gottes unschuldig
                                            J. Pachelbel [PA 2:44;4:00]

SENIOR CHOIR:
Behold the Lamb of God [John 1:29]   G.F. Handel

JUNIOR CHOIR:
Behold That Star (IBC 78)

HYMNS:
Lord, Enthroned in Heavenly Splendor [John 1:29-36] (324HB)
Hail, Thou Once Despised Jesus [John 1:29-35] (478HB)
O Love, How Deep, How Broad, How High [John 1:29-34] (100HB)
Songs of Thankfulness and Praise (St.2) [John 1:29-34] (433HB)

DATE: Third Sunday after the Epiphany

READINGS:
Isaiah 9:1-4
Psalm 27:1, 4-9
1 Corinthians 1:10-18
Matthew 4:12-23

ORGAN MUSIC:
Premier Livre d'Orgue   N. DeGrigny [23:00]
Prelude   Kyrie
             Fugue
             Cromorne en taille
             Trio en dialogue
             Dialogue sur les Grands Jeux
             Et in terra pax   [pp.5-15]
Offertory   Duo   [p.17]
Postlude   Dialogue sur les Grands Jeux   [p.63]

SENIOR CHOIR:
Break Forth, O Beauteous Heavenly Light (HB 402)   J.S. Bach
Gloria in Excelsis [Isaiah 9:6]   K. Bissell
Glory Be to God on High [Christmas] [U]   H. Willan

JUNIOR CHOIR:
Every Star Shall Sing a Carol (HB 428)

HYMNS:
Christ, Whose Glory Fills the Skies [Isaiah 9:2] (362HB)
I Love Your Kingdom, Lord [Ps.26:8] (296LW)
Dear Lord and Father of Mankind [Matthew 4:18-22] (249HB)
They Cast Their Nets in Galilee [Matthew 4:18-22] (661TH)

DATE: Fourth Sunday after the Epiphany

READINGS:
Micah 6:1-8
Psalm 15
1 Corinthians 1:18-31
Matthew 5:1-12

ORGAN MUSIC:
Prelude   Sonata I in Eb Major   J.S. Bach [16:00]
Offertory   O Jesu, wie ist dein Gestalt
            (O Jesus, How Thy Face)   Bach [BN 12;2:30]
Postlude   Fugue in B Minor on a Theme of Corelli   Bach [5:00]

SENIOR CHOIR:
Blessed Are They That Mourn [Matthew 5:4]   J. Brahms

JUNIOR CHOIR:
Shalom, chaverim (SFGP 114)

HYMNS:
Sing, My Tongue, the Glorious Battle [1 Cor.1:18-25] (446HB)
O Christ, the Word Incarnate (St.1) [1 Cor.1:30] (22SFGP)
Blest Are the Pure in Heart [Matthew 5:8] (58HB)

DATE: Fifth Sunday after the Epiphany

READINGS:
Isaiah 58:1-9a, (9b-12)
Psalm 112:1-9(10)
1 Corinthians 2:1-12, (13-16)
Matthew 5:13-20

ORGAN MUSIC:
Prelude	Prelude and Fugue in C Major	G. Böhm [5:00]
	Prelude in G Major	N. Bruhns [10:00]
Offertory	Fugue in C Minor	W.F. Bach [2:00]
Postlude	Fugue in Eb Major	W.F. Bach [3:00]

SENIOR CHOIR:
Eye of Man Hath Not Seen [1 Cor.2:9]	O. Lasso
I Am the Light of the World [Epiphany] [U]	P. Bouman

JUNIOR CHOIR:
Shout for God (AGCS 48)

HYMNS:
Once in Royal David's City [1 Cor.2:9] (112HB)

DATE: Sixth Sunday after the Epiphany

READINGS:
Deuteronomy 30:15-20 or Sirach 15:15-20
Psalm 119:1-8
1 Corinthians 3:1-9
Matthew 5:21-37

ORGAN MUSIC:
Prelude   Prelude and Fugue in C Minor   J.S. Bach [12:00]
Offertory   O Herre Gott, dein Göttlich Wort
             (O Lord God, Thy Godly Word)   Bach [BN 48;2:00]
Postlude   Canzona in D Minor   Bach [5:00]

SENIOR CHOIR:
Blessed Are the Undefiled [Ps.119:1,2,33]   H. Willan

JUNIOR CHOIR:
If You're Happy and You Know It (AGCS 26)

HYMNS:
[None available]

DATE: Seventh Sunday after the Epiphany

READINGS:
Leviticus 19:1-2, 9-18
Psalm 119:33-40
1 Corinthians 3:10-11, 16-23
Matthew 5:38-48

ORGAN MUSIC:
Prelude	Vater unser im Himmelreich	
	(The Lord's Prayer)	J.S. Bach [BCL 58;8:00]
		[BCL 66;1:30]
		[BO 64;2:30]
		G. Böhm [BS 96;4:30]
		F. Peeters [PH 19:8]
Offertory	Vater unser im Himmelreich	Böhm [BS 100;2:00]
Postlude	Vater unser im Himmelreich	Böhm [BS 102;3:30]

SENIOR CHOIR:
Teach Me, O Lord [Ps.119:33]   T. Attwood

JUNIOR CHOIR:
Lord, I Want to Be a Christian (PH 372)

HYMNS:
Love, Love, Love Your God [Lev.19:18] (43SFGP)
Blest Are the Pure in Heart [1 Cor.3:16] (58HB)
Come Down, O Love Divine [1 Cor.3:16] (67HB)
The Church's One Foundation [1 Cor.3:11] (146HB)
The Servant Song [Matthew 5:41] (133SFGP)

DATE: Eighth Sunday after the Epiphany

READINGS:
Isaiah 49:8-16a
Psalm 131
1 Corinthians 4:1-5
Matthew 6:24-34

ORGAN MUSIC:
Prelude   Concerto after Albinoni   J. Walther [6:00]
             Fantasia on B-A-C-H   J. Sweelinck [9:30]
Offertory   O Jesu Christ, mein's Lebens Licht
             (O Jesus Christ, the Light of My Life)
                                            Walther [WO 119;2:00]
Postlude   Toccata and Fugue in Bb Major   J. Pachelbel

SENIOR CHOIR:
Seek Ye First God's Own Kingdom [Matt.6:33]   W.A. Mozart

JUNIOR CHOIR:
Seek Ye First the Kingdom of God [Matt.6:33] (SFGP 83)

HYMNS:
I Will Never Forget You, My People [Is.49:15-16] (71SFGP)
O God of Bethel, By Whose Hand [Matthew 6:25-33] (263HB)
All Things Bright and Beautiful [Matthew 6:28-29] (86HB)

DATE: Ninth Sunday after the Epiphany

READINGS:
Deuteronomy 11:18-21, 26-28
Psalm 31:1-5, 19-24
Romans 1:16-17; 3:22b-28 (29-31)
Matthew 7:21-29

ORGAN MUSIC:
Prelude	Fantasia and Fugue in C Minor	J.S. Bach [13:00]
Offertory	Alle Menschen müssen sterben	
	(All Men Must Die)	Bach [BO 74;2:00]
Postlude	Fantasia in B Minor	Bach [4:00]

SENIOR CHOIR:
Lord, in Thee Do I Put My Trust [Ps.31:1-2]   H. Schütz

JUNIOR CHOIR:
I Love My Lord (LP 90)

HYMNS:
Hail, Thou Once Despised Jesus [Romans 3:23-25a] (478HB)
Amazing Grace! How Sweet the Sound [Romans 3:23-24] (67SFGP)
How Firm a Foundation, Ye Saints of the Lord [Matthew 7:24-27] (139HB)
Glorious Things of Thee Are Spoken [Matthew 7:24-25] (144HB)

DATE: Last Sunday after the Epiphany
                   (Transfiguration Sunday)

READINGS:
Exodus 24:12-18
Psalm 2 or Psalm 99
2 Peter 1:16-21
Matthew 17:1-9

ORGAN MUSIC:
Prelude   Wie schön leuchtet der Morgenstern [2 Peter 1:19]
             (How Brightly Beams the Morning Star)
                                    D. Buxtehude [BC 142;8:00]
                                    G. Telemann [HP 5:38;3:00]
                                    J. Praetorius [PO I:194;1:30]
                                    J. Bender [HP 13:18]
Offertory   Wie schön leuchtet der Morgenstern
                                    A. Armsdorff [GT 3:171;2:30]
Postlude   Wie schön leuchtet der Morgenstern
                                    J. Pachelbel [PA 3:78;3:00]

SENIOR CHOIR:
This Is My Beloved Son [Matt.17:5]   K. Nystedt

JUNIOR CHOIR:
Let Us Praise the God of Truth (SFGP 4)

HYMNS:
Songs of Thankfulness and Praise [2 Peter 1:17-18] (433HB)
Christ, Whose Glory Fills the Skies [2 Peter 1:19] (362HB)
O Christ, the Word Incarnate (St.1) [2 Peter 1:19] (22SFGP)
Songs of Thankfulness and Praise (St.4) [Matthew 17:1-2] (443HB)
Christus Paradox (St.2) [Matthew 17:1-2] (64SFGP)

DATE: First Sunday in Lent

READINGS:
Genesis 2:15-17; 3:1-7
Psalm 32
Romans 5:12-19
Matthew 4:1-11

ORGAN MUSIC:
Prelude   Ach, was soll ich Sünder machen
             (Ah, What Shall I, a Sinner, Do)
                                     J.S. Bach [BP 104;11:00]
                                     J. Pachelbel [PA 4:38;5:00]
Offertory   Ach, was soll ich Sünder machen
                                     F.W. Marpurg [MC 10;1:00]
Postlude   Ach, was soll ich Sünder machen
                                     J. Walther [WO 7;5:00]

SENIOR CHOIR:
Be Gone, Satan [Matt.4:10]   J. Bender
Lord Jesus, We Give Thanks to Thee [Lent] [U]   M. Drischner

JUNIOR CHOIR:
Joy Shall Come (SFGP 68)

HYMNS:
Creator of the Stars of Night [Genesis 3:1-8; Romans 5:12-21]
(462HB)
Amazing Grace! How Sweet the Sound [Romans 5:18-21] (67SFGP)
Forty Days and Forty Nights [Matthew 4:1-11] (438HB)
O Love, How Deep, How Broad, How High [Matthew 4:1-11]
(100HB)

DATE: Second Sunday in Lent

READINGS:
Genesis 12:1-4a
Psalm 121
Romans 4:1-5, 13-17
John 3:1-17 or Matthew 17:1-9

ORGAN MUSIC:
Prelude   Ach Gott vom Himmel sieh' darein
                (O God From Heaven, Look Down, Behold)
                         J.P. Sweelinck [SA 19;5:00]
                             J. Walther [WO 6;2:00]
                                   [GG2:87;2:00]
                       J. Pachelbel [PA 3:64;1:30]
                            N. Hanff [HS 4;2:30]
                         S. Scheidt [EK 1:1;1:00]
Offertory   Ach Gott vom Himmel sieh' darein
                          J.L. Krebs [GT 1:8;2:00]
Postlude   Ach Gott vom Himmel sieh' darein
                          J.S. Bach [BU 4;4:00]

SENIOR CHOIR:
So God Loved the World [John 3:14]   O. Gibbons
Lift Thine Eyes [Ps.121] [SSA]   F. Mendelssohn
O Christ, Thou Lamb of God [Lent] [U]   J. Bender

JUNIOR CHOIR:
Many and Great, O Lord, Are Your Works (SFGP 80)

HYMNS:
To Abraham and Sarah [Genesis 12:1-3] (123SFGP)
I to the Hills Will Lift My Eyes [Psalm 121] (430WB)
Now There Is No Male or Female (St.3) [John 3:5] (62SFGP)
Lift High the Cross [John 3:14-15] (321HB)
Christus Paradox (St.2) [Matthew 17:1-2] (64SFGP)

DATE: Third Sunday in Lent

READINGS:
Exodus 17:1-7
Psalm 95
Romans 5:1-11
John 4:5-42

ORGAN MUSIC:
Prelude   Variations on Sei gegrüsset, Jesu gütig
               (Hail to Thee, My Jesu, Lowly)
                                        J.S. Bach [BP 32;18:00]
Offertory   Ach wie nichtig, ach wie flüchtig
               (Ah, How Futile, How Inutile)   Bach [BO 76;2:00]
Postlude   Prelude and Fugue in A Minor   Bach [5:00]

SENIOR CHOIR:
O Come Let Us Sing [Ps.95]   K. Bissell
Oh, Sing to God Your Joyful Praise [Ps.95:1-2]   G.F. Handel
O Christ, Our King, Creator, Lord [Lent] [U]   C. Jennings

JUNIOR CHOIR:
When I Needed a Neighbour (SFGP 131)

HYMNS:
Glorious Things of Thee Are Spoken [Exodus 17:1-6; John 4:7-14]
(144HB)
Guide Me, O Thou Great Jehovah [Exodus 17:6] (269HB)
From East to West [Psalm 95:1-6] (403HB)
Come Down, O Love Divine [Romans 5:5] (67HB)
My Song Is Love Unknown [Romans 5:8-11] (442HB)
Jesus, Lover of My Soul [John 4:13-14] (77HB)

DATE: Fourth Sunday in Lent

READINGS:
1 Samuel 16:1-13
Psalm 23
Ephesians 5:8-14
John 9:1-41

ORGAN MUSIC:
Prelude   Herr Jesu Christ, du höchstes Gut
               (Lord Jesus Christ, Thou Highest Good)
                                        J.S. Bach [BN 56;3:00]
                                        J. Walther [WO 54;6:30]
                                        J.L. Krebs [GT 2:44;5:30]
Offertory   Herr Jesu Christ, du höchstes Gut
                                        D. Buxtehude [BC 38;2:30]
Postlude   Herr Jesu Christ, du höchstes Gut
                                        J. Pachelbel [PA 3:90;4:00]

SENIOR CHOIR:
Brother James's Air [Ps.23]   G. Jacob
Brother James's Air [Ps.23] [U]   A. Trew

JUNIOR CHOIR:
My Shepherd Is the Living Lord [Ps.23] (SFGP 75)

HYMNS:
The Lord's My Shepherd: I'll Not Want [Psalm 23] (131HB)
My Shepherd Is the Living Need [Psalm 23] (75SFGP)
O For a Thousand Tongues to Sing [John 9:1-14] (48HB)
Thou, Whose Almighty Word [John 9:1-41] (235HB)
I Heard the Voice of Jesus Say (St.3) [John 9:5] (115HB)

DATE: Fifth Sunday in Lent

READINGS:
Ezekiel 37:1-14
Psalm 130
Romans 8:6-11
John 11:1-45

ORGAN MUSIC:
Prelude	Sonata III (based on	
	Aus tiefer Not)	F. Mendelssohn [10:00]
	Aus tiefer Not [Ps.130]	
	(In Deepest Need, I Call to Thee)	
		J.S. Bach [BCL 74;6:00]
Offertory	Aus tiefer Not	S. Scheidt [GT 1:63;1:00]
Postlude	Aus tiefer Not	Bach [BCL 78;5:00]

SENIOR CHOIR:
In Deep Despair [Ps.130]   F. Mendelssohn
Let Shouts of Gladness Rise [General] [U]   D. Buxtehude

JUNIOR CHOIR:
When God Delivered Israel (SFGP 98)

HYMNS:
From Depths of Woe I Cry to You [Psalm 130] (230LW)
Creator Spirit, by Whose Aid [Romans 8:9] (167LW)
O For a Thousand Tongues to Sing [John 11:1-44] (48HB)
Jesus the Christ Said (St.4) [John 11:25] (73SFGP)

DATE: Sixth Sunday in Lent
                          (Passion Sunday or Palm Sunday)

READINGS: Liturgy of the Palms
Matthew 21:1-11
Psalm 118:1-2, 19-29
                          Liturgy of the Passion
Isaiah 50:4-9a
Psalm 31:9-16
Philippians 2:5-11
Matthew 26:14 - 27:66 or Matthew 27:11-54

ORGAN MUSIC:
Prelude   Passion Chorale [Matt.27:27-54]
                                          J. Walther [WP 60;12:00]
                                          F. Peeters [PC 3:22]
Offertory   Passion Chorale   D. Buxtehude [BC 4;2:00]
Postlude   Valet will ich dir geben
               (All Glory, Laud and Honour)   J.S. Bach [BU 84;4:30]

SENIOR CHOIR:
Hosanna to the Son of David [Matt.21:9]   T.L. Victoria

JUNIOR CHOIR:
Holy, Holy, Holy, Lord (SFGP 117)

HYMNS:
All Glory, Laud and Honour [Matthew 21:1-11; Psalm 118:26]
(447HB)
Ride On! Ride On in Majesty [Matthew 21:1-11; Psalm 118:26]
(449HB)
Hosanna, Loud Hosanna [Matthew 21:8-9] (448HB)
Ah, Holy Jesus, How Hast Thou Offended [Matthew 27:15-26]
(443HB)
My Song Is Love Unknown [Matthew 27:15-26] (442HB)

DATE: Holy Thursday

READINGS:
Exodus 12:1-4 (5-10) 11-14
Psalm 116:1-2, 12-19
1 Corinthians 11:23-26
John 13:1-17, 31b-35

ORGAN MUSIC:
Herzliebster Jesu (Ah, Holy Jesus)   J. Brahms [BE 10,2:00]

SENIOR CHOIR:
We Adore Thee   G.P. Palestrina

JUNIOR CHOIR:

HYMNS:
At the Lamb's High Feast We Sing [Exodus 12:1-28; 1 Cor.11:23-26]
(174TH)
Bread of the World in Mercy Broken [1 Cor.11:23-26] (326HB)
Now, My Tongue, the Mystery Telling [1 Cor.11:23-26] (341HB)

DATE: Good Friday

READINGS:
Isaiah 52:13 - 53:12
Psalm 22
Hebrews 10:16-25 or Hebrews 4:14-16
John 18:1 - 19:42

ORGAN MUSIC:
Prelude   Herzliebster Jesu [Passion]
               (Ah, Holy Jesus)   J. Brahms [BE 10;2:00]
                                          G.F. Kauffmann [GG 2:132;1:00]
                                               J.C. Oley [PO I:65;1:00]
                                               J.S. Bach [BN 10;2:00]
               Mach's mit mir, Gott, nach deiner Güt
               (According to Thy Kindness, God)
                                               J. Walther [WO 88;9:30]
Postlude   Mach's mit mir, Gott, nach deiner Güt
                                               Bach [BN 64;2:30]

SENIOR CHOIR:
Surely He Hath Borne Our Griefs [Is.53:4-5]   G.F. Handel

JUNIOR CHOIR:

HYMNS:
My Song Is Love Unknown [Isaiah 52:13-53:12; John 19:38-42]
(442HB)
Ah, Holy Jesus, How Hast Thou Offended [Isaiah 53:1-12] (443HB)
God, When I Stand [Ps.22:1-2] (125SFGP)
O Sacred Head, Sore Wounded [John 19:17-37] (452HB)
Sing, My Tongue, the Glorious Battle [John 19:17-37] (446HB)
Were You There When They Crucified My Lord [John 19:2-5]
(460HB)

DATE: Easter Day

READINGS:
Acts 10:34-43 or Jeremiah 31:1-6
Psalm 118:1-2, 14-24
Colossians 3:1-4 or Acts 10:34-43
John 20:1-18 or Matthew 28:1-10

ORGAN MUSIC:
Prelude   Christ lag in Todesbanden [Easter]
               (In Death's Strong Grasp the Saviour Lay)
                                              J.S. Bach [BS 48;8:00]
                                                   [BU 16;9:00]
Offertory   Christ lag in Todesbanden   Bach [BO 46;1:30]
Postlude   Christ lag in Todesbanden
                              J. Pachelbel [PA 2:48;5:00]

SENIOR CHOIR:
Praise to God, Who Rules the Earth [Easter]   G.F. Handel
Alleluia   R. Thompson
Christ Is Risen [Easter] [U]   K. Bissell

JUNIOR CHOIR:
Come, Children, Join to Sing (SFGP 38)

HYMNS:
"Welcome, Happy Morning!" Age to Age Shall Say [Acts 10:39-40]
(462HB)
Hail Thee, Festival Day [Acts 10:39-40] (461HB)
Good Christians All, Rejoice and Sing [John 20:1-18; Matt.28:1-10]
(469HB)
Jesus Christ Is Risen Today [John 20:1-18; Matt.28:1-10] (465HB)
The Strife Is O'er, the Battle Done [John 20:1-18; Matt.28:1-10]
(468HB)
That Easter Day With Joy Was Bright [Matt.28:1-10] (474HB)
The Day of Resurrection [John 20:1-18; Matt.28:1-10] (374HB)

DATE: Second Sunday of Easter

READINGS:
Acts 2:14a, 22-32
Psalm 16
1 Peter 1:3-9
John 20:19-31

ORGAN MUSIC:

Prelude	Toccata and Fugue in F Major	J.S. Bach [15:00]
Offertory	Heut triumphieret Gottes Sohn [1 Peter 1:3-5]	
	(Today God's Only-Gotten Son)	
		Bach [BO 56;2:00]
Postlude	In dir ist Freude [1 Peter 1:6-8]	
	(In Thee Is Gladness)	Bach [BO 27]

SENIOR CHOIR:
The One Who Died by Sinners' Hands [Acts 2:14a, 22-32]   C. Tye
The Whole Bright World Rejoices [Easter]   E. Hill
Christ Jesus Is Arisen [Easter] [U]   M. Drischner

JUNIOR CHOIR:
Morning Has Broken (SFGP 103)

HYMNS:
This Joyful Eastertide [Acts 2:22-36; Ps.16:9] (471HB)
Christ the Lord Is Risen Today [Acts 2:29-32] (466HB)
O Sons and Daughters, Let Us Sing [John 20:19-31] (467HB)
That Easter Day With Joy Was Bright [John 20:19-31] (474HB)
Lo! He Comes, With Clouds Descending [John 20:24-29] (393HB)

DATE: Third Sunday of Easter

READINGS:
Acts 2:14a, 36-41
Psalm 116:1-4, 12-19
1 Peter 1:17-23
Luke 24:13-35

ORGAN MUSIC:
Prelude   Jesu, meine Freude [1 Peter 1:18-19]
             (Jesu, Priceless Treasure)
                    J. Walther [GT 2:113;15:00]
Offertory   Jesu, meine Freude   Walther [GG 1:33;2:00]
Postlude   Ach bleib' bei uns, Herr Jesu Christ [Luke 24:29]
             (Lord Jesus Christ, With Us Abide)
                     J.S. Bach [BSC 95;3:00]

SENIOR CHOIR:
The Man We Crucified [Acts 2:14a,36-47]   C. Tye
Amen [Easter]   J. Hairston
At the Lamb's High Feast We Sing [Easter] [U]   M. Drischner

JUNIOR CHOIR:
Sing Alleluia (LP 204)

HYMNS:
The Head That Once Was Crowned With Thorns [Acts 2:36] (108HB)
Hark! a Thrilling Voice Is Sounding [1 Peter 1:18-21] (59TH)
Jesus, Priceless Treasure [1 Peter 1:18-19] (270LW)
The Church's One Foundation [1 Peter 1:18-19] (146HB)
O Brother Man [1 Peter 1:20] (299HB)
Good Christians All, Rejoice and Sing [Luke 24:13-27] (469HB)
The Strife Is O'er, the Battle Done [Luke 24:13-27] (468HB)

DATE: Fourth Sunday of Easter

READINGS:
Acts 2:42-47
Psalm 23
1 Peter 2:19-25
John 10:1-10

ORGAN MUSIC:
Prelude   Allein zu dir, Herr Jesu Christ [1 Peter 2:24]
             (Lord Christ, On Thee My Hope Is Stayed]
                                    J. Pachelbel [PA 3:13;5:00]
                                    J. Sweelinck [SA 2:23;2:30]
                                    J. Walther [WO 16;2:00]
                                    [GG 2:89;2:00]
                                    D. Erich [45:14;4:30]
Offertory   Allein zu dir, Herr Jesu Christ
                                    F.W. Zachau [HP 19;2:00]
Postlude   Allein zu dir, Herr Jesu Christ
                                    J.S. Bach [BN 24;2:30]

SENIOR CHOIR:
The Lord Is My Shepherd [Ps.23]   J. Rutter
God Is My Shepherd [Ps.23] [U]   A. Dvorak

JUNIOR CHOIR:
The King of Glory (JS 40)

HYMNS:
In Heavenly Love Abiding [Ps.23] (230MH)
Saviour, Like a Shepherd Lead Us [Ps.23:1-4] (93SFGP)
The Strife Is O'er, the Battle Done [1 Peter 2:21-24] (468HB)
Come, Thou Fount of Every Blessing (St.2) [1 Peter 2:21-25]
(52SFGP)
The King of Love My Shepherd Is [Ps.23; John 10:1-30] (132HB)

DATE: Fifth Sunday of Easter

READINGS:
Acts 7:55-60
Psalm 31:1-5, 15-16
1 Peter 2:2-10
John 14:1-14

ORGAN MUSIC:

Prelude	Prelude and Fugue in A Major		J.S. Bach [7:00]
	Gott der Vater wohn uns bei [Ps.31:1-3]		
	(God, Our Father, Dwells Within)		
			J. Pachelbel [PA 2:60;5:00]
			D. Buxtehude [BC 32;3:00]
Offertory	Gott der Vater wohn uns bei		S. Scheidt [80:34;1:30]
Postlude	Gott der Vater wohn uns bei		
			J. Walther [GG 2:137;4:30]

SENIOR CHOIR:
Christ, Our Passover [Easter]   H. Willan

JUNIOR CHOIR:
Jesus the Christ Said [John 14:6] (SFGP 73)

HYMNS:
Christ Is Made the Sure Foundation [1 Peter 2:4-8; John 14:13-14] (145HB)
The Church's One Foundation [1 Peter 2:4-8] (145HB)
Seek Ye First the Kingdom of God [John 14:13-14] (711TH)
How Sweet the Name of Jesus Sounds [John 14:6] (116HB)

DATE: Sixth Sunday of Easter

READINGS:
Acts 17:22-31
Psalm 66:8-20
1 Peter 3:13-22
John 14:15-21

ORGAN MUSIC:
Prelude   Allein Gott in der Höh sei Ehr
            (All Glory Be to God on High)
                                           J.S. Bach [B18:67;9:00]
                                                    [B18:79;6:00]
Offertory   Allein Gott in der Höh sei Ehr
                                           J. Pachelbel [PA 2:24;2:00]
Postlude   Allein Gott in der Höh sei Ehr
                                           Pachelbel [PA 2:27;3:00]

SENIOR CHOIR:
If Ye Love Me [John 14:15-17]   T. Tallis

JUNIOR CHOIR:
Here Comes Jesus (SS 26)

HYMNS:
"Welcome Happy Morning!" Age to Age Shall Say [1 Peter 3:18-20]
(462HB)
My Song Is Love Unknown [1 Peter 3:18] (442HB)
Rejoice, the Lord Is King [1 Peter 3:22] (44HB)
Love Divine, All Loves Excelling [John 14:15-21] (241HB)
Come Down, O Love Divine [John 14:16] (67HB)

DATE: Seventh Sunday of Easter

READINGS:
Acts 1:6-14
Psalm 68:1-10, 32-35
1 Peter 4:12-14; 5:6-11
John 17:1-11

ORGAN MUSIC:
Prelude	Chorale No. 2	C. Franck [17:00]
Offertory	A solis ortus	N. DeGrigny [p.91;2:00]
Postlude	Carillon-Sortie	H. Mulet

SENIOR CHOIR:
The Parting Word the Saviour Spoke [Acts 5:1-14]   C. Tye
O Clap Your Hands Together All Ye People [Ascension]   M. Shaw
Ascended Is Our God and Lord [Ascension] [U]   M. Drischner

JUNIOR CHOIR:
Like a Mighty River Flowing (LP 145)

HYMNS:
Hail Thee, Festival Day [Acts 1:9] (476HB)
All Beautiful the March of Days [Acts 1:11] (388HB)
All Creatures of Our God and King [1 Peters 5:7] (1HB)

DATE: Day of Pentecost

READINGS:
Acts 2:1-21 or Numbers 11:24-30
Psalm 104:24-34, 35b
1 Corinthians 12:3b-13 or Acts 2:1-21
John 20:19-23 or John 7:37-39

ORGAN MUSIC:
Prelude   Komm, heiliger Geist, Herre Gott [Acts 2:4]
            (Come, holy Spirit, Lord God)
                                    J.S. Bach [B18:3;6:30]
                                        [B18:13;10:00]
Offertory   Komm, heiliger Geist, Herre Gott
                        G.F. Kauffmann [GG 2:142;2:00]
Postlude   Komm, heiliger Geist, Herre Gott
                        D. Buxtehude [BC 55;3:00]
                                    [BC 58;3:30]

SENIOR CHOIR:
There Came Jesus [John 20:19-20]   J. Handl
I Will Sing to the Lord [Ps.104:25,31-34] [U]   C. Schalk

JUNIOR CHOIR:
We Are One in the Spirit (LP 254)

HYMNS:
Hail Thee, Festival Day [Acts 2:1-42] (481HB)
She Flies On (St.5) [Acts 2:1-4] (126SFGP)
Spirit, Spirit of Gentleness (St.3) [Acts 2:1-4] (St.4) [Acts 2:16-21]
(108SFGP)
Come, Holy Ghost, Our Souls Inspire [Acts 2:1-3] (245HB)
Spirit Divine, Attend Our Prayers [Acts 2:1-3] (60HB)
This Is My Father's World [Ps.104:24-30] (82HB)
Immortal, Invisible [Ps.104:24-30] (26HB)
O Bread of Life [John 20:19-23] (68SFGP)

DATE: Trinity Sunday (First Sunday after Pentecost)

READINGS:
Genesis 1:1-2:4a
Psalm 8
2 Corinthians 13:11-13
Matthew 28:16-20

ORGAN MUSIC:
Prelude   Prelude and Fugue in Eb Major   J.S. Bach [17:00]
Offertory   Der Du bist drei in Einigkeit [Trinity]
             (Thou Who Art Three in One)
                                          J. Walther [GG2: 102;2:00]
Postlude   Der Du bist drei in Einigkeit
                                          J. Sweelinck [SA 46;4:30]

SENIOR CHOIR:
How Excellent Thy Name [Ps.8:1]   G.F. Handel
O Lord, Our Master, How Glorious Is
Thy Name [Ps. 8:1] [U]   G.P. Telemann
Holy, Holy, Holy [Trinity] [U]   H. Willan

JUNIOR CHOIR:

HYMNS:
All Things Bright and Beautiful [Gen.1:1-2:3] (86HB)
I Sing the Mighty Power of God [Gen 1:1-2:3] (94HB)
This Is My Father's World [Gen 1:1-2:3] (82HB)
For the Beauty of the Earth [Ps.8] (199HB)
Many and Great, O God, Are Your Works [Ps.8:1-4] (80SFGP)
Alleluia! Sing to Jesus (St.2) [Matthew 28:16-20] (49HB)

DATE: Sunday between May 29 and June 4 inclusive

READINGS:
Genesis 6:9-22; 7:24; 8:14-19 or Deuteronomy 11:18-21, 26-28
Psalm 46 or Psalm 31:1-5, 19-24
Romans 1:16-17, 3:22b-28, (29-31)
Matthew 7:21-29

ORGAN MUSIC:
Prelude   Prelude and Fugue in C Major
                (BWV 545)   J.S. Bach [7:00]
                In dich hab' ich gehoffet, Herr [Ps.31]
                (In Thee, Lord, Have I Put My Trust)
                                                          J.S. Bach [BU 48;3:00]
                                                          J.C.Bach [80:45;1:30]
                                                          J. Walther [WO 94;2:30]
                                                          J. Pachelbel [PA3:43;1:00]
Offertory   In dich hab' ich gehoffet, Herr
                                                          J. M. Bach [HP 28: 1:30]
Postlude   Mitten wir im Leben sind [Gen.7:21-24]
                (In the Midst of Life Are We)   Walther [GG1:46;2:30]

SENIOR CHOIR:
God Is Our Refuge [Ps.46:1]   W.A. Mozart
There Is a River [Ps.46:4] [U]   B. Marcello

JUNIOR CHOIR:

HYMNS:
Hail, Thou Once Despised Jesus [Romans 3:23-25a] (478HB)
Amazing Grace! How Sweet the Sound [Romans 3:23-24] (67SFGP)
How Firm a Foundation, Ye Saints of the Lord [Matthew 7:24-27]
(139HB)
Glorious Things of Thee Are Spoken [Matthew 7:24-25] (144HB)

DATE: Sunday between June 5 and June 11 inclusive

READINGS:
Genesis 12:1-9 or Hosea 5:15-6:6
Psalm 33:1-12 or Psalm 50:7-15
Romans 4:13-25
Matthew 9:9-13, 18-26

ORGAN MUSIC:

Prelude	Prelude and Fugue in E Major	D. Buxtehude [8:00]	
	Prelude, Fugue and Chaconne in C Major	[5:00]	
Offertory	O Mensch, willst du leben seliglich		
	(O Man, Will You Lead the Holy Life)		
		Buxtehude [BC 76;1:30]	
Postlude	Canzona in G Major	Buxtehude [3:30]	

SENIOR CHOIR:
Rejoice in the Lord [Ps.33:1-3]   L. Viadana

JUNIOR CHOIR:

HYMNS:
To Abraham and Sarah [Genesis 12:1-3] (123SFGP)
Lead On, O King Eternal [Hosea 6:3] (173HB)
When in Our Music God Is Glorified [Ps.33] (264PH)
Many and Great, O God, Are Your Works [Ps.33:4-9] (80SFGP)
There's a Wideness in God's Mercy [Ps.33:4-5] (76HB)
O For a Thousand Tongues to Sing [Matthew 9:18-26] (48HB)

DATE: Sunday between June 12 and June 18 inclusive

READINGS:
Genesis 18:1-15, (21:1-7) or Exodus 19:2-8a
Psalm 116:1-2, 12-19 or Psalm 100
Romans 5:1-8
Matthew 9:35 - 10:8, (9-23)

ORGAN MUSIC:

Prelude	Tiento del Quinto Tono	A. Cabezon [5:00]
	Tiento 5° tono	J. Cabanilles [4:00]
	Tiento	F. Araujo [5:30]
	Diferencias sobre el Canto del Caballero	Cabezon
Offertory	Tiento de falsas	Cabanilles [2:00]
Postlude	Tiento del Quinto Tono Transportado	Cabezon [3:00]

SENIOR CHOIR:
The Hundredth Psalm   R. Vaughan Williams

JUNIOR CHOIR:

HYMNS:
All People That on Earth Do Dwell [Ps.100] (12HB)
Come Down, O Love Divine [Romans 5:5] (67HB)
Come, Holy Spirit, Heavenly Dove [Romans 5:5] (244HB)
Come, Labor On [Matthew 9:37-38] (541TH)

DATE: Sunday between June 19 and June 25 inclusive

READINGS:
Genesis 21:8-21 or Jeremiah 20:7-13
Psalm 86:1-10, 16-17 or Psalm 69:7-10, (11-15), 16-18
Romans 6:1b-11
Matthew 10:24-39

ORGAN MUSIC:

Prelude	Prelude and Fugue in D Major	J.S. Bach [13:00]
Offertory	Hilf Gott, das mir's gelinge	
	(O Help Me, Lord, to Praise Thee)	Bach [BO 44;2:00]
Postlude	Fugue in E Minor	W.F. Bach [2:00]

SENIOR CHOIR:

Christ Being Raised From the Dead [General]	K. Bissell
With a Voice of Singing [General]	M. Shaw

JUNIOR CHOIR:

HYMNS:
Now There Is No Male or Female (St.2,3) [Romans 6:1-11] (62SFGP)
Out of Deep Unordered Water [Romans 6:1-11] (78SFGP)
On This Day, the First of Days [Romans 6:3-11] (373HB)
Good Christians All, Rejoice and Sing (St.4) [Romans 6:9-10] (469HB)

DATE: Sunday between June 26 and July 2 inclusive

READINGS:
Genesis 22:1-14 or Jeremiah 28:5-9
Psalm 13 or Psalm 89:1-4, 15-18
Romans 6:12-23
Matthew 10:40-42

ORGAN MUSIC:
Prelude	Suite for a Musical Clock	G.F. Handel [6:30]
	Voluntary No.8 in C Minor	M. Greene [4:00]
	Verse in F Major	H. Purcell [1:30]
	Voluntary No.13	Greene [2:30]
Offertory	Voluntary in A Major	J. Blow [2:00]
Postlude	Trumpet Tune	Purcell

SENIOR CHOIR:
I Have Trusted in Thy Mercy [Ps.13:5]   H. Willan

JUNIOR CHOIR:

HYMNS:
O Laughing Light (St.2) [Ps.89:15] (101SFGP)
There's a Spirit in the Air [Matthew 10:40-42] (433PH)
Where Cross the Crowded Ways of Life [Matthew 10:42] (303HB)

DATE: Sunday between July 3 and July 9 inclusive

READINGS:
Genesis 24:34-38, 42-49, 58-67 or Zechariah 9:9-12
Psalm 45:10-17 or Psalm 145:8-14
Romans 7:15-25a
Matthew 11:16-19, 25-30

ORGAN MUSIC:
Prelude	Toccata and Fugue in F Major	D. Buxtehude [5:00]
	Prelude and Fugue in E Minor	[4:30]
	Ich dank dir schon durch deinen Sohn	
	(I Give Thee Thanks Through Thy Son)	[BC 44;5:30]
Offertory	Prelude and Fugue in E Minor	J. Pachelbel [2:00]
Postlude	Toccata in G Minor	Pachelbel

SENIOR CHOIR:
Come Unto Me, All You That Labour and Are Heavy Laden
[Matt.11:18-30] [S or A solo]   H. Willan

JUNIOR CHOIR:

HYMNS:
Ride On, Ride on in Majesty [Zechariah 9:9] (449HB)
O Morning Star, How Fair and Bright [Ps.45] (112HU)
Ye Servants of God (St.1) [Ps.145:10-13] (94SFGP)
I Heard the Voice of Jesus Say (St.1) [Matthew 11:28] (115HB)
Jesus Shall Reign [Matthew 11:28] (164HB)

DATE: Sunday between July 10 and July 16 inclusive

READINGS:
Genesis 25:19-34 or Isaiah 55:10-13
Psalm 119:105-112 or Psalm 65:(1-8), 9-13
Romans 8:1-11
Matthew 13:1-9, 18-23

ORGAN MUSIC:
Prelude	Prelude and Fugue in G Minor	J.S. Bach [7:30]
	Toccata and Fugue in G Minor	J. Eberlin [5:30]
Offertory	Fantasia	J. Pachelbel [2:00]
Postlude	Fugue in F Minor	W.F. Bach

SENIOR CHOIR:
Thou Visitest the Earth [Ps.65:9-11] [SA Duet]   M. Greene

JUNIOR CHOIR:

HYMNS:
O Word of God Incarnate [Ps.119:105] (335LW)
O Beautiful for Spacious Skies [Ps.65:9-13] (68HU)
Sing to the Lord of Harvest [Ps.65:9-13] (382HB)
Sent Forth by God's Blessing [Matthew 13:1-9, 18-23] (96SFGP)
Come, Labor On [Matthew 13:3-43] (541TH)

DATE: Sunday between July 17 and July 23 inclusive

READINGS:
Genesis 28:10-19a or Wisdom of Solomon 12:13, 16-19 or Isaiah 44:6-8
Psalm 139:1-12, 23-24 or Psalm 86:11-17
Romans 8:12-25
Matthew 13:24-30, 36-43

ORGAN MUSIC:
Prelude   Was Gott tut, das ist wohlgetan [Rom.8:28]
               (What God Does Is Well Done)
                              J. Pachelbel (Partita) [PA 4:30;10:30]
                                       J.L. Krebs [GT 3:126;5:00]
                                       F.W. Marpurg [MC 55;2:00]
                                       J. Walther [WO 129;3:00]
Offertory   Was Gott tut, das ist wohlgetan
                                       J.S. Bach [BN 60;2:00]
Postlude   Was Gott tut, das ist wohlgetan
                                       J.P. Kellner [GT 3:122;3:30]

SENIOR CHOIR:
Bow Down Thine Ear, O Lord [Ps.86] [SA]   A.S. Arensky

JUNIOR CHOIR:

HYMNS:
O God of Bethel, By Whose Hand [Genesis 28:10-22] (263HB)
We Are Climbing Jacob's Ladder [Genesis 28:10-17] (418UM)
Abide With Me [Ps.139:11-12] (180HB)
In Christ There Is No East or West [Romans 8:14-17] (149HB)
Father Eternal, Ruler of Creation [Romans 8:18-23] (279HB)
For the Healing of the Nations (St.4) [Romans 8:18-23] (23SFGP)
Come, Labor On [Matthew 13:3-43] (541TH)
Come, You Thankful People, Come [Matthew 13:24-30, 36-43]
(384HB)

DATE: Sunday between July 24 and July 30 inclusive

READINGS:
Genesis 29:15-28 or 1 Kings 3:5-12
Psalm 105:1-11, 45b or Psalm 128 or Psalm 119:129-136
Romans 8:26-39
Matthew 13:31-33, 44-52

ORGAN MUSIC:

Prelude	Jesu, meine Freude [Matt.13:44-46]	
	(Jesus, Priceless Treasure)	
		F.W. Zachau [GT 2:109;5:00]
		J.S. Bach [BO 19;3:00]
		[BU 54;4:00]
		[BN 38;1:30]
Offertory	Jesu, meine Freude	F.W. Marpurg [MC 22;2:00]
Postlude	Postlude in D Minor	A. Bruckner [2:00]

SENIOR CHOIR:
Offer Thanks Unto the Lord [Ps.105:1-2] [SAB]   W. Croft

JUNIOR CHOIR:

HYMNS:
Guide Me, O Thou Great Jehovah [Ps.105] (269HB)
Immortal, Invisible, God Only Wise [Ps.105:1-2] (26HB)
God Moves in a Mysterious Way [Romans 8:28] (159HB)
What God Ordains Is Always Good [Romans 8:28] (422LW)
Soldiers of Christ, Arise [Romans 8:37] (171HB)
Jesus, Priceless Treasure [Matthew 13:44-46] (270LW)

DATE: Sunday between July 31 and August 6 inclusive

READINGS:
Genesis 32:22-31 or Isaiah 55:1-5
Psalm 17:1-7, 15 or Psalm 145:8-9, 14-21
Romans 9:1-5
Matthew 14:13-21

ORGAN MUSIC:
Prelude   Toccata and Fugue in E Major   J.S. Bach [12:00]
             Kommt her zu mir, spricht Gottes Sohn
             (Come Unto Me, Said God's Son)
                                         J. Walther [WO 75;3:00]
Offertory   Kommt her zu mir, spricht Gottes Sohn
                                    Walther [GG 1:38;1:30]
Postlude   Fugue in C Major   J. Pachelbel [2:00]

SENIOR CHOIR:
Give Ear Unto Me [Ps.17]   B. Marcello
Lord Jesus Christ, Be Present Now [General] [U]   M. Drischner

JUNIOR CHOIR:

HYMNS:
Come Let Us Sing (St.2) [Isaiah 55:1] (90SFGP)
Break Now the Bread of Life [Matthew 14:13-21] (86SFGP)
Love Divine, All Loves Excelling [Matthew 14:14] (241HB)

DATE: Sunday between August 7 and August 13 inclusive

READINGS:
Genesis 37:1-4, 12-28 or 1 Kings 19:9-18
Psalm 105:1-6, 16-22, 45b or Psalm 85:8-13
Romans 10:5-15
Matthew 14:22-32

ORGAN MUSIC:

Prelude	Prelude and Fugue in F Major	D. Buxtehude [6:30]
	Nimm von uns, Herr, du treuer Gott	
	(Take From Us, Lord, Thou True God)	[BC 82;6:00]
	Werde munter, mein Gemüte	
	(Jesu, Joy of Man's Desiring)	J. Pachelbel [4:00]
Offertory	Werde munter, mein Gemüte	J. Walther [WO 134;3:00]
Postlude	Toccata in C Minor	Pachelbel [2:00]

SENIOR CHOIR:
How Lovely Are the Messengers [Romans 10:15]   F. Mendelssohn

JUNIOR CHOIR:

HYMNS:
Dear Lord and Father of Mankind [1 Kings 19:9-12] (249HB)
Guide Me, O Thou Great Jehovah [Ps.105] (269HB)
Rejoice, Ye Pure in Heart [Ps.105:1-3] (156HU)
Immortal, Invisible, God Only Wise [Ps.105:1-2] (26HB)
At the Name of Jesus [Romans 10:8-13] (39HB)
Eternal Father, Strong to Save [Matthew 14:22-33] (221HB)

DATE: Sunday between August 14 and August 20 inclusive

READINGS:
Genesis 45:1-15 or Isaiah 56:1, 6-8
Psalm 133 or Psalm 67
Romans 11:1-2a, 29-32
Matthew 15:(10-20), 21-28

ORGAN MUSIC:

Prelude	Prelude and Fugue in E Major	D. Buxtehude [6:00]
	O Herr Gott, dein Göttlich Wort	
	(O Lord God, Thy Godly Word)	
		J. Walther [WO 112;9:00]
Offertory	Straf mich nicht in deiner Zorn	
	(Strike Me Not in Thy Anger)	Walther [GG 1:62;1:00]
Postlude	O Ewigkeit, du Donnerwort	
	(O Eternity, Thou Thundrous Word)	
		Walther [GG 1:54;3:00]

SENIOR CHOIR:
God Be Merciful Unto Us and Bless Us [Ps.67]   H. Willan

JUNIOR CHOIR:

HYMNS:
Behold, How Pleasant [Ps.133] (120SFGP)
God of Grace and God of Glory [Ps.67] (223HB)

DATE: Sunday between August 21 and August 27 inclusive

READINGS:
Exodus 1:8 - 2:10 or Isaiah 51:1-6
Psalm 124 or Psalm 138
Romans 12:1-8
Matthew 16:13-20

ORGAN MUSIC:

Prelude	Voluntary No. 6 in D Minor	W. Walond	[8:30]
	Voluntary for Double Organ	H. Purcell	[5:30]
Offertory	Prelude on "Martyrdom"	H. Willan	[WH 2:33;2:00]
Postlude	Prelude on "Hyfrydol"	Willan	[WH 1:10]

SENIOR CHOIR:
A Living Sacrifice [Romans 12:1-2]   R.M. Johnson

JUNIOR CHOIR:

HYMNS:
To Show By Touch and Word (St.2) [Romans 12:1-2] (134SFGP)
Many Are the Lightbeams (Sts.3-5) [Romans 12:1-2] (104SFGP)
The Church's One Foundation [Matthew 16:15-18] (146HB)
Glorious Things of Thee Are Spoken [Matthew 16:18] (144HB)

DATE: Sunday between August 28 and September 3 inclusive

READINGS:
Exodus 3:1-15 or Jeremiah 15:15-21
Psalm 105:1-6, 23-26, 45c or Psalm 26:1-8
Romans 12:9-21
Matthew 16:21-28

ORGAN MUSIC:
Prelude	Prelude and Fugue in C Major	
	(BWV 531)	J.S. Bach [7:00]
	Prelude and Fugue in G Major	
	(BWV 550)	[8:00]
Offertory	Alle Menschen müssen sterben	
	(All Men Must Die)	Bach [BN 62;2:00]
Postlude	Mach's mit mir, Gott, nach deinen Güt	
	(According to Thy Goodness, Lord)	Bach [BN 64;2:30]

SENIOR CHOIR:
O Lord, I Cry to Thee [Ps.26]   J. Arcadelt

JUNIOR CHOIR:

HYMNS:
The God of Abraham Praise [Exodus 3:6, 14] (450LW)
Go Down, Moses [Exodus 3:7-12] (143HB)
Guide Me, O Thou Great Jehovah [Ps.105] (269HB)
Rejoice, Ye Pure in Heart [Ps.105:1-3] (156HU)
Immortal, Invisible, God Only Wise [Ps.105:1-2] (26HB)
We Love the Place, O Lord [Ps.26] (355HB)
The Servant Song (St.4) [Romans 12:15] (133SFGP)
New Every Morning Is the Love [Matthew 16:24] (360HB)

DATE: Sunday between September 4 and September 10 inclusive

READINGS:
Exodus 12:1-14 or Ezekiel 33:7-11
Psalm 149 or Psalm 119:33-40
Romans 13:8-14
Matthew 18:15-20

ORGAN MUSIC:

Prelude	Voluntary in A Minor	J. Stanley [6:00]
		[Hinrichsen 1035:5]
	Voluntary in F Major	[4:00]
	Echo Voluntary in G Major	J. Blow [4:00]
Offertory	Prelude on "St. Columba"	H. Willan [WH 1:32;2:00]
Postlude	Voluntary in G Major	Stanley [4:30]
		[Hinrichsen 1033:16]

SENIOR CHOIR:

Sing to the Lord [Ps.149]   J.P. Sweelinck
O Jesu, Joy of Loving Hearts [General] [U]   J. Brahms

JUNIOR CHOIR:

HYMNS:
At the Lamb's High Feast We Sing [Exodus 12:1-28] (174TH)
To Show By Touch and Word (St.3) [Romans 13:8-10] (134SFGP)
Christ Is Made the Sure Foundation [Matthew 18:19-20] (145HB)
There's a Quiet Understanding [Matthew 18:20] (66SFGP)

DATE: Sunday between September 11 and September 17 inclusive

READINGS:
Exodus 14:19-31 or Genesis 50:15-21
Psalm 114 or Exodus 15:1b-11, 20-21 or Psalm 103:(1-7), 8-13
Romans 14:1-12
Matthew 18:21-35

ORGAN MUSIC:

Prelude	Messe pour les Couvents	F. Couperin [15:00]
	Plein Jeu	[p.3]
	Fugue sur la Trompette	[p.4]
	Récit de Chromhorne	[p.6]
	Dialogue	[p.10]
	Chromhorne sur la Taille	[p.18]
	Dialogue sur la Voix humaine	[p.20]
	Recit de tierce	[p.24]
	Dialogue sur les grands jeux	[p.26]
	Elevation	[p.36]
	Dialogue sur les grands jeux	[p.40]
Offertory	Duo	N. DeGrigny [2:00]
Postlude	Postlude II	J. Langlais

SENIOR CHOIR:

Psalm 114	Z. Kodály∗
Let Shouts of Gladness Rise [General] [U]	D. Buxtehude

JUNIOR CHOIR:
This Little Gospel Light of Mine (LOSP 103)

HYMNS:
Come, Ye Faithful, Raise the Strain [Exodus 14:21-15:21] (464HB)
The Day of Resurrection [Exodus 14:21-15:21] (374HB)
Crown Him With Many Crowns [Romans 14:9] (480HB)
Where Charity and Love Prevail (St.4) [Matthew 18:21-35] (6SFGP)
Help Us Accept Each Other (St.3) [Matthew 18:21-22] (8SFGP)

DATE: Sunday between September 18 and September 24 inclusive

READINGS:
Exodus 16:2-15 or Jonah 3:10-4:11
Psalm 105:1-6, 37-45 or Psalm 145:1-8
Philippians 1:21-30
Matthew 20:1-16

ORGAN MUSIC:
Prelude   Sonata No.2 in C Major   J.S. Bach [14:00]
Offertory   Gott ist mein Heil, mein Hilf und Trost
             (God Is My Saviour, My Help and Comfort)
                                                        Bach [BN 39;2:30]
Postlude   Toccata in G Minor   J. Pachelbel [2:00]

SENIOR CHOIR:
O God, My King [Ps.145:1,3,8,21]   J. Amner
I Come Like a Beggar [General] [U]   S. Carter

JUNIOR CHOIR:
He's Got the Whole Word in His Hands (HB 84)

HYMNS:
Glorious Things of Thee Are Spoken [Exodus 16:4-17:6] (144HB)
Lord, Enthroned in Heavenly Splendor [Exodus 15:4-17:6] (324HB)
Guide Me, Oh Thou Great Jehovah [Exodus 16:4-35] (269HB)
Rejoice, Ye Pure in Heart [Ps.105:1-3] (156HU)
Immortal, Invisible, God Only Wise [Ps.105:1-2] (26HB)
Hark, the Voice of Jesus Calling [Matthew 20:1-16] (318LW)

DATE: Sunday between September 25 and October 1 inclusive

READINGS:
Exodus 17:1-7 or Ezekiel 18:1-4, 25-32
Psalm 78:1-4, 12-16 or Psalm 25:1-9
Philippians 2:1-13
Matthew 21:23-32

ORGAN MUSIC:

Prelude	Auf meinen lieben Gott [Ps.25:1-8]	
	(In God, My Faithful God)	
		G. Böhm [BS 28;9:00]
		D. Buxtehude [80:10;4:30]
		J. Pachelbel [PA 3:88;2:30]
		F.W. Zachau [GG 1:10;1:00]
		N. Hanff [HS 6;1:00]
Offertory	Auf meinen lieben Gott	J.S. Bach [BSC 90;2:00]
Postlude	Auf meinen lieben Gott	Bach [BU 103;3:30]

SENIOR CHOIR:

At the Name of Jesus [Phil.2:10,11]	J. Handl
Beautiful Savior [General] [U]	H. Willan

JUNIOR CHOIR:
Holy, Holy, Holy Is the Lord (LP 74)

HYMNS:
Glorious Things of Thee Are Spoken [Exodus 17:1-6] (144HB)
Guide Me, O Thou Great Jehovah [Exodus 17:6] (269HB)
In God, My Faithful God [Ps.25:1-8] (421LW)
All Hail the Power of Jesus' Name [Phil.2:5-11] (42HB)
At the Name of Jesus [Phil.2:5-11] (39HB)
Rejoice, the Lord Is King [Phil.2:9-11] (44HB)

DATE: Sunday between October 2 and October 8 inclusive

READINGS:
Exodus 20:1-4, 7-9, 12-20 or Isaiah 5:1-7
Psalm 19 or Psalm 80:7-15
Philippians 3:4b-14
Matthew 21:33-46

ORGAN MUSIC:
Prelude	Cortège et Litanie	M. Dupré [9:00]
	Antiphons II, III	[6:00]
Offertory	Antiphon V	[2:30]
Postlude	Antiphon I	[3:00]

SENIOR CHOIR:
The Heavens Are Telling [Ps.19]   L. Beethoven
The Heavens Declare the Creator's Glory [U]   L. Beethoven

JUNIOR CHOIR:
I Will Sing, I Will Sing (LP 99)

HYMNS:
O Come, O Come, Emmanuel [Exodus 20:1-20] (390HB)
All Beautiful the March of Days [Ps.19] (388HB)
The Spacious Firmament on High [Ps.19] (85HB)
Holy, Holy, Holy! [Ps.19:1-6] (50HB)
Be Thou My Vision [Phil.3:7] (253HB)
Awake, My Soul, Stretch Every Nerve [Phil.3:12-14] (546TH)

DATE: Sunday between October 9 and October 15

READINGS:
Exodus 32:1-14 or Isaiah 25:1-9
Psalm 106:1-6, 19-23 or Psalm 23
Philippians 4:1-9
Matthew 22:1-14

ORGAN MUSIC:

Prelude	Schmücke dich, o liebe Seele [Matt.22:1-14]	
	(Deck Thyself, My Soul, With Gladness)	
		G.P. Telemann [HP 38:20;2:30]
		J. Walther [WO 122;6:30]
		J.S. Bach [B18:26;5:30]
Offertory	Schmücke dich, o liebe Seele	J. Brahms [BE 18;1:30]
Postlude	Schmücke dich, o liebe Seele	
		F.W. Marpurg [MC 59;2:30]

SENIOR CHOIR:

Rejoice in the Lord Alway [Phil.4:4-7]	J. Redford
Praise to the Lord, the Almighty [General] [U]	M. Drischner

JUNIOR CHOIR:
Like a Mighty River Flowing [Phil.4:7] (LP 145)

HYMNS:
Jesus, Lover of My Soul [Isaiah 25:4] (77HB)
Guide Me, O Thou Great Jehovah [Ps.106] (269HB)
Now Thank We All Our God [Ps.106:1] (197HB)
Come, You Faithful, Raise the Strain [Ps.106:1-12] (464HB)
Rejoice, the Lord Is King [Phil.4:4] (44HB)
Deck Thyself, My Soul, With Gladness [Matt.22:1-14] (333HB)

DATE: Sunday between October 16 and October 22 inclusive

READINGS:
Exodus 33:12-23 or Isaiah 45:1-7
Psalm 99 or Psalm 96:1-9 (10-13)
1 Thessalonians 1:1-10
Matthew 22:15-22

ORGAN MUSIC:

Prelude	Prelude and Fugue in A Minor	D. Buxtehude [6:00]
	Partita on "St. Flavian"	H. Willan [WH 1:17;5:30]
	Chorale	R. Turner [2:30]
Offertory	Prelude	Turner [2:00]
Postlude	Prelude on "Old 124th"	Willan [WH 2:22]

SENIOR CHOIR:
Jesus and the Pharisees [Matt.22:20-22]   M. Franck
Eternal Father, Who Hast Called Us [General] [U]
                                              R. Vaughan Williams

JUNIOR CHOIR:
Morning Has Broken (SFGP 103)

HYMNS:
God the Omnipotent [Isaiah 45:5-8] (273HB)
Oh, For a Thousand Tongues to Sing [Ps.96:1-3] (48HB)
This Is the Threefold Truth [1 Thess.1:2-10] (99SFGP)

DATE: Sunday between October 23 and October 29 inclusive

READINGS:
Deuteronomy 34:1-12 or Leviticus 19:1-2, 15-18
Psalm 90:1-6, 13-17 or Psalm 1
1 Thessalonians 2:1-8
Matthew 22:34-46

ORGAN MUSIC:
Prelude	Prelude and Fugue in E Minor [BWV 548]	
		J.S. Bach [15:00]
Offertory	Wo Gott der Herr nicht bei uns hält	
	(If Lord God Dwell Not With Us)	
		J. Pachelbel [PA 3:77;2:00]
Postlude	Prelude and Fugue in C Minor	A. Bruckner [3:00]

SENIOR CHOIR:
Turn Thee Again, O Lord [Ps.90:13]	T. Attwood
If God Himself Be For Me [General] [U]	M. Drischner

JUNIOR CHOIR:
All Things Bright and Beautiful (HB 86)

HYMNS:
Love, Love, Love Your God [Lev.19:18] (43SFGP)
Our God, Our Help in Ages Past [Ps.90] (133HB)
Immortal, Invisible, God Only Wise [Ps.90:4-7] (46HB)
Rise Up, Ye Saints of God [Matthew 22:37-40] (172HB)
All Hail the Power of Jesus' Name [Matthew 22:41-46] (42HB)

DATE: Sunday between October 30 and November 5 inclusive

READINGS:
Joshua 3:7-17 or Micah 3:5-12
Psalm 107:1-7, 33-37 or Psalm 43
1 Thessalonions 2:9-13
Matthew 23:1-12

ORGAN MUSIC:
Prelude	Suite du 1er Ton	L.-N. Clérambault [15:00]
Offertory	Guide Me, O Thou Great Jehovah	
		F. Peeters [PH 20:1]
Postlude	Toccata	C. Widor [5:00]

SENIOR CHOIR:
Oh, Send Out Thy Light [Ps.43:3,4]   H. Willan

JUNIOR CHOIR:
I Sing a Song of the Saints of God [All Saints] (P481)

HYMNS:
Guide Me, O Thou Great Jehovah [Joshua 3:17] (269HB)

DATE: Sunday between November 6 and November 12 inclusive

READINGS:
Joshua 24:1-3a, 14-25 or Wisdom of Solomon 6:12-16 or Amos
5:18-24
Psalm 78:1-7 or Wisdom of Solomon 6:17-20 or Psalm 70
1 Thessalonians 4:13-18
Matthew 25:1-13

ORGAN MUSIC:
Prelude	Prelude in D Minor	G. Böhm [5:30]
	Wachet auf, ruft uns die Stimme [Matt.25:1-13]	
	("Sleepers, Wake!" the Watch Are Calling)	
		J.S. Bach [BSC 86;5:00]
		J. Walther [GG 1:70;4:00]
Offertory	Wachet auf, ruft uns die Stimme	
		S. Scheidt [EK 3:234;1:30]
Postlude	Prelude and Fugue in A Minor	Böhm [3:00]

SENIOR CHOIR:
Rejoice, Rejoice, Believers [Matt.25:1-13]	M. Praetorius
Sleepers, Wake! [Matt.25:6]	F. Mendelssohn
Wake, Awake, For Night Is Flying [Matt.25:6] [U]	M. Drischner

JUNIOR CHOIR:
Give Me Oil in My Lamp [Matt.25:1-13] (SFGP 130)

HYMNS:
Guide Me, O Thou Great Jehovah [Joshua 24:3] (269HB)
Once to Every Man and Nation [Joshua 24:14-15] (167HB)
Our Father, by Whose Name [Joshua 24:15] (219HB)
Lo! He Comes, With Clouds Descending [1 Thess.4:16-17]
"Sleepers, Wake!" the Watch Are Calling [Matthew 25:1-13]
(394HB)
Rejoice, Rejoice, Believers [Matthew 25:1-13] (68TH)

DATE: Sunday between November 13 and November 19 inclusive

READINGS:
Judges 4:1-7 or Zephaniah 1:7, 12-18
Psalm 123 or Psalm 90:1-8, (9-11), 12
1 Thessalonians 5:1-11
Matthew 25:14-30

ORGAN MUSIC:

Prelude	Prelude and Fugue in F Major	V. Lübeck [3:30]
	Concerto in D Minor	J.S. Bach [11:00]
Offertory	Christe, der du bist Tag und Licht	
	(O Christ, Who Art the Light and Day)	
		Bach [BN 70;2:30]
Postlude	Concerto in C Major	Bach [4:00]

SENIOR CHOIR:

Turn Back, O Man [General]	G. Holst
Commit Whatever Grieves Thee [General] [U]	M. Drischner

JUNIOR CHOIR:
Gloria, Gloria (UM 72)

HYMNS:
Eternal Ruler of the Ceaseless Round [1 Thess.5:8] (252HB)
Soldiers of Christ, Arise [1 Thess.5:8] (171HB)
God, Whose Giving Knows No Ending (St.2) [Matthew 25:14-30]
(56SFGP)
Come, Labor On [Matthew 25:14-30] (415PH)

DATE: Sunday between November 20 and November 26 inclusive
(Christ the King)

READINGS:
Ezekial 34:11-16, 20-24
Psalm 100 or Psalm 95:1-7a
Ephesians 1:15-23
Matthew 25:31-46

ORGAN MUSIC:

Prelude	Passacaglia in G Minor	G. Muffat [16:30]
	Du Friedefürst, Herr Jesu Christ	
	(Thou Prince of Peace, Our Christ and Lord)	
		J.S. Bach [BN 33;3:00]
Offertory	Du Friedefürst, Herr Jesu Christ	
		J.B. Bach [GT 1:123;1:30]
		[GG 2:106;1:00]
Postlude	Prelude on "Rejoice the Lord Is King"	
		H. Willan [WP 1:8]

SENIOR CHOIR:

Serve the Lord With Gladness [Ps.100]	A. Caldara
Before Him [Matthew 25:32-33] [U]	K. Nystedt

JUNIOR CHOIR:
When I Needed a Neighbour [Matt.25:31-46] (SFGP 131)

HYMNS:
All People That on Earth Do Dwell [Ps.100] (12HB)
Christus Paradox (St.3) [Ephesians 1:20-22] (64SFGP)
All Glory Be to God on High [Ephesians 1:20; Matthew 25:31-46]
(421TH)
Christ Is Made the Sure Foundation [Ephesians 1:22-23] (145HB)
Rejoice, the Lord Is King [Matthew 25:31-46] (44HB)
Crown Him With Many Crowns [Matthew 25:31] (480HB)

DATE: All Saints (November 1 or the First Sunday in November)

READINGS:
Revelation 7:9-17
Psalm 34:1-10, 22
1 John 3:1-3
Matthew 5:1-12

ORGAN MUSIC:
[See October 30]

SENIOR CHOIR:
Let Us Now Praise Famous Men [All Saints] [U]

R. Vaughan Williams

JUNIOR CHOIR:
Lord, I Want to Be a Christian [1 John 3:2] (UM 402)

HYMNS:
Jerusalem the Golden [Rev.7:9-17] (184HB)
Lord, Enthroned in Heavenly Splendor [Rev.7:9-17] (324HB)
Ye Holy Angels Bright [Rev.7:9-17] (6HB)
Ye Watchers and Ye Holy Ones [Rev.7:9-17) (7HB)

DATE: Thanksgiving

READINGS:
Deuteronomy 8:7-18
Psalm 65
2 Corinthians 9:6-15
Luke 17:11-19

ORGAN MUSIC:
Prelude	Toccata Undecima	G. Muffat [6:00]
	Herr Gott, dich loben alle wir	
	(Old Hundredth)	J. Blow [HP 18:15;3:00]
		H. Willan [WH 1:28;2:30]
		H. Purcell [Works,16;3:00]
		J.C. Bach [PO I:117;1:00]
Offertory	Herr Gott, dich loben alle wir	
		J. Pachelbel [GT 2:13;2:00]
Postlude	Herr Gott, dich loben alle wir	
		J. Walther [GT 2:15,16;3:00]

SENIOR CHOIR:
Laudate Dominum [Ps.65]   K. Bissell
Thanks Be to Thee [General] [U]   G.F. Handel

JUNIOR CHOIR:
Let All Things Now Living   arr. Davis

HYMNS:
I Sing the Mighty Power [Ps.65:5-13] (81HB)
All Creatures of Our God and King [Ps.65:8-13] (436LW)
O Beautiful For Spacious Skies [Ps.65:9-13] (68HU)
Sing to the Lord of Harvest [Ps.65:9-13] (382HB)
Amazing Grace! How Sweet the Sound [2 Cor.9:8] (67SFGP)
Come, Ye Thankful People, Come [2 Cor.9:10-12] (384HB)

YEAR B

Begins on the First Sunday of Advent 1996, 1999, 2002, 2005

DATE: First Sunday of Advent

READINGS:
Isaiah 64:1-9
Psalm 80:1-7, 17-19
1 Corinthians 1:3-9
Mark 13:24-37

ORGAN MUSIC:

Prelude	Noels 4, 5, 6	M.-A. Charpentier [13:30]
Offertory	Noel 1	Charpentier [2:30]
Postlude	Noel 2	Charpentier [3:00]

SENIOR CHOIR:
O Blessed Lord, Our God [Matt.13:33-37]   H. Schütz
Creator of the Stars of Night [Advent] [U]   M. Drischner

JUNIOR CHOIR:
Down to Earth, as a Dove (HB 425)
On This Day Earth Shall Ring (UM 46)

HYMNS:
O Come, O Come, Emmanuel [Ps.80:14-19] (390HB)
Lo! He Comes, With Clouds Descending [Mark 13:24-27] (393HB)
Rejoice! Rejoice, Believers [Mark 13:32-37] (68TH)
"Sleepers, Wake!" the Watch Are Calling [Mark 13:32-37] (394HB)

DATE: Second Sunday of Advent

READINGS:
Isaiah 40:1-11
Psalm 85:1-2, 8-13
2 Peter 3:8-15a
Mark 1:1-8

ORGAN MUSIC:
Prelude   Freu dich sehr, o meine Seele [Is.40:1-8]
               (Comfort, Comfort These My People)
                                           G. Böhm [BS 58:16]
                                    J. Pachelbel [PA 4:48;6:00]
Offertory   Freu dich sehr, o meine Seele
                                      J.C. Oley [GT 1:16;1:30]
Postlude   Freu dich sehr, o meine Seele
                                      J. Walther [WO 40;4:30]

SENIOR CHOIR:
And the Glory of the Lord [Is.40:5]   G.F. Handel
For Unto Us a Child Is Born [Is.40:6]   Handel

JUNIOR CHOIR:
Infant Holy, Infant Lowly (UM 229)

HYMNS:
Comfort, Comfort These My People [Isaiah 40:1-8; Mark 1:1-4]
(28LW)
There's a Voice in the Wilderness Crying [Isaiah 40:1-11; Mark 1:1-4]
(153HB)
Herald, Sound the Note of Judgement [Isaiah 40:1-5; Mark 8:1-8]
(103HB)
On Jordan's Bank the Baptist's Cry [Isaiah 40:1-5,7; Mark 8:1-8]
(391HB)
Songs of Thankfulness and Praise (St.2) [Mark 1:1-11] (443HB)

DATE: Third Sunday of Advent

READINGS:
Isaiah 61:1-4, 8-11
Psalm 126 or Luke 1:47-55
1 Thessalonians 5:16-24
John 1:6-8, 19-28

ORGAN MUSIC:
Prelude	Noels 5, 6, 7	C. Daquin [14:30]
Offertory	Come, Thou Long-Expected Jesus	
		J. Bender [PO 12:68]
Postlude	Noel 8	Daquin [4:00]

SENIOR CHOIR:
Over the Hills Young Mary Hastes [Luke 1:47-55]   J. Eccard
O Lord, How Shall I Meet Thee [Advent] [U]   M. Drischner

JUNIOR CHOIR:
'Twas in the Moon of Winter Time (HB 412)

HYMNS:
I Am the Light of the World [Isaiah 61:1-3] (24SFGP)
Come, Thou Long-Expected Jesus [Isaiah 61:1-2] (389HB)
Hark, the Herald Angels Sing [Isaiah 61:1-3] (407HB)
Songs of Thankfulness and Praise [Isaiah 61:1-3] (433HB)
Herald, Sound the Note of Judgment [John 1:15-28] (103HB)
Hark! a Thrilling Voice Is Sounding [John 1:19-36] (59TH)

DATE: Fourth Sunday of Advent

READINGS:
2 Samuel 7:1-11, 16
Luke 1:47-55 or Psalm 89:1-4, 19-26
Romans 16:25-27
Luke 1:26-38

ORGAN MUSIC:
Prelude   Album of Noels   A.P.F. Boely [15:00]
                Quel étonnement vient saisir mon âme
                Seigneur Dieu ouvre la porte
                Réveillez-vous pastoureaux
                Esprits divins
                Ici je ne bâtis pas
                Sus, sus qu'on se réveille
                Le vermeil du Soleil
                Lyre ce n'est pas en ce chant
                Voici la première entrée
                Muses soeurs de la peinture
                Sus bergers en campagne

Offertory   Prelude on "This Endris Nyght"
                                    H. Willan [WH 2:19;2:00]
Postlude   Lob sei dem allmächtigen Gott [Luke 1:26-38]
                (To God We Render Thanks and Praise)
                                    J.S. Bach [BU 62;1:00]
                                        [BO 7;1:00]

SENIOR CHOIR:
The Angel Gabriel [Luke 1:26-38]   [Carol]
Rejoice, Rejoice, Believers [Advent] [U]   M. Drischner

JUNIOR CHOIR:
Mary Had a Baby (LOSP 90)

HYMNS:
God of the Prophets [Romans 16:25-26] (62HU)
Creator of the Stars of Night [Luke 1:26-38] (396HB)

Lo, How a Rose E'er Blooming [Luke 1:26-38] (81TH)
Of the Father's Love Begotten (St.2) [Luke 1:26-38] (429HB)
She Flies On (St.3) [Luke 1:26-38] (126SFGP)
[For Luke 1:47-55, see Advent 3: Year A, and Advent 4: Year C]

DATE: Christmas Eve

READINGS:

ORGAN MUSIC:
Prelude   Vom Himmel hoch, da komm ich her [Luke 2:1-20]
           (From Heaven on High to Earth I Come)
                                          J.S. Bach [BO 13;1:00]
                                          [BU 92,94,96;6:30]
                                          G. Böhm [BS 106;1:30]
                                          F.W. Marpurg [MC 7;2:30]
                                          F.W. Zachau [GG 1:65;3:00]
Offertory Vom Himmel kam der Engel schar
           (From Heaven Came the Angel Host)
                                          Bach [BO 14;2:00]
Postlude   Ave Maris Stella   N. DeGrigny [Works p.83]

SENIOR CHOIR:
Gloria from "Harmoniemesse"   F.J. Haydn
Joseph, Dearest Joseph Mine [Christmas] [U]   M. Drischner

JUNIOR CHOIR:
Christmas Song   G. Holst

HYMNS:
Carols

DATE: Christmas Day

READINGS: [Proper II; for Proper I, see Year A]
Isaiah 62:6-12
Psalm 97
Titus 3:4-7
Luke 2:(1-7), 8-20

ORGAN MUSIC:
Prelude   Lobt Gott, ihr Christen, allzugleich [Luke 2:1-20]
              (Let All Together Praise Our God)
                                          J. Walther [WB 19;7:30]
                                          V. Lübeck [ADW 8;1:30]
                                          D. Buxtehude [BC 62;1:30]
                                          J.C. Bach [GT 2:147;1:00]
              Christmas Carol   A. Cabezon [HOR 6:3;2:00]
Offertory   Lobt Gott, ihr Christen, allzugleich
                                          J.S. Bach [BO 18;1:00]
                                                    [BU 64;1:00]
Postlude   Verbum Supernum   N. DeGrigny [Works, p.74]

SENIOR CHOIR:
Glory to God in the Highest [Luke 2:8-20]   G.B. Pergolesi
The Seed Is the Word of God [Luke 2:11,15] [U]   H. Willan

JUNIOR CHOIR:
Go, Tell It on the Mountain (JS 9)

HYMNS:
Carols [See list under Luke 2:1-20 in Part II]

DATE: First Sunday after Christmas

READINGS:
Isaiah 61:10 - 62:3
Psalm 148
Galatians 4:4-7
Luke 2:22-40

ORGAN MUSIC:
Prelude   Mit Fried und Freud ihr fahr dahin [Luke 2:29-37]
               (In Peace and Joy I Now Depart) [Nunc Dimittis]
                              D. Buxtehude [BC 77;7:30]
                                    J.S. Bach [BO 30;2:30]
                              F.W. Zachau [HP 32:40;1:30]
               Herr Gott, nun schleuss den Himmel auf [Luke 2:29-32]
               (Lord God, Unlock Now Heaven's Gate)
                                    Bach [BO 32;3:00]
Offertory   Herr Gott, nun schleuss den Himmel auf
                                    Bach [BN 8;2:00]
Postlude   Herr Gott, nun schleuss den Himmel auf
                                    J. Walther [WO 44;2:30]

SENIOR CHOIR:
Nunc Dimittis [Luke 2:22-40]   H. Willan
O Jesus So Sweet, O Jesus So Mild [Christmas] [U]
                                                    M. Drischner

JUNIOR CHOIR:
Mary Had a Baby [Christmas] [U]   D. Walker

HYMNS:
Come Thou, Almighty King [Isaiah 61:10] (62HB)
Ye Watchers and Ye Holy Ones [Psalm 148] (7HB)
Hark the Herald Angels Sing [Galatians 4:4-5] (407HB)
Angels, From the Realms of Glory (St.4) [Luke 2:22-38] (408HB)
Brightest and Best of the Sons of the Morning [Luke 2:22-35] (432HB)
Come, O Long-Expected Jesus [Luke 2:29-32] (389HB)

DATE: Epiphany of the Lord

READINGS: [Same as Year A]
Isaiah 60:1-6
Psalm 72:1-7, 10-14
Ephesians 3:1-12
Matthew 2:1-12

ORGAN MUSIC: See Year A

SENIOR CHOIR:

JUNIOR CHOIR:

HYMNS:

DATE: Baptism of the Lord
(First Sunday after the Epiphany)

READINGS:
Genesis 1:1-5
Psalm 29
Acts 19:1-7
Mark 1:4-11

ORGAN MUSIC:
Prelude   Prelude in G Minor   N. Bruhns [5:00]
                 Christ, unser Herr, zum Jordan kam [Mark 1:4-11]
                 (Christ, our Lord, to Jordan came)
                                      D. Buxtehude [BC 6;3:30]
                                        J. Bender [HP 5:32;1:30]
                                       J.S. Bach [BCL 68;6:30]
Offertory   Christ, unser Herr, zum Jordan kam
                               F.W. Zachau [GG 2:99;1:30]
Postlude   Christ, unser Herr, zum Jordan kam
                               J. Pachelbel [PA 3:10;2:00]

SENIOR CHOIR:
Give to Jehovah [Ps.29:1-2]   H. Schütz
Christians, Awake [U]   R.J. Powell

JUNIOR CHOIR:
Oh, How Beautiful the Sky (JS 22)

HYMNS:
I Sing the Mighty Power of God [Genesis 1] (81HB)
All Things Bright and Beautiful [Genesis 1:1-2:3] (86HB)
Many and Great, O God, Are Thy Works [Genesis 1:1-17] (80SFGP)
Morning Has Broken [Genesis 1:1-5] (103SFGP)
Come, Gracious Spirit, Heavenly Dove [Mark 1:10] (265HB)
Come, Holy Spirit, Heavenly Dove [Mark 1:10] (244HB)

DATE: Second Sunday after the Epiphany

READINGS:
1 Samuel 3:1-10, (11-20)
Psalm 139:1-6, 13-18
1 Corinthians 6:12-20
John 1:43-51

ORGAN MUSIC:

Prelude	Prelude and Fugue in G Minor	D. Buxtehude	[7:30]
	Passacaglia in D Minor		[6:00]
Offertory	Es spricht der Unweise Mund wohl		
		Buxtehude	[BC 21;2:30]
	(The Fool Hath Said) [Ps.14]		
Postlude	Canzonetta in G Major	Buxtehude	[2:30]

SENIOR CHOIR:
O Christ, Thou Bright and Morning Star [Epiphany]   C. Tye
                                                            J. S. Bach
What Cheer? Good Cheer! [Christmas] [U]   P. Warlock

JUNIOR CHOIR:
O How Joyfully, O How Merrily (JS 25)

HYMNS:
Teach Me, God to Wonder [1 Samuel 3:1-10] (36SFGP)
Come Down, O Love Divine [1 Cor.6:19] (67HB)
By All Your Saints Still Striving [John 1:43-46] (231TH)

DATE: Third Sunday after the Epiphany

READINGS:
Jonah 3:1-5, 10
Psalm 62:5-12
1 Corinthians 7:29-31
Mark 1:14-20

ORGAN MUSIC:
Prelude	Prelude in F# Major	J.L. Krebs [7:00]
	Prelude and Fugue in D Minor	F. Mendelssohn [8:30]
Offertory	Prelude on "Aberystwyth"	H. Willan [WH 1:34;2:00]
Postlude	Prelude on "Richmond"	Willan [WH 1:6;2:00]

SENIOR CHOIR:
Truly My Soul Waiteth Upon God [Ps.62:1,2,7a]   Willan

JUNIOR CHOIR:
Still, Still, Still (PH 47)

HYMNS:
Dear Lord and Father of Mankind (St.2) [Mark 1:16-20] (249HB)
By All Your Saints Still Striving [Mark 1:16-18] (231TH)
They Cast Their Nets in Galilee [Mark 1:16-20] (661TH)

DATE: Fourth Sunday after the Epiphany

READINGS:
Deuteronomy 18:15-20
Psalm 111
1 Corinthians 8:1-13
Mark 1:21-28

ORGAN MUSIC:

Prelude	Sonata III in D Minor	J.S. Bach [16:00]
Offertory	Ehre sei dir, Christe	
	(Glory to Thee, Christ)	Bach [BN 18:2:00]
Postlude	Fugue in C Minor	J. Pachelbel [2:00]

SENIOR CHOIR:
O Thou the Central Orb [Epiphany]   O. Gibbons

JUNIOR CHOIR:
Kum Bah Yah (UM 494)

HYMNS:
Silence, Frenzied, Unclean Spirit [Mark 1:21-28] (74SFGP)
Thine Arm, O Lord, in Days of Old [Mark 1:21-2:12] (567TH)

DATE: Fifth Sunday after the Epiphany

READINGS:
Isaiah 40:21-31
Psalm 147:1-11, 20c
1 Corinthians 9:16-23
Mark 1:29-39

ORGAN MUSIC:

Prelude	Toccata per l'Elevazione	G. Frescobaldi [2:30]
	All'Elevatione	G. Martini [3:00]
	Le Banquet Céleste	O. Messiaen [4:00]
	Toccata Sesta	Frescobaldi [5:00]
Offertory	Canzona	Frescobaldi [2:00]
Postlude	Pasticcio	J. Langlais [3:00]

SENIOR CHOIR:
Blest Are They Whose Spirits Long [Is.40:31]   G.F. Handel

JUNIOR CHOIR:

HYMNS:
Praise to the Lord, the Almighty [Isaiah 40:21] (29HB)
Father Eternal, Ruler of Creation [Isaiah 40:23] (279HB)
Arise, Your Light Is Come (St.4) [Isaiah 40:31] (19SFGP)
Rejoice, Ye Pure in Heart [Ps.147:1] (160UM)

DATE: Sixth Sunday after the Epiphany

READINGS:
2 Kings 5:1-14
Psalm 30
1 Corinthians 9:24-27
Mark 1:40-45

ORGAN MUSIC:

Prelude	Concerto in G Minor	T. Arne [15:00]
Offertory	Voluntary in G Major	H. Purcell [3:00]
Postlude	Voluntary I	W. Boyce [3:30]

SENIOR CHOIR:
Let Nothing Ever Grieve Thee [General]   J. Brahms

JUNIOR CHOIR:

HYMNS:
God, You Meet Us (St.2) [Ps.30:5] (124SFGP)
Fight the Good Fight With All Thy Might [1 Cor.9:24-27] (175HB)
Awake, My Soul, Stretch Every Nerve [1 Cor.9:24-25] (357HB)

DATE: Seventh Sunday after the Epiphany

READINGS:
Isaiah 43:18-25
Psalm 41
2 Corinthians 1:18-22
Mark 2:1-12

ORGAN MUSIC:
Prelude   Fantasia and Fugue in G Minor   J.S. Bach [11:30]
             Wo Gott zum Haus nicht gibt sein Gunst
             (The House That Has Not God's Favour)
                                              J. Pachelbel [PA 3;4:00]
Offertory   Wo Gott zum Haus nicht gibt sein Gunst
                                           J. Walther [GG 2:167;1:00]
Postlude   Toccata in C Major   Pachelbel [3:00]

SENIOR CHOIR:
I Was Like a Lamb in Innocence [Ps.41:7]   Victoria

JUNIOR CHOIR:

HYMNS:
Come, Thou Fount of Every Blessing [2 Cor.1:21-22] (686TH)
Songs of Thankfulness and Praise (St.3) [Mark 1:1-12] (443HB)

DATE: Eighth Sunday after the Epiphany

READINGS:
Hosea 2:14-20
Psalm 103:1-13, 22
2 Corinthians 3:1-6
Mark 2:13-22

ORGAN MUSIC:

Prelude	Concerto after Meck	J. Walther [8:30]
	Lobe den Herren [Psalm 103]	
	(Praise to the Lord, the Almighty)	
		M. Reger [NT 20;1:00]
		Merkel [NT 21;1:00]
		J.S. Bach [BSC 98;3:30]
Offertory	Lobe den Herren	Walther [GG 1:40;2:00]
Postlude	Lobe den Herren	Micheelsen [NT 24;2:30]

SENIOR CHOIR:
Praise Ye the Lord [Ps.103:1-6]   H. Distler

JUNIOR CHOIR:

HYMNS:
Praise, My Soul, the King of Heaven [Ps.103] (30HB)
Praise to the Lord, the Almighty [Ps.103] (29HB)
Amazing Grace! How Sweet the Sound [Ps.103:8] (49SFGP)
By All Your Saints Still Striving [Mark 2:13-14] (231TH)

DATE: Ninth Sunday after the Epiphany

READINGS:
Deuteronomy 5:12-15
Psalm 81:1-10
2 Corinthians 4:5-12
Mark 2:23-3:6

ORGAN MUSIC:
Prelude	Prelude and Fugue on B-A-C-H	F. Liszt [15:00]
Offertory	Wenn den Unglück tut greifen an	
	(When Misfortune Seizes You)	J.S. Bach [BN 37;1:30]
Postlude	Fugue on B-A-C-H	R. Schumann

SENIOR CHOIR:
Sing We Merrily [Ps.81:1-3]   Symons
Sing We Merrily   Campbell

JUNIOR CHOIR:

HYMNS:
Make a Joyful Noise Unto the Lord [Ps.81:1] (710TH)
Christ, Whose Glory Fills the Skies [2 Cor.4:6] (362HB)
Let There Be Light [2 Cor.4:6] (274HB)
Songs of Thankfulness and Praise (St.3) [Mark 3:1-12] (433HB)

DATE: Last Sunday after the Epiphany
(Transfiguration Sunday)

READINGS:
2 Kings 2:1-12
2 Corinthians 4:3-6
Psalm 50:1-6
Mark 9:2-9

ORGAN MUSIC:

Prelude	Christ, der du bist der Helle Tag [Transfiguration] (Christ, Thou Who Art the Bright Day)	
	Partita	J.S. Bach [BP 114;9:00]
	Chorale Prelude	G. Böhm [BS 40;8:00]
Offertory	Christ, der du bist der Helle Tag	Bach [BN 70;1:00]
Postlude	Christ, der du bist der Helle Tag	
		H. Distler [GG3:253;1:00]

SENIOR CHOIR:
The Mighty God [Ps.50:1,3,4]   B. Marcello

JUNIOR CHOIR:

HYMNS:
Swing Low, Sweet Chariot [2 Kings 2;11] (703UM)
The Glory of These Forty Days [2 Kings 2:11-12] (143LW)
O Wondrous Type! O Vision Fair [Mark 9:2-8] (136TH)
Songs of Thankfulness and Praise (St.4) [Mark 9:2-8] (433HB)

DATE: First Sunday in Lent

READINGS:
Genesis 9:8-17
Psalm 25:1-10
1 Peter 3:18-22
Mark 1:9-15

ORGAN MUSIC:
Prelude   Toccata undecima   G. Muffat [HOR 1:84;6:00]
               Intermezzo   M. Reger [3:30]
               Herzlich lieb hab ich dich, O Herr [Lent]
               (I love Thee with all my heart, O Lord)
                                                  J.F. Alberti [GT 2:51;1:30]
                                                  J.L. Krebs [GT 2:52;3:00]
                                                  J. Walther [WO 52;3:00]
                                                  [GG 2:130;2:30]
Offertory   Herzlich lieb hab ich dich, O Herr
                                             G. Kauffmann [GG 2:129;2:00]
Postlude   Herzlich lieb hab ich dich, O Herr
                                             J.S. Bach [BN 58;3:00]

SENIOR CHOIR:
Call to Remembrance [Ps.25:5,6]   R. Farrant
Lord Jesus Christ [Lent] [U]   L. Viadana

JUNIOR CHOIR:

HYMNS:
Lead Us, O Father, in the Paths of Peace [Ps.25:3] (703TH)
"Welcome Happy Morning!" Age to Age Shall Say [1 Peter 3:18-20] (462HB)
My Song Is Love Unknown [1 Peter 3:18] (442HB)
Rejoice, the Lord Is King [1 Peter 3:22] (44HB)
Forty Days and Forty Nights [Mark 1:12-15] (438HB)
O Love, How Deep, How Broad, How High [Mark 1:12-13] (100HB)
The Glory of These Forty Days [Mark 1:12-13] (143TH)

DATE: Second Sunday in Lent

READINGS:
Genesis 17:1-7, 15-16
Psalm 22:23-31
Romans 4:13-25
Mark 8:31-38 or Mark 9:2-9

ORGAN MUSIC:
Prelude   Christus, der ist mein Leben [Lent]
            (Christ, Who Is My Life's Salvation)
                                        J. Pachelbel [PA 4;10:00]
                                    F.W. Marpurg [MC 16;3:00]
                                        J. Walther [GG 1:14;1:30]
Offertory   Christus, der ist mein Leben   J.S. Bach [BN 52;1:30]
Postlude   Christus, der ist mein Leben   J. Walther [WO 22;2:30]

SENIOR CHOIR:
My God, my God, O Lord, My God [Ps.22]   H. Schütz

JUNIOR CHOIR:

HYMNS:
Take Up Thy Cross [Mark 8:34-35] (165HB)
He Who Would Valiant Be [Mark 8:34]
New Every Morning Is the Love [Mark 8:34] (360HB)
Songs of Thankfulness and Praise (St.4) [Mark 9:2-8] (433HB)

DATE: Third Sunday in Lent

READINGS:
Exodus 20:1-17
Psalm 19
1 Corinthians 1:18-25
John 2:13-22

ORGAN MUSIC:
Prelude   Prelude and Fugue in G Major (BWV 541)
                                        J.S. Bach [8:00]
             Dies sind die heil'gen zehn Gebot [Exodus 20:1-17]
             (These Are the Holy Ten Commandments)
                                        J.S. Bach [BCL 42;5:30]
                                        J. Walther [GG 2:137;1:30]
Offertory   Dies sind die heil'gen zehn Gebot   Bach [BO 62;2:00]
Postlude   Dies sind die heil'gen zehn Gebot   Bach [BCL 49;2:00]

SENIOR CHOIR:
The Heavens Are Telling [Ps.19]   F.J. Haydn
God, Who Madest Earth and Heaven [General] [U]   M. Drischner

JUNIOR CHOIR:

HYMNS:
All Beautiful the March of Days [Ps.19] (388HB)
O Lord of Every Shining Constellation [Ps.19] (83HB)
The Spacious Firmament on High [Ps.19] (85HB)
Holy, Holy Holy! [Ps.19:1-6] (50HB)
Sing, My Tongue, the Glorious Battle [1 Cor.1:18-25] (446HB)
When I Survey the Wondrous Cross [1 Cor.1:18] (109HB)

DATE: Fourth Sunday in Lent

READINGS:
Numbers 21:4-9
Psalm 107:1-3, 17-22
Ephesians 2:1-10
John 3:14-21

ORGAN MUSIC:
Prelude   Was mein Gott will, das g'scheh allzeit
             (Let Happen E'er What My God Wills)
                              J.E. Kindermann [80:74;2:00]
                              F.W. Marpurg [MC 51;3:00]
                              F. Zachau [HP 41:2;2:30]
             Wenn wir in höchsten Nöten sein [Lent]
             (When in the Hour of Utmost Need)
                              J.S. Bach [BO 71;1:30]
                                       [B18:212;5:00]
                              Scheidt [PO 7:9;1:00]
Offertory   Wenn wir in höchsten Nöten sein
                              J. Walther [WO 133;2:00]
Postlude   Wenn wir in höchsten Nöten sein
                              J. Pachelbel [PA 3:46;4:00]

SENIOR CHOIR:
For God So Loved the World [John 3:16]   H. Distler
God So Loved the World [John 3:16] [U]   K. Bissell

JUNIOR CHOIR:
All I Really Need (AGCS)

HYMNS:
Now Thank We All Our God [Ps.107:21-22] (197HB)
Amazing Grace! How Sweet the Sound [Eph.2:4-10] (49SFGP)
From Deepest Woe I Cry to Thee [Eph.2:8-9] (151TH)
Lift High the Cross [John 3:14-15] (321HB)
Help Us Accept Each Other (St.3) [John 3:21] (8SFGP)

DATE: Fifth Sunday in Lent

READINGS:
Jeremiah 31:31-34
Psalm 51:1-12 or Psalm 119:9-16
Hebrews 5:5-10
John 12:20-33

ORGAN MUSIC:
Prelude   Chromatic Fantasy   J.P. Sweelinck [9:00]
               Erhalt uns, Herr, bei deinem Wort [Ps.119:10]
               (Lord, Keep Us Steadfast in Thy Word)
                                               G. Böhm [BS 56;2:30]
                                          D. Buxtehude [BC 8;1:30]
                                        J. Praetorius [PO I:48;1:00]
                                             J.S. Bach [BN 36;1:30]
Offertory   Erhalt uns, Herr, bei deinem Wort
                                          J. Walther [WO 30;2:00]
Postlude   Erhalt uns, Herr, bei deinem Wort
                                       J. Pachelbel [GT 1:151;2:30]

SENIOR CHOIR:
O Lord, Increase My Faith [General]   Loosemore
A Lamb Goes Uncomplaining Forth [Lent] [U]   H.F. Micheelsen

JUNIOR CHOIR:
Now the Green Blade Rises [John 12:24] (SFGP 100)

HYMNS:
Jesus, Lover of My Soul [Ps.41:1-2] (77HB)
O For a Closer Walk with God [Ps.51:12] (396PH)
Rise Up, O Saints of God (St.5) [John 12:24-25] (47SFGP)
O Jesus, I Have Promised [John 12:26] (304HB)

DATE: Sixth Sunday in Lent
                           (Passion Sunday or Palm Sunday)

READINGS: Liturgy of the Palms
Mark 11:1-11 or John 12:12-16
Psalm 118:1-2, 19-29
                           Liturgy of the Passion
Isaiah 50:4-9a
Psalm 31:9-16
Philippians 2:5-11
Mark 14:1 - 15:47 or Mark 15:1-39, (40-47)

ORGAN MUSIC:
Prelude   Passion Chorale [Mark 15:16-39]
                                          J.S. Bach [BN 28;2:00]
                                                   [BU 46;2:00]
                                          J. Pachelbel [PA 3:17,18;4:30]
                                                   Kuhnau [GT 2:80;2:00]
                                          J. Brahms [BE 30;3:00]
Offertory   Passion Chorale   Brahms [BE 28;1:30]
Postlude   Valet will ich dir geben [Mark 11:1-10]
               (All Glory, Laud and Honor)   J.S. Bach [BU 77;3:30]

SENIOR CHOIR:
Hosanna to the Son of David [Mark 11:1]   O. Gibbons

JUNIOR CHOIR:

HYMNS:
All Glory, Laud and Honor [Mark 11:1-10; John 12:12-15] (447HB)
Hark! the Glad Sound! the Savior Comes (St.4) [Mark 11:1-10; John
2:12-15] (395HB)
Hosanna, Loud Hosanna [Mark 11:1-10] (448HB)
My Song Is Love Unknown [Mark 11:1-10; John 12:12-15] (442HB)
Ride On! Ride On in Majesty [Mark 11:1-10; John 12:12-15] (449HB)
O Sacred Head, Now Wounded [Isaiah 50:6; Mark 15:16-39] (452HB)
All Hail the Power of Jesus' Name [Phil.2:5-11] (42HB)
At the Name of Jesus [Phil.2:5-11] (39HB)
Ah, Holy Jesus, How Hast Thou Offended [Mark 15:6-15] (443HB)

DATE: Holy Thursday (A,B,C)

READINGS:
Exodus 12:1-4 (5-10) 11-14
Psalm 116:1-2, 12-19
1 Corinthians 11:23-26
John 13:1-17, 31b-35

ORGAN MUSIC:
Ich ruf zu dir, Herr Jesu Christ
(Lord, Hear the Voice of My Complaint)   J.S. Bach [BO 68;3:30]

SENIOR CHOIR:
Darkness Had Fallen There   M.A. Ingegneri

JUNIOR CHOIR:

HYMNS:
At the Lamb's High Feast We Sing [Exodus 12:1-28; 1 Cor.11:23-26]
(174TH)
Bread of the World in Mercy Broken [1 Cor.11:23-26] (326HB)
Now, My Tongue, the Mystery Telling [1 Cor.11:23-26] (341HB)

DATE: Good Friday (A,B,C)

READINGS:
Isaiah 52:13 - 53:12
Psalm 22
Hebrews 10:165-25 or Hebrews 4:14-16
John 18:1 - 19:42

ORGAN MUSIC:
Prelude   Chorale Prelude and Fugue on "O Traurigkeit, O Herze-
               lied" (O Sorrow, O Heart's Song)
                                   J. Brahms [Peters 6333a:25;5:00]
               Ich ruf zu dir, Herr Jesu Christ [Prayer]
               (Lord, Hear the Voice of My Complaint)
                                        J.S. Bach [BO 68;3:30]
                                        J. Pachelbel [PA 3:32;3:30]
                                        S. Scheidt [GT 2:87;2:30]
                                        V. Lübeck [LS 48;10:00]

SENIOR CHOIR:
And With His Stripes We Are Healed [Is.53:5]   G.F. Handel

JUNIOR CHOIR:

HYMNS:
My Song Is Love Unknown [Isaiah 52:13-53:12; John 19:38-42]
(442HB)
Ah, Holy Jesus, How Hast Thou Offended [Isaiah 53:1-12] (443HB)
God, When I Stand [Ps.22:1-2] (125SFGP)
O Sacred Head, Sore Wounded [John 19:17-37] (452HB)
Sing, My Tongue, the Glorious Battle [John 19:17-37] (446HB)
Were You There When They Crucified My Lord [John 19:2-5]
(460HB)

DATE: Easter Day

READINGS:
Acts 10:34-43 or Isaiah 25:6-9
Psalm 118:1-2, 14-24
1 Corinthians 15:1-11 or Acts 10:34-43
John 20:1-18 or Mark 16:1-8

ORGAN MUSIC:
Prelude   Toccata, Adagio and Fugue in C Major
                                          J.S. Bach [14:00]
Offertory   O Filii et Filiae
             (O Sons and Daughters)   LeBegue [LC 200;2:00]
Postlude   Prelude on "O Filii et Filiae"
                                          H. Willan [WH 1:34;3:30]

SENIOR CHOIR:
Ye Sons and Daughters of the King [Easter]   V. Leisring
Instruments Waken and Publish Your Gladness [Easter] D. Buxtehude
Good Christian Men, Rejoice and Sing [Easter] [U]   M. Drischner

JUNIOR CHOIR:
We Welcome Glad Easter (JS 57)

HYMNS:
"Welcome, Happy Morning!" Age to Age Shall Say [Acts 10:39-40]
(462HB)
Hail Thee, Festival Day [Acts 10:39-40] (461HB)
The Strife Is O'er [1 Cor.15; John 20:1-18] (468HB)
Jesus Christ Is Risen Today [1 Cor.15:3-4; John 20:1-18] (465HB)
The Day of Resurrection [John 20:1-18] (374HB)

DATE: Second Sunday of Easter

READINGS:
Acts 4:32-35
Psalm 133
1 John 1:1 - 2:2
John 20:19-31

ORGAN MUSIC:
Prelude   Adagio, Allegro (and Adagio)   W.A.Mozart [12:00]
             Jesus Christus, unser Heiland, der den Tod [Easter]
             (Jesus Christ, Our Saviour, Who Overcame Death)
                                        J.S. Bach [BO 48;1:00]
                                     J. Pachelbel [PA 2:52;2:00]
                                     J. Walther [EK 2:114;1:00]
Offertory   Jesus Christus, unser Heiland
                                     D. Buxtehude [BC 54;2:00]
Postlude   Finale Jubilante   H. Willan

SENIOR CHOIR:
Because You Have Seen Me, Thomas [John 20:29]   L. Marenzio

JUNIOR CHOIR:
I Danced in the Morning (HB 106)

HYMNS:
Good Christians All, Rejoice and Sing! [Acts 4:33] (469HB)
Behold, How Pleasant [Ps.133] (120SFPG)
Jesus, Lover of My Soul [1 John 1:5-7] (77HB)
O Sons and Daughters, Let Us Sing [John 20:19-31] (467HB)
That Easter Day With Joy Was Bright [John 20:19-31] (474HB)
Lo! He Comes, With Clouds Descending [John 20:24-29] (393HB)

DATE: Third Sunday of Easter

READINGS:
Acts 3:12-19
Psalm 4
1 John 3:1-7
Luke 24:36b-48

ORGAN MUSIC:
Prelude   O Filii et Filiae
               (O Sons and Daughters)   Dandrieu [5:30]
               Erschienen ist der herrliche Tag [Lk.24:36-43]
               (The Glorious Day Now Appears)
                                              J.S. Bach [BO 55;1:30]
                                              J. Walther [WO 32;9:30]
                                              D. Buxtehude [BC 148;1:30]
Offertory   Erschienen ist der herrliche Tag
                                              Walther [GG 1:18;1:00]
                                       G.F. Kauffmann [HP 24:24;1:00]
Postlude   Toccata on "O Filii et Filiae"   L. Farnum

SENIOR CHOIR:
God's Power Still Indwelling Him [Acts 3:13-15]   C. Tye
Awake, My Heart, With Gladness [Easter] [U]   H. Peter

JUNIOR CHOIR:
A Spring Carol (CS 42)   H. Willan

HYMNS:
My Song Is Love Unknown [Acts 3:14-15] (442HB)
Lord, I Want to Be a Christian [1 John 3:2] (372PH)
That Easter Day With Joy Was Bright [Luke 24:36-43] (474HB)

DATE: Fourth Sunday of Easter

READINGS:
Acts 4:5-12
Psalm 23
1 John 3:16-24
John 10:11-18

ORGAN MUSIC:
Prelude   Chorale No. 1   C. Franck [13:00]
Offertory   Récit de Cromone   N. DeGrigny [2:00]
Postlude   For Lo, the Winter Is Past [Antiphon IV]   M. Dupré

SENIOR CHOIR:
The Lord's My Shepherd [Ps.23]   H. Willan
I Am the Good Shepherd [John 10:14] [U]   R. Wetzler

JUNIOR CHOIR:
Jesus the Christ Said [John 10:11] (73SFGP)

HYMNS:
Christ Is Made the Sure Foundation [Acts 4:11-12] (145HB)
The Church's One Foundation [Acts 4:11-12] (146HB)
At the Name of Jesus [Acts 4:12] (39HB)
Oh, For a Thousand Tongues to Sing [Acts 4:12] (48HB)
The King of Love My Shepherd Is [Psalm 23] (132HB)
We Give Thee But Thine Own [1 John 3:17-18] (296HB)

DATE: Fifth Sunday of Easter

READINGS:
Acts 8:26-40
Psalm 22:25-31
1 John 4:7-21
John 15:1-8

ORGAN MUSIC:
Prelude   Herr Christ, der ein'ge Gottes Sohn [1 Jn.4:9]
             (Lord Christ, God's Only-Begotten Son)
                                        J.S. Bach [BU 35;1:30]
                                        D. Buxtehude [BC 34;4:30]
                                        J.P. Sweelinck [SA 32;4:30]
                                        J. Walther [WO 43;1:30]
                                        [GG 2:124;2:00]
                                        H. Scheidemann [HP 6:14;2:00]
Offertory   Herr Christ, der ein'ge Gottes Sohn   Bach [BO 6;2:00]
Postlude   Herr Christ, der ein'ge Gottes Sohn
                                        J. Pachelbel [PA 2:8;3:00]

SENIOR CHOIR:
Beloved, Let Us Love One Another [John.4:7-8,10]   J. Langlais

JUNIOR CHOIR:
Simple Gifts (AGCS 64)

HYMNS:
Where Charity and Love Prevail [1 John 4:7-21] (6SFGP)
Love Divine, All Love's Excelling [1 John 4:7-17] (241HB)
Father Eternal, Ruler of Creation [1 John 4:11-21] (279HB)
Lord, Dismiss Us With Thy Blessing [John 15:1-8,16] (308HB)

DATE: Sixth Sunday of Easter

READINGS:
Acts 10:44-48
Psalm 98
1 John 5:1-6
John 15:9-17

ORGAN MUSIC:

Prelude	Allein Gott in der Höh sei Ehr [1 John 5:4-9]	
	(All Glory Be to God on High)	
		J.S. Bach [BCL 33;7:00]
		[B18 72;7:00]
		[BU 14;1:30]
Offertory	Allein Gott in der Höh sei Ehr	Bach [BCL 41;1:30]
Postlude	Allein Gott in der Höh sei Ehr	Bach [BCL 30;3:00]

SENIOR CHOIR:
O Sing Unto the Lord a New Song [Ps.98]   H. Willan

JUNIOR CHOIR:
Come, Children, Join to Sing [John 15:15] (SFGP 38)

HYMNS:
Sing, My Tongue [Ps.98:1-2] (446HB)
All Creatures of Our God and King [Ps.98:1,4-9] (1HB)
All Glory Be to God on High [1 John 5:4-9] (215LW)
I Come With Joy [John 15:12-17] (60SFGP)
Crown Him With Many Crowns [John 15:13] (480HB)

DATE: Seventh Sunday of Easter

READINGS:
Acts 1:15-17, 21-26
Psalm 1
1 John 5:9-13
John 17:6-19

ORGAN MUSIC:
Prelude	Sonata VI	F. Mendelssohn [15:30]
	(based on "Vater unser im Himmelreich")	
Offertory	Vater unser im Himmelreich	
	(The Lord's Prayer)	F. Zachau [GT 3:79;2:00]
Postlude	Vater unser im Himmelreich	D. Buxtehude [6:30]

SENIOR CHOIR:
Blessed Is the Man [Ps.1]   S. Lekberg
Dear Christians, One and All, Rejoice [Ascension] [U]
                                                         M. Drischner

JUNIOR CHOIR:

HYMNS:
Sing to the Lord of Harvest [Ps.1] (382HB)
Break Now the Bread of Life (St.3) [John 17:17] (86SFGP)
Thou, Who at Thy First Eucharist Didst Pray [John 17:1-26] (315TH)

DATE: Day of Pentecost

READINGS:
Acts 2:1-21 or Ezekiel 37:1-14
Psalm 104:24-34, 35b
Romans 8:22-27 or Acts 2:1-21
John 15:26-27; 16:4b-15

ORGAN MUSIC:
Prelude   Ciacona in F Minor   J. Pachelbel [6:30]
               Komm, Gott Schöpfer, heiliger Geist [Acts 2:1-3]
               (Come, O Creator Spirit Blest)
                                                         J.S. Bach [BO 58;1:00]
                                                    J. Titelouze [PO 8:36;2:30]
                                                    J. Walther [EK 2:119;1:30]
                                                              [GG 2:140;2:00]
                                                      F. Zachau [HP 12:32;1:00]
Offertory   Komm, Gott Schöpfer, heiliger Geist
                                                    Pachelbel [PA 2:58;2:00]
Postlude   Komm, Gott Schöpfer, heiliger Geist
                                                        Bach [B18:94;3:00]

SENIOR CHOIR:
Come, Holy Ghost, Creator Blest [Pentecost]   H. Distler
O Come, Creator Spirit, Come [Pentecost] [U]   M.-A. Charpentier

JUNIOR CHOIR:

HYMNS:
Hail Thee, Festival Day [Acts 2:1-42] (481HB)
She Flies On (St.5) [Acts 2:1-4] (126SFGP)
Come, Holy Ghost, Our Souls Inspire [Acts 2:1-3] (245HB)
This Is My Father's World [Ps.104:24-30] (82HB)
Come Down, O Love Divine [Romans 8:26-27] (67HB)
Come, Gracious Spirit, Heavenly Dove [John 16:13-15] (265HB)

DATE: Trinity Sunday
                              (First Sunday after Pentecost)

READINGS:
Isaiah 6:1-8
Psalm 29
Romans 8:12-17
John 3:1-17

ORGAN MUSIC:
Prelude   Herr Jesu Christ, dich zu uns wend [Is.6:3]
               (Lord Jesus Christ, Be Present Now)

                                        G. Böhm [BS 76;9:00]
                                        J. Walther [WO 46;8:30]
Offertory   Herr Jesu Christ, dich zu uns wend

                                        J.S. Bach [BO 59;2:00]
Postlude   Herr Jesu Christ, dich zu uns wend

                                        Bach [B18:31;4:30]

SENIOR CHOIR:
Holy Is God [Is.6:3]   C.P.E. Bach
Spirit of Life, O Spirit of God [Pentecost] [U]   M. Drischner

JUNIOR CHOIR:
Every Time I Feel the Spirit [Romans 8:15-17]   B. Trant

HYMNS:
Let All Mortal Flesh Keep Silence [Isaiah 6:1-3] (332HB)
The God of Abraham Praise [Isaiah 6:1-3] (401TH)
God the Omnipotent! King, Who Ordainest [Ps.29:10-100] (273HB)
In Christ There Is No East or West [Romans 8:14-17] (149HB)
Lift High the Cross [John 3:14-15] (321HB)

DATE: Sunday betwen May 29 and June 4 inclusive

READINGS:
1 Samuel 3:1-10 (11-20) or Deuteronomy 5:12-15
Psalm 139:1-6, 13-18 or Psalm 81:1-10
2 Corinthians 4:5-12
Mark 2:23 - 3:6

ORGAN MUSIC:
Prelude	Prelude and Fugue in B Minor	J.S. Bach [12:30]
	Herr Jesu Christ, dich zu uns wend	
	(Lord Jesus Christ, Be Present Now)	
		Bach [BU 43;3:00]
Offertory	Herr Jesu Christ, dich zu uns wend	Bach [BU 45;1:00]
Postlude	Fughetta on "Iste Confessor"	
		H. Willan [WH 3:10;3:30]

SENIOR CHOIR:
Almighty and Everlasting God [General]	O. Gibbons
Come, Souls, Behold Today [Pentecost] [U]	H. Willan

JUNIOR CHOIR:

HYMNS:
Open My Eyes That I May See (St.2) [1 Sam.3:1-10] (82SFGP)
Teach Me, God to Wonder [1 Sam.3:1-10] (36SFGP)
We Have This Ministry [2 Cor.4:1-12] (76SFGP)
Let There Be Light [2 Cor.4:6] (274HB)
Songs of Thankfulness and Praise (St.3) [Mark 2:1-12] (443HB)

DATE: Sunday between June 5 and June 11 inclusive

READINGS:
1 Samuel 8:4-11 (12-15) 16-20 (11:14-15) or Genesis 3:8-15
Psalm 138 or Psalm 130
2 Corinthians 4:13-5:1
Mark 3:20-35

ORGAN MUSIC:

Prelude	Echo Fantasy	J.P. Sweelinck [3:30]
	Durch Adams Fall ist ganz verderbt [Gen.3:8-15]	
	(Through Adam's Fall Is All Undone)	
		J.S. Bach [BO 65;2:00]
		[BN 30;3:00]
		D. Buxtehude [BC 30;3:00]
		J. Walther [WO 29;3:00]
		J. Pachelbel [PA 3:21;4:00]
Offertory	Durch Adams Fall ist ganz verderbt	
		Walther [GG 2:106;2:00]
Postlude	Durch Adams Fall ist ganz verderbt	
		Sweelinck [SA 26;5:00]

SENIOR CHOIR:
From the Depths Have I Called Unto Thee [Ps.130]   W.A. Mozart
Lord, as Thou Wilt, Deal Thou With Me [General] [U]

M. Drischner

JUNIOR CHOIR:

HYMNS:
O What Their Joy and Their Glory Must Be [2 Cor.4:16-5:10]
(186HB)

DATE: Sunday between June 12 and June 18 inclusive

READINGS:
1 Samuel 15:34 - 16:13 or Ezekiel 17:22-24
Psalm 20 or Psalm 92:1-4, 12-15
2 Corinthians 5:6-10, (11-13), 14-17
Mark 4:26-34

ORGAN MUSIC:
Prelude	Sonata VI	C.P.E. Bach [14:00]
Offertory	Trio 1	J. Rheinberger [2:00]
Postlude	Fugue in Bb Major	W.F. Bach

SENIOR CHOIR:
Psalm XX [Ps.20]   H. Schütz

JUNIOR CHOIR:

HYMNS:
Only-Begotten, Word of God Eternal [Ps.20:1-5] (256HB)
Jerusalem, My Happy Home [2 Cor.5:8] (620TH)
Make Me a Captive, Love [2 Cor.5:14-15] (242HB)
Come, Ye Thankful People, Come (St.2) [Mark 4:26-29]

DATE: Sunday between June 19 and June 25 inclusive

READINGS:
1 Samuel 17: (1a, 4-11, 19-23), 32-49 or Job 38:1-11
Psalm 9:9-20 or 1 Samuel 17:57-18:5, 10-16 or Psalm 107:1-3, 23-32
2 Corinthians 6:1-13
Mark 4:35-41

ORGAN MUSIC:

Prelude	Toccata in F Major	D. Buxtehude [8:00]
	Prelude and Fugue in G Minor	[7:00]
Offertory	Fantasia in D Minor	J. Pachelbel [2:00]
Postlude	Canzonetta in G Major	Buxtehude [2:30]

SENIOR CHOIR:
Let Their Celestial Concerts All Unite [General]   G.F. Handel

JUNIOR CHOIR:

HYMNS:
Lead Us, Heavenly Father, Lead Us [2 Cor.6:3-10] (268HB)
Morning Glory, Starlit Sky (St.4) [2 Cor.6:3-10] (13SFGP)
Eternal Father, Strong to Save [Mark 4:35-41] (221HB)

DATE: Sunday between June 26 and July 2 inclusive

READINGS:
2 Samuel 1:1, 17-27 or Wisdom of Solomon 1:13-15; 2:23-24
Psalm 130 or Lamentations 3:23-33 or Psalm 30
2 Corinthians 8:7-15
Mark 5:21-43

ORGAN MUSIC:
Prelude   Theme and Variations   Martini [GRV 6;5:00]
             Sonata No. 8   G. Valeri [7:30]
Offertory   Canzon Francese on "Martin Menoit"
                                             A. Gabrieli [2:30]
Postlude   Ricercar on "Martin Menoit"   Gabrieli

SENIOR CHOIR:
Then David Mourned [2 Sam.1:17]   T. Tomkins

JUNIOR CHOIR:

HYMNS:
From Depths of Woe I Cry to You [Ps.130] (230LW)
Great Is Thy Faithfulness [Lam.3:22-23] (95SFGP)
O Jesus, Crowned With All Renown [2 Cor.8:8-15] (292TH)
Morning Glory, Starlit Sky (St.4) [2 Cor.8:9] (13SFGP)
O For a Thousand Tongues to Sing [Mark 5:21-43] (48HB)

DATE: Sunday between July 3 and July 9 inclusive

READINGS:
2 Samuel 5:1-5, 9-10 or Ezekiel 2:1-5
Psalm 48 or Psalm 123
2 Corinthians 12:2-10
Mark 6:1-13

ORGAN MUSIC:

Prelude	Voluntary in C Major	J. Stanley [9:00]
	Voluntary in A Minor	[5:30]
Offertory	Voluntary No. 5	G.F. Handel [2:00]
Postlude	Voluntary in E Minor	Stanley

SENIOR CHOIR:
O Had I Jubal's Lyre [General] [S solo]   Handel

JUNIOR CHOIR:

HYMNS:
Glorious Things of Thee Are Spoken [Ps.48:1-14] (144HB)
The Day That Thou Gavest, Lord, Is Ended [Ps.48:9] (366HB)
God, You Meet Us (St.1) [2 Cor.12:7-10] (124SFGP)
Soldiers of Christ, Arise [2 Cor.12:9] (171HB)
Break Thou the Bread of Life [Mark 6:3] (329PH)

DATE: Sunday between July 10 and July 16 inclusive

READINGS:
2 Samuel 6:1-5, 12b-19 or Amos 7:7-15
Psalm 24 or Psalm 85:8-13
Ephesians 1:3-14
Mark 6:14-29

ORGAN MUSIC:
Prelude	Prelude and Fugue in G Minor	V. Lübeck [7:30]
	Pange Lingua	J. Titelouze [7:00]
Offertory	Elevation in G Major	N. LeBegue [1:30]
Postlude	Toccata	E. Gigout

SENIOR CHOIR:
Lift Up Your Heads, O Ye Gates [Ps.24] (SA)   K. Bissell

JUNIOR CHOIR:

HYMNS:
Lift Up Your Heads, Ye Mighty Gates [Ps.24] (436TH)
This Is My Father's World [Ps.24] (82HB)
Amazing Grace! How Sweet the Sound [Eph.1:4-6] (47SFGP)
There's a Wideness in God's Mercy [Eph.1:7-8] (76HB)

DATE: Sunday between July 17 and July 23 inclusive

READINGS:
2 Samuel 7:1-14a or Jeremiah 23:1-6
Psalm 89:20-37 or Psalm 23
Ephesians 2:11-22
Mark 6:30-34, 53-56

ORGAN MUSIC:

Prelude	Fugue in C Minor	W.F. Bach [6:00]
	Prelude and Fugue in G Minor	J. S. Bach [8:00]
Offertory	Trio No. 2	J. Rheinberger [2:00]
Postlude	Fugue in F Major	W.F. Bach [4:00]

SENIOR CHOIR:
The Bird's Song [Ps.23] (S Solo)   R. Vaughan Williams

JUNIOR CHOIR:

HYMNS:
Hail to the Lord's Anointed [2 Sam.7:12] (154HB)
Christus Paradox (St.1) [Eph.2:14-17] (64SFGP)
Hail, Thou Once Despised Jesus [Eph.2:14-16] (478HB)
Christ Is Made the Sure Foundation [Eph.2:19-22] (145HB)
The Church's One Foundation [Eph.2:19-22] (146HB)
Hope of the World, Thou Christ of Great Compassion [Mark 6:34] (472TH)

DATE: Sunday between July 24 and July 30 inclusive

READINGS:
2 Samuel 11:1-15 or 2 Kings 4:42-44
Psalm 14 or Psalm 145:10-18
Ephesians 3:14-21
John 6:1-21

ORGAN MUSIC:

Prelude	Prelude in G Minor	D. Buxtehude [7:00]
	Toccata in D Minor	\ [7:00]
Offertory	Elevation in Bb Major	LeBegue [1:30]
Postlude	Toccata in G Major	Buxtehude [2:30]

SENIOR CHOIR:
Thanks Be To Thee [General] (B solo)   G.F. Handel

JUNIOR CHOIR:

HYMNS:
Our Father, By Whose Name [Eph.3:14-15] (219HB)
Just as I Am, Without One Plea [Eph.3:14-19] (284HB)
Eternal Father, Strong to Save [John 6:16-21] (221HB)

DATE: Sunday between July 31 and August 6 inclusive

READINGS:
2 Samuel 11:26 - 12:13a or Exodus 16:2-4, 9-15
Psalm 51:1-12 or Psalm 78:23-29
Ephesians 4:1-16
John 6:24-35

ORGAN MUSIC:

Prelude	Voluntary in D Minor	J. Stanley [7:00]
	Voluntary No. 4 in D Major	W. Walond [7:00]
Offertory	Voluntary No. 10	G. F. Handel [2:00]
Postlude	Voluntary in E Minor	Stanley [4:00]

SENIOR CHOIR:
O God, Have Mercy [Ps.51] (SB)   Handel/Hopson
Create in Me a Clean Heart, O God [Ps.51:10-12] [U]   H. Willan

JUNIOR CHOIR:

HYMNS:
Jesus, Lover of My Soul [Ps.51:1-2] (77HB)
Just as I Am, Without One Plea [Ps.51:1-2] (284HB)
Eternal Ruler of the Ceaseless Round [Eph.4:4-6]
The Church's One Foundation (St.2) [Eph.4:4-6] (146HB)
Your Hand, O God, Has Guided [Eph.4:4-6] (152HB)

DATE: Sunday between August 7 and August 13 inclusive

READINGS:
1 Samuel 18:5-9, 15, 31-33 or 1 Kings 19:4-8
Psalm 130 or Psalm 34:1-8
Ephesians 4:25 - 5:2
John 6:35, 41-51

ORGAN MUSIC:
Prelude   Kyrie - Christe - Kyrie [John 6:41-51]
             (Lord Have Mercy, Christ Have Mercy, Lord Have
             Mercy)
                                     J.S. Bach [BCL 16;11:00]
Offertory   Kyrie, Gott heiliger Geist
             (Have Mercy, God, Holy Spirit)
                                  Wolfrum [GG 2:214,215;2:00]
Postlude   Kyrie - Christe - Kyrie   Bach [BCL 27;4:30]

SENIOR CHOIR:
I Will Alway Give Thanks [Ps.34:1] [SA]   King

JUNIOR CHOIR:

HYMNS:
From Depths of Woe I Cry to You [Ps.130] (230LW)
O Brother Man [Eph.4:31-32; 5:1-2] (299HB)
Bread of the World [John 6:35-58] (326HB)
Let All Mortal Flesh Keep Silence [John 6:35-58] (332HB)
Deck Thyself, My Soul, With Gladness [John 6:35] (333HB)
I Heard the Voice of Jesus Say [John 6:35] (115HB)
Jesus the Christ Said (St.1) [John 6:48-51] (73SFGP)

DATE: Sunday between August 14 and August 20 inclusive

READINGS:
1 Kings 2:10-12; 3:3-14 or Proverbs 9:1-6
Psalm 111 or Psalm 34:9-14
Ephesians 5:15-20
John 6:51-58

ORGAN MUSIC:

Prelude	Jesus Christus, unser Heiland, der von uns [Jn.6:50-57]
	(Jesus Christ, Our Saviour, Who Gave His Life For Us)
	F. Tunder [45:37;9:30]
	J.S. Bach [B18:87;4:00]
	[BCL 81;4:00]
	[BCL 89;5:00]
Offertory	Jesus Christus, unser Heiland
	J. Pachelbel [PA 3:24;3:00]
Postlude	Jesus Christus, unser Heiland Bach [B18:91;3:00]

SENIOR CHOIR:
Fear the Almighty [Ps.111] [SS]   H. Schütz

JUNIOR CHOIR:

HYMNS:
O God of Earth and Space [Ps.111] (274PH)
There's a Spirit in the Air [Eph.5:18-20] (30SFGP)
When in Our Music God Is Glorified [Eph.5:19] (420TH)
Bread of the World [John 6:51] (326HB)

DATE: Sunday between August 21 and August 27 inclusive

READINGS:
1 Kings 8:(1,6,10-11), 22-30, 41-43 or Joshua 24:1-2a, 14-18
Psalm 84 or Psalm 34:15-22
Ephesians 6:10-20
John 6:56-69

ORGAN MUSIC:
Prelude   Von Gott will ich nicht lassen [Joshua 24:16]
             (From God Shall Naught Divide Me)
                                        J.S. Bach [B18:51;4:00]
                                        D. Buxtehude [BC 136;4:00]
                                        J.L. Krebs [GT 3:100;4:30]
                                        N. Hanff [HS 14;1:30]
Offertory   Von Gott will ich nicht lassen
                                        F.W. Marpurg [MC 37;1:30]
Postlude   Von Gott will ich nicht lassen
                                        J. Walther [WO 128;2:30]

SENIOR CHOIR:
Hear the Voice and Prayer [1 Kings 8:28-32]   T. Tallis
God Is Ever Sun and Shield [Ps.84:11] [U]   J.S. Bach

JUNIOR CHOIR:

HYMNS:
Only-Begotten, Word of God Eternal [1 Kings 8:27-30] (356HB)
How Lovely Is Thy Dwelling Place [Ps.84] (517TH)
Soldiers of Christ, Arise! [Eph.6:10-18] (171HB)
Eternal Ruler of the Ceaseless Round [Eph.6:10-17] (252HB)
A Mighty Fortress [Eph.6:10-12] (135HB)
Rise Up, O Saints of God (St.5) [John 6:63] (47SFPG)

DATE: Sunday between August 28 and September 3 inclusive

READINGS:
Song of Solomon 2:8-13 or Deuteronomy 4:1-2, 6-9
Psalm 45:1-2, 6-9 or Psalm 15
James 1:17-27
Mark 7:1-8, 14-15, 21-23

ORGAN MUSIC:
Prelude   Partita on "O Gott, du frommer Gott"
            (O God, Thou Faithful God)   J.S. Bach [BP 122;15:00]
Offertory   O Gott, du frommer Gott   M. Reger [GG 3:226;1:30]
Postlude   O Gott, du frommer Gott   J. Brahms [BE 22;5:00]

SENIOR CHOIR:
Molded in Grace Are Thy Lips [Ps.45:2,8]   G.B. Nanino

JUNIOR CHOIR:

HYMNS:
Come Away to the Skies [Song of Solomon 2:10-13] (213TH)
O Jesus, King Most Wonderful [Ps.45:1-3] (121HB)
Fairest Lord Jesus [Ps.45:2] (46HB)
For the Beauty of the Earth [James 1:17] (199HB)
We Plow the Fields and Scatter [James 1:17] (383HB)
O Brother Man [James 1:27] (299HB)
As a Chalice Cast of Gold [Mark 7:1-8,14-15,21-23] (336PH)

DATE: Sunday between September 4 and September 10 inclusive

READINGS:
Proverbs 22:1-2, 8-9, 22-23 or Isaiah 35:4-7a
Psalm 125 or Psalm 146
James 2:1-10, (11-13), 14-17
Mark 7:24-37

ORGAN MUSIC:

Prelude	Chaconne in E Minor	D. Buxtehude [5:30]
	Prelude and Fugue in D Major	[5:00]
	Ich dank dir, lieber Herr	
	(I Thank You, Dear Lord)	[BC 40;5:00]
Offertory	Wär Gott nicht mit uns diese Zeit	
	(Were God Not On Our Side)	
		Buxtehude [BC 140;2:00]
Postlude	Prelude and Fugue in G Major	Buxtehude [3:00]

SENIOR CHOIR:
He Hath Done All Things Well [Mark 7:37]   J. Bender
This Day at Thy Creating Word [General] [U]   M. Drischner

JUNIOR CHOIR:

HYMNS:
In Christ There Is No East or West [James 2:1] (149HB)
Thine Arm, O Lord, in Days of Old [Mark 7:24-37] (567TH)
O For a Thousand Tongues to Sing [Mark 7:31-37] (48HB)

DATE: Sunday between September 11 and September 17 inclusive

READINGS:
Proverbs 1:20-22 or Isaiah 50:4-9a
Psalm 19 or Wisdom of Solomon 7:26 - 8:1 or Psalm 116:1-9
James 3:1-12
Mark 8:27-38

ORGAN MUSIC:

Messe des Paroisses		F. Couperin	[20:00]
Prelude	Kyrie		[p.3;1:00]
	Fugue		[p.4;2:00]
	Récit de Chromhorne		[p.6;1:00]
	Dialogue sur la Trompette et le Chromhorne		[p.8;2:00]
	Duo sur les Tierces		[p.13;1:30]
	Dialogue en trio du Cornet et de la Tierce		[p.25;2:00]
	Dialogue sur les Grands Jeux		[p.28;1:30]
	Dialogue sur les Grands Jeux		[p.43;2:00]
Offertory	Benedictus		[p.39;1:30]
Postlude	Offertoire sur les Grands Jeux		[p.30;6:00]

SENIOR CHOIR:
Psalm XIX [Ps.19]   B. Marcello
Tarry No Longer; Toward Thine Heritage [General] [U] W.H. Harris

JUNIOR CHOIR:

HYMNS:
Before Thy Throne, O God, We Kneel [James 3:1-5:6] (574TH)
Take Up Your Cross, The Saviour Said [Mark 8:34] (176HB)
He Who Would Valiant Be [Mark 8:34] (414WB)
New Every Morning Is the Love [Mark 8:34] (360HB)

DATE: Sunday between September 18 and September 24 inclusive

READINGS:
Proverbs 31:10-31 or Wisdom of Solomon 1:16-2:1, 12-22 or Jeremiah 11:18-20
Psalm 1 or Psalm 54
James 3:13 - 4:3, 7-8a
Mark 9:30-37

ORGAN MUSIC:
Prelude	Trio in D Minor	J.S. Bach [5:00]
	Sonata No.4 in E Minor	Bach [10:00]
Offertory	Ich hab mein Gott heimgestellt	
	(I Have Placed God in My Home)	Bach [BN 54;2:30]
Postlude	Herr Gott, dich loben wir	
	(Lord God, We Praise Thee)	
		J. Walther [GG 2:127;2:30]

SENIOR CHOIR:
Psalm 1 (SA)	H. Schütz
The Smiling Dawn of Happy Days [General] [U]	G.F.Handel

JUNIOR CHOIR:

HYMNS:
Sing to the Lord of Harvest [Ps.1] (382HB)
The Man Is Ever Blessed [Ps.1] (388LW)
O Master, Let Me Walk with Thee [Mark 9:35] (301HB)

DATE: Sunday between September 25 and October 1 inclusive

READINGS:
Esther 7:1-6, 9-10; 9:20-22 or Numbers 11:4-6, 10-16, 24-29
Psalm 124 or Psalm 19:7-14
James 5:13-20
Mark 9:38-50

ORGAN MUSIC:

Prelude	Ciacona in D Minor	J. Pachelbel [6:00]
	Prelude and Fugue in C Minor	F. Mendelssohn [8:00]
Offertory	Gott Vater, der du deine Sohn	
	(Father God, Who Gave Thy Son)	
		Pachelbel [PA 3:54;1:30]
Postlude	Gott hat das Evangelium	
	(God Sent the Evangel)	Pachelbel [PA 3:93;3:00]

SENIOR CHOIR:
Let the Words of My Mouth [Ps.19:14] (TTB)   H. Purcell
Let My Prayer Come Up [General] (SSATB)   Purcell
We Praise Thee, O God [General] [U]   H.G. Ley

JUNIOR CHOIR:

HYMNS:
There's a Spirit in the Air [Mark 9:40-41] (433PH)
Where Cross the Crowded Ways of Life [Mark 9:41] (303HB)

DATE: Sunday between October 2 and October 8 inclusive

READINGS:
Job 1:1, 2:1-10 or Genesis 2:18-24
Psalm 26 or Psalm 8
Hebrews 1:1-4, 2:5-12
Mark 10:2-16

ORGAN MUSIC:

Prelude	Prelude and Fugue in E Minor	J.S. Bach [7:00]	
	Liebster Jesu, wir sind hier [Mark 10:13-16]		
	(Dearest Jesus, We Are Here)	Bach [BO 60;1:30]	
		[BU 59,60;2:30]	
		J. Walther [WO 78;3:00]	
		[EK 2:127;1:00]	
Offertory	Liebster Jesu, wir sind hier	Bach [BU 61;2:00]	
Postlude	Prelude on "Ebenezer"	H. Willan [WH 2:6]	

SENIOR CHOIR:
O Lord, Our Governor [Ps.8:1] [U]   B. Marcello

JUNIOR CHOIR:

HYMNS:
We Love the Place, O Lord [Ps.26] (355HB)
Rejoice, the Lord Is King [Hebrews 1:3] (44HB)
All Hail the Power of Jesus' Name [Hebrews 2:5-9] (42HB)
Crown Him With Many Crowns [Hebrews 2:9] (480HB)
When Jesus Left His Father's Throne [Mark 10:13-16] (480TH)
Jesus Loves Me! [Mark 10:13-15] (123HB)

DATE: Sunday between October 9 and October 15 inclusive
[see Thanksgiving]

READINGS:
Job 23:1-9, 16-17 or Amos 5:6-7, 10-15
Psalm 22:1-15 or Psalm 90:12-17
Hebrews 4:12-16
Mark 10:17-31

ORGAN MUSIC:

SENIOR CHOIR:

JUNIOR CHOIR:

HYMNS:

DATE: Sunday between October 16 and October 22 inclusive

READINGS:
Job 38:1-7 (34-41) or Isaiah 53:4-12
Psalm 104:1-9, 24, 35c or Psalm 91:9-16
Hebrews 5:1-10
Mark 10:35-45

ORGAN MUSIC:
Prelude	Prelude in A Minor	D. Buxtehude [6:00]
	Da Jesus an dem Kreuze stund' [Heb.5:7]	
	(When On the Cross the Savior Hung)	
		S.Scheidt [GT 1:116;3:30]
		J.C.F. Fischer [GT 1:114;2:30]
		J. Pachelbel [PA 2:42;2:30]
Offertory	Da Jesus an dem Kreuze stund' J.S. Bach [BO 39;2:00]	
Postlude	Variations on the Milanese Galliard	A. Cabezon

SENIOR CHOIR:
All We Like Sheep [Is.53:6]   G.F. Handel

JUNIOR CHOIR:
Many and Great, O God, Are Your Works [Ps.104] (SFGP 80)

HYMNS:
Brightest and Best of the Sons of the Morning [Job 38:7] (432HB)
The Singer and the Song [Job 38:7] (54SFGP)
Eternal Father, Strong to Save [Job 38:8-11] (221HB)
God Moves in a Mysterious Way [Job 38:22-23] (159HB)
Guide Me, O Thou Great Jehovah [Ps.104] (269HB)
O Worship the King, All Glorious Above [Ps.104] (458LW)
Immortal, Invisible, God Only Wise [Ps.104:1-5] (26HB)
O Master, Let Me Walk with Thee [Mark 10:35-40] (301HB)

DATE: Sunday between October 23 and October 29 inclusive

READINGS:
Job 42:1-6, 10-17 or Jeremiah 31:7-9
Psalm 34:1-8, (19-22) or Psalm 126
Hebrews 7:23-28
Mark 10:46-52

ORGAN MUSIC:
Prelude	Concerto in C Major	J.S. Bach [20:00]
Offertory	Es spricht der unweisen Mund wohl (The Fool Hath Said) [Ps.14]	
		J. Walther [GG 2:108;2:00]
Postlude	Es spricht der unweisen Mund wohl	
		J. Pachelbel [PA 3:66;3:30]

SENIOR CHOIR:
O Taste and See [Ps.34:8]   R. Vaughan Williams
The Song of the Tree of Life [General] [U or 2-part]
                                                      Vaughan Williams

JUNIOR CHOIR:

HYMNS:
Through All the Changing Scenes of Life [Ps.34] (137HB)
At the Lamb's High Feast We Sing [Hebrews 7:11-28] (174TH)
O For a Thousand Tongues to Sing [Mark 10:46-52] (48HB)

DATE: Sunday between October 30 and November 5 inclusive
[see All Saints]

READINGS:
Ruth 1:1-18 or Deuteronomy 6:1-9
Psalm 146 or Psalm 119:1-8
Hebrews 9:11-14
Mark 12:28-34

ORGAN MUSIC:

SENIOR CHOIR:

JUNIOR CHOIR:

HYMNS:

DATE: Sunday between November 6 and November 12 inclusive

READINGS:
Ruth 3:1-5; 4:13-17 or 1 Kings 17:8-16
Psalm 127 or Psalm 146
Hebrews 9:24-28
Mark 12:38-44

ORGAN MUSIC:

Prelude	Sonata I	P. Hindemith [17:00]
Offertory	Trio No. 3	J. Rheinberger [2:00]
Postlude	Fugue in G Minor	J. Pachelbel

SENIOR CHOIR:
Then Round About the Starry Throne [General]   G.F. Handel

JUNIOR CHOIR:

HYMNS:
Unless the Lord the House Shall Build [Ps.127] (238PH)
Lord, Enthroned in Heavenly Splendor [Hebrews 9:23-26] (324HB)

DATE: Sunday between November 13 and November 19 inclusive

READINGS:
1 Samuel 1:4-20 or Daniel 12:1-3
1 Samuel 2:1-10 or Psalm 16
Hebrews 10:11-14 (15-18) 19-25
Mark 13:1-8

ORGAN MUSIC:
Prelude	Suite Médievale	J. Langlais [16:00]
Offertory	Elevation in G Major	LeBegue [2:00]
Postlude	Toccata from Suite Gothique	L. Boëllmann

SENIOR CHOIR:
Achieved Is the Glorious Work [General]   F.J. Haydn

JUNIOR CHOIR:

HYMNS:
Tell Out, My Soul, the Greatness of the Lord [1 Sam.2:1-10] (495HB)
Lord, Enthroned in Heavenly Splendor [Hebrews 10:1-22] (324HB)
At the Lamb's High Feast We Sing [Hebrews 10:10-22] (174TH)
Lord Christ, When First Thou Cam'st to Earth (St.2) [Mark 13:1-2]
(598TH)

DATE: Sunday between November 20 and November 26 inclusive
(Christ the King)

READINGS:
2 Samuel 23:1-7 or Daniel 7:9-10, 13-14
Psalm 132:1-12 (13-18) or Psalm 93
Revelation 1:4b-8
John 18:33-37

ORGAN MUSIC:
Prelude   Passacaglia and Fugue in C Minor   J.S. Bach [14:00]
Offertory   Prelude on Deo Gracias   H. Willan [WH 2:14;2:00]
Postlude   Tiento del Octavo Tono   A. Cabezon

SENIOR CHOIR:
How Excellent Thy Name [John 18:33-37]   G.F. Handel

JUNIOR CHOIR:

HYMNS:
Glorious Things of Thee Are Spoken [Ps.132:13-18] (144HB)
Let All Mortal Flesh Keep Silence (St.2) [Rev.1:4-7] (332HB)
Lord, Enthroned in Heavenly Splendor [Rev.1:5-6] (324HB)
Lo, He Comes With Clouds Descending [Rev.1:7] (393HB)
Come Thou, Almighty King [Rev.1:8] (62HB)

DATE: November 1 or the First Sunday in November
                        (All Saints)

READINGS:
Wisdom of Solomon 3:1-19 or Isaiah 25:6-9
Psalm 24
Revelation 21:1-6a
John 11:32-44

ORGAN MUSIC:

Suite du 2me Ton		L.-N. Clérambault [17:00]
Prelude	Plein jeu	[2:00]
	Duo	[2:00]
	Trio	[2:00]
	Flûtes	[3:00]
	Récit de Nazard	[2:30]
Offertory	Basse de Cromorne	[2:00]
Postlude	Caprice sur les Grands Jeux	

SENIOR CHOIR:
For All the Saints [All Saints]   R. Vaughan Williams
Let Saints on Earth in Concert Sing [All Saints] [U]   A. Ridout

JUNIOR CHOIR:
Jesus the Christ Said [John 11:25] (73SFGP)

HYMNS:
For Ourselves No Longer Living (St.2) [Ps.24:1] (119SFGP)
All Glory, Laud and Honor [Ps.24:7-9] (447HB)
Jerusalem the Golden [Rev.21:2-22:5] (184HB)
For the Healing of the Nations [Rev.21:2-22:5] (428UM)
O What Their Joy and Their Glory Must Be [Rev.21:2-22:5] (186HB)
Glorious Things of Thee Are Spoken [Rev.21:2-3] (144HB)

DATE: Thanksgiving Day

READINGS:
Joel 2:21-27
Psalm 126
1 Timothy 2:1-7
Matthew 6:25-33

ORGAN MUSIC:

Prelude	Nun freut euch, lieben Christen g'mein I	
	(Be Glad Now, All Ye Christian Folk)	
		J.S. Bach [BU 70;3:00]
		J. Praetorius [PRC 32;13:00]
		J.L. Krebs [GT 3:6;1:00]
Offertory	Nun freut euch, lieben Christen g'mein	
		Bach [GG 1:22;2:30]
Postlude	Nun freut euch, lieben Christen g'mein	
		J. Pachelbel [PA 2:54;2:30]

SENIOR CHOIR:

Sing to the Lord of Harvest [Thanksgiving]	H. Willan
Lord, Hear Our Thanks [General] [U]	G.F. Handel

JUNIOR CHOIR:
Seek Ye First the Kingdom of God [Matthew 6:33] (83SFGP)

HYMNS:
Rejoice, O Land, in God Your Lord [Joel 2:21] (331HT)
Christ, by Heavenly Hosts Adored [1 Timothy 2:1-3] (499LW)
O God of Bethel, by Whose Hand [Matthew 6:25-33] (263HB)
All Things Bright and Beautiful [Matthew 6:28-29] (86HB)
When God Delivered Israel [Ps.126] (98SFPG)

YEAR C

Begins on the First Sunday of Advent in 1994, 1997, 2000, 2003

DATE: First Sunday of Advent

READINGS:
Jeremiah 33:14-16
Psalm 25:1-10
1 Thessalonians 3:9-13
Luke 21:25-36

ORGAN MUSIC:

Prelude	Conditor alme siderum	
	(Creator of the Stars of Night)	J. Titelouze [5:00]
		F. Peeters [PG 1:3]
	Noels	J.-F. Dandrieu
	Ou s'en vont ces gais bergers	[5:30]
Offertory	Noël cette journée	[2:30]
Postlude	Vous qui desirez sans fin	[3:00]

SENIOR CHOIR:

O Come, O Come, Emmanuel	Z. Kodály
The Angel Gabriel [Advent] [U]	R.J. Powell

JUNIOR CHOIR:

HYMNS:
O Heavenly Word, Eternal Light [1 Thess.3:11-13] (63TH)
The Day Is Surely Drawing Near [Lk.21:25-36] (462LW)
Lo! He Comes With Clouds Descending [Lk.21:25-28] (393HB)
Jesus Came, Adored by Angels [Lk.21:25-28] (454TH)

134

DATE: Second Sunday of Advent

READINGS:
Baruch 5:1-9 or Malachi 3:1-4
Luke 1:68-79
Philippians 1:3-11
Luke 3:1-6

ORGAN MUSIC:
Prelude	Pastorale in F Major	J.S. Bach [13:30]
Offertory	Aria Pastorella	
		V. Rathgeber [ADW 16;1:00]
Postlude	Prelude on "Lo, He Comes with Clouds	
	Descending"	A. Ridout [CPE 2]

SENIOR CHOIR:
But Who May Abide the Day of His Coming   G.F. Handel
[Malachai 3:2-3] (B or S Solo)
And He Shall Purify ("Messiah") [Advent]

JUNIOR CHOIR:

HYMNS:
On Jordan's Bank the Baptist's Cry [Mal.3:1] (391HB)
There's a Voice in the Wilderness Crying [Mal.3:1] (153HB)
Herald, Sound the Note of Judgment [Mal.3:1] (103HB)
Sing, My Tongue [Luke 1:68-79] (446HB)

DATE: Third Sunday of Advent

READINGS:
Zephaniah 3:14-20
Isaiah 12:2-6
Philippians 4:4-7
Luke 3:7-18

ORGAN MUSIC:

Prelude	Noels 9, 10, 11	C.L. Daquin [14:00]
Offertory	Veni Emmanuel	F. Peeters [PH 1:1;2:00]
Postlude	Noel 12	Daquin [4:30]

SENIOR CHOIR:

Rejoice in the Lord Alway [Phil.4:4-7]	H. Purcell
Wake, Awake, for Night Is Flying [Advent] [U]	F. Tunder

JUNIOR CHOIR:

HYMNS:
O For a Thousand Tongues to Sing [Is.12:4-5] (48HB)
Rejoice, the Lord Is King [Phil.4:4] (44HB)
Rejoice, Ye Pure in Heart [Phil.4:4] (145PH)
Like a Mighty River Flowing [Phil.4:7] (32HT)
Prepare the Way, O Zion [Luke 3:4-5] (65TH)

DATE: Fourth Sunday of Advent

READINGS:
Micah 5:2-5a
Luke 1:47-55 or Psalm 80:1-7
Hebrews 10:5-10
Luke 1:39-45, (46-55)

ORGAN MUSIC:
Prelude   Magnificat (Meine Seele erhebet den Herren) [Luke
               1:46-55]

                                               D. Buxtehude [BC 73;2:30]
                                               J. Walther [EK 2:139;6:30]
                                               J.S. Bach [BSC 91;3:00]
Offertory   Magnificat   J. Pachelbel [PA 2:32;3:00]
Postlude   Fugue on the Magnificat   Bach [BU 65;4:00]

SENIOR CHOIR:
Magnificat [Luke 1:39-45] [U]   J. Duke

JUNIOR CHOIR:
Shepherds Watched Their Flocks by Night (CS 32)   H. Willan

HYMNS:
O Little Town of Bethlehem [Micah 5:2] (421HB)
Tell Out, My Soul, the Greatness of the Lord [Luke 1:46-55] (495HB)
Song of Mary [Luke 1:46-55] (600PH)
Lord, Enthroned in Heavenly Splendor [Heb.10:1-22] (324HB)

DATE: Christmas Eve

READINGS:

ORGAN MUSIC:
Prelude   Puer natus in Bethlehem
            (A Boy Is Born in Bethlehem)
                                    J.S. Bach [BO 8;1:00]
                                    D. Buxtehude [BC 121;1:00]
                                    G.F. Kauffmann [AWK 31;2:30]
                                    J. Walther [WO 120;3:00]
            Vom Himmel hoch, da komm ich her
            (From Heaven on High, to Earth I Come)
                                    J.H. Buttstedt [AWK 35;1:00]
                                    J. Heuschel [AWK 36;1:00]
            O Jesulein süss
            (O Jesus Sweet)   S. Scheidt [PO 6:25;1:00]
                                    G.F. Kauffmann [AWK 40;1:00]
                                    J.C.F. Fischer [GT 3:38;1:00]
                                    Anonymous [AWK 42;1:00]
            Es ist ein Ros entsprungen
            (Lo, How a Rose E'er Blooming)
                                    J. Brahms [BE 26;2:00]
            Adeste fideles   Adam [GRV 1;1:00]
Offertory   This Endris Nyght   H. Willan [WH 2:19;2:00]
Postlude   Ave Maris Stella   M. Dupré [2:30]

SENIOR CHOIR:
Joseph, Dearest Joseph Mine [Christmas]   Bodenschatz
Carol of the Russian Children [Christmas]   Gaul
Let Our Gladness Have No End [Christmas] [U]   J. Ferguson

JUNIOR CHOIR:
O Mary, Where Is Your Baby? [Christmas] [U w/d]   D. Walker

HYMNS:
Carols

DATE: Christmas Day

READINGS: [Proper III (A,B,C); for Propers I and II, see Years A and B, respectively]
Isaiah 52:7-10
Psalm 98
Hebrews 1:1-4, (5-12)
John 1:1-14

ORGAN MUSIC:
Prelude   Allein Gott in der Höh sei Ehr [Luke 2:1-20]
              (All Glory Be to God on High)
                                          J.S. Bach [BU 8,11;6:00]
                                          J. Walther [WO 12;3:30]
                                          G. Böhm [BS 26;3:30]
Offertory   Allein Gott in der Höh sei Ehr
                                          F.W. Marpurg [MC 20;2:00]
Postlude   Allein Gott in der Höh sei Ehr
                                          Walther [GG 1:8;3:00]

SENIOR CHOIR:
Christmas Day [Christmas]   G. Holst
Beside Thy Manger Here I Stand [Christmas] [U]   M. Koler

JUNIOR CHOIR:
Shepherds in Judea [Christmas] [U w/d]   D. Walker

HYMNS:
Come, Thou Long-Expected Jesus [Is.52:7] (389HB)
Joy to the World [Ps.98] (401HB)
O Come, All Ye Faithful (St.2) [Heb.1:1-12] (415HB)
Angels, From the Realms of Glory [Heb.1:6] (408HB)
Hark! the Herald Angels Sing (Sts.2 & 3) [John 1:1-18] (407HB)
Once in Royal David's City [John 1:1-18] (112HB)
Break Forth, O Beauteous Heavenly Light [John 1:4-5] (402HB)

DATE: First Sunday after Christmas Day

READINGS:
1 Samuel 2:18-20, 26
Psalm 148
Colossians 3:12-17
Luke 2:41-52

ORGAN MUSIC:

Prelude	Organ Carols	H. Schroeder [6:00]
	Sleep Softly, Softly Beautiful Jesus	[p.1]
	The Shadows Are Falling	[p.14]
	Now Sing We, Now Rejoice	[p.20]
	In Bethlehem a Wonder	[p.21]
	Now to This Babe So Tender	[p.22]
	Delicate Child of Royal Line	[p.23]

Helft mir Gottes Güte preisen
(Help Me Praise God's Goodness)
                                    J.S. Bach [BO 24;2:00]
                            G.F. Kauffmann [AWK 44;2:30]
Das alte Jahr vergangen ist [New Years]
(The Old Year Now Hath Passed Away)
                                    Bach [BO 25;2:00]
                            J. Walther [GG 2:102;1:30]

Offertory	Das alte Jahr vergangen ist	Bach [BN 6;2:00]
Postlude	Gloria from Ave Maris Stella	M. Dupré

SENIOR CHOIR:
In Thee Is Gladness [Christmas]   Gastoldi
Of the Father's Love Begotten [Christmas] [U]   Plainsong

JUNIOR CHOIR:
The Little Cradle Rocks Tonight in Glory [Christmas] [U]
                                                         D. Walker

HYMNS:
All Creatures of Our God and King [Ps.148] (1HB)
Ye Watchers and Ye Holy Ones [Ps.148] (7HB)
Songs of Praise the Angels Sang [Ps.148:1-2; Col.3:16] (447LW)
When in Our Music God Is Glorified [Col.3:16] (420TH)

DATE: Epiphany of the Lord (A,B,C)

READINGS: [See Year A]
Isaiah 60:1-6
Psalm 72:1-7, 10-14
Ephesians 3:1-12
Matthew 2:1-12

ORGAN MUSIC:

SENIOR CHOIR:

JUNIOR CHOIR:

HYMNS:

DATE: Baptism of the Lord
                              (First Sunday after the Epiphany)

READINGS:
Isaiah 43:1-7
Psalm 29
Acts 8:14-17
Luke 3:15-17, 21-22

ORGAN MUSIC:
Prelude   Prelude and Fugue in C Minor   V. Lübeck [5:00]
              Wir glauben all an einem Gott [Is.43:1-7]
              (We All Believe in One True God)
                                             J.C. Bach [GT 3:177;1:00]
                                             J.S. Bach [BCL 57;1:30]
                                             J. Pachelbel [PA 3:4;4:00]
                                             S. Scheidt [80:80;2:30]
                                             J. Walther [HP 42:32;1:00]
                                             F. Zachau [GG 2:165;1:30]
Offertory   Wir glauben all an einem Gott   J.S. Bach [BN 20;2:00]
Postlude   Wir glauben all an einem Gott
                                             J.S. Bach [BCL 52;3:00]

SENIOR CHOIR:
Bethlehem Down [Epiphany]   P. Warlock
Now Let Us Come Before Him [Epiphany] [U]   M. Drischner

JUNIOR CHOIR:
From a Distant Home (PH 64)

HYMNS:
How Firm a Foundation [Is.43:1-7] (139HB)
We All Believe in One True God, Maker [Is.43:1-7] (213LW)
We Praise You, O God (St.2) [Is.43:1,2] (59SFGP)
God the Omnipotent! King, Who Ordainest [Ps.29:10-11] (273HB)
Help Us Accept Each Other (St.3) [Lk.3:21] (27SFGP)

DATE: Second Sunday after the Epiphany

READINGS:
Isaiah 62:1-5
Psalm 36:5-10
1 Corinthians 12:1-11
John 2:1-11

ORGAN MUSIC:
Prelude	Pastorale	C. Franck [9:00]
	Première Elevation	N. LeBègue [1:30]
	Préambule	L. Vierne [3:30]
Offertory	Canzon Francese on "Pour ung Plaisir"	
		A. Gabrieli [2:00]
Postlude	Ave Maris Stella	J. Titelouze [6:00]

SENIOR CHOIR:
Here Are We in Bethlehem [Epiphany]	H. Willan
Rejoice and Be Merry [Christmas] [U]	R.J. Powell

JUNIOR CHOIR:
Many Are the Lightbeams [1 Cor.12:4-13] (SFGP 104)

HYMNS:
All Hail the Power of Jesus' Name [Is.62:3] (42HB)
Immortal, Invisible, God Only Wise [Ps.36:6] (26HB)
Christ, From Whom All Blessings Flow [1 Cor.12:4-31] (550UM)
Songs of Thankfulness and Praise (St.2) [John 2:1-11] (433HB)

DATE: Third Sunday after the Epiphany

READINGS:
Nehemiah 8:1-3, 5-6, 8-10
Psalm 19
1 Corinthians 12:12-31a
Luke 4:14-21

ORGAN MUSIC:

Prelude	Prelude and Fugue in Eb Major	C. Saint-Saëns [7:30]
	Gottes Sohn ist kommen [Lk.4:17-19]	
	(The Son of God Is Come)	J.S. Bach [BO 4;1:00]
		J.H. Buttstedt [GT 2:9;2:00]
		G.F. Kauffmann [GG 2:116;2:00]
		Walther [GG 2:118;1:30]
Offertory	Gottes Sohn ist kommen	Walther [WO 42;2:00]
Postlude	Gottes Sohn ist kommen	Bach [BU 33,34;2:30]

SENIOR CHOIR:
Here Is the Little Door [Epiphany]   H. Howells
Sing, O Sing [Christmas] [U]   J.R. Powell

JUNIOR CHOIR:
I Am the Light of the World [Lk.4:18-19] (SFGP 24)

HYMNS:
All Beautiful the March of Days [Ps.19] (388HB)
The Spacious Firmament on High [Ps.19] (85HB)
Holy, Holy, Holy! [Ps.19:1-6] (50HB)
Jesus Shall Reign [Ps.19:4-6] (164HB)
Hark! the Glad Sound! the Savior Comes [Lk.4:16-21] (395HB)

DATE: Fourth Sunday after the Epiphany

READINGS:
Jeremiah 1:4-10
Psalm 71:1-6
1 Corinthians 13:1-13
Luke 4:21-30

ORGAN MUSIC:
Prelude   Toccata and Fugue (Dorian) in D Minor, BWV 538
                                              J.S. Bach [13:00]
Offertory   Fantasia in Eb Major   J. Pachelbel [2:00]
Postlude   Fugue in A Minor   Pachelbel [2:30]

SENIOR CHOIR:
Light for the Child [Epiphany]   N. Telfer

JUNIOR CHOIR:
He Whom Joyous Shepherds Praised   H. Willan

HYMNS:
Rock of Ages, Cleft For Me [Ps.71:3] (79HB)
Morning Glory, Starlit Sky (St.2-3) [1 Cor.13:4-7] (13SFGP)

DATE: Fifth Sunday after the Epiphany

READINGS:
Isaiah 6:1-8, (9-13)
Psalm 138
1 Corinthians 15:1-11
Luke 5:1-11

ORGAN MUSIC:
Prelude	Sonata V	C.P.E. Bach [19:30]
Offertory	Trio No. 4	J. Rheinberger [2:00]
Postlude	Fugue in G Major	D. Buxtehude

SENIOR CHOIR:
Holy, Holy, Holy [Is.6:3]   Cimarosa

JUNIOR CHOIR:
Holy, Holy, Holy Lord [Is.6:3] (SFGP 117)

HYMNS:
Let All Mortal Flesh Keep Silence [Is.6:1-3] (332HB)
The God of Abraham Praise [Is.6:1-3] (401TH)
Amazing Grace! How Sweet the Sound [1 Cor.15:10] (49SFGP)
They Cast Their Nets in Galilee [Lk.5:1-11] (661TH)
Dear Lord and Father of Mankind (St.2) [Lk.5:11] (249HB)

DATE: Sixth Sunday after the Epiphany

READINGS:
Jeremiah 17:5-10
Psalm 1
1 Corinthians 15:12-20
Luke 6:17-26

ORGAN MUSIC:

Prelude	Prelude in C Major	D. Buxtehude [3:00]
	Prelude and Fugue in G Minor	[7:30]
	Canzona in C Major	[5:30]
Offertory	Toccata in C Major	J. Pachelbel [2:00]
Postlude	Fugue in Bb Major	Buxtehude

SENIOR CHOIR:
Lord of All Hopefulness [General]   H. Willan

JUNIOR CHOIR:
Jesus the Christ Said [Lk.6:20] (SFGP 73)

HYMNS:
How Blest Are They Who Hear God's Word [Ps.1:1-3] (222LW)
Hope of the World [1 Cor.15:19] (360PH)

DATE: Seventh Sunday after the Epiphany

READINGS:
Genesis 45:3-13, 15
Psalm 37:1-11, 39-40
1 Corinthians 15:35-38, 42-50
Luke 6:27-38

ORGAN MUSIC:
Prelude	Prelude and Fugue in Eb Major	V. Lübeck [5:30]
	Jesus, meine Zuversicht [1 Cor.15:35 ff]	
	(Jesus Christ, My Sure Defense)	
		J. Walther [WO 72;6:30]
		N. Raasted [EK 2:118;1:30]
Offertory	Jesus, meine Zuversicht	Bach [BU 48;2:00]
Postlude	Prelude in F Major	Lübeck

SENIOR CHOIR:
Commit Your Life to the Lord [Ps.37:5]   Liebhold

JUNIOR CHOIR:

HYMNS:
Jesus Christ, My Sure Defense [1 Cor.15:35ff] (266LW)

DATE: Eighth Sunday after the Epiphany

READINGS:
Sirach 27:4-7 or Isaiah 55:10-13
Psalm 92:1-4, 12-15
1 Corinthians 15:51-58
Luke 6:39-49

ORGAN MUSIC:
Prelude	Nun lasst uns Gott dem Herrn dank sagen [Ps.92:1]
	(Now Let Us Sing Thanks Unto the Lord God)

                                                       V. Lübeck [LS 60;7:00]

                                                       J. Walther [WO 102;8:00]

                                                     J. Pachelbel [PA 3:38;1:30]

Offertory	Nun lasst uns Gott dem Herrn dank sagen

                                                     F. Zachau [GG 1:52;2:00]

Postlude	Nun lasst uns Gott dem Herrn dank sagen

                                                   H. Willan [WS 3:37;2:30]

SENIOR CHOIR:
But Thanks Be to God [1 Cor.15:55-57]   G.F. Handel

JUNIOR CHOIR:

HYMNS:
Awake, My Soul, and With the Sun [Ps.92:1-4] (357HB)
When in Our Music God Is Glorified [Ps.92:1-4] (264PH)
Alleluia! The Strife Is O'er [1 Cor.15:51-54] (468HB)
Rejoice, the Lord Is King [1 Cor.15:51-52] (44HB)
Lord, Dismiss Us With Thy Blessing [Luke 6:43-45] (308HB)
How Firm a Foundation, Ye Saints of the the Lord [Luke 6:47-49] (139HB)

DATE: Ninth Sunday after the Epiphany

READINGS:
1 Kings 8:22-23, 41-43
Psalm 96:1-9
Galatians 1:1-12
Luke 7:1-10

ORGAN MUSIC:

Prelude	Voluntary in D Minor	H. Purcell [4:00]
	Voluntary in G Minor	J. Stanley [6:00]
	Voluntary in D Minor	Stanley [3:30]
Offertory	Voluntary No. 1	G.F. Handel [2:00]
Postlude	Voluntary in D Major	Stanley

SENIOR CHOIR:
I, O Lord, Am Not Worthy [Luke 7:1-10]   Victoria

JUNIOR CHOIR:

HYMNS:
Oh, For a Thousand Tongues to Sing [Ps.96:1-3; Luke 7:1-17] (48HB)
Thine Arm, O Lord, in Days of Old [Luke 7:1-23] (567TH)

DATE: Last Sunday after the Epiphany
                   (Transfiguration Sunday)

READINGS:
Exodus 34:29-35
Psalm 99
2 Corinthians 3:12 - 4:2
Luke 9:28-36, (37-43)

ORGAN MUSIC:

Prelude	Prelude and Fugue in G Major	V. Lübeck [5:30]
	Prelude and Fugue in C Minor	J.S. Bach [7:30]
Offertory	Trio No. 6	J. Rheinberger [2:00]
Postlude	Fugue in C Major	J. Pachelbel

SENIOR CHOIR:
We Saw His Glory [Transfiguration]   Mauersberger

JUNIOR CHOIR:

HYMNS:
For the Healing of the Nations (St.4) [2 Cor.3:18] (23SFGP)
From Glory to Glory Advancing, We Praise Thee, O Lord [2
Cor.3:18] (307HB)
Love Divine, All Love's Excelling [2 Cor.3:18] (241HB)
Songs of Thankfulness and Praise (St.4) [Luke 9:28-36] (433HB)
Oh, Wondrous Type! Oh, Vision Fair [Luke 9:28-36] (87LW)
Christ Upon the Mountain Peak [Luke 9:28-36] (129TH)

DATE: First Sunday in Lent

READINGS:
Deuteronomy 26:1-11
Psalm 91:1-2, 9-16
Romans 10:8b-13
Luke 4:1-13

ORGAN MUSIC:

Prelude	Canzona in D Minor	D. Buxtehude [4:00]
	Prelude and Fugue in A Minor	J.S. Bach [11:00]
Offertory	Trio No. 5	J. Rheinberger [2:00]
Postlude	Prelude in F Major	Buxtehude

SENIOR CHOIR:
O Christ, Thou Lamb of God [Lent]   J.N. David
O Lamb of God Most Holy [Lent] [U]   M. Drischner

JUNIOR CHOIR:

HYMNS:
Sing Praise to God, Who Reigns Above [Ps.91] (483PH)
O God of Bethel, By Whose Hand [Ps.91:1-4] (263HB)
At the Name of Jesus [Romans 10:8-13] (39HB)
Forty Days and Forty Nights [Luke 4:1-13] (437HB)
She Flies On (St.4) [Luke 4:1-13] (126SFGP)

DATE: Second Sunday in Lent

READINGS:
Genesis 15:1-12, 17-18
Psalm 27
Philippians 3:17 - 4:1
Luke 13:31-35 or Luke 9:28-36

ORGAN MUSIC:

Prelude	Prelude and Fugue in F Major	V. Lübeck [5:30]
	Ach Gott und Herr [Confession]	
	(Ah, God and Lord)	J. Walther [WO 2;5:30]
		[HP 12:8;1:30]
		J.S. Bach [BU 3;1:00]
		D. Buxtehude [BC 2;2:00]
Offertory	Ach Gott und Herr	Walther [GG 1:3;2:00]
Postlude	Ach Gott und Herr	Bach [BN 2;2:00]

SENIOR CHOIR:
Hide Not Thou Thy Face From Us, O Lord [Ps.27:9]   R. Farrant

JUNIOR CHOIR:

HYMNS:
God Is My Strong Salvation [Ps.27] (179PH)
I Love Your Kingdom, Lord [Ps.27:4] (296LW)
God of Grace and God of Glory [Ps.27:14] (223HB)
Songs of Thankfulness and Praise (St.4) [Luke 9:28-36] (433HB)

DATE: Third Sunday in Lent

READINGS:
Isaiah 55:1-9
Psalm 63:1-8
1 Corinthians 10:1-13
Luke 13:1-9

ORGAN MUSIC:
Prelude   Fugue on a Theme of Legrenzi   J.S. Bach [7:00]
            O Mensch, bewein dein' Sünde gross [Lent]
            (O Man, Thy Grievous Sin Bemoan)
                                        J.P. Sweelinck [SA 49;2:30]
                                              Bach [BO 60;4:30]
Offertory   O Mensch, bewein dein' Sünde gross
                                        D. Hellmann [EK 3:193;2:00]
Postlude   O Mensch, bewein dein' Sünde gross
                                        J. Pachelbel [PA 2:36;4:00]

SENIOR CHOIR:
O God, Thou Art My God [Ps.63:1-5,8]   H. Purcell

JUNIOR CHOIR:

HYMNS:
Come, Let Us Sing (St.2) [Isaiah 55:1] (90SFGP)
O God, You Are My God [Ps.63] (198PH)
Glorious Things of Thee Are Spoken [1 Cor.10:1-4] (144HB)
Guide Me, O Thou Great Jehovah [1 Cor.10:1-4] (269HB)
Lord, Enthroned in Heavenly Splendor [1 Cor.10:3-4] (324HB)

DATE: Fourth Sunday in Lent

READINGS:
Joshua 5:9-12
Psalm 32
2 Corinthians 5:16-21
Luke 15:1-3, 11b-32

ORGAN MUSIC:
Prelude   Prelude and Fugue in G Minor   J. Brahms [9:00]
                 O Welt, ich muss dich lassen
                 (O World, I Now Must Leave Thee)
                                          Anonymous [GG 1:60;1:00]
                                          J.S. Bach [PO I:126;1:00]
                                          Brahms [BE 12;2:30]
                                          H. Isaac [HP 3:34;1:00]
                                  G.F. Kauffmann [HP 18:21;1:30]
Offertory   O Welt, ich muss dich lassen J. Walther [GG 1:60;1:30]
Postlude   O Welt, ich muss dich lassen   Brahms [BE 34;2:30]

SENIOR CHOIR:
Let Down the Bars, O Death [Lent]   S. Barber
When I Survey the Wondrous Cross [Lent] [U]   M. Drischner

JUNIOR CHOIR:

HYMNS:
Rejoice, Ye Pure in Heart [Ps.32:12] (556TH)
The Church's One Foundation [2 Cor.5:17] (146HB)
Now the Silence, Now the Peace [Luke 15:11-32] (48SFGP)

DATE: Fifth Sunday in Lent

READINGS:
Isaiah 43:16-21
Psalm 126
Philippians 3:4b-14
John 12:1-8

ORGAN MUSIC:
Prelude   Sonata I   F. Mendelssohn [15:00]
               (based on "Was mein Gott will, das g'scheh allzeit)
Offertory   Was mein Gott will, das g'scheh allzeit [Lent]
               (Let Happen What E'er My God Wills)
                                                    J. Walther [GG 1:76;2:30]
Postlude   Was mein Gott will, das g'scheh allzeit
                                                    J. Pachelbel [PA 3:40;3:00]

SENIOR CHOIR:
When My Last Hour Is Close at Hand [Lent]   Gumpeltzhaimer
O Sacred Head Now Wounded [Lent] [U]   G.F. Handel

JUNIOR CHOIR:

HYMNS:
In Suffering Love (St.5) [Ps.126] (53SFGP)
Bless Us and Keep Us, God [Ps.126:5,6] (132SFGP)
Be Thou My Vision [Phil.3:7] (253HB)
Awake, My Soul, Stretch Every Nerve [Phil.3:12-14] (546TH)

DATE: Sixth Sunday in Lent
                           (Passion Sunday or Palm Sunday)

READINGS: Liturgy of the Palms
Luke 19:28-40
Psalm 118:1-2, 19-29
                          Liturgy of the Passion
Isaiah 50:4-9a
Psalm 31:9-16
Philippians 2:5-11
Luke 22:14 - 23:56 or Luke 23:1-49

ORGAN MUSIC:
Prelude   Passion Chorale [Luke 23:11,26-49]
                                         J.P. Kellner [45:21;5:00]
                                    J.P. Kirnberger [GT 2:72;2:00]
                                    F.W. Marpurg [MC 33;2:30]
                                    G.P. Telemann [GT 2:75;2:30]
                                      F.W. Zachau [GT 2:81;2:30]
                                       D. Strungk [GT 2:73;1:30]
Offertory   Valet will ich dir geben [Luke 19:29-39]
             (All Glory, Laud and Honour)
                                  G.F. Kauffmann [GG 2:160;2:00]
Postlude   Valet will ich dir geben   J. Bender [BK 1:44]
                                          N.O. Raasted [EK 3:217]

SENIOR CHOIR:
Alleluia from "Brazilian Psalm"   J. Berger

JUNIOR CHOIR:

HYMNS:
All Glory, Laud and Honor [Luke 19:29-39; Ps.118:26] (447HB)
Hark! the Glad Sound! the Savior Comes (St.4) [Luke 19:29-39]
(395HB)
My Song Is Love Unknown [Luke 19:29-39] (442HB)
Ride On! Ride on in Majesty [Luke 19:29-39; Ps.118:26] (449HB)
O Sacred Head, Now Wounded [Isaiah 50:6] (452HB)
The Servant Song [Phil.2:5] (133SFPG)

Go to Dark Gethsemane (St.1) [Luke 22:39-46] (451HB)
Lord Christ, When First Thou Cam'st to Earth [Luke 23:11] (598TH)
Ah, Holy Jesus, How Hast Thou Offended [Luke 23:18-25] (443HB)

DATE: Holy Thursday (A,B,C)

READINGS:
Exodus 12:1-4 (5-10) 11-14
Psalm 116:1-2, 12-19
1 Corinthians 11:23-26
John 13:1-17, 31b-35

ORGAN MUSIC:
Ich ruf zu dir (I Cry to Thee)   J.P. Sweelinck [SA 37;9:30]

SENIOR CHOIR:
Behold the Saviour of Mankind [Passion]   C. Tye

JUNIOR CHOIR:

HYMNS:
At the Lamb's High Feast We Sing [Exodus 12:1-28; 1 Cor.11:23-26]
(174TH)
Bread of the World in Mercy Broken [1 Cor.11:23-26] (326HB)
Now, My Tongue, the Mystery Telling [1 Cor.11:23-26] (341HB)

DATE: Good Friday (A,B,C)

READINGS:
Isaiah 52:13 - 53:12
Psalm 22
Hebrews 10:16-25 or Hebrews 4:14-16
John 18:1 - 19:42

ORGAN MUSIC:
Jesu, Kreuz, Leiden und Pein [Lent]
(Jesus' Cross and Anguish Sore)   J. Walther [WO 69;1:30]
                                                        [WO 70;2:30]

Ich ruf zu dir [Lent]
(I Cry to Thee)   J.P. Sweelinck [SA 37;9:30]
                                             D. Buxtehude [BC 48;3:00]
                                             J.L. Krebs [EK 2:90;3:00]
                                      G.F. Kauffmann [GG 2:133;1:30]

SENIOR CHOIR:
Surely He Has Borne Our Griefs [Is.53:4] (S,B)   A. Lotti

JUNIOR CHOIR:

HYMNS:
My Song Is Love Unknown [Isaiah 52:13-53:12; John 18:28-19:16]
(442HB)
Ah, Holy Jesus, How Hast Thou Offended [Isaiah 53:1-12; John 18:15-
27] (443HB)
O Sacred Head, Sore Wounded [Isaiah 53:1-12] (452HB)
Lord, When I Stand [Ps.22:1-2] (125SFGP)
Lord, Enthroned in Heavenly Splendor [Hebrews 10:1-22] (324HB)
At the Lamb's High Feast We Sing [Hebrews 10:10-12] (174TH)
Go to Dark Gethsemane (St.2) [John 18:12-19:16] (451HB)

DATE: Easter Day

READINGS:
Acts 10:34-43 or Isaiah 65:17-25
Psalm 118:1-2, 14-24
1 Corinthians 15:19-26 or Acts 10:34-43
John 20:1-18 or Luke 24:1-12

ORGAN MUSIC:

Prelude	Toccata and Fugue in D Minor	J.S. Bach [9:00]
	Christ ist erstanden [Easter]	
	(Christ Is Risen)	Bach [BO 49;5:30]
		J.H. Buttstedt [GG 2:94;1:30]
		J.C.F. Fischer [GG 2:95;1:30]
		H. Bach [GT 1:77;1:30]
Offertory	Christ ist erstanden	S. Scheidt [PO I:24;1:30]
Postlude	Christ ist erstanden	H. Willan [WH 3:126;3:00]

SENIOR CHOIR:

Since By Man Came Death [1 Cor.15:21,22]	G.F. Handel
Festival Te Deum	B. Britten
Alleluia [Easter] [U]	G.P. Telemann

JUNIOR CHOIR:

HYMNS:
Hail Thee, Festival Day [Acts 10:39-40] (461HB)
"Welcome, Happy Morning!" Age to Age Shall Say [Acts 10:39-40] (462HB)
This Is the Day [Ps.118] (40SFGP)
The Day of Resurrection [Ps.118:15; John 20:1-18] (374HB)
Jesus Christ Is Risen Today [1 Cor.15:20; John 20:1-18] (465HB)
Come, Ye Faithful, Raise the Strain [1 Cor.15:20-22] (464HB)
Good Christians All, Rejoice and Sing [John 20:1-18] (469HB)
The Strife Is O'er, the Battle Done [John 20:1-18] (468HB)

DATE: Second Sunday of Easter

READINGS:
Acts 5:27-32
Psalm 118:14-29 or Psalm 150
Revelation 1:4-8
John 20:19-31

ORGAN MUSIC:
Prelude   Chorale No. 3   C. Franck [12:30]
Offertory   Erstanden ist der heil'ge Christ [Easter]
             (Arisen Is the Holy Christ)   J.S. Bach [BO 54;1:00]
Postlude   Voluntary No. 4   G. F. Handel

SENIOR CHOIR:
Psalm 150   Franck
Unto Him That Loved Us [Rev.1:5,6] [U]   R. Vaughan Williams

JUNIOR CHOIR:
O Sing to the Lord [Ps.150] (PH 472)

HYMNS:
The Head That Once Was Crowned With Thorns [Acts 5:30-31]
(108HB)
Welcome, Happy Morning [Acts 5:30-31] (462HB)
The Day of Resurrection [Ps.118:15] (374HB)
Good Christian Friends, Rejoice and Sing [Ps.118:24] (469HB)
Let All Mortal Flesh Keep Silence (St.2) [Rev.1:4-7] (332HB)
Jesus Christ Is Risen Today [Rev.1:5-6] (465HB)
Lord, Enthroned in Heavenly Splendor [Rev.1:5-6] (324HB)
O Sons and Daughters, Let Us Sing [John 20:19-31] (467HB)
That Easter Day With Joy Was Bright [John 20:19-31] [474HB]

DATE: Third Sunday of Easter

READINGS:
Acts 9:1-6, (7-20)
Psalm 30
Revelation 5:11-14
John 21:1-19

ORGAN MUSIC:

Prelude	Prelude in D Minor	V. Lübeck [9:00]
	Fugue in A Minor "Alla Capella"	W. F. Bach [5:00]
Offertory	Trio No. 7	J. Rheinberger [2:00]
Postlude	Fugue in C Major	J. Pachelbel

SENIOR CHOIR:
Worthy Is the Lamb [Rev.5:12-13]   G.F. Handel
Christ Whose Glory Fills the Skies [Morning] [U]   K. Bissell

JUNIOR CHOIR:

HYMNS:
By All Your Saints Still Striving [Acts 9:1-22; John 21:15-17] (231TH)
God, You Meet Us (St.2) [Ps.30:5] (124SFGP)
Alleluia! Sing to Jesus [Rev.5:6-14] (49HB)
Crown Him With Many Crowns [Rev.5:6-14] (480HB)
Hail, Thou Once Despised Jesus [Rev.5:6-14] (478HB)
Lord, Enthroned in Heavenly Splendor [Rev.5:6-14] (324HB)

DATE: Fourth Sunday of Easter

READINGS:
Acts 9:36-43
Psalm 23
Revelation 7:9-17
John 10:22-30

ORGAN MUSIC:
Prelude   Sonata VI in G Major   J.S. Bach [18:00]
Offertory   Canzon Francese on "Orsus au Loup"
                                                  A. Gabrieli [2:00]
Postlude   Ricercar on "Orsus au Loup"   A. Gabrieli

SENIOR CHOIR:
Revelation Motet [Rev.7:13-17]   M. Franck
I Am the Good Shepherd [U]   R.I. Wetzler

JUNIOR CHOIR:

HYMNS:
The Lord's My Shepherd: I'll Not Want [Ps.23] (131HB)
Lord, Enthroned in Heavenly Splendor [Rev.7:9-17] (324HB)
Ye Holy Angels Bright [Rev.7:9-17] (6HB)
Ye Watchers and Ye Holy Ones [Rev.7:9-17] (7HB)
Crown Him With Many Crowns [Rev.7:9-12] (480HB)
All Hail the Power of Jesus' Name [Rev.7:9-11] (42HB)

DATE: Fifth Sunday of Easter

READINGS:
Acts 11:1-18
Psalm 148
Revelation 21:1-6
John 13:31-35

ORGAN MUSIC:
Prelude	Prelude and Fugue in A Minor	J.S. Bach [6:00]
	Prelude and Fugue in Ab Minor	J. Brahms [5:30]
Offertory	Trio No. 8	J. Rheinberger [2:00]
Postlude	Voluntary No. 8	G. F. Handel

SENIOR CHOIR:
Christ the Lord Is Risen Today [Easter]   R. Williams

JUNIOR CHOIR:

HYMNS:
All Creatures of Our God and King [Ps.148] (1HB)
Ye Watchers and Ye Holy Ones [Ps.148] (7HB)
For the Healing of the Nations [Rev.21:10-22:5] (23SFGP)

DATE: Sixth Sunday of Easter

READINGS:
Acts 16:9-15
Psalm 67
Revelation 21:10, 21:22-22:5
John 14:23-29 or John 5:1-9

ORGAN MUSIC:
Prelude   Prelude in G Major   V. Lübeck [6:30]
               Es wolle Gott uns gnädig sein [Ps.67]
               (God Be Merciful Unto Us)   J. Walther [662:110;2:30]
                                            S. Scheidt [80:30;1:00]
                                      J. Pachelbel [PA 3:74;3:00]
Offertory   Voluntary No. 6   G.F. Handel [2:00]
Postlude   Fugue in G Major   J. Pachelbel

SENIOR CHOIR:
Let the People Praise Thee, O God [Ps.67]   W. Matthias
Let the People Praise Thee, O God [Ps.67:4-7] [U]
                                                  A. Hammerschmidt

JUNIOR CHOIR:

HYMNS:
From Greenland's Icy Mountains [Acts 16:9] (322LW)
God of Grace and God of Glory [Ps.67] (223HB)
Jerusalem the Golden [Rev.21:2-22:5] (184HB)
O Holy City, Seen of John [Rev.21:2-22:5] (160HB)
Oh What Their Joy and Their Glory Must Be [Rev.21:2-22:5] (186HB)

DATE: Seventh Sunday of Easter

READINGS:
Acts 16:16-34
Psalm 47 or Psalm 110
Ephesians 1:15-23
Luke 24:44-53

ORGAN MUSIC:

Prelude	Sonata No. 6	G. Valeri [5:00]
	Concerto in G Major	J.S. Bach [8:00]
Offertory	Trio No. 9	J. Rheinberger [2:00]
Postlude	Psalm 19	B. Marcello

SENIOR CHOIR:
God Is Gone Up With a Shout [Ps.47]   H. Willan

JUNIOR CHOIR:

HYMNS:
Our Father, By Whose Name [Acts 16:32-34] (219HB)
A Hymn of Glory Let Us Sing [Ps.47:5-9] (149LW)
Christus Paradox (St.3) [Eph.1:20-22] (64SFGP)
Christ Is Made the Sure Foundation [Eph.1:22-23] (145HB)
Alleluia, Alleluia, Give Thanks (St.2) [Luke 24:46-47] (34SFGP)
Sent Forth By God's Blessing [Luke 24:47-53] (247LW)
Alleluia! Sing to Jesus (St.2) [Luke 24:50-51] (49HB)
Hail the Day That Sees Him Rise [Luke 24:50-51] (477HB)

DATE: Day of Pentecost

READINGS:
Acts 2:1-21 or Genesis 11:1-9
Psalm 104:24-34, 35b
Romans 8:14-17 or Acts 2:1-21
John 14:8-17, (25-27)

ORGAN MUSIC:
Prelude   Nun bitten wir den Heiligen Geist [Pentecost]
             (Now, Holy Spirit, We Pray to Thee)
                                      G. Böhm [BS 94;2:30]
                                      D. Buxtehude [BC 80;2:30]
                                                 [BC 90;2:00]
                                      J. Walther [WO 96;2:30]
                                      H. Scheidemann [PO 8:39;1:30]
                                      J. Bender [BK 2:38;1:30]
                                      E. Pepping [HP 12:36;1:00]
             Komm, heiliger Geist, Herre Gott [Acts 2:4]
             (Come, Holy Spirit, Lord God)
                                      J. Walther [GG 2:143;3:30]
                                      J. Pachelbel [PA 2:57;1:00]
Offertory   Komm, heiliger Geist, Herre Gott
                                      F. Zachau [80:49;2:00]
Postlude   Komm, heiliger Geist, Herre Gott
                                      G.P. Telemann [PO I:85;3:00]

SENIOR CHOIR:
The Spirit of the Lord [Pentecost]   H. Willan
Holy Spirit, Enter In [Pentecost] [U]   M. Drischner

JUNIOR CHOIR:

HYMNS:
Hail Thee, Festival Day [Acts 2:1-42] (481HB)
She Flies On (St.5) [Acts 2:1-4] (126SFGP)
God of Grace and God of Glory [Acts 2:17-18] (223HB)
This Is My Father's World [Ps.104:24-30] (82HB)
In Christ There Is No East or West [Rom.8:14-17] (149HB)

Christ Is Made the Sure Foundation [John 14:13-14] (145HB)
Come Down, O Love Divine [John 14:16,23,26] (67HB)
Come, Holy Ghost, Our Souls Inspire [John 14:26] (245HB)

DATE: Trinity Sunday
                        (First Sunday after Pentecost)

READINGS:
Proverbs 8:1-14, 22-31
Psalm 8
Romans 5:1-5
John 16:12-15

ORGAN MUSIC:
Prelude   Prelude and Fugue in D Minor   D. Buxtehude [5:00]
            Es ist das Heil uns kommen her [Romans 5:1-2]
            (Salvation Now Is Come to Us)
                                    Anonymous [GT 1:154;3:00]
                                    J.S. Bach [BO 66;1:00]
                                    J.P. Sweelinck [SA 29;3:00]
                                    F. Zachau [GT 1:156;2:30]
Offertory   Es ist das Heil uns kommen her
                                    J. Walther [GG 1:19;2:30]
Postlude   Es ist das Heil uns kommen her
                                    Buxtehude [BC 19;3:00]

SENIOR CHOIR:
Father, We Praise Thee [Trinity]   H. Willan
Holy, Holy, Holy [Trinity] [U]   J. Bender

JUNIOR CHOIR:

HYMNS:
God Is Love, Let Heaven Adore Him [Proverbs 8:29] (379TH)
For the Beauty of the Earth [Ps.8] (199HB)
O God, Beneath Your Guiding Hand [Ps.8] (495WB)
Many and Great, O Lord, Are Your Works [Ps.8:1-4]
Come Down, O Love Divine [Romans 5:5] (67HB)
Come, Holy Spirit, Heavenly Dove [Romans 5:5] (244HB)
Come, Gracious Spirit, Heavenly Dove [John 16:13-15] (265HB)

DATE: Sunday between May 29 and June 4 inclusive

READINGS:
1 Kings 18:20-21, (22-29), 30-39 or 1 Kings 8:22-23, 41-43
Psalm 96 or Psalm 96:1-9
Galatians 1:1-12
Luke 7:1-10

ORGAN MUSIC:
Prelude	Veni Creator	J. Titelouze [6:00]
	Prelude and Fugue in F Minor	J.S. Bach [8:00]
Offertory	Elevation in A Major	N. LeBègue [1:30]
Postlude	Voluntary No. 9	G.F. Handel

SENIOR CHOIR:
Sing Ye Unto the Lord [Ps.96:1-3]   H.L. Hassler
Litany to the Holy Spirit [Pentecost] [U]   P. Hurford

JUNIOR CHOIR:

HYMNS:
As Now the Sun Shines Down at Noon [1 Kings 18:27] (18TH)
Oh, For a Thousand Tongues to Sing [Ps.96:1-3; Luke 7:1-17]
(48HB)
The Royal Banners Forward Go [Ps.96:10] (103LW)
Thine Arm, O Lord, in Days of Old [Luke 7:1-23] (567TH)

DATE: Sunday between June 5 and June 11 inclusive

READINGS:
1 Kings 17:8-16, (17-24) or 1 Kings 17:17-24
Psalm 146 or Psalm 30
Galatians 1:11-24
Luke 7:11-17

ORGAN MUSIC:
Prelude	Toccata in G Major	D. Buxtehude [5:30]
	Prelude in A Minor	[4:00]
	Prelude and Fugue in A Major	[5:30]
Offertory	Trio No. 1	J. Rheinberger [2:00]
Postlude	Canzonetta in E Minor	Buxtehude [2:30]

SENIOR CHOIR:
Hallelujah, Amen from "Judas Maccabeus" [General]   G.F.Handel

JUNIOR CHOIR:

HYMNS:
I'll Praise My Maker While I've Breath [Ps.146] (121SFGP)
Praise the Almighty [Ps.146] (445LW)
O Jesus, King Most Wonderful [Ps.146:10] (121HB)
By All Your Saints Still Striving [Gal.1:11-24] (231TH)
O For a Thousand Tongues to Sing [Luke 7:1-17] (48HB)

DATE: Sunday between June 12 and June 18 inclusive

READINGS:
1 Kings 21:1-10 (11-14) 15-21a or 2 Samuel 11:26-12:10, 13-15
Psalm 5:1-8 or Psalm 32
Galatians 2:15-21
Luke 7:36 - 8:3

ORGAN MUSIC:

Prelude	Prelude in C Major	D. Buxtehude [5:30]
	Prelude in G Major	[5:00]
	Prelude and Fugue in B Major	C. Saint-Saëns
Offertory	St. Agnes	W. Held [HPP 14]
Postlude	Fugue in E Minor	J. Pachelbel

SENIOR CHOIR:
Give Ear, O Lord [Ps.5:2] (SS)   H. Schütz

JUNIOR CHOIR:

HYMNS:
Lead Me, Lord [Ps.5:8] (473UM)
O Jesus Christ, Grow Thou in Me (St.2) [Gal.2:20] (27SFGP)
By All Your Saints Still Striving [Luke 8:1-3] (231TH)
Thine Arm, O Lord, in Days of Old [Luke 8:2] (567TH)

DATE: Sunday between June 19 and June 25 inclusive

READINGS:
1 Kings 19:1-4, (5-7), 8-15a or Isaiah 65:1-9
Psalm 42 and 43 or Psalm 22:19-28
Galatians 3:23-29
Luke 8:26-39

ORGAN MUSIC:
Prelude   Voluntary in D Minor   H. Purcell [4:00]
             Voluntary in E Minor   J. Stanley [4:00]
                                               [Hinrichsen 1033:21]

             Preludes on Welsh Hymn Tunes
                                     R. Vaughan Williams [8:30]
Offertory   First Elevation   N. LeBègue [1:30]
Postlude   Voluntary No. 11   G.F. Handel

SENIOR CHOIR:
Like as the Hart [Ps.42]   H. Willan

JUNIOR CHOIR:

HYMNS:
Dear Lord and Father of Mankind [1 Kings 19:9-12] (249HB)
As Longs the Deer for Cooling Streams [Ps.42] (658TH)
As Longs the Hart [Ps.42:1-5] (89SFGP)
As Pants Hart [Ps.42:1-5] (37SFGP)
In Christ There Is No East or West [Gal.3:27-28] (149HB)
Now There Is No Male or Female (St.1) [Gal.3:27] (62SFGP)
Thine Arm, O Lord, in Days of Old [Luke 8:26-56] (567TH)

DATE: Sunday between June 26 and July 2 inclusive

READINGS:
1 Kings 2:1-2, 6-14 or 1 Kings 19:15-16, 19-21
Psalm 77:1-2, 11-20 or Psalm 16
Galatians 5:1, 13-25
Luke 9:51-62

ORGAN MUSIC:
Prelude	Preludes in F Major, G Major and C Major	
		F. Tunder [13:00]
Offertory	Elevation in G Minor	N. LeBègue [1:30]
Postlude	Prelude in G Minor	Tunder [3:30]

SENIOR CHOIR:
Strike the Cymbal, Bow the String [General]   F. Schubert

JUNIOR CHOIR:

HYMNS:
God Moves in a Mysterious Way [Ps.77:19] (159HB)
Now There Is No Male or Female (St.1) [Gal.5:1] (62SFGP)
The Servant Song [Gal.5:13] (133SFGP)
For the Fruit of All Creation (St.3) [Gal.5:22] (58SFGP)
Love, Joy and Peace [Gal.5:22] (57SFGP)
Lead Us, Heavenly Father, Lead Us [Luke 9:51] (268HB)
O Jesus, I Have Promised [Luke 9:57] (304HB)
My Song Is Love Unknown [Luke 9:58] (442HB)
He Who Would Valiant Be [Luke 9:62] (564TH)

DATE: Sunday between July 3 and July 9 inclusive

READINGS:
2 Kings 5:1-14 or Isaiah 66:10-14
Psalm 30 or Psalm 66:1-9
Galatians 6:(1-6), 7-16
Luke 10:1-11, 16-20

ORGAN MUSIC:
Prelude	Prelude in G Major	D. Buxtehude [6:30]
	Prelude in G Minor	[5:00]
Offertory	Elevation in G Major	N. LeBègue [2:00]
Postlude	Prelude in A Major	Buxtehude [4:30]

SENIOR CHOIR:
Where'er You Walk [General] (U)   G.F. Handel

JUNIOR CHOIR:

HYMNS:
God, You Made Us (St.2) [Ps.30:5] (124SFGP)
The Servant Song [Gal.6:2] (133SFGP)
For the Fruit of All Creation (St.3) [Gal.6:8] (58SFGP)
Ask Me What Great Thing I Know [Gal.6:14] (163UM)

DATE: Sunday between July 10 and July 16 inclusive

READINGS:
Amos 7:7-17 or Deuteronomy 30:9-14
Psalm 82 or Psalm 25:1-10
Colossians 1:1-14
Luke 10:25-37

ORGAN MUSIC:

Prelude	Six Trios	M. Reger [16:00]
Offertory	Fantasy	P. Hofhaymer [HOR I:3;1:30]
Postlude	Voluntary No. 12	G.F. Handel

SENIOR CHOIR:
Cast Thy Burden Upon the Lord [Ps.25:3]

F. Mendelssohn

JUNIOR CHOIR:

HYMNS:
The Lord Will Come and Not Be Slow [Ps.82] (468MH, 462TH)
Judge Eternal, Throned in Splendor [Ps.82:8] (213HB)
God of Grace and God of Glory [Col.1:9-12] (223HB)
Lord, Dismiss Us With Thy Blessing [Col.1:9-10] (308HB)
From Glory to Glory Advancing, We Praise Thee, O Lord [Col.1:11-12] (307HB)
Rise Up, Ye Saints of God [Luke 10:27] (172HB)

DATE: Sunday between July 17 and July 23 inclusive

READINGS:
Amos 8:1-12 or Genesis 18:1-10a
Psalm 52 or Psalm 15
Colossians 1:15-28
Luke 10:38-42

ORGAN MUSIC:
Prelude	Fugue	F. Zachau [4:00]
	Prelude and Fugue	[3:00]
	Fantasie	[6:00]
Offertory	Elevation in G Major	N. LeBègue [1:30]
Postlude	Fugue in B Minor	J. Pachelbel

SENIOR CHOIR:
What God Ordains Is Always Good [General] [U]   Pachelbel

JUNIOR CHOIR:

HYMNS:
All Glory Be to God on High [Col.1:15-20] (421TH)
Of the Father's Love Begotten [Col.1:15-20] (429HB)
Christ Is Made the Sure Foundation [Col.1:18] (145HB)
Lord, Enthroned in Heavenly Splendor [Col.1:18] (324HB)
Hail, Thou Once Despised Jesus [Col.1:19-23] (478HB)
Our Father, By Whose Name [Luke 10:38-39] (219HB)

DATE: Sunday between July 24 and July 30 inclusive

READINGS:
Hosea 1:2-10 or Genesis 18:20-32
Psalm 85 or Psalm 138
Colossians 2:6-15, (16-19)
Luke 11:1-13

ORGAN MUSIC:
Prelude   Vater unser im Himmelreich [Luke 11:2-4]
               (The Lord's Prayer)   J. Praetorius [PRC 19;12:00]
                                           S. Scheidt [GT 3:78;1:30]
                                           J. Pachelbel [PA 3:8;2:00]
Offertory   Vater unser im Himmelreich
                                           D. Buxtehude [BC 134;2:00]
Postlude   Vater unser im Himmelreich
                                           J.P. Sweelinck [SA 52;5:30]

SENIOR CHOIR:
Our Father, Thron'd in Heaven High [General] [SA]   M. Praetorius
Beautiful Saviour [General] [U]   H. Willan

JUNIOR CHOIR:

HYMNS:
God of Grace, and God of Glory [Ps.85:7-8] (223HB)
Love Divine, All Love Excelling [Ps.85:7-8] (241HB)
The Lord Will Come and Not Be Slow [Ps.85] (468MH, 462TH)
Now Thank We All Our God [Col.2:7] (197HB)
On This Day, the First of Days [Col.2:12-14] (373HB)
Father Eternal, Ruler of Creation (Refrain) [Luke 11:2] (279HB)
"Thy Kingdom Come!" on Bended Knee [Luke 11:2] (615TH)
Thy Kingdom Come, O God [Luke 11:2] (276HB)
Seek Ye First the Kingdom of God [Luke 11:9] (83SFGP)

DATE: Sunday between July 31 and August 6 inclusive

READINGS:
Hosea 11:1-11 or Ecclesiastes 1:2, 12-14; 2:18-23
Psalm 107:1-9, 43 or Psalm 49:1-12
Colossians 3:1-11
Luke 12:18-34

ORGAN MUSIC:
Prelude	Prelude in D Major	D. Buxtehude [6:00]
	Prelude in D Minor	[5:30]
	Voluntary No. 7	G.F. Handel [3:00]
Offertory	Plein Jeu	L. Marchand [HOR 1:108;2:00]
Postlude	Canzona	A. Gabrieli [3:00]

SENIOR CHOIR:
Grant Peace, We Pray [General]   F. Mendelssohn

JUNIOR CHOIR:

HYMNS:
O Love That Wilt Not Let Me Go (St.1) [Hosea 11:1-9] (110SFGP)
Jesus, Thou Joy of Loving Hearts [Ps.107:9] (343HB)
In Christ There Is No East or West [Col.3:11] (149HB)
O God of Bethel, by Whose Hand [Luke 12:22-31] (263HB)

DATE: Sunday between August 7 and August 13 inclusive

READINGS:
Isaiah 1:1, 10-20 or Genesis 15:1-6
Psalm 50:1-8, 22-23 or Psalm 33:12-22
Hebrews 11:1-3, 8-16
Luke 12:32-40

ORGAN MUSIC:

Prelude	Sonata de I° tono	J. Lidon [4:00]
	Allegro	J. Carvalho [5:00]
	Cançao	Ypes [3:00]
	Tiento	J. Cabanilles [HOR VI:37;2:30]
Offertory	Partita	B. Pasquini [2:00]
Postlude	La Romanesca	A. Valente [1:30]

SENIOR CHOIR:
Psalm 50 (SAB)   C. LeJeune

JUNIOR CHOIR:

HYMNS:
Jesus, Lover of My Soul [Isaiah 1:18] (77HB)
Faith of Our Fathers [Hebrews 11] (187HB)
O What Their Joy and Their Glory Must Be [Hebrews 11:13-16] (186HB)
Guide Me, O Thou Great Jehovah [Hebrews 11:13] (269HB)

DATE: Sunday between August 14 and August 20 inclusive

READINGS:
Isaiah 5:1-7 or Jeremiah 23:23-29
Psalm 80:1-2, 8-19 or Psalm 82
Hebrews 11:29 - 12:2
Luke 12:49-56

ORGAN MUSIC:
Prelude	Prelude and Fugue in F# Minor	D. Buxtehude [8:00]
	Chaconne in C Minor	[6:00]
Offertory	Kommt her zu mir, spricht Gottes Sohn	
	(Come Unto Me, Said God's Son)	
		Buxtehude [BC 60;2:00]
Postlude	Fugue in C Major ("Jig")	Buxtehude [3:00]

SENIOR CHOIR:
Welcome as the Cheerful Light [General] (SS)   G.F. Handel
The Sun Shall Be No More Thy Light [General] [U]   M. Greene

JUNIOR CHOIR:

HYMNS:
God of Grace and God of Glory [Ps.80:14-19] (223HB)
All Who Would Valiant Be [Hebrews 11:33-40] (383LW)
Awake, My Soul, Stretch Every Nerve [Hebrews 12:1-2] (546TH)
Fight the Good Fight With All Thy Might [Hebrews 12:1] (175HB)
I Sing a Song of the Saints of God [Hebrews 12:1] (364PH)
They Cast Their Nets in Galilee [Luke 12:51-53] (661TH)

DATE: Sunday between August 21 and August 27 inclusive

READINGS:
Jeremiah 1:4-10 or Isaiah 58:9b-14
Psalm 71:1-6 or Psalm 103:1-8
Hebrews 12:18-29
Luke 13:10-17

ORGAN MUSIC:
Prelude   Nun lob, mein Seel, den Herren [Ps.103]
                  (Now Praise the Lord, O My Soul)
                                      D. Buxtehude [BC 110;6:00]
                                                  [BC 116;3:30]
                                    J. Pachelbel [PA 3:28;2:00]
                                    J. Praetorius [GT 3:26;2:30]
                                    J. Walther [WO 110;3:00]
Offertory   Nun lob, mein Seel, den Herren
                                    Buxtehude [BC 119;2:30]
Postlude   Nun lob, mein Seel, den Herren
                                    Buxtehude [BC 106;4:30]

SENIOR CHOIR:
O Praise the Lord, My God [Ps.103:1-4]   Ippolitof-Ivanov

JUNIOR CHOIR:

HYMNS:
Rock of Ages, Cleft For Me [Ps.71:3] (79HB)
Thine Arm, O Lord, in Days of Old [Luke 13:10-17] (567TH)

DATE: Sunday between August 28 and September 3 inclusive

READINGS:
Jeremiah 2:4-13 or Sirach 10:12-18 or Proverbs 25:6-7
Psalm 81:1, 10-16 or Psalm 112
Hebrews 13:1-8, 15-16
Luke 14:1, 7-14

ORGAN MUSIC:
Prelude   Wer nur den lieben Gott lässt walten [Heb.13:5]
              (If You But Trust in God to Guide You)
                                          J.S. Bach [BO 72;3:00]
                                              [BSC 92;3:30]
                                          G. Böhm [BS 108;7:00]
                                          J. Walther [WO 136;6:00]
                                          F.W. Marpurg [MC 62;2:30]
Offertory   Wer nur den lieben Gott lässt walten
                                          Bach [BU 98;3:00]
Postlude   Wer nur den lieben Gott lässt walten
                                          J.L. Krebs [GT 3:150;3:30]

SENIOR CHOIR:
O Happy Man [Ps.112] (SATB)   H. Purcell

JUNIOR CHOIR:

HYMNS:
When I Needed a Neighbor [Hebrews 13:1-3] (131SFGP)
O Jesus, I Have Promised [Hebrews 13:5-6] (304HB)
How Firm a Foundation, Ye Saints of the Lord [Hebrews 13:5]
(139HB)
If You But Trust in God to Guide You [Hebrews 13:5] (420LW)
All My Hope on God Is Founded [Hebrews 13:15] (134HB)

DATE: Sunday between September 4 and September 10 inclusive

READINGS:
Jeremiah 18:1-11 or Deuteronomy 30:15-20
Psalm 139:1-6, 13-18 or Psalm 1
Philemon 1:21
Luke 14:25-33

ORGAN MUSIC:

Prelude	Voluntary in A Major	J. Stanley [5:00]
	Voluntary in E Major	[4:00]
	Voluntary II	W. Walond [5:00]
Offertory	Voluntary in C Major	H. Purcell [1:30]
Postlude	Voluntary in G Major	Stanley
		[Hinrichsen 1035:38]

SENIOR CHOIR:
Lord, Thou Hast Searched Me Out [Ps.139]   H. Willan

JUNIOR CHOIR:

HYMNS:
In the Cross of Christ [Luke 14:27] (113HB)
Take Up Your Cross, the Savior Said [Luke 14:27] (176HB)

DATE: Sunday between September 11 and September 17 inclusive

READINGS:
Jeremiah 4:11-12, 22-28 or Exodus 32:7-14
Psalm 14 or Psalm 51:1-10
1 Timothy 1:12-17
Luke 15:1-10

ORGAN MUSIC:

Prelude	Variations sur un thème de Janequin	
		J. Alain [6:30]
	Le Jardin suspendu	[3:30]
	Chorale Phrygien	[3:00]
Offertory	Chorale Dorien	Alain [2:00]
Postlude	Litanies	Alain

SENIOR CHOIR:

Miserere Mei [Ps.51]	A. Lotti
I Have Trusted In Thy Mercy [General] [U]	H. Willan

JUNIOR CHOIR:

HYMNS:
Immortal, Invisible, God Only Wise [1 Tim.1:17] (26HB)
The King of Love My Shepherd Is [Luke 15:3-7] (132HB)

DATE: Sunday between September 18 and September 24 inclusive

READINGS:
Jeremiah 8:18 - 9:1 or Amos 8:4-7
Psalm 79:1-9 or Psalm 113
1 Timothy 2:1-7
Luke 16:1-13

ORGAN MUSIC:

Prelude	Sonata V in G Major	J.S. Bach [16:00]
Offertory	Erbarm dich mein, O Herre Gott	
	(O God, Be Merciful to Me)	Bach [BU 28;2:00]
Postlude	Fugue in G Minor	Bach [4:00]

SENIOR CHOIR:
Sing to the Lord [Ps.113]   C. Tye

JUNIOR CHOIR:
Praise God, Praise God (AGCS 16)

HYMNS:
By All Your Saints Still Striving [Jer.8:22] (231TH)
Lord, Speak to Me That I May Speak [1 Tim.2:2] (302HB)
Stand Up, Stand Up For Jesus [1 Tim.2:3-4] (174HB)
Soldiers of Christ, Arise [1 Tim.2:3] (171HB)
Thine Arm, O Lord, in Days of Old [Luke 6:6-11] (567TH)
Dear Lord and Father of Mankind (St.3) [Luke 6:12] (249HB)

DATE: Sunday between September 25 and October 1 inclusive

READINGS:
Jeremiah 32:1-3a, 6-15 or Amos 6:1a, 4-7
Psalm 91:1-6, 14-16 or Psalm 146
1 Timothy 6:6-19
Luke 16:19-31

ORGAN MUSIC:

Prelude	Prelude and Fugue in G Minor	M. Dupré [10:00]
	Préambule	L. Vierne [3:30]
Offertory	Trio	N. DeGrigny [2:00]
Postlude	Postlude I	J. Langlais

SENIOR CHOIR:

Simple Gifts [General] [SA]	A. Copland
Verily, Verily, I Say Unto You [General] [U]	H. Willan

JUNIOR CHOIR:
We Love Because God First Loved Us (AGCS 77)

HYMNS:
O God of Bethel, By Whose Hand [Ps.91:1-4] (263HB)
Praise to the Lord, the Almighty [Ps.91:4] (29HB)
Faith of Our Fathers [1 Tim.6:12] (187HB)
Fight the Good Fight [1 Tim.6:12] (175HB)
The Son of God Goes Forth to War [1 Tim.6:12] (304LW)
Crown Him With Many Crowns [1 Tim.6:14-16] (480HB)
Come, O Almighty King [1 Tim.6:14-16] (169LW)
Immortal, Invisible, God Only Wise [1 Tim.6:15-16] (26HB)
All My Hope on God Is Founded [1 Tim.6:17] (134HB)

DATE: Sunday between October 2 and October 8 inclusive

READINGS:
Lamentations 1:1-6 or Habakkuk 1:1-4; 2:1-4
Lamentations 3:19-26 or Psalm 137 or Psalm 37:1-9
2 Timothy 1:1-14
Luke 17:5-10

ORGAN MUSIC:

Prelude	An Wasserflüssen Babylon [Ps.137]	
	(By the Waters of Babylon)	
		J.S. Bach [B18:22;5:00]
		J. Pachelbel [PA 3:50;5:00]
		J. Walther [WO 26;4:00]
Offertory	An Wasserflüssen Babylon	F. Zachau [GG 1:9;1:30]
Postlude	An Wasserflüssen Babylon	J.R. Ahle [EK 1:42;3:00]

SENIOR CHOIR:
Rejoice, Ye Pure in Heart [General]   H. Willan

JUNIOR CHOIR:
By the Babylonian Rivers [Ps.137] (SFGP 137)

HYMNS:
Go to Dark Gethsemane [Lam.3:19] (451HB)
Great Is Thy Faithfulness [Lam.3:22-23] (95SFGP)
Morning Has Broken [Lam.3:22-23] (103SFGP)
New Every Morning Is the Love [Lam.3:22-23] (360HB)

DATE: Sunday between October 9 and October 15 inclusive

READINGS:
Jeremiah 29:1, 4-7 or 2 Kings 5:1-3, 7-15c
Psalm 66:1-12 or Psalm 111
2 Timothy 2:8-15
Luke 17:11-19

[See Thanksgiving]

ORGAN MUSIC:

SENIOR CHOIR:

JUNIOR CHOIR:

HYMNS:

DATE: Sunday between October 16 and October 22 inclusive

READINGS:
Jeremiah 31:27-34 or Genesis 32:22-31
Psalm 119:97-104 or Psalm 121
2 Timothy 3:14 - 4:5
Luke 18:1-8

ORGAN MUSIC:

Livre d'Orgue		P. Dumage [18:30]
Prelude	Plein Jeu	
	Fugue	
	Trio	
	Tierce en Taille	
	Basse de Trompette	
	Récit	
Offertory	Duo	
Postlude	Grand jeu	

SENIOR CHOIR:
He, Watching Over Israel [Ps.121:4]   F. Mendelssohn

JUNIOR CHOIR:
What Does the Lord Require? (AGCS 67)

HYMNS:
Lamp of Our Feet, Whereby We Trace [2 Tim.3:14-17] (627TH)
All Glory Be to God on High [2 Tim.4:1] (421TH)
Faith of Our Fathers [2 Tim.4:3-4] (187HB)

DATE: Sunday between October 23 and October 29 inclusive

READINGS:
Joel 2:23-32 or Sirach 35:12-17 or Jeremiah 14:7-10, 19-22
Psalm 65 or Psalm 84:1-7
2 Timothy 4:6-8, 16-18
Luke 18:9-14

ORGAN MUSIC:
Prelude   Prelude and Fugue in C Major [BWV 547]
                                              J.S. Bach [11:30]
Offertory   Jesu, meines Lebens Leben
             (Jesus, My Life)   Bach [BN 42:2:00]
Postlude   Fugue in G Major ("Gigue")   Bach [4:30]

SENIOR CHOIR:
Two Men Betook Themselves to Pray in the Temple   H. Schütz
[Luke 18:9-14]

JUNIOR CHOIR:
Make Me a Channel of Your Peace (SFGP 2)

HYMNS:
She Flies On (St.2) [Joel 2:28-32] (126SFGP)
Spirit, Spirit of Gentleness (St.4) [Joel 2:28-32] (108SFGP)
I Sing the Mighty Power [Ps.65:5-13] (81HB)
All Creatures of Our God and King [Ps.65:8-13] (1HB)
Sing to the Lord of Harvest [Ps.65:9-13] (65HB)
By All Your Saints Still Striving [2 Tim.4:7-8] (231TH)
Fight the Good Fight With All Thy Might [2 Tim.4:7-8] (175HB)
For All the Saints, Who From Their Labors Rest [2 Tim.4:7-8]
(501HB)
Lead On, O King Eternal [2 Tim.4:7-8] (173HB)

DATE: Sunday between October 30 and November 5 inclusive

READINGS:
Habakkuk 1:1-4, 2:1-4 or Isaiah 1:10-18
Psalm 119:137-144 or Psalm 32:1-7
2 Thessalonians 1:1-4, 11-12
Luke 19:1-10

[See All Saints]

ORGAN MUSIC:

SENIOR CHOIR:

JUNIOR CHOIR:

HYMNS:

DATE: Sunday between November 6 and November 12 inclusive

READINGS:
Haggai 1:15b - 2:9 or Job 19:23-27a
Psalm 145:1-5, 17-21 or Psalm 98 or Psalm 17:1-9
2 Thessalonians 2:1-5, 13-17
Luke 20:27-38

ORGAN MUSIC:

Prelude	Sonata II	P. Hindemith [11:30]
	Echo Fantasy (Dorian)	J.S. Sweelinck [4:00]
Offertory	Mache dich, mein Geist, bereit	
	(Up, My Soul, Gird Thee With Power)	
		J. Walther [WO 2;2:00]
Postlude	Fugue in Bb Major	W.F. Bach [2:30]

SENIOR CHOIR:
I Know That My Redeemer Lives [Job 19:25-27]   J.S. Bach

JUNIOR CHOIR:
Rise and Shine (LOSP 66)

HYMNS:
O Come, O Come Emmanuel [Haggai 2:7] (390HB)
Come, Thou Long-Expected Jesus [Haggai 2:7] (389HB)
O For a Thousand Tongues to Sing (St.1) [Ps.145:1,2] (1SFPG)
All Creatures of Our God and King [Ps.145:1] (1HB)
Sing Praise to Our Creator [2 Thess.2:13] (295TH)

DATE: Sunday between November 13 and November 19 inclusive

READINGS:
Isaiah 65:17-25 or Malachi 4:1-2a
Isaiah 12 or Psalm 98
2 Thessalonians 3:6-13
Luke 21:5-19

ORGAN MUSIC:

Prelude	Concerto in A Minor	J.S. Bach [12:00]
	Fantasia in C Major	[3:00]
Offertory	Werde munter, mein Gemüte	
	(Jesu, Joy of Man's Desiring)	Bach [BN 66;2:00]
Postlude	Allabreve in D Major	Bach [5:00]

SENIOR CHOIR:

Sing a New Song to the Lord [Ps.98]	V. Archer
I Will Sing New Songs of Gladness [General] [U]	A. Dvorak

JUNIOR CHOIR:
Seek Ye First (SFGP 83)

HYMNS:
Jerusalem, My Happy Home [Isaiah 65:17-19] (620TH)
Jerusalem the Golden [Isaiah 65:17-19] (184HB)
O For a Thousand Tongues to Sing [Isaiah 12:4-5] (48HB)
Awake, My Soul, and With the Sun [2 Thess.3:6-15] (357HB)
Lord Christ, When First Thou Cam'st to Earth (St.2) [Luke 21:6] (598TH)

DATE: Sunday between November 20 and November 26
(Christ the King)

READINGS:
Jeremiah 23:1-6
Luke 1:68-79 or Psalm 46
Colossians 1:11-20
Luke 23:33-43

ORGAN MUSIC:

Prelude	Ein feste Burg [Ps.46] (A Mighty Fortress)	
		J. S. Bach [BU 24:4:00]
		D. Buxtehude [BC 15;2:30]
		F.W. Marpurg [MC 25;3:00]
		N. Hanff [HS 8;2:30]
		G.F. Kauffmann [NT 4;2:30]
		J. Praetorius [80:22;4:00]
		M. Reger [NT 3;1:30]
		J. Walther [WO 24;3:00]
Offertory	Ein feste Burg	J. Walther [GG 1:16;2:00]
Postlude	Ein feste Burg	J. Pachelbel [PA 3:69;4:30]

SENIOR CHOIR:
A Mighty Fortress Is Our God [Ps.46]   F. Tunder and Bach
A Mighty Fortress Is Our God [Ps.46] [U]   F. Tunder

JUNIOR CHOIR:
Jesus Bids Us Shine

HYMNS:
Sing, My Tongue [Luke 1:68-79] (446HB)
Christ, Whose Glory Fills the Skies [Luke 1:78-79] (362HB)
O Come, O Come, Emmanuel [Luke 1:78-79] (390HB)
Lead Us, O Father, in the Paths of Peace [Luke 1:79] (703TH)
From Glory to Glory Advancing, We Praise Thee, O Lord [Col.1:11-12] (307HB)
Of the Father's Love Begotten [Col.1:15-20] (429HB)
Christ Is Made the Sure Foundation [Col.1:18] (145HB)
Lord, Enthroned in Heavenly Splendor [Col.1:18] (324HB)

DATE: All Saints
                    (November 1 or First Sunday in November)

READINGS:
Daniel 7:1-3, 15-18
Psalm 149
Ephesians 1:11-23
Luke 6:20-31

ORGAN MUSIC:
Prelude	Concerto after Torelli	J. Walther [7:30]
	Prelude in C Major	V. Lübeck [6:30]
Offertory	Aus meines Herzens Grunde	
	(With All My Heart's New Power)	
		Walther [GG 1:10;2:00]
Postlude	Concerto after Torelli	Walther [3:00]

SENIOR CHOIR:
Sing to the Lord a New Song [Ps.149:1-2]   G. Pitoni
O What Their Joy and Their Glory Must Be [All Saints]

H. Willan

JUNIOR CHOIR:
One More Step (AGCS 52)

HYMNS:
Earth and All Stars [Ps.149:1-3] (438LW)
Walls That Divide [Eph.1:12-14] (32SFGP)
Christ Is Made the Sure Foundation [Eph.1:22-23] (145HB)
Jesus the Christ Said (St.2) [Luke 6:20] (73SFGP)

DATE: Thanksgiving Day (A,B,C)

READINGS:
Deuteronomy 26:1-11
Psalm 100
Philippians 4:4-9
John 6:25-35

ORGAN MUSIC:

Prelude	Fantasy in G Major	J.S. Bach [9:00]
	Nun danket alle Gott [Ps.100]	
	(Now Thank We All Our God)	
		J. Bender [PO 9:32;2:00]
		Bach [B18:46;4:30]
		J.C. Oley [NT 26;1:00]
		M. Reger [NT 32;1:00]
Offertory	Nun danket alle Gott	
		G.F. Kauffmann [GG 2:150;2:00]
Postlude	Nun danket alle Gott	S. Karg-Elert

SENIOR CHOIR:

Sing to the Lord of Harvest [Thanksgiving]	H. Willan
We Praise Thee, O God [Thanksgiving] [U]	H. Willan

JUNIOR CHOIR:
Thanks a Lot (AGCS 90)

HYMNS:
As Those of Old Their First Fruits Brought [Deut.26:1-11] (705TH)
For the Fruit of All Creation [Deut.26:2-3] (58SFGP)
All People That On Earth Do Dwell [Ps.100] (12HB)
Before the Lord Jehovah's Throng [Ps.100] (454LW)
Now Thank We All Our God [Ps.100:4] (197HB)
Rejoice, the Lord Is King [Philippians 4:4] (44HB)
Rejoice, Ye Pure in Heart [Philippians 4:4] (145PH)
Like a Mighty River Flowing [Philippians 4:7] (32HT)
Guide Me, O Thou Great Jehovah [John 6:25-59] (269HB)

II. A SCRIPTURAL INDEX
OF HYMN TEXTS

Introduction

The choice of hymns corresponding to particular scripture readings represents one of the most important tasks in planning a worship service. Individual hymnals contain scriptural indices of varying comprehensiveness. The index which follows draws on a number of sources and lists hymn texts from more than one hymnal. Often, a suitable text, not found in a given hymnal, may be available in another, and it may be possible, having obtained the appropriate copyright permissions, to print the text in the program and sing the hymn to a familiar tune.

Scriptural citations are listed in the following order: entire chapter, largest portion of chapter, individual verse, thus: Ps.23; Ps.23:1-20; Ps.23:1-10; Ps.23:1; Ps.23:2.

No attempt has been made to verify the individual citations. Worship planners will naturally wish to compare the individual hymn texts with the lections in order to determine their suitability in the context of a particular worship service.

Scriptural Index of Hymn Texts

Scripture	Hymn	Hymn Title

Genesis

1	272PH	God of the Sparrow
	158HB	God, Who Stretched the Spangled Heavens
	285PH	God, You Spin the Whirling Planets
	81HB	I Sing the Mighty Power of God
	273PH	O God the Creator
1:1-2:3	86HB	All Things Bright and Beautiful
	81HB	I Sing the Mighty Power of God
	94HB	Thanks to God Whose Word Was Spoken
	82HB	This Is My Father's World
	386TH	We Sing of God, the Mighty Source
1:1-17	385TH	Many and Great, O God, Are Thy Works
1:1-3,26-27	443UM	O God Who Shaped Creation
1:1-5	151UM	God Created Heaven and Earth
	688UM	God, That Madest Earth and Heaven
	51TH	We the Lord's People, Heart and Voice Uniting
1:1-4	140MH	Father, I Stretch My Hands to Thee
	492LW	God, Who Made the Earth and Heaven
1:1-3	39HB	At the Name of Jesus
	317LW	God, Whose Almighty Word
	235HB	Thou, Whose Almighty Word
1:1-2	579TH	Almighty Father, Strong to Save
	279HB	Father Eternal, Ruler of Creation
	469PH	Morning Has Broken
	14HU	O Splendor of God's Glory
	373HB	On This Day, the First of Days
1:1,3,20	273HU	Eternal Father, Strong to Save (St.3)

1:1	134PH	Creating God, Your Fingers Trace
1:2-4	78SFGP	Out of Deep Unordered Water (St.1)
	54SFGP	The Singer and the Song
	134SFGP	To Show By Touch and Word (St.1)
1:2	167LW	Creator Spirit, by Whose Aid
	113SFGP	God of Many Names
	554PH	Let All Things Now Living
	246HB	O Holy Spirit, By Whose Breath
	176TH	Over the Chaos of the Empty Waters
	506TH	Praise the Spirit in Creation
	126SFGP	She Flies On (St.1)
1:3-19	28HB	Let Us, With a Gladsome Mind
1:3-5	38TH	Jesus, Redeemer of the World
	8TH	Morning Has Broken
	48TH	O Day of Radiant Gladness
	101SFGP	O Laughing Light (St.1)
	52TH	This Day at Thy Creating Word
1:3-4	31TH	Most Holy God, the Lord of Heaven
	27TH	O Blest Creator, Source of Light
1:3	235HB	God Whose Almighty Word
	275HB	O Day of God, Draw Nigh
	378HT	Ring From Your Steeple
	380HT	This Is the Day of Light
	328LW	Thy Strong Word Did Cleave the Darkness
1:11-18	199HB	For the Beauty of the Earth
1:14-19	38TH	Jesus, Redeemer of the World
	31TH	Most Holy God, the Lord of Heaven
	27TH	O Blest Creator, Source of Light
1:26-27	279HB	Father Eternal, Ruler of Creation
	373HB	On This Day, the First of Days
1:26	23SFGP	For the Healing of the Nations (St.4)
1:27	642UM	As Man and Woman We Were Made
	83HB	O Lord of Every Shining Constellation
	100LW	On My Heart Imprint Your Image
1:31	86HB	All Things Bright and Beautiful
2	272PH	God of the Sparrow
	285PH	God, You Spin the Whirling Planets
2:4-14	86HB	All Things Bright and Beautiful
	81HB	I Sing the Mighty Power of God

2:4-14	82HB	This Is My Father's World
	386TH	We Sing of God, the Mighty Source
2:4-9	103SFGP	Morning Has Broken
2:4b-9	283PH	God Marked a Line and Told the Sea
2:7	358TH	Christ the Victorious, Give to Your Servants
	373HB	On This Day, the First of Days
2:10	244TH	Come, Pure Hearts, in Joyful Measure (St.2)
2:15-17	283PH	God Marked a Line and Told the Sea
2:15	434PH	Today We All Are Called to Be Disciples
2:24	350TH	O God of Love, to Thee We Bow
	352TH	O God, to Those Who Here Profess
3:1-15	462HB	Welcome, Happy Morning
3:1-8	396HB	Creator of the Stars of Night
	270TH	Gabriel's Message Does Away
	401HB	Joy to the World! (St.3)
	88TH	Sing, O Sing, This Blessed Morn (St.3)
	295TH	Sing Praise to Our Creator
3:8	292LW	In Adam We Have All Been One
3:19	358TH	Christ the Victorious, Give to Your Servants
4:1-16	180HU	Am I My Brother's Keeper
4:10	98LW	Glory Be to Jesus
5:24	512LW	Lord, Take My Hand and Lead Me
	683TH	O For a Closer Walk with God
7:21-24	265LW	In the Very Midst of Life
8:22	383HB	We Plow the Fields and Scatter
11:1-9	230TH	A Mighty Sound From Heaven
	279HB	Father Eternal, Ruler of Creation
11:9	427HB	It Came Upon the Midnight Clear
12:1-3	123SFGP	To Abraham and Sarah

14:18	397HT	Behold the Eternal King and Priest
21:6	107SFGP	Give to Us Laughter
22:1-14	173TH	O Sorrow Deep (St.2)
28:10-22	254HB	Nearer, My God, to Thee
	263HB	O God of Bethel, by Whose Hand
	35HT	O God of Jacob, by Whose Hand
28:10-17	453TH	As Jacob With Travel Was Weary One Day
	418UM	We Are Climbing Jacob's Ladder
28:16-18	327LW	How Blessed Is This Place, O Lord
28:16	168HB	All Who Love and Serve Your City
28:17	356HB	Only-Begotten, Word of God Eternal
28:18-22	479LW	O Holy, Blessed Trinity
28:20-22	263HB	O God of Bethel, by Whose Hand
31:42	401TH	The God of Abraham, Praise
31:49	540PH	God Be With You Till We Meet Again
	469LW	Holy Father, in Your Mercy
32:22-30	638TH	Come, O Thou Traveler Unknown

Exodus

3:6	450LW	The God of Abraham Praise
3:7-12	143HB	Go Down, Moses
3:13-17	401TH	The God of Abraham Praise
	386TH	We Sing of God, the Mighty Source
3:13-14	330PH	Deep in the Shadows of the Past
	439TH	What Wondrous Love Is This
3:14	113SFGP	God of Many Names
	450LW	The God of Abraham Praise
3:15	718TH	God of Our Fathers, Whose Almighty Hand
3:21-22	173HB	Lead on, O King Eternal
5:1	648TH	When Israel Was in Egypt's Land

6:2-4	269HB	Guide Me, O Thou Great Jehovah
	393TH	Praise Our Great and Gracious Lord
6:7	123SFGP	To Abraham and Sarah
7:16	648TH	When Israel Was in Egypt's Land
8:1,20	648TH	When Israel Was in Egypt's Land
9:1,13	648TH	When Israel Was in Egypt's Land
10:3	648TH	When Israel Was in Egypt's Land
11:4	648TH	When Israel Was in Egypt's Land
12:1-28	174TH	At the Lamb's High Feast We Sing
	202TH	The Lamb's High Banquet Called to Share
12:22	126LW	At the Lamb's High Feast We Sing
	374HB	The Day of Resurrection
12:26-27	374HB	The Day of Resurrection
13:21-22	363TH	Ancient of Days, Who Sittest Throned in Glory
	149TH	Eternal Lord of Love, Behold Your Church
	144HB	Glorious Things of Thee Are Spoken
	393TH	Praise Our Great and Gracious Lord
	187TH	Through the Red Sea Brought at Last
13:21	46MH	Captain of Israel's Host
	220LW	Guide Me Ever, Great Redeemer
	269HB	Guide Me, O Thou Great Jehovah
14:21-15:21	174TH	At the Lamb's High Feast We Sing
	363TH	Ancient of Days, Who Sittest Throned in Glory
	464HB	Come, Ye Faithful, Raise the Strain
	425TH	Sing Now With Joy Unto the Lord
	374HB	The Day of Resurrection
	202TH	The Lamb's High Banquet Called to Share
	187TH	Through the Red Sea Brought at Last
14:22	144HB	Glorious Things of Thee Are Spoken

14:22	78SFGP	Out of Deep, Unordered Water
14:24	149TH	Eternal Lord of Love, Behold Your Church
	269HB	Guide Me, O Thou Great Jehovah
	393TH	Praise Our Great and Gracious Lord
14:29	464HB	Come, Ye Faithful, Raise the Strain
15	464HB	Come, Ye Faithful, Raise the Strain
15:1-2	438LW	Earth and All Stars
15:2	530WB	O Where Are Kings and Empires Now
15:11	50HB	Holy, Holy, Holy!
15:13	386LW	Jesus, Still Lead On
15:13-18	370LW	Blest the Children of Our God
15:21	134UM	O Mary, Don't You Weep
16:4-17:6	144HB	Glorious Things of Thee Are Spoken
	324HB	Lord, Enthroned in Heavenly Splendor
	322HB	O God, Unseen Yet Ever Near
	343TH	Shepherd of Souls, Refresh and Bless
16:4-35	269HB	Guide Me, O Thou Great Jehovah
	308TH	O Food to Pilgrims Given
17:1-6	144HB	Glorious Things of Thee Are Spoken
	79HB	Rock of Ages, Cleft For Me
17:6	269HB	Guide Me, O Thou Great Jehovah
19:4	143UM	On Eagle's Wings
19:9-13	390HB	Oh, Come, Oh, Come, Emmanuel
19:16	310LW	Look Toward the Mountains
20:1-20	390HB	O Come, O Come, Emmanuel
20:1-17	539HT	Father of All, Whose Laws Have Stood
	331LW	Here Is the Tenfold Sure Command
	477LW	Lord, Help Us Ever to Retain
23:16	171HU	As Men of Old
23:19	705TH	As Those of Old Their First Fruits Brought
	296HB	We Give Thee But Thine Own

| 33:14 | 59SFGP | We Praise You, O God (St.2) |
| 33:20 | 50HB | Holy, Holy, Holy |

| 34:1-35 | 390HB | O Come, O Come, Emmanuel |
| 34:28 | 143TH | The Glory of These Forty Days (St.2) |

| 40:38 | 269HB | Guide Me, O Thou Great Jehovah |

Leviticus

| 6:13 | 552HT | O Lord, Who Came From Realms Above |
| | 239HB | O Thou Who Camest from Above |

| 8:35 | 413UM | A Charge to Keep I Have |

| 19:18 | 43SFGP | Love, Love, Love Your God |

| 23:9-14 | 705TH | As Those of Old Their First Fruits Brought |

| 25 | 411PH | Arise, Your Light Is Come! |
| 25:8-17 | 379UM | Blow Ye the Trumpet, Blow |

Numbers

6:24	624WB	We Gather Together to Ask the Lord's Blessing
6:24-26	308HB	Lord, Dismiss Us with Your Blessing
	596PH	May the Lord, Mighty God
6:25	391HB	On Jordan's Bank the Baptist's Cry

| 9:15 | 144HB | Glorious Things of Thee Are Spoken |

20:8-13	269HB	Guide Me, O Thou Great Jehovah
20:11	144HB	Glorious Things of Thee Are Spoken
	324HB	Lord, Enthroned in Heavenly Splendor
	79HB	Rock of Ages, Cleft For Me
	343TH	Shepherd of Souls, Refresh and Bless

24:17	68PH	What Star Is This, With Beams So Bright
32:32	269HB	Guide Me, O Thou Great Jehovah
	393TH	Praise Our Great and Gracious Lord
34:2	269HB	Guide Me, O Thou Great Jehovah
	393TH	Praise Our Great and Gracious Lord

Deuteronomy

1:21	178HU	He Who Would Valiant Be
6:5	43SFGP	Love, Love, Love Your God
	172HB	Rise Up, Ye Saints of God
	85SFGP	Spirit of God, Descend Upon My Heart (St.1,3)
	581TH	Where Charity and Love Prevail
8:3	144HB	Glorious Things of Thee Are Spoken
	627TH	Lamp of Our Feet, Whereby We Trace
	83SFGP	Seek Ye First the Kingdom of God (St.2)
	343TH	Shepherd of Souls, Refresh and Bless
	70SFGP	What Is the Place (St.2)
8:14-18	586UM	Let My People Seek Their Freedom
10:12	397LW	O God of Mercy, God of Light
21:8	93LW	Savior, when in Dust to You
26:1-11	705TH	As Those of Old Their First Fruits Brought
26:1-8	558PH	Come, Sing a Song of Harvest
26:2-3	553PH	For the Fruit of All Creation
30:11-14	94SFGP	Ye Servants of God (St.2)
31:6-8	139HB	How Firm a Foundation, Ye Saints of the Lord

32:3	452LW	Sing Praise to God, the Highest Good
	126UM	Sing Praise to God Who Reigns Above
	174LW	The Lord, My God, Be Praised
32:4	422LW	What God Ordains Is Always Good
32:11	118UM	The Care the Eagle Gives Her Young
33:26	159HB	God Moves in a Mysterious Way
33:27	340PH	Eternal Light, Shine in My Heart
	133UM	Lean on the Everlasting Arms
	13SFGP	Morning Glory, Starlit Sky (St.6)
	183HB	O Lord of Life, Where'er They Be
	290HU	What a Fellowship
34	575HT	There Is a Land of Pure Delight

Joshua

1:16	247LW	Sent Forth by God's Blessing
3:14	220LW	Guide Me Ever, Great Redeemer
	269HB	Guide Me, O Thou Great Jehovah
3:17	269HB	Guide Me, O Thou Great Jehovah
5:6	184HB	Jerusalem the Golden
10:12-14	18TH	As Now the Sun Shines Down at Noon
24:3	269HB	Guide Me, O Thou Great Jehovah
	393TH	Praise Our Great and Gracious Lord
24:14-15	167HB	Once to Every Man and Nation
24:15	219HB	Our Father, by Whose Name
24:15b	467LW	Oh, Blest the House
24:16	409LW	From God Can Nothing Move Me

Judges

5:21	243MH	March On, O Soul, with Strength

Ruth

| 1:16 | 167HB | Once to Every Man and Nation |
| 1:17 | 351HB | O Perfect Love |

1 Samuel

2:1-10	495HB	Tell Out, My Soul, the Greatness of the Lord
3:1-10	274MH	Master, Speak! Thy Servant Heareth
	82SFGP	Open My Eyes That I May See (St.2)
	274MH	Speak, O Lord, Your Servant Listens
	36SFGP	Teach Me, God to Wonder
3:10	253HT	Speak, Lord in the Stillness
7:12	52SFGP	Come, Thou Fount of Every Blessing (St.2)
	333HB	Deck Yourself, My Soul, with Gladness
	456LW	God Brought Me to This Time and Place
20:3	265LW	In the Very Midst of Life
20:42	469LW	Holy Father, in Your Mercy

2 Samuel

7:12	154HB	Hail to the Lord's Anointed
7:22-24	199LW	We Worship You, O God of Might
12:18	269LW	Jesus, Shepherd, in Your Arms
22:3	408LW	I Am Trusting You, Lord Jesus
22:7-20	159HB	God Moves in a Mysterious Way
22:29-33	335LW	O Word of God Incarnate

1 Kings

| 3:5 | 433LW | Come, My Soul, with Every Care |

3:5	371LW	O God, My Faithful God
8	561HT	God of Light and Life's Creation
8:27-30	356HB	Only-Begotten, Word of God Eternal
8:36a	401LW	Forgive Us, Lord, for Shallow Thankfulness
8:66	247LW	Sent Forth by God's Blessing
9:3	290LW	Christ Is Our Cornerstone
18:27	18TH	As Now the Sun Shines Down at Noon
18:44-45	541UM	See How Great a Flame Aspires
19:8	143TH	The Glory of These Forty Days (St.2)
19:9-12	249HB	Dear Lord and Father of Mankind
19:11-12	506TH	Praise the Spirit in Creation

2 Kings

2:9-15	258LW	God of the Prophets, Bless the Prophets' Sons
2:11-12	143LW	The Glory of These Forty Days (St.2)
2:11	703UM	Swing Low, Sweet Chariot

1 Chronicles

16:4-36	449LW	When in Our Music God Is Glorified
16:23-36	29HB	Praise to the Lord, the Almighty
16:31-36	448LW	Oh, That I Had a Thousand Voices
17:16-17	378UM	Amazing Grace! How Sweet the Sound
29:5	182MH	Lord, in the Strength of Grace
29:14	383HB	We Plow the Fields, and Scatter
29:14b	588UM	All Things Come of Thee
29:20	238LW	O Lord, We Praise You

2 Chronicles

5:13-14	486PH	When the Morning Stars Together
6:18-21	145HB	Christ Is Made the Sure Foundation
7:1,12-16	145HB	Christ Is Made the Sure Foundation
14:11	446HT	We Trust in You
15:15	391UM	O Happy Day, That Fixed My Choice
20:12	428LW	When in the Hour of Deepest Need

Ezra

3:11	29HB	Praise to the Lord, the Almighty
9:15	234LW	To You, Omniscient Lord of All

Nehemiah

9:5-6	447LW	Jehovah, Let Me Now Adore You
9:5	45HB	Stand Up and Bless the Lord
9:6	29HB	Praise to the Lord, the Almighty
9:19-20	269HB	Guide Me, O Thou Great Jehovah
9:19	363TH	Ancient of Days, Who Sittest Throned in Glory
	149TH	Eternal Lord of Love, Behold Your Church
	144HB	Glorious Things of Thee Are Spoken
	393TH	Praise Our Great and Gracious Lord
	187TH	Through the Red Sea Brought at Last
10:35	705TH	As Those of Old Their First Fruits Brought

Job

1:21	429LW	I Leave All Things to God's Direction
8:21	107SFGP	Give to Us Laughter
11:7-9	476TH	Can We by Searching Find Out God
19:25-27	264LW	I Know That My Redeemer Lives
	266LW	Jesus Christ, My Sure Defense
26	554PH	Let All Things Now Living
26:14	214HB	O God of Earth and Altar
28	287PH	God Folds the Mountains Out of Rock
28:23-28	159HB	God Moves in a Mysterious Way
33:4	505TH	O Spirit of Life, O Spirit of God
37:2-5	273HB	God the Omnipotent! King, Who Ordainest
37:23	159HB	God Moves in a Mysterious Way
38	554PH	Let All Things Now Living
38:1-41	159HB	God Moves in a Mysterious Way
38:4-7	426TH	Songs of Praise the Angels Sang
38:4	379TH	God Is Love, Let Heaven Adore Him
38:7	432HB	Brightest and Best of the Sons of the Morning
	346LW	O Kingly Love, That Faithfully
	190LW	Stars of the Morning, So Gloriously Bright
	54SFGP	The Singer and the Song
	486PH	When the Morning Stars Together
38:8-11	579TH	Almighty Father, Strong to Save
	221HB	Eternal Father, Strong to Save
38:22-23	159HB	God Moves in a Mysterious Way

Psalms

1	382HB	Sing to the Lord of Harvest
	158PH	The One Is Blest
	388LW	The Man Is Ever Blessed
	214MH	The Righteous Ones

1:1-3	222LW	How Blest Are They Who Hear God's Word
2	159PH	Why Are Nations Raging
3:5	485LW	Now Rest Beneath Night's Shadow
	503LW	Now the Light Has Gone Away
3:8	308HB	Lord, Dismiss Us With Thy Blessing
4	160PH	Psalm 4
4:8	473UM	Lead Me, Lord
	485LW	Now Rest Beneath Night's Shadow
	541PH	Now the Day Is Over
	503LW	Now the Light Has Gone Away
5	161PH	As Morning Dawns
	267HT	Lord, as I Wake, I Turn to You
5:3	479LW	O Holy, Blessed Trinity
5:8	473UM	Lead Me, Lord
	512LW	Lord, Take My Hand and Lead Me
5:11-12	174LW	The Lord, My God, Be Praised
7:1	421LW	In God, My Faithful God
	170LW	Triune God, Oh, Be Our Stay
8	199HB	For the Beauty of the Earth
	50SFGP	How Great Thou Art (St.1)
	466WB	Lord of the Strong, When Earth You Trod
	163PH	Lord, Our Lord, Thy Glorious Name
	495WB	O God, Beneath Your Guiding Hand
	274PH	O God of Earth and Space
	35HU	O How Glorious, Full of Wonder
	162PH	O Lord, Our God, How Excellent
	515WB	O Lord, Our Lord, in All the Earth
8:1-4	80SFGP	Many and Great, O God, Are Your Works
9	568WB	Sing Praise to God, Who Reigns Above
10:1	125SFGP	God, When I Stand (St.2)

13:5-6	342PH	By Gracious Powers
15	164PH	Lord, Who May Dwell Within Your House
16	165PH	When in the Night I Meditate
16:1	170LW	Triune God, Oh, Be Our Stay
16:5-6	196LW	When All Your Mercies, O My God
16:6	333LW	God's Word Is Our Great Heritage
16:8	306HB	Forth in Your Name, O Lord, I Go
16:9	487LW	O Trinity, O Blessed Light
	471HB	This Joyful Eastertide
16:11-12	174LW	The Lord, My God, Be Praised
16:11	107SFGP	Give to Us Laughter (St.4)
17	374HT	O Lord, Our Guardian and Our Guide
17:15	337WB	Come, My Soul, You Must Be Waking
18	475HT	I Love You, O Lord, You Alone
	413LW	Lord, You I Love with All My Heart
18:1-2	135HB	A Mighty Fortress
18:1	279LW	How Sweet the Name of Jesus Sounds
18:2-3	184LW	Now Let Us Come Before Him
18:18	170LW	Triune God, Oh, Be Our Stay
18:46-49	136LW	Today in Triumph Christ Arose
19	388HB	All Beautiful the March of Days
	415WB	Heaven and Earth, and Sea, and Air
	149UM	Let's Sing Unto the Lord
	83HB	O Lord of Every Shining Constellation
	85HB	The Spacious Firmament on High
	431TH	The Stars Declare His Glory
19:1-6	50HB	Holy, Holy, Holy!
	166PH	The Heavens Above Declare God's Praise
	254HT	The Heavens Declare Your Glory, Lord
19:1-4	434TH	Nature With Open Volume Stands
19:4-6	164HB	Jesus Shall Reign
19:7-14	167PH	God's Law Is Perfect and Gives Life
19:7-8	329LW	The Law of God Is Good and Wise
19:7	336LW	Grant, Holy Ghost, that We Behold

19:10	22SFGP	O Christ, the Word Incarnate (St.2)
19:14	344HU	Let the Words of My Mouth
	347HU	May the Words of Our Mouths
20	169PH	In the Day of Need
20:1-5	356HB	Only-Begotten, Word of God Eternal
20:4,5	455LW	Rejoice, O Pilgrim Throng (Rejoice, Ye Pure in Heart)
20:6	394WB	God of Our Fathers, Whose Almighty Hand
21:3-6	286TH	Who Are These Like Stars Appearing
22	168PH	Lord, Why Have You Forsaken Me
22:1-2	125SFGP	God, When I Stand (St.2)
22:1	406PH	Why Has God Forsaken Me?
22:3-5	324LW	As Moses, Lost in Sinai's Wilderness
22:6-8	452HB	O Sacred Head, Now Wounded
22:28	274LW	O Jesus, King Most Wonderful
23	128UM	He Leadeth Me: O Blessed Thought
	230MH	In Heavenly Love Abiding
	75SFGP	My Shepherd Is the Living Lord
	172PH	My Shepherd Will Supply My Need
	518UM	O Thou, in Whose Presence
	173PH	Psalm 23
	132HB	The King of Love My Shepherd Is
	663TH	The Lord My God My Shepherd Is
	45HT	The Lord My Shepherd Rules My Life
	175PH	The Lord's My Shepherd: All My Need
	131HB	The Lord's My Shepherd: I'll Not Want
23:1-4	93SFGP	Saviour, Like a Shepherd Lead Us
23:4	280LW	Jesus, Your Boundless Love So True
	308HB	Lord, Dismiss Us With Thy Blessing
24	436TH	Lift Up Your Heads, Ye Mighty Gates
	177PH	Psalm 24
	176PH	The Earth and All That Dwell Therein
	82HB	This Is My Father's World
24:1	119SFGP	For Ourselves No Longer Living (St.2)

	82HB	This Is My Father's World
24:1	119SFGP	For Ourselves No Longer Living (St.2)
24:1	90HB	God of Concrete
24:7-10	477HB	Hail the Day That Sees Him Rise
	76HU	Lift Up Your Heads
	65TH	Prepare the Way, O Zion
	75HU	The King of Glory
24:7-9	447HB	All Glory, Laud, and Honor
	27LW	Prepare the Royal Highway
24:7	83LW	O God of God, O Light of Light
25	178PH	Lord, to You My Soul Is Lifted
25:1-8	421LW	In God, My Faithful God
25:3	703TH	Lead Us, O Father, in the Paths of Peace
25:4-5	386LW	Jesus, Still Lead On
	255LW	My Maker, Now Be Nigh
25:7	498LW	O God of Love, O King of Peace
26	355HB	We Love the Place, O Lord
26:8	325LW	For Many Years, O God of Grace
	296LW	I Love Your Kingdom, Lord
26:12	494LW	We Praise You, O God
27	179PH	God Is My Strong Salvation
27:1-4	424LW	Rejoice, My Heart, Be Glad
27:4-6	207LW	To Your Temple, Lord, I Come
27:4-5	325LW	For Many Years, O God of Grace
27:4	296LW	I Love Your Kingdom, Lord
27:8	520PH	Here, O Our Lord, We See You Face to Face
27:9	413LW	Lord, You I Love with All My Heart
27:11	512LW	Lord, Take My Hand and Lead Me
27:14	223HB	God of Grace and God of Glory
28:2	209LW	Kyrie, God Father
29	180PH	The God of Heaven
29:10-11	273HB	God the Omnipotent! King, Who Ordainest
	262HU	O God of Love

30:5	268HU	Lift Thy Head, O Zion
	110SFGP	O Love That Wilt Not Let Me Go (St.3)
30:10-12	17LW	O Lord of Light, Who Made the Stars
31:1-3	170LW	Triune God, Oh, Be Our Stay
31:1-5	406LW	In You, Lord, I Have Put My Trust
31:3	386LW	Jesus, Still Lead On
31:9-16	182PH	Psalm 31: 9-16
31:16	208LW	Lamb of God, Pure and Sinless
32	184PH	How Blest Are Those
32:5	233LW	Lord, to You I Make Confession
32:12	556TH	Rejoice, Ye Pure in Heart
33	185PH	Psalm 33
	264PH	When in Our Music God Is Glorified
33:1	196LW	When All Your Mercies, O My God
33:3-6	419LW	Evening and Morning
33:3	412TH	Earth and All Stars
33:4-11	107UM	Righteous and Just Is the Word of Our Lord
33:4-9	80SFGP	Many and Great, O God, Are Your Works
33:4-5	76HB	There's a Wideness in God's Mercy
33:5	196LW	When All Your Mercies, O My God
33:8	475TH	God Himself Is With Us
33:12	499LW	Christ, by Heavenly Hosts Adored
33:22	208LW	Lamb of God, Pure and Sinless
34	41HT	Tell His Praise in Song and Story
	137HB	Through All the Changing Scenes of Life
34:8	240LW	Draw Near and Take the Body of the Lord
34:9-22	187PH	Psalm 34:9-22
34:11	470LW	Lord Jesus Christ, the Children's Friend
34:15-17	433LW	Come, My Soul, With Every Care
34:17	434LW	Christians, While on Earth Abiding
34:18	124SFGP	God, You Meet Us (St.2)
35:28	48HB	O For a Thousand Tongues to Sing
36	186PH	Thy Mercy and Thy Truth, O Lord

36	186PH	Thy Mercy and Thy Truth, O Lord
36:6	26HB	Immortal, Invisible, God Only Wise
36:7	485LW	Now Rest Beneath Night's Shadow
37	669TH	Commit Thou All That Grieve Thee
	188PH	Fret Not For those Who Do Wrong Things
37:3	464UM	I Will Trust in the Lord
37:5-7	286PH	Give to the Winds Thy Fears
37:5	427LW	Entrust Your Days and Burdens
38:4	232LW	Alas, My God, My Sins Are Great
38:21-22	372LW	O God, Forsake Me Not
39:8	134HB	All My Hope on God Is Founded
42	658TH	As Longs the Deer for Cooling Streams
	190PH	Psalm 42
42:1-7	189PH	As Deer Long For the Streams
42:1-5	89SFGP	As Longs the Hart
	37SFGP	As Pants the Hart
42:2	307LW	Jerusalem, My Happy Home
42:8	485LW	Now Rest Beneath Night's Shadow
42:4-11	510LW	Be Still, My Soul
43:3	83LW	O God of God, O Light of Light
43:3-4	201LW	We Worship You, O God of Might
43:4-5	327LW	How Blessed Is This Place, O Lord
44	54MH	O Lord, Our Fathers Oft Have Told
44:1-8	501LW	God of Our Fathers
	326LW	Our Fathers' God in Years Long Gone
44:1-3	109SFGP	O God of Love, O Power of Peace (St.2)
45	112HU	O Morning Star, How Fair and Bright
45:1-3	121HB	O Jesus, King Most Wonderful
45:2	507LW	Beautiful Savior
	46HB	Fairest Lord Jesus
	178MH	What Grace, O Lord, and Beauty Shone
45:3	169LW	Come, O Almighty King

46	135HB	A Mighty Fortress Is Our God
	283WB	All Glory Be to God on High
	191PH	God Is Our Refuge and Our Strength
	527HT	God Is Our Strength and Refuge
	396WB	God of the Ages, by Whose Hand
	192PH	God, Our Help and Constant
	193PH	Psalm 46
46:5	275TH	Hark! the Sound of Holy Voices
46:8,9	109SFGP	O God of Love, O Power of Peace (St.1)
46:9	498LW	O God of Love, O King of Peace
46:10	31SFGP	Be Still, My Soul
	607TH	O God of Every Nation
	578TH	O God of Love, O King of Peace
	276HB	Thy Kingdom Come, O God
47	194PH	Peoples, Clap Your Hands!
47:5-9	149LW	A Hymn of Glory Let Us Sing
48:1-14	144HB	Glorious Things of Thee Are Spoken
48:9	366HB	The Day Thou Gavest, Lord, Is Ended
49:7-8	34LW	Come, O Precious Ransom
50:10-12	82HB	This Is My Father's World
50:14	385LW	How Can I Thank You, Lord
51	195PH	Have Mercy on Us, Living Lord
	48HB	O For a Thousand Tongues
	196PH	Psalm 51
51:1-2	77HB	Jesus, Lover of My Soul
	284HB	Just as I Am, Without One Plea
51:1	392WB	God of Compassion, in Mercy Befriend Us
51:2	226MH	Savior, More Than Life to Me
51:3	234LW	To You, Omniscient Lord of All
51:3-11	233LW	Lord, to You I Make Confession
51:6-12	231LW	Lord Jesus, Think on Me
51:8-17	126SFGP	She Flies On (St.2)
51:10	417UM	O For a Heart to Praise My God
	502UM	Thy Holy Wings, O Savior
51:12	396PH	O For a Closer Walk With God

51:15	82SFGP	Open My Eyes That I May See (St.3)
54:4	357WB	Eternal God, Whose Power Upholds
55	286PH	Give to the Winds Thy Fears
55:18	257LW	Let Me Be Yours Forever
55:22-23	282PH	If Thou But Trust in God to Guide Thee
55:22	323WB	Cast Your Burden on the Lord
	210HM	If Thou But Suffer God to Guide Thee
	420LW	If You But Trust in God to Guide You
	451WB	Let There Be Light, Lord God of Hosts
56	286PH	Give to the Winds Thy Fears
56:8	424LW	Rejoice, My Heart, Be Glad
57:1	484LW	All Praise to Thee, My God, This Night
	77HB	Jesus, Lover of My Soul
59:16	464WB	Lord of All Majesty and Might
59:16-17	357HB	Awake, My Soul, and With the Sun
	479LW	O Holy, Blessed Trinity
60:4	321HB	Lift High the Cross
61	365HT	Listen to My Prayer, Lord
	523UM	Saranam, Saranam (Refuge)
61:2	223HB	God of Grace and God of Glory
	245MH	O Sometimes the Shadows Are Deep
61:3	133HB	Our God, Our Help in Ages Past
61:8	357HB	Awake, My Soul, and With the Sun
62	197PH	My Soul in Silence Waits for God
63	198PH	O God, You Are My God
	514WB	O Lord, Our God, Most Earnestly
	199PH	O Lord, You Are My God
65	201PH	Praise Is Your Right, O God, in Zion
	290HT	The Earth Is Yours O God
	200PH	To Bless the Earth

65:2	498MH	At Thy Feet, Our God and Father
65:4	207LW	To Your Temple, Lord, I Come
65:5-13	81HB	I Sing the Mighty Power
65:8-13	436LW	All Creatures of Our God and King
65:9-13	496LW	Lord, to You Immortal Praise
	68HU	O Beautiful For Spacious Skies
	382HB	Sing to the Lord of Harvest
	512MH	To Bless the Earth, God Sendeth
65:9-11	86UM	Mountains Are All Aglow
65:11	183LW	Greet Now the Swiftly Changing Year
65:13	524MH	To Thee, O Lord, Our Hearts We Raise
66:1-2	1HU	From All That Dwell
	378WB	Glorious Is Your Name, Most Holy
	1SFGP	O For a Thousand Tongues to Sing (St.5)
66:1	446WB	Joyful, Joyful, We Adore Thee
	710TH	Make a Joyful Noise Unto the Lord
67	223HB	God of Grace and God of Glory
	538TH	God of Mercy, God of Grace
	456WB	Lord, Bless and Pity Us
	330HT	May God Be Gracious to Us
	288LW	May God Embrace Us With His Grace
	202PH	Psalm 67
67:2	539TH	O Zion, Haste, Thy Mission High Fulfilling
67:4	467WB	Lord Our God, With Praise We Come
67:5-6	382HB	Sing to the Lord of Harvest
67:6-7	42HU	Come, Ye Thankful People, Come
68:18	215TH	See the Conqueror Mounts in Triumph
	492TH	Sing, Ye Faithful, Sing With Gladness
68:19	356PH	Come, Thou Fount of Every Blessing
	496LW	Lord, to You Immortal Praise
	197HB	Now Thank We All Our God
	196LW	When All Your Mercies, O My God
71:3	79HB	Rock of Ages, Cleft For Me
72	205PH	All Hail to God's Anointed

72	154HB	Hail to the Lord's Anointed
	164HB	Jesus Shall Reign Where'er the Sun
	204PH	Psalm 72
72:1-8	65TH	Prepare the Way, O Zion
72:19	63UM	Blessed Be the Name
73:23	409LW	From God Can Nothing Move Me
	423LW	When I Suffer Pains and Losses
73:25-26	109SFGP	O God of Love, O Power of Peace (St.3)
73:25	253HB	Be Thou My Vision
73:26	502UM	Thy Holy Wings, O Savior
77:19	159HB	God Moves in a Mysterious Way
78	472LW	Let Children Hear the Mighty Deeds
78:1-8	470LW	Lord Jesus Christ, the Children's Friend
78:52-54	10HU	O God, Beneath Thy Guiding Hand
79:9	301LW	Lord of Our Life
80	206PH	O Hear Our Cry, O Lord
80:8-19	273LW	Amid the World's Bleak Wilderness
80:14-19	223HB	God of Grace and God of Glory
	390HB	Oh, Come, Oh, Come, Emmanuel
81:1	710TH	Make a Joyful Noise Unto the Lord
82	468MH	The Lord Will Come and Not Be Slow
82:8	213HB	Judge Eternal, Throned in Splendor
	462TH	The Lord Will Come and Not Be Slow
84	25MH	Great God, Attend, While Zion Sings
	517TH	How Lovely Is Thy Dwelling Place
	207PH	How Lovely, Lord
	208PH	Psalm 84
84:1	325LW	For Many Years, O God of Grace
85	468MH	The Lord Will Come and Not Be Slow
85:5	401LW	Forgive Us, Lord, for Shallow Thankful-ness

85:7-8	223HB	God of Grace and God of Glory
	286LW	Love Divine, All Love Excelling
85:7	208LW	Lamb of God, Pure and Sinless
85:8	221LW	Savior, Again to Your Dear Name
85:11,13	462TH	The Lord Will Come and Not Be Slow
86	462TH	The Lord Will Come and Not Be Slow
86:3-6	17LW	O Lord of Light, Who Made the Stars
86:3	93LW	Savior, When in Dust to You
86:9-10	462TH	The Lord Will Come and Not Be Slow
86:10	50SFGP	How Great Thou Art (St.1)
87	294LW	Glorious Things of You Are Spoken
87:3	144HB	Glorious Things of Thee Are Spoken
89	209PH	My Song Forever Shall Record
	47HT	Timeless Love! We Sing the Story
	628WB	We Sing the Mighty Power of God
89:1	51HU	I Will Sing of the Mercies
89:9	579TH	Almighty Father, Strong to Save
89:9	221HB	Eternal Father, Strong to Save
89:15	101SFGP	O Laughing Light (St.2)
90	211PH	Lord, You Have Been Our Dwelling Place
	133HB	Our God, Our Help in Ages Past
90:1-2	326LW	Our Fathers' God in Years Long Gone
90:1	165HU	We Come Unto Our Fathers' God
90:2	412PH	Eternal God, Whose Power Upholds
90:4-7	46HB	Immortal, Invisible, God Only Wise
90:17	462WB	Lord, Look Upon Our Working Days
91	322WB	Call Jehovah Your Salvation
	375TH	Give Praise and Glory Unto God
	445HT	Safe in the Shadow of the Lord
	483PH	Sing Praise to God, Who Reigns Above
	270HU	The Man Who Once Has Found Abode
	212PH	Within Your Shelter, Loving God
91:1-12	489LW	Before the Ending of the Day
91:1-4	263HB	O God of Bethel, By Whose Hand
91:1	184LW	Now Let Us Come Before Him

91:4	484LW	All Praise to Thee, My God, This Night
	29HB	Praise to the Lord, the Almighty
	502UM	Thy Holy Wings, O Savior
92	377HT	Sweet Is the Work, My God, My King
92:1-2	482LW	Father, We Praise You
	387LW	Praise and Thanks and Adoration
92:1-4	357HB	Awake, My Soul, and With the Sun
	174LW	The Lord, My God, Be Praised
	264PH	When in Our Music God Is Glorified
92:5	519LW	How Great Thou Art
93	213PH	God, Our Lord, a King Remaining
	403WB	God, the Lord, a King Remaineth
95	215PH	Come, Sing With Joy to God
	24MH	Come, Sound His Praise Abroad
	16HT	Come With All Joy to Sing to God
	18HT	Come Worship God Who Is Worthy of Honour
	214PH	O Come and Sing Unto the Lord
95:1-7	91UM	Canticle of Praise to God (Venite Exultemus)
	399TH	To God With Gladness Sing
95:1-6	403HB	From East to West
	290LW	Christ Is Our Cornerstone
	494LW	We Praise You, O God
95:1-2	204LW	Come, Let Us Join Our Cheerful Songs
95:1	90SFGP	Come, Let Us Sing (St.1)
95:2	201LW	Lord Jesus Christ, Be Present Now
	710TH	Make a Joyful Noise Unto the Lord
95:4-5	271PH	Many and Great, O God, Are Thy Things
95:6	644WB	You, Holy Father, We Adore
95:7-8	105MH	God Calling Yet! Shall I Not Hear
96	467PH	How Great Thou Art
	39MH	Let All on Earth Their Voices Raise
	216PH	O Sing a New Song to the Lord
	217PH	Psalm 96
96:1	438LW	Earth and All Stars

96:1-3	48HB	Oh, For a Thousand Tongues to Sing
96:1-5	321LW	Spread the Reign of God the Lord
96:1-8	452LW	Sing Praise to God, the Highest Good
96:3-9	290PH	God Created Earth and Heaven
96:3	322LW	From Greenland's Icy Mountains
96:9,13	91UM	Canticle of Praise to God (Venite Exulte-mus)
96:10	103LW	The Royal Banners Forward Go
97	152PH	Earth's Scattered Isles and Contoured Hills
	183HT	The Lord Is King! Lift Up Your Voice
98	401HB	Joy to the World
	468PH	Let All the World in Every Corner Sing
	413TH	New Songs of Celebration Render
	349HT	Sing a New Song to the Lord
	352HT	Sing to God New Songs of Worship
	219PH	To God Compose a Song of Joy
	264PH	When in Our Music God Is Gloried
98:1	1HB	All Creatures of Our God and King
	412TH	Earth and All Stars
98:1-2	446HB	Sing, My Tongue
	468HB	The Strife Is O'er, the Battle Done
98:3-4	33LW	Let the Earth Now Praise the Lord
98:4-9	1HB	All Creatures of Our God and King
98:6	186HT	Blow Upon the Trumpet
100	12HB	All People That on Earth Do Dwell
	454LW	Before the Lord Jehovah's Throne
	391TH	Before the Lord's Eternal Throne
	17HT	Come, Rejoice Before Your Maker
	12HU	O Be Joyful
	205LW	Oh, Sing Jubilee to the Lord
	484PH	Sing With Hearts
100:1	710TH	Make a Joyful Noise Unto the Lord
100:3	23SFGP	For the Healing of the Nations (St.4)
100:4	198LW	Open Now Thy Gates of Beauty
	197HB	Now Thank We All Our God
100:4-5	385LW	How Can I Thank You, Lord

102:25-26	180HB	Abide With Me
103	453LW	My Soul, Now Praise Your Maker
	34HT	O Bless the Lord, My Soul
	223PH	O My Soul, Bless Your Redeemer
	7HU	O My Soul, Bless God
	30HB	Praise, My Soul, the King of Heaven
	29HB	Praise to the Lord, the Almighty
	222PH	Psalm 103
103:1-7	457LW	Oh, Bless the Lord, My Soul
103:3	432WB	I'm So Glad Troubles Don't Last Always
103:8	296WB	Amazing Grace! How Sweet the Sound
103:16-17	523WB	O My Soul, Bless God, the Father
	629WB	We Thank You, Lord, for Strength of Arm
103:17	76HB	There's a Wideness in God's Mercy
103:19	30HB	Ye Servants of God, Your Master Proclaim
104	224PH	Bless the Lord, My Soul and Being
	269HB	Guide Me, O Thou Great Jehovah
	80SFGP	Many and Great, O God, Are Your Works
	458LW	O Worship the King, All Glorious Above
104:1-5	26HB	Immortal, Invisible, God Only Wise
104:5	379TH	God Is Love, Let Heaven Adore Him
104:24-30	148UM	Many and Great
	82HB	This Is My Father's World
104:24	419LW	Evening and Morning
104:31-35	26HB	Immortal, Invisible, God Only Wise
105	269HB	Guide Me, O Thou Great Jehovah
105:1-3	156HU	Rejoice, Ye Pure in Heart
105:1-2	26HB	Immortal, Invisible, God Only Wise
105:7	452PH	O Day of God, Draw Nigh
106	269HB	Guide Me, O Thou Great Jehovah
106:1	197HB	Now Thank We All Our God
	387LW	Praise and Thanks and Adoration
106:1-12	464HB	Come, You Faithful, Raise the Strain

106:4	241HB	Love Divine, All Loves Excelling
106:44-47	401LW	Forgive Us, Lord, for Shallow Thankfulness
107:1-3	370LW	Blest the Children of Our God
107:4-8	324LW	As Moses, Lost in Sinai's Wilderness
107:8	183LW	Greet Now the Swiftly Changing Year
107:9	343HB	Jesus, Thou Joy of Loving Hearts
107:10-22	48LW	Come, Your Hearts and Voices Raising
107:16	509HT	Lift Up Your Heads, You Gates of Brass
107:21-22	197HB	Now Thank We All Our God
	326LW	Our Fathers' God in Years Long Gone
107:22	385LW	How Can I Thank You, Lord
107:23-32	221HB	Eternal Father, Strong to Save
107:31-38	496LW	Lord, to You Immortal Praise
	403LW	Praise and Thanksgiving
107:31-32	494LW	We Praise You, O God
107:32	30HB	Ye Servants of God, Your Master Proclaim
108:1-2	357HB	Awake, My Soul, and With the Sun
108:13	564TH	He Who Would Valiant Be
110:2	221LW	Savior, Again to Your Dear Name
111	274PH	O God of Earth and Space
113	225PH	Praise the Lord!
	17SFGP	Praise to the Lord
	226PH	Sing Praise Unto the Name of God
113:1	30HB	Ye Servants of God, Your Master Proclaim
113:2-3	366HB	The Day Thou Gavest, Lord, Is Ended
113:3	292WB	All Praise to Thee, Our God, This Night
	487LW	O Trinity, O Blessed Light
115	227PH	Not Unto Us, O Lord of Heaven
115:18	4SFGP	Ba ni ngyeti Ba Yawe
116	228PH	O Thou, My Soul, Return in Peace

119:18	82SFGP	Open My Eyes That I May See
119:33	392LW	Oh, That the Lord Would Guide My Ways
119:105,		
130	627TH	Lamp of Our Feet, Whereby We Trace
	22SFGP	O Christ, the Word Incarnate (St.1)
119:105	332LW	How Precious Is the Book Divine
	499WB	O God of Light, Your Word, a Lamp Unfailing
	335LW	O Word of God Incarnate
	601UM	Thy Word Is a Lamp
119:111	333LW	God's Word Is Our Great Heritage
119:114	502UM	Thy Holy Wings, O Savior
119:129-		
132	329LW	The Law of God Is Good and Wise
119:133	231LW	Lord Jesus, Think on Me
	392LW	Oh, That the Lord Would Guide My Ways
119:140	197LW	Lord, Open Now My Heart to Hear
119:164	46SFGP	When Morning Gilds the Skies
119:176	392LW	Oh, That the Lord Would Guide My Ways
120:1-2	515UM	Out of the Depths I Cry to You
121	181LW	Across the Sky the Shades of Night
	489LW	Before the Ending of the Day
	492LW	God, Who Made the Earth and Heaven
	430WB	I to the Hills Will Lift My Eyes
	48HT	Unto the Hills Around
	57MH	Unto the Hills I Lift Mine Eyes
121:3-4	408TH	Sing Praise to God Who Reigns Above (St.2)
121:4	452LW	Sing Praise to God, the Highest Good
121:4-7	512LW	Lord, Take My Hand and Lead Me
121:8	221HB	Eternal Father, Strong to Save
122	235PH	With Joy I Heard My Friends Exclaim
122:1	325LW	For Many Years, O God of Grace
122:6-8	498LW	O God of Love, O King of Peace
124	236PH	Now Israel May Say

125:1	427LW	Entrust Your Days and Burdens
126	53SFGP	In Suffering Love (St.5)
	98SFGP	When God Delivered Israel
126:2	107SFGP	Give to Us Laughter
126:3	448LW	Oh, That I Had a Thousand Voices
126:5,6	132SFGP	Bless and Keep Us, God
127	238PH	Unless the Lord the House Shall Build
127:1	251LW	O Father, All Creating
128	239PH	How Happy Is Each Child of God
	466LW	Oh, Blessed Home Where Man and Wife
128:3-6	470LW	Lord Jesus Christ, the Children's Friend
130	230LW	From Depths of Woe I Cry to You
	459WB	Lord, from the Depths to You I Cry
	666TH	Out of the Depths I Call
	526MH	Out of the Depths I Cry to Thee
131	670TH	Lord, For Ever at Thy Side
132:13-18	144HB	Glorious Things of Thee Are Spoken
133	120SFGP	Behold, How Pleasant
	241PH	Behold the Goodness of Our Lord
	9SFGP	Blest Be the Tie That Binds
	497HT	How Good a Thing It Is
133:1	41SFGP	What a Goodly Thing
134	242PH	Come, All You Servants of the Lord
134:2	332HU	Come, Bless the Lord
136	31HT	Give to Our God Immortal Praise
	23HT	Let Us Gladly With One Mind
	28HB	Let Us with a Gladsome Mind
	243PH	We Thank You, Lord, For You Are Good
136:1-9	556PH	The World Abounds With God's Free Grace

137	55SFGP	By the Babylonian Rivers
	245PH	By the Waters of Babylon
	296LW	I (We) Love Your Kingdom, Lord
137:1-6	307LW	Jerusalem, My Happy Home
138	247PH	I Will Give Thanks With My Whole Heart
139	275PH	God of Our Life
	460WB	Lord God of Hosts, Whose Purpose
	248PH	You Are Before Me, Lord
139:1-11	702TH	Lord, Thou Hast Searched Me and Dost Know
139:7-10	233LW	Lord, to You I Make Confession
139:10	404PH	Precious Lord, Take My Hand
139:11-12	180HB	Abide With Me
139:11	485LW	Now Rest Beneath Night's Shadow
139:18	264MH	Still, Still with Thee
139:23-24	396PH	O For a Closer Walk With God
141	249PH	O Lord, Make Haste to Hear My Cry
141:2	327LW	How Blessed Is This Place, O Lord
	494MH	Softly Now the Light of Day
142:1	498UM	My Prayer Rises to Heaven
142:5	49SFGP	Amazing Grace, How Sweet the Sound
143	250PH	When Morning Lights the Eastern Skies
143:8	197LW	Lord, Open Now My Heart to Hear
143:10	255LW	My Maker, Now Be Nigh
144:9	412TH	Earth and All Stars
145	88SFGP	Holy God, We Praise Your Name (St.2)
	404TH	We Will Extol You, Ever-blessed Lord
145:1-13	252PH	O Lord, You Are My God and King
145:1-12	414TH	God, My King, Thy Might Confessing
145:1,2	1SFGP	O For a Thousand Tongues to Sing (St.1)
145:1	1HB	All Creatures of Our God and King
	500LW	Before You, Lord, We Bow
145:10-13	94SFGP	Ye Servants of God (St.1)

	441LW	We Sing the Almighty Power of God
149:1-3	438LW	Earth and All Stars
149:1-2	494LW	We Praise You, O God
149:2-4	439LW	I Will Sing My Maker's Praises
150	430TH	Come, O Come, Our Voices Raise
	412TH	Earth and All Stars
	432TH	O Praise Ye the Lord! Praise Him in the Height
	472PH	O Sing to the Lord
	552WB	Praise the Lord, His Glories Show
	96UM	Praise the Lord Who Reigns Above
	29HB	Praise to the Lord, the Almighty
	258PH	Praise Ye the Lord
	354HT	Sing Praise to the Lord
	484PH	Sing With Hearts
	449LW	When in Our Music God Is Glorified
150:1	55HB	Praise God, From Whom All Blessings Flow

Proverbs

3:24	491LW	Now the Day Is Over
4:18	362HB	Christ, Whose Glory Fills the Skies
6:23	372MH	O Word of God Incarnate
8:1-31	390HB	O Come, O Come, Emmanuel
8:29	379TH	God Is Love, Let Heaven Adore Him
10:22	415LW	All Depends on Our Possessing
18:24	114HB	What a Friend We Have in Jesus

Ecclesiastes

| 2:11,18 | 73HB | Turn Back, O Man |

3:11	86HB	All Things Bright and Beautiful
11:7-10	415LW	All Depends on Our Possessing
50:22-24	197HB	Now Thank We All Our God

Song of Solomon

1:3	279LW	How Sweet the Name of Jesus Sounds
1:4	153LW	Draw Us to You
2:10-13	213TH	Come Away to the Skies
5:10-16	83MH	Majestic Sweetness Sits Enthroned

Isaiah

1:18	77HB	Jesus, Lover of My Soul
	284HB	Just as I Am, Without One Plea
	347LW	Today Your Mercy Calls Us
2:1-4	426UM	Behold a Broken World
2:2-3	310LW	Look Toward the Mountains
2:4	542TH	Christ Is the World's True Light
	276HB	Thy Kingdom Come, O God
	434PH	Today We All Are Called to Be Disciples
2:12-17	492WB	O Day of Grace, Draw Nigh
2:12	260HU	O Day of God, Draw Nigh
4:5-6	144HB	Glorious Things of Thee Are Spoken
5:1-7	273LW	Amid the World's Bleak Wilderness
6:1-7	50HB	Holy, Holy, Holy!
6:1-4	578HT	Bright the Vision That Delighted
	214LW	Isaiah, Mighty Seer, in Spirit Soared
6:1-3	88SFGP	Holy God, We Praise Thy Name (St.2)
	332HB	Let All Mortal Flesh Keep Silence
	643TH	My God, How Wonderful Thou Art
	364TH	O God, We Praise Thee and Confess

6:1-3	367TH	Round the Lord in Glory Seated
	401TH	The God of Abraham Praise
6:2-3	199LW	We Worship You, O God of Might
6:3	687UM	Day Is Dying in the West
	97SFGP	Holy, Holy Lord
	117SFGP	Holy, Holy, Holy Lord
	201LW	Lord Jesus Christ, Be Present Now
	48TH	O Day of Radiant Gladness
	203LW	O Day of Rest and Gladness
6:6	45HB	Stand Up and Bless the Lord
6:7	261LW	Lord of the Church, We Humbly Pray
6:8-9	525PH	Here I Am, Lord
6:8	344PH	Christ of the Upward Way
	318LW	Hark, the Voice of Jesus Calling
	419PH	How Clear Is Our Vocation, Lord
	497UM	Send Me, Lord
	436UM	The Voice of God Is Calling
	582UM	Whom Shall I Send?
7:14	407HB	Hark! the Herald Angels Sing (St.2)
	496TH	How Bright Appears the Morning Star
	390HB	Oh, Come, Oh, Come, Emmanuel
	346LW	O Kingly Love, That Faithfully
	88TH	Sing, O Sing, This Blessed Morn (St.3)
	54SFGP	The Singer and the Song (St.4)
9:2-7	402HB	Break Forth, O Beauteous Heavenly Light
	68HT	The Darkness Turns to Dawn
	125TH	The People Who in Darkness Walked
	381TH	Thy Strong Word Did Cleave the Darkness
	64HT	To Us a Child of Royal Birth
9:2	362HB	Christ, Whose Glory Fills the Skies
	77LW	The People That in Darkness Sat
9:3	384HB	Come, You Faithful People, Come
9:4-5	427HB	It Came Upon the Midnight Clear
9:6	542TH	Christ Is the World's True Light
	389HB	Come, O Long-Expected Jesus
	407HB	Hark! The Herald Angels Sing
	88TH	Sing, O Sing, This Blessed Morn (St.1)
	382HB	Sing to the Lord of Harvest

9:6	640TH	Watchman, Tell Us of the Night
9:27	402HB	Break Forth, O Beauteous
11	337PH	Isaiah the Prophet Has Written of Old
11:1-10	117HB	How Bright Appears the Morning Star
	324HB	Lord, Enthroned in Heavenly Splendor
11:1	69PH	O Morning Star, How Fair and Bright
	390HB	Oh, Come, Oh, Come, Emmanuel
11:1-2	67LW	Lo, How a Rose Is Growing
11:2-3	118SFGP	Come, Holy Spirit
11:2	245HB	Come, Holy Ghost, Our Souls Inspire
	226TH	Come, Thou Holy Spirit Bright
	167LW	Creator Spirit, By Whose Aid
	156LW	Creator Spirit, Heavenly Dove
	160LW	O Holy Spirit, Enter In
	501TH	O Holy Spirit, By Whose Breath
	263LW	Send, O Lord, You Holy Spirit
11:6-9	597TH	O Day of Peace That Dimly Shines
11:9	245HB	Come, Holy Ghost, Our Souls Inspire
	412PH	Eternal God, Whose Power Upholds
	534TH	God Is Working His Purpose Out
12	78LW	Jesus Has Come and Brings Pleasure
12:2-6	678TH	Surely It Is God Who Saves Me
12:2	408LW	I Am Trusting You, Lord Jesus
12:4-5	48HB	O For a Thousand Tongues to Sing
21:11-12	640TH	Watchman, Tell Us of the Night
22:22	390HB	O Come, O Come, Emmanuel
25:4	53SFGP	In Suffering Love (St.1)
	77HB	Jesus, Lover of My Soul
25:6-8	96LW	Come to Calvary's Holy Mountain
25:8	123LW	Christ Jesus Lay in Death's Strong Bonds
26:2-4	198LW	Open Now Thy Gates of Beauty
26:4	635TH	If Thou But Trust in God to Guide Thee
28:12	440HB	Beneath the Cross of Jesus

28:16	145HB	Christ Is Made the Sure Foundation
	139HB	How Firm a Foundation
	146HB	The Church's One Foundation
29:18-19	48HB	O For a Thousand Tongues to Sing
30:15	249HB	Dear Lord and Father of Mankind
32:2	440HB	Beneath the Cross of Jesus
	53SFGP	In Suffering Love (St.2)
	77HB	Jesus, Lover of My Soul
32:6-7	77HB	Jesus, Lover of My Soul
33:20-21	144HB	Glorious Things of Thee Are Spoken
35	200HT	When the King Shall Come Again
	198HT	Let the Desert Sing
	18PH	The Desert Shall Rejoice
35:1-10	53SFGP	In Suffering Love (St.5)
35:1-2,6	65SFGP	Joy Shall Come
35:1-2	233UM	Cold December Flies Away
	90SFGP	Come, Let Us Sing (St.4)
	216UM	Lo, How a Rose E'er Blooming
	126SFGP	She Flies On (St.2)
35:5-6	1SFGP	O For a Thousand Tongues to Sing (St.4)
35:10	392TH	Come, We That Love the Lord
	184HB	Jerusalem, the Golden
40:1-11	153HB	There's a Voice in the Wilderness Crying
40:1-8	21LW	"Come, Comfort," Says the Voice
	28LW	Comfort, Comfort These My People
40:1-5	59TH	Hark! a Thrilling Voice Is Sounding
	103HB	Herald, Sound the Note of Judgment
	391HB	On Jordan's Bank the Baptist's Cry
	65TH	Prepare the Way, O Zion
40:3-5	210UM	All Earth Is Waiting
40:3-4	27LW	Prepare the Royal Highway
40:3	395HB	Hark the Glad Sound
	207UM	Prepare the Way of the Lord

40:6-8	453LW	My Soul, Now Praise Your Maker
40:7	391HB	On Jordan's Bank the Baptist's Cry
40:9	99TH	Go Tell It on the Mountain (Refrain)
40:11	139HB	How Firm a Foundation
	517LW	I Am Jesus' Little Lamb
	478TH	Jesus, Our Mighty Lord
	297HU	O, Rise and Shine
	93SFGP	Savior, Like a Shepherd Lead Us
	471LW	Shepherd of Tender Youth
40:21	29HB	Praise to the Lord, the Almighty
40:23	279HB	Father Eternal, Ruler of Creation
40:26	501LW	God of Our Fathers
40:31	19SFGP	Arise, Your Light Is Come (St.4)
41:10	139HB	How Firm a Foundation
41:13	404PH	Precious Lord, Take My Hand
42:10-12	438LW	Earth and All Stars
43:1-7	139HB	How Firm a Foundation
	213LW	We All Believe in One True God, Maker
43:1,2	53SFGP	In Suffering Love (St.1)
	59SFGP	We Praise You, O God (St.2)
43:2	512LW	Lord, Take My Hand and Lead Me
45:5-8	273HB	God the Omnipotent
45:7	134PH	Creating God, Your Fingers Trace
45:23	39HB	At the Name of Jesus
	396HB	Creator of the Stars of Night
	252TH	Jesus! Name of Wondrous Love
46:16-17	209LW	Kyrie, God Father
49:12	149HB	In Christ There Is No East or West
49:15-16	71SFGP	I Will Never Forget You, My People
49:16	296LW	I Love Your Kingdom, Lord
50:6	452HB	O Sacred Head, Now Wounded
51:12-15	379TH	God Is Love, Let Heaven Adore Him

51:13-16	158HB	God, Who Stretched the Spangled Heavens
52:1-8	394HB	"Sleepers, Wake!" a Voice Astounds Us
52:1	177LW	Wake, Awake, For Night Is Flying
52:7	389HB	Come, Thou Long-Expected Jesus
	319LW	O God, O Lord of Heaven and Earth
	539TH	O Zion, Haste, Thy Mission High Fulfilling
52:8-10	640TH	Watchman, Tell Us of the Night
52:8	315LW	Awake, Thou Spirit of the Watchmen
52:9	42LW	Let Us All With Gladsome Voice
52:9-10	446HB	Sing, My Tongue
	134LW	With High Delight Let Us Unite
52:10	207UM	Prepare the Way of the Lord
52:13-53:12	442HB	My Song Is Love Unknown
53	103PH	Deep Were His Wounds, and Red
	165UM	Hallelujah! What a Savior
	137HT	See, Christ Was Wounded For Our Sake
	120LW	Upon the Cross Extended
53:1-12	443HB	Ah, Holy Jesus, How Hast Thou Offended
	452HB	O Sacred Head, Sore Wounded
53:3-5	78PH	Alas! And Did My Savior Bleed
	116LW	Stricken, Smitten, and Afflicted
53:3	130HT	Man of Sorrows, What a Name
53:4-5	336LW	Grant, Holy Ghost, That We Behold
	95LW	Grant, Lord Jesus, That My Healing
	132LW	Make Songs of Joy
53:4-7	111LW	A Lamb Alone Bears Willingly
53:5	468HB	The Strife Is O'er, the Battle Done
53:6-7	208LW	Lamb of God, Pure and Sinless
53:6	85PH	What Wondrous Love Is This
53:10-12	53SFGP	In Suffering Love (Sts.3,4)
54:7-8	159HB	God Moves in a Mysterious Way
55:1-2	350UM	Come, All of You
55:1	90SFGP	Come, Let Us Sing (St.2)
55:6-11	124UM	Seek the Lord
55:6	399PH	We Walk by Faith and Not by Sight

55:13	401HB	Joy to the World
56:6-7	51TH	We the Lord's People, Heart and Voice Uniting
57:15	291LW	Built on the Rock
	643TH	My God, How Wonderful Thou Art
58:5-10	145TH	Now Quit Your Care
59:20	390HB	Oh, Come, Oh, Come, Emmanuel
60	313LW	Rise, Crowned With Light
60:1-22	543TH	O Zion, Tune Thy Voice
60:1-3	725UM	Arise, Shine Out, Your Light Has Come
	314LW	O Christ, Our Light, O Radiance True
60:1-6	85LW	Arise and Shine in Splendor
60:1	19SFGP	Arise, Your Light Is Come
	187UM	Rise, Shine, You People
	47SFGP	Rise Up, O Saints of God
60:2	672TH	O Very God of Very God
60:3-6	84LW	Hail, O Source of Every Blessing
60:19-20	101SFGP	O Laughing Light (St.2)
60:19	435HB	As With Gladness Men of Old
61	332PH	Live Into Hope
61:1-3	19SFGP	Arise, Your Light Is Come!
	24SFGP	I Am the Light of the World
	407HB	Hark! The Herald Angels Sing
	433HB	Songs of Thankfulness and Praise
61:1-2	389HB	Come, Thou Long-Expected Jesus
	395HB	Hark the Glad Sound
	115SFGP	The Spirit of the Lord
61:1	539TH	O Zion, Haste, Thy Mission High Fulfilling
61:3	222LW	How Blest Are They Who Hear God's Word
61:10	169LW	Come, O Almighty King
	362LW	Jesus, Your Blood and Righteousness

62:2-3	206LW	God Himself Is Present
62:3	42HB	All Hail the Power of Jesus' Name
62:5-12	177LW	Wake, Awake, For Night Is Flying
62:6-7	315LW	Awake, Thou Spirit of the Watchmen
64:1	32LW	O Savior, Rend the Heavens Wide
64:8	170HU	Have Thine Own Way, Lord
65:17-19	620TH	Jerusalem, My Happy Home
	184HB	Jerusalem the Golden
65:17	296TH	We Know That Christ Is Raised and Dies No More
65:25	450PH	O Day of Peace

Jeremiah

7:23	123SFGP	To Abraham and Sarah
8:22	231TH	By All Your Saints Still Striving
	676TH	There Is a Balm in Gilead
10:12-13	271PH	Many and Great, O God, Are Thy Things
10:23	703TH	Lead Us O Father, in the Paths of Peace
17:7	408LW	I Am Trusting You, Lord Jesus
18:6	382UM	Have Thine Own Way, Lord
23:4	263LW	Send, O Lord, Your Holy Spirit
23:29	441HT	O Come, Our All-Victorious Lord
29:7	499LW	Christ, By Heavenly Hosts Adored
31:3	110SFGP	O Love That Wilt Not Let Me Go (St.1)
31:6	394HB	"Sleepers, Wake!" A Voice Astounds Us
31:31	482HT	Loved With Everlasting Love
33:11	326LW	Our Fathers' God in Years Long Gone

| 50:5 | 606UM | Come, Let Us Use the Grace Divine |

Lamentations

1:12	454HB	Alone Thou Goest Forth, O Lord
	442HB	My Song Is Love Unknown
2:22-23	260HT	Great Is Your Faithfulness
	270HT	New Every Morning Is the Love
3	240HU	Good Is the Lord
3:19	451HB	Go to Dark Gethsemane
3:22-23	95SFGP	Great Is Thy Faithfulness
	145UM	Morning Has Broken
	360HB	New Every Morning Is the Love
5:19	366HB	The Day Thou Gavest, Lord Is Ended

Ezekiel

1:4-28	235TH	Come Sing, Ye Choirs Exultant (St.2)
1:26	449HB	Ride On, Ride On in Majesty
10:9-22	235TH	Come Sing, Ye Choirs Exultant (St.2)
18:31-32	346UM	Sinners, Turn: Why Will You Die
31:1-31	478TH	Jesus, Our Mighty Lord
33:11	235LW	As Surely as I Live, God Said
34:16	213HB	Judge Eternal, Throned
34:26	383HB	We Plow the Fields and Scatter
36:26-28	67HB	Come Down, O Love Divine
36:26	483HT	O For a Heart to Praise My God
36:27	160LW	O Holy Spirit, Enter In

37:5-6	314PH	Like the Murmur of the Dove's Song
47:1-12	78SFGP	Out of Deep Unordered Water
48:35	168HB	All Who Love and Serve Your City

Daniel

2:22	159HB	God Moves in a Mysterious Way
3:29-34	373HU	Blessed Art Thou, O Lord
4:13	7HB	Ye Watchers and Ye Holy Ones
7:9-14	363TH	Ancient of Days
	62HB	Come, Thou Almighty King
	26HB	Immortal, Invisible, God Only Wise
	401TH	The God of Abraham Praise
7:9	27HB	O Worship the King, All Glorious Above
7:12-14	454TH	Jesus Came, Adored by Angels
7:13-14	393HB	Lo! He Comes, With Clouds Descending
7:14	289PH	O God of Every Nation
8:15-17	282TH	Christ, the Fair Glory of the Holy Angels (St.3)
9:3	143TH	The Glory of These Forty Days (St.3)
9:10-23	282TH	Christ, the Fair Glory of the Holy Angels (St.3)
9:17-19	434LW	Christians, While on Earth Abiding
	428LW	When in the Hour of Deepest Need
9:18-19	234LW	To You, Omniscient Lord of All
10:10-21	282TH	Christ, the Fair Glory of the Holy Angels (St.2)
12:1-4	282TH	Christ, the Fair Glory of the Holy Angels (St.2)

Hosea

6:3	173HB	Lead On, O King Eternal
11:1-9	110SFGP	O Love That Wilt Not Let Me Go (St.1)
12:6	73HB	Turn Back, O Man
13:14	188TH	Love's Redeeming Work Is Done

Joel

2:12	73HB	Turn Back, O Man
2:21	331HT	Rejoice, O Land, in God Your Lord
2:28-32	126SFGP	She Flies On (St.2)
	108SFGP	Spirit, Spirit of Gentleness (St.4)
3:10	542TH	Christ Is the World's True Light

Amos

3:3	128SFGP	Let There Be Peace on Earth
5:23-24	427PH	Lord, Whose Love Through Humble Service
5:24	434PH	Today We All Are Called to Be Disciples

Micah

4:1-4	426UM	Behold a Broken World
	498WB	O God of Every Nation
4:3-4	105SFGP	Vine and Fig Tree
4:3	542TH	Christ Is the World's True Light
	295PH	O God of Love, O God of Peace
	503WB	O God, Whose Will Is Life and Peace
	434PH	Today We All Are Called to Be Disciples
	276HB	Thy Kingdom Come, O God
5:2	421HB	O Little Town of Bethlehem

6:6-8	605TH	What Does the Lord Require
6:8	397LW	O God of Mercy, God of Light
	631WB	What Makes a City Great and Strong?
7:18	241HB	Love Divine, All Loves Excelling

Habakkuk

2:14	534TH	God Is Working His Purpose Out
2:20	206LW	God Himself Is Present
	475TH	God Himself Is With Us
	332HB	Let All Mortal Flesh Keep Silence
	329HU	The Lord Is in His Holy Temple
3:17-18	496LW	Lord, to You Immortal Praise
	667TH	Sometimes a Light Surprises (St.4)

Zephaniah

1:14	349LW	Delay Not, Delay Not, O Sinner, Draw Near

Haggai

2:7	389HB	Come, Thou Long-Expected Jesus
	390HB	O Come, O Come, Emmanuel

Zechariah

2:13	332HB	Let All Mortal Flesh Keep Silence
9:9	449HB	Ride On, Ride On in Majesty
	12LW	The Advent of Our God
12:10	393HB	Jesus Comes With Clouds Descending
13:1	686TH	Come, Thou Fount of Every Blessing

13:1	96LW	Come to Calvary's Holy Mountain
	77HB	Jesus, Lover of My Soul
	144HT	There Is a Fountain Filled with Blood
	506LW	There Stands a Fountain Where for Sin

Malachi

1:11	487LW	O Trinity, O Blessed Light
3:1	408HB	Angels, From the Realms of Glory (St.4)
	67TH	Comfort, Comfort Ye My People
	103HB	Herald, Sound the Note of Judgment
	241HB	Love Divine, All Loves Excelling
	391HB	On Jordan's Bank the Baptist's Cry
	65TH	Prepare the Way, O Zion
	153HB	There's a Voice in the Wilderness Crying
3:10	301WB	As Men of Old Their Firstfruits Brought
3:17	256LW	Yours Forever, God of Love
4:2	362HB	Christ, Whose Glory Fills the Skies
	407HB	Hark! the Herald Angels Sing (St.3)
	490TH	I Want to Walk as a Child of the Light
	213HB	Judge Eternal, Throned in Splendor
	672TH	O Very God of Very God
	667TH	Sometimes a Light Surprises
	235HB	Thou, Whose Almighty Word

Matthew

1	608WB	To Abraham the Promise Came
1:10-11	40LW	Oh, Rejoice, All Christians, Loudly
1:18-25	231TH	By All Your Saints Still Striving
	261TH	By the Creator, Joseph Was Appointed
	260TH	Come Now, and Praise the Humble Saint
	252TH	Jesus! Name of Wondrous Love 1:18-25
	81TH	Lo, How a Rose E'er Blooming
	250TH	Now Greet the Swiftly Changing Year (St.2)
	55TH	Redeemer of the Nations, Come

1:18-25	54TH	Savior of the Nations, Come
	248TH	To the Name of Our Salvation
1:21-23	39HB	At the Name of Jesus
1:21	182LW	Jesus! Name of Wondrous Love
1:22-23	63SFGP	Let Us Talents and Tongues Employ
	68SFGP	O Bread of Life
	390HB	O Come, O Come, Emmanuel
1:23	204UM	Emmanuel, Emmanuel
	282HU	God Himself Is with Us
	117HB	How Bright Appears the Morning Star
	265TH	The Angel Gabriel From Heaven Came
	54SFGP	The Singer and the Song
2:1-12	64PH	From a Distant Home
	418HB	In the Bleak Midwinter (St.4)
	79LW	O Jesus, King of Glory
	92TH	On This Day Earth Shall Ring (St.3)
	237UM	Sing We Now of Christmas
	410HB	The First Nowell the Angel Did Say
	412HB	'Twas in the Moon of Wintertime
	124TH	What Star Is This, with Beams So Bright
	131TH	When Christ's Appearing Was Made Known (Sts. 1 & 2)
	491TH	Where Is This Stupendous Stranger
2:1-11	435HB	As With Gladness Men of Old
	432HB	Brightest and Best of the Stars of the Morning
	431HB	Earth Has Many a Noble City
	54LW	He Whom Shepherds Once Came Praising
	56LW	I Am So Glad When Christmas Comes
	65PH	Midnight Stars Make Bright the Sky
	254UM	We Three Kings
	61LW	What Child Is This
	100HT	Wise Men, They Came to Look for Wisdom
2:1-3	408HB	Angels From the Realms of Glory
2:1-2	76LW	O Chief of Cities, Bethlehem
	421HB	O Little Town of Bethlehem
	433HB	Songs of Thankfulness and Praise
2:1,11	312WB	Born in the Night, Mary's Child

2:1	324HB	Lord, Enthroned in Heavenly Splendor
	452TH	Glorious the Day When Christ Was Born
2:8-12	27PH	Gentle Mary Laid Her Child
2:9	81LW	When Christ's Appearing was Made Known
2:9-10	114HU	O Thou, Who by a Star Did Guide
2:10-12	21PH	All My Heart Today Rejoices
	408HB	Angels, From the Realms of Glory
	52PH	Sheep Fast Asleep
2:10-11	417HB	All Poor Men and Humble
	76LW	O Chief of Cities, Bethlehem
2:11	55LW	Angels We Have Heard on High
	62PH	Bring We the Frankincense of Our Love
	84LW	Hail, O Source of Every Blessing
2:13-23	231TH	By All Your Saints Still Striving
	261TH	By the Creator, Joseph Was Appointed
	260TH	Come Now, and Praise the Humble Saint
2:13-18	98TH	Unto Us a Boy Is Born (St.3)
	113TH	Oh, Sleep Now, Holy Baby
2:13-16	188LW	Sweet Flowerets of the Martyr Band
2:13-15	45PH	O Sleep, Dear Holy Baby
2:16-18	192LW	By All Your Saints in Warfare
	246TH	In Bethlehem a Newborn Boy
	247TH	Lully, Lullay, Thou Little Tiny Child
3:1-12	59TH	Hark! a Thrilling Voice Is Sounding
	103HB	Herald, Sound the Note of Judgment
	391HB	On Jordan's Bank the Baptist's Cry
	69TH	What Is the Crying at Jordan
3:1-3	67TH	Comfort, Comfort Ye My People
3:1-3	153HB	There's a Voice in the Wilderness Crying
3:3	65TH	Prepare the Way, O Zion
3:4	143TH	The Glory of These Forty Days (St.3)
3:7-9	409PH	Wild and Lone the Prophet's Voice
3:11	245HB	Come, Holy Ghost, Our Souls Inspire
	500TH	Creator Spirit, By Whose Aid
	513TH	Like the Murmur of the Dove's Song
	501TH	O Holy Spirit, By Whose Breath
	239HB	O Thou Who Camest From Above

3:11	60HB	Spirit Divine, Attend Our Prayers
3:13-17	116TH	"I Come," the Great Redeemer Cries
	121TH	Christ, When For Us You Were Baptized
	71PH	Lord, When You Came to Jordan
	100HB	O Love, How Deep, How Broad, How High
	433HB	Songs of Thankfulness and Praise (St.2)
	120TH	The Sinless One to Jordan Came
	131TH	When Christ's Appearing Was Made Known
	252UM	When Jesus Came to Jordan
	139TH	When Jesus Went to Jordan's Stream
3:16	265HB	Come, Gracious Spirit, Heavenly Dove
	244HB	Come, Holy Spirit, Heavenly Dove
	513TH	Like the Murmur of the Dove's Song
	60HB	Spirit Divine, Attend Our Prayers
	591WB	The Lone, Wild Bird
4:1-17	120TH	The Sinless One to Jordan Came (St.4)
4:1-11	438HB	Forty Days and Forty Nights
	443TH	From God Christ's Deity Came Forth
	81PH	Lord, Who Throughout These Forty Days
	146TH	Now Let Us All With One Accord
	92LW	O Lord, Throughout These Forty Days
	100HB	O Love, How Deep, How Broad, How High
	284TH	O Ye Immortal Throng (St.3)
	93LW	Savior, When in Dust to You
	433HB	Songs of Thankfulness and Praise
	142TH	The Glory of These Forty Days
4:4	83SFGP	Seek Ye First the Kingdom of God (St.2)
	70SFGP	What Is the Place (St.2)
4:16	143HU	Christ Is the World's True Light
	55HU	Comfort, Comfort Ye My People
	77LW	The People That in Darkness Sat
	381TH	Thy Strong Word Did Cleave the Darkness
4:18-22	249HB	Dear Lord and Father of Mankind
	276TH	For Thy Blest Saints, a Noble Throng (St.2)
	166HB	Jesus Calls Us, O'er the Tumult

4:18-22	377PH	Lord, You Have Come to the Lakeshore
	661TH	They Cast Their Nets in Galilee
4:18-20	231TH	By All Your Saints Still Striving
	166HB	Jesus Calls Us; O'er the Tumult
4:23-25	567TH	Thine Arm, O Lord, in Days of Old
	139TH	When Jesus Went to Jordan's Stream (St.2)
4:23-24	303HB	Where Cross the Crowded Ways of Life
5:3-12	560TH	Remember Your Servants, Lord
5:8	58HB	Blest Are the Pure in Heart
5:14-16	385UM	Let Us Please For Faith Alone
5:14	370LW	Blest the Children of Our God
5:17	62HU	God of the Prophets
5:41	133SFGP	The Servant Song
6:1-2	438HB	Forty Days and Forty Nights
6:9-13	434LW	Christians, While on Earth Abiding
	358HT	Father God in Heaven, Lord Most High
	571PH	Our Father in Heaven
	590PH	Our Father, Lord of Heaven and Earth
	589PH	Our Father, Which Art in Heaven
	430LW	Our Father, Who From Heaven Above
	271UM	The Lord's Prayer
	12SFGP	The Lord's Prayer
	10SFGP	The Lord's Prayer
	349PH	Let All Who Pray the Prayer Christ Taught
6:9	547WB	Our Father, Which Art in Heaven
6:10	615TH	"Thy Kingdom Come!" on Bended Knee
	279HB	Father Eternal, Ruler of Creation (Refrain)
	340TH	For the Bread Which You Have Broken
	425PH	Lord of Light, Your Name Outshining
	389LW	May We Your Precepts, Lord, Fulfill
	425LW	The Will of God Is Always Best
	276HB	Thy Kingdom Come, O God
6:11	263HB	O God of Bethel, By Whose Hand
6:12-15	674TH	"Forgive Our Sins As We Forgive"
	581TH	Where Charity and Love Prevail
6:19-34	415LW	All Depends on Our Possessing

6:25-34	352PH	Great Are Your Mercies, O My Maker
6:25-33	263HB	O God of Bethel, By Whose Hand
	667TH	Sometimes a Light Surprises (St.3)
6:28-29	86HB	All Things Bright and Beautiful
6:33	83SFGP	Seek Ye First the Kingdom of God (St.1)
7:7	83SFGP	Seek Ye First the Kingdom of God (St.3)
7:7-8	114HB	What a Friend We Have in Jesus
7:14	64SFGP	Christus Paradox (St.3)
7:15-20	392TH	Come, We That Love the Lord
	308HB	Lord, Dismiss Us With Thy Blessing
7:24-28	379PH	My Hope Is Built on Nothing Less
7:24-27	139HB	How Firm a Foundation, Ye Saints of the Lord
7:24-25	144HB	Glorious Things of Thee Are Spoken
	174HU	We Would Be Building
8:1-17	567TH	Thine Arm, O Lord, in Days of Old
8:3	367UM	He Touched Me
8:5-13	443HB	Songs of Thankfulness and Praise (St.3)
8:8	407HT	I Am Not Worthy, Holy Lord
8:11-12	464LW	A Multitude Comes
8:17	103PH	Deep Were His Wounds, and Red
8:19	338UM	Where He Leads Me
8:20	442HB	My Song Is Love Unknown
8:23-27	31SFGP	Be Still, My Soul
	221HB	Eternal Father, Strong to Save
	373PH	Lonely the Boat
	512UM	Stand By Me
8:26	513LW	Jesus, Savior, Pilot Me
8:28-9:8	567TH	Thine Arm, O Lord, in Days of Old
9:1-8	443HB	Songs of Thankfulness and Praise (St.3)
9:9	193LW	By All Your Saints in Warfare
	281TH	He Sat to Watch O'er Customs Paid
9:18-35	567TH	Thine Arm, O Lord, in Days of Old
9:18-26	48HB	O For a Thousand Tongues to Sing
9:20-21	434WB	Immortal Love, Forever Full
9:20-22	266UM	Heal Us, Emmanuel, Hear Our Prayer

9:20-22	590TH	O Jesus Christ, May Grateful Hymns Be Rising
9:27-30	48HB	O For a Thousand Tongues to Sing
	633TH	Word of God, Come Down to Earth
9:36	472TH	Hope of the World, Thou Christ of Great Compassion
9:37-38	540TH	Awake, Thou Spirit of the Watchmen
	541TH	Come, Labor On
	339MH	Lord of the Harvest, Hear
10:7-8	528TH	Lord, You Give the Great Commission
	114HB	What a Friend We Have in Jesus
10:8	389UM	Freely, Freely
10:10	424TH	For the Fruit of All Creation
10:22	304HB	O Jesus, I Have Promised
10:34-36	661TH	They Cast Their Nets in Galilee
10:34	64SFGP	Christus Paradox (St.1)
10:38-39	572TH	Weary of All Trumpeting (St.3)
10:38	484TH	Praise the Lord Through Every Nation
	675TH	Take up Your Cross, the Savior Said
10:40-42	433PH	There's a Spirit in the Air
10:42	303HB	Where Cross the Crowded Ways of Life
11:2-6	442HB	My Song Is Love Unknown
	139TH	When Jesus Went to Jordan's Stream (St.2)
11:2-5	1SFGP	O For a Thousand Tongues to Sing (St.3)
11:7-15	271TH	The Great Forerunner of the Morn (St.4)
11:7-10	67TH	Comfort, Comfort Ye My People
	103HB	Herald, Sound the Note of Judgment
	391HB	On Jordan's Bank the Baptist's Cry
	65TH	Prepare the Way, O Zion
	153HB	There's a Voice in the Wilderness Crying
11:15	536TH	God Has Spoken to His People
11:28-30	74TH	Blest Be the King Whose Coming (St.4)
	44SFGP	Part of the Family (St.3)
	76SFGP	We Have This Ministry (St.3)
	303HB	Where Cross the Crowded Ways of Life
11:28	350UM	Come, All of You
	96LW	Come to Calvary's Holy Mountain

11:28	345LW	Come Unto Me, Ye Weary
	116HB	How Sweet the Name of Jesus Sounds
	115HB	I Heard the Voice of Jesus Say (St.1)
	164HB	Jesus Shall Reign
	342TH	O Bread of Life, For Sinners Broken
	350LW	The Savior Calls; Let Every Ear
11:30	306HB	Forth in Your Name, O Lord, I Go
12:9-22	567TH	Thine Arm, O Lord, in Days of Old
12:22	48HB	O For a Thousand Tongues to Sing
	633TH	Word of God, Come Down on Earth
12:33-35	392TH	Come, We That Love the Lord
	308HB	Lord, Dismiss Us With Thy Blessing
13:1-9	96SFGP	Sent Forth by God's Blessing
13:3-43	588TH	Almighty God, Your Word Is Cast
	541TH	Come, Labor On
13:3	217LW	On What Has Now Been Sown
13:8	338LW	When Seed Falls on Good Soil
13:9	536TH	God Has Spoken to His People
13:18-23	96SFGP	Sent Forth By God's Blessing
13:19	217LW	On What Has Now Been Sown
13:23	217LW	On What Has Now Been Sown
	338LW	When Seed Falls on Good Soil
13:24-30	384HB	Come, You Thankful People, Come
13:31-33	24TH	The Day That Thou Gavest, Lord, Is Ended
	275UM	The Kingdom of God
13:36-43	384HB	Come, You Thankful People, Come
13:38	383HB	We Plow the Fields and Scatter
13:43	536TH	God Has Spoken to His People
13:44-46	270LW	Jesus, Priceless Treasure
13:55	231TH	By All Your Saints Still Striving
	260TH	Come Now, and Praise the Humble Saint
14:13-21	86SFGP	Break Now the Bread of Life (Sts.1,2)
14:14	241HB	Love Divine, All Loves Excelling
14:17	377WB	Give to the Winds Your Fears
14:22-33	221HB	Eternal Father, Strong to Save
	689TH	I Sought the Lord, and Afterward I Knew

14:34-36	590TH	O Jesus Christ, May Grateful Hymns Be Rising
	567TH	Thine Arm, O Lord in Days of Old
15:22	234LW	To You, Omniscient Lord of All
15:29-39	86SFGP	Break Now the Bread of Life (Sts.1,2)
15:30-31	567TH	Thine Arm, O Lord, in Days of Old
15:32	472TH	Hope of the World, Thou Christ of Great Compassion
	303HB	Where Cross the Crowded Ways of Life
16:2-3	618WB	We Are Living, We Are Dwelling
16:13-20	443TH	From God Christ's Deity Came Forth
16:13-19	254TH	You Are the Christ, O Lord
16:15-18	146HB	The Church's One Foundation
16:16	598PH	This Is the Good News
16:18	154HU	Founded on Thee
	144HB	Glorious Things of Thee Are Spoken
	178HB	Onward, Christian Soldiers
16:19	235LW	As Surely as I Live, God Said
16:24-26	572TH	Weary of All Trumpeting (St.3)
16:24-25	277PH	O God, Our Faithful God
	110SFGP	O Love That Wilt Not Let Me Go (St.4)
16:24	379LW	"Come, Follow Me," Said Christ, the Lord
	176HB	"Take Up Your Cross," The Savior Said
	381LW	Let Us Ever Walk With Jesus
	360HB	New Every Morning Is the Love
	387LW	Praise and Thanks and Adoration
	484TH	Praise the Lord Through Every Nation
	47SFGP	Rise Up, O Saints of God (St.5)
17:1-2	303HB	Where Cross the Crowded Ways of Life
	129TH	Christ Upon the Mountain Peak
	64SFGP	Christus Paradox (St.2)
	133TH	O Light of Light, Love Given Birth
	87LW	Oh, Wondrous Type! Oh, Vision Fair
	443HB	Songs of Thankfulness and Praise (St.4)
	73PH	Swiftly Pass the Clouds of Glory
	89LW	How Good, Lord to Be Here

21:1-11	395HB	Hark! the Glad Sound! the Savior Comes (St.4)
	442HB	My Song Is Love Unknown
	65TH	Prepare the Way, O Zion
	449HB	Ride On! Ride On in Majesty
	50TH	This Is the Day the Lord Hath Made (Sts.3-5)
	480TH	When Jesus Left His Father's Throne
21:1-9	424HB	A Stable Lamp Is Lighted (St.2)
	19LW	O Lord, How Shall I Meet You
	571WB	So Lowly Does the Savior Ride
21:5	34LW	Come, O Precious Ransom
	20LW	O Bride of Jesus, Rejoice
21:6-9	447HB	All Glory, Laud and Honor
21:8-9	279UM	Filled with Excitement
	448HB	Hosanna, Loud Hosanna
	442HB	My Song Is Love Unknown
	19LW	O Lord, How Shall I Meet You
	27LW	Prepare the Royal Highway
	277UM	Tell Me the Stories of Jesus
21:9	97SFGP	Holy, Holy Lord
	117SFGP	Holy, Holy, Holy Lord
	16LW	Hosanna Now Through Advent
	460LW	When Morning Gilds the Skies
21:13	51TH	We the Lord's People, Heart and Voice Uniting
21:14-17	38SFGP	Come, Children, Join to Sing (St.1)
21:15	447HB	All Glory, Laud, and Honor
	448HB	Hosanna, Loud Hosanna
21:16	447HB	All Glory, Laud, and Honor
21:22	145HB	Christ Is Made the Sure Foundation
	114HB	What a Friend We Have in Jesus
22:1-14	333HB	Deck Thyself, My Soul, With Gladness
	346LW	O Kingly Love, That Faithfully
22:9-10	321LW	Spread the Reign of God the Lord
22:9	303HB	Where Cross the Crowded Ways of Life
22:32	401TH	The God of Abraham Praise
22:37-40	172HB	Rise Up, Ye Saints of God
	581TH	Where Charity and Love Prevail

22:37-39	43SFGP	Love, Love, Love Your God
22:37	85SFGP	Spirit of God, Descend Upon My Heart (Sts.1,3)
	579WB	Take Thou Our Minds, Dear Lord
22:39	58SFGP	For the Fruit of All Creation (St.2)
22:41-46	42HB	All Hail the Power of Jesus' Name
23:37-39	590TH	O Jesus Christ, May Grateful Hymns Be Rising
24:1-2	598TH	Lord Christ, When First Thou Cam'st to Earth (St.2)
24:12-13	53TH	Once He Came in Blessing
24:29-30	449PH	My Lord! What a Morning
24:30	454TH	Jesus Came, Adored by Angels
	393HB	Lo! He Comes, With Clouds Descending
24:31	368LW	My Hope Is Built on Nothing Less
25:1-13	130SFGP	Give Me Oil (St.1)
	394HB	"Sleepers, Wake!" A Voice Astounds Us
	68TH	Rejoice! Rejoice, Believers
	177LW	Wake, Awake, for Night Is Flying
25:5	302LW	Rise, My Soul, to Watch and Pray
25:6	176LW	The Bridegroom Soon Will Call Us
25:6-7	177LW	Wake, Awake, for Night Is Flying
25:10	177LW	Wake, Awake, for Night Is Flying
25:13	302LW	Rise, My Soul, to Watch and Pray
25:14-30	56SFGP	God, Whose Giving Knows No Ending (St.2)
	410PH	When I Had Not Yet Learned of Jesus
25:23	415PH	Come, Labor On
25:31-46	421TH	All Glory Be to God on High
	124SFGP	God, You Meet Us (St.3)
	610TH	Lord, Whose Love Through Humble Service
	44HB	Rejoice, the Lord Is King
	36SFGP	Teach Me, Lord, to Wonder
	30SFGP	There's a Spirit in the Air (Sts.3,5)
	131SFGP	When I Needed a Neighbour
25:31-46	434UM	When the Poor Ones

	303HB	Where Cross the Crowded Ways of Life
25:31-34	462LW	The Day Is Surely Drawing Near
25:31	480HB	Crown Him With Many Crowns
	26LW	The King Shall Come
25:35-36	407PH	When a Poor One
25:40	395LW	O Fount of Good, for All Your Love
	397LW	O God of Mercy, God of Light
26:26-29	126LW	At the Lamb's High Feast We Sing
	209HU	Broken Bread and Outpoured
	305TH	Come, Risen Lord, and Deign to Be Our Guest
	340TH	For the Bread Which You Have Broken
	60SFGP	I Come With Joy
	15SFGP	Jesus, to Your Table Led (St.2)
	528TH	Lord, You Give the Great Commission (St.3)
	341HB	Now, My Tongue, the Mystery Telling
	244LW	O Living Bread From Heaven
	107LW	The Death of Jesus Christ, Our Lord
	51TH	We the Lord's People, Heart and Voice Uniting
	322TH	When Jesus Died to Save Us
	320TH	Zion, Praise Thy Savior, Singing
26:26-28	94PH	An Upper Room Did Our Lord Prepare
	243LW	Here, O My Lord, I See You Face to Face
26:28	332HB	Let All Mortal Flesh Keep Silence
26:30	420TH	When in Our Music God Is Glorified (St.4)
26:36-46	451HB	Go to Dark Gethsemane (St.1)
26:36-38	511LW	In the Hour of Trial
26:39-42	68SFGP	O Bread of Life
26:41	302LW	Rise, My Soul, to Watch and Pray
26:56	443HB	Ah, Holy Jesus, How Hast Thou Offended
	454HB	Alone Thou Goest Forth, O Lord
26:57-27:31	451HB	Go to Dark Gethsemane (St.2)
26:64-67	94LW	Christ, the Life of All the Living
26:69-75	443HB	Ah, Holy Jesus, How Hast Thou Offended
	231TH	By All Your Saints Still Striving

26:69-75	640WB	When We Are Tempted to Deny Your Song
27:15-26	443HB	Ah, Holy Jesus, How Hast Thou Offended
	442HB	My Song Is Love Unknown
27:24	180HU	Am I My Brother's Keeper
27:27-54	452HB	O Sacred Head, Sore Wounded
27:27-31	598TH	Lord Christ, When First Thou Cam'st to Earth
	100HB	O Love, How Deep, How Broad, How High
	170TH	To Mock Your Reign, O Dearest Lord
27:32-54	451HB	Go to Dark Gethsemane (St.3)
27:33-61	172TH	Were You There When They Crucified My Lord
27:33-54	446HB	Sing, My Tongue, the Glorious Battle
27:33-46	94LW	Christ, the Life of All the Living
27:33-37	101HB	There Is a Green Hill Far Away
27:33-35	96LW	Come to Calvary's Holy Mountain
27:35	95PH	He Never Said a Mumbalin' Word
27:37	100LW	On My Heart Imprint Your Image
27:45-50	18TH	As Now the Sun Shines Down at Noon
27:45	466HB	Christ the Lord Is Risen Today
	16TH	Now Let Us Sing Our Praise to God
	126SFGP	She Flies On (St.5)
	163TH	Sunset to Sunrise Changes Now
	23TH	The Fleeting Day Is Nearly Gone
27:46	112LW	Jesus, in Your Dying Woes
	99PH	Throned Upon the Awful Tree
	406PH	Why Has God Forsaken Me?
27:50	93LW	Savior, When in Dust to You
27:57-66	442HB	My Song Is Love Unknown
27:57-60	122LW	O Darkest Woe
27:60	93LW	Savior, When in Dust to You
27:62-66	173TH	O Sorrow Deep
27:63	468HB	The Strife Is O'er, the Battle Done
27:66	464HB	Come, You Faithful, Raise the Strain
28:1-10	291WB	All Praise to God in Highest Heaven
	231TH	By All Your Saints Still Striving

28:1-10	107PH	Celebrate with Joy and Singing
	327WB	Christ Jesus Lay in Death's Strong Bands
	184TH	Christ the Lord Is Risen Again
	183TH	Christians, to the Paschal Victim
	464HB	Come, Ye Faithful, Raise the Strain
	469HB	Good Christians All, Rejoice and Sing
	180TH	He Is Risen, He Is Risen
	465HB	Jesus Christ Is Risen Today
	190TH	Lift Your Voice Rejoicing, Mary
	196TH	Look There! the Christ, Our Brother, Comes
	467HB	O Sons and Daughters, Let Us Sing
	201TH	On Earth Has Dawned This Day of Days
	474HB	That Easter Day with Joy Was Bright
	374HB	The Day of Resurrection
	468HB	The Strife Is O'er, the Battle Done
28:1-8	673TH	The First One Ever, Oh Ever, to Know (St.3)
28:1-7	474HB	That Easter Day With Joy Was Bright
28:1	452TH	Glorious Day When Christ Was Born
	203LW	O Day of Rest and Gladness
	48TH	O Day of Radiant Gladness
	373HB	On This Day, the First of Days
	52TH	This Day at Thy Creating Word
	50TH	This Is the Day the Lord Hath Made
28:2-7	284TH	O Ye Immortal Throng (St.6)
28:2-3	41HB	Thine Is the Glory
28:6	713TH	Christ Is Arisen
	466HB	Christ the Lord Is Risen Today
	480HB	Crown Him With Many Crowns
	505LW	Were You There
28:7	34SFGP	Alleluia, Alleluia, Give Thanks (St.2)
28:9,16-17	474HB	That Easter Day With Joy Was Bright
28:16-20	320LW	On Galilee's High Mountain
	222TH	Rejoice, the Lord of Life Ascends
	49HB	Alleluia! Sing to Jesus (St.2)
28:18-20	389UM	Freely, Freely
	429PH	Lord, You Give the Great Commission
	621WB	We Bear the Strain of Earthly Care
28:18	220TH	O Lord Most High, Eternal King

28:19-29	48HB	O For a Thousand Tongues to Sing
28:19-20	571UM	Go, Make of All Disciples
	297TH	Descend O Spirit, Purging Flame
	422PH	God, Whose Giving Knows No Ending
	528TH	Lord, You Give the Great Commission
	531TH	O Spirit of the Living God
	139TH	When Jesus Went to Jordan's Stream (St.3)
	583UM	You Are the Seed
28:19	224LW	Baptized Into Your Name Most Holy
	68HB	I Bind Unto Myself Today
	539TH	O Zion, Haste, Thy Mission High Fulfilling
	223LW	To Jordan Came the Christ, Our Lord
28:20	182TH	Christ Is Alive! Let Christians Sing
	342TH	O Bread of Life, For Sinners Broken

Mark

1:1-11	116TH	"I Come," the Great Redeemer Cries
	121TH	Christ, When For Us You Were Baptized
	100HB	O Love, How Deep, How Broad, How High
	443HB	Songs of Thankfulness and Praise (St.2)
	120TH	The Sinless One to Jordan Came
	131TH	When Christ's Appearing Was Made Known
	139TH	When Jesus Went to Jordan's Stream
1:1-8	103HB	Herald, Sound the Note of Judgment
	391HB	On Jordan's Bank the Baptist's Cry
	69TH	What Is the Crying at the Jordan
1:1-5	59TH	Hark! a Thrilling Voice Is Sounding
1:1-4	67TH	Comfort, Comfort Ye My People
	153HB	There's a Voice in the Wilderness Crying
1:1-3	65TH	Prepare the Way, O Zion
1:6	143TH	The Glory of These Forty Days (St.3)
1:9-13	126SFGP	She Flies On (St.4)
1:9-11	71PH	Lord, When You Came to Jordan
	223LW	To Jordan Came the Christ, Our Lord

1:9-11	252UM	When Jesus Came to Jordan
1:10	265HB	Come, Gracious Spirit, Heavenly Dove
	244HB	Come, Holy Spirit, Heavenly Dove
	513TH	Like the Murmur of the Dove's Song
	60HB	Spirit Divine, Attend Our Prayers
1:12-15	120TH	The Sinless One to Jordan Came (St.4)
1:12-13	438HB	Forty Days and Forty Nights
	443TH	From God Christ's Deity Came Forth
	142TH	Lord, Who Throughout These Forty Days
	146TH	Now Let Us All With One Accord
	92LW	O Lord, Throughout These Forty Days
	100HB	O Love, How Deep, How Broad, How High
	284TH	O Ye Immortal Throng (St.3)
	143TH	The Glory of These Forty Days
1:16-20	276TH	For Thy Blest Saints, a Noble Throng (St.2)
	249HB	Dear Lord and Father of Mankind (St.2)
	377PH	Lord, You Have Come to the Lakeshore
	661TH	They Cast Their Nets in Galilee
1:16-18	231TH	By All Your Saints Still Striving
	166HB	Jesus Calls Us; O'er the Tumult
1:17	249HB	Dear Lord and Father of Mankind (St.2)
1:21-2:12	567TH	Thine Arm, O Lord, in Days of Old
1:21-28	74SFGP	Silence, Frenzied, Unclean Spirit
1:24	421TH	All Glory Be to God on High
1:32-34	314HT	At Evening, When the Sun Had Set
1:41	367UM	He Touched Me
2:1-12	443HB	Songs of Thankfulness and Praise (St.3)
2:13-14	231TH	By All Your Saints Still Striving
	281TH	He Sat to Watch O'er Customs Paid
2:14-17	706TH	In Your Mercy, Lord, You Called Me
3:1-12	433HB	Songs of Thankfulness and Praise (St.3)
	567TH	Thine Arm, O Lord, in Days of Old
3:9-10	590TH	O Jesus Christ, May Grateful Hymns Be Rising
4:2-20	588TH	Almighty God, Your Word Is Cast

4:2-20	541TH	Come, Labor On
4:9,23	536TH	God Has Spoken to His People
4:14	374PH	Lord, Make Us Servants of Your Peace
4:18-20	257LW	Let Me Be Yours Forever
4:26-32	588TH	Almighty God, Your Word Is Cast
4:26-29	216LW	Almighty Father, Bless the Word
	384HB	Come, Ye Thankful People, Come (St.2)
	217LW	On What Has Now Been Sown
4:28	338LW	When Seed Falls on Good Soil
4:30-32	366HB	The Day Thou Gavest, Lord, Is Ended
	275UM	The Kingdom of God
4:35-41	221HB	Eternal Father, Strong to Save
	509UM	Jesus, Savior, Pilot Me
	373PH	Lonely the Boat
	512UM	Stand By Me
5:1-43	567TH	Thine Arm, O Lord, in Days of Old
5:15	249HB	Dear Lord and Father of Mankind (St.1)
5:21-43	48HB	O For a Thousand Tongues to Sing
5:25-34	266UM	Heal Us, Emmanuel, Hear Our Prayer
	590TH	O Jesus Christ, May Grateful Hymns Be Rising
6:3	661TH	Christ the Worker
	586TH	Jesus, Thou Divine Companion
6:34	472TH	Hope of the World, Thou Christ of Great Compassion
6:41	329PH	Break Thou the Bread of Life
6:47-52	221HB	Eternal Father, Strong to Save
6:53-56	567TH	Thine Arm, O Lord, in Days of Old
	26SFGP	Your Hands, O Christ
6:56	590TH	O Jesus Christ, May Grateful Hymns Be Rising
7:1-8	336PH	As a Chalice Cast of Gold
7:14-15	336PH	As a Chalice Cast of Gold
7:21-23	336PH	As a Chalice Cast of Gold
7:24-37	567TH	Thine Arm, O Lord, in Days of Old
7:31-37	48HB	O For a Thousand Tongues to Sing
	633TH	Word of God, Come Down on Earth

7:32-37	400LW	O Son of God, in Galilee
8:22-26	48HB	O For a Thousand Tongues to Sing
	567TH	Thine Arm, O Lord, in Days of Old
	633TH	Word of God, Come Down on Earth
8:27-30	254TH	You Are the Christ, O Lord
8:34-36	572TH	Weary of All Trumpeting (St.3)
8:34-35	176HB	Take Up Thy Cross
8:34	414WB	He Who Would Valiant Be
	360HB	New Every Morning Is the Love
	484TH	Praise the Lord Through Every Nation
	176HB	Take Up Your Cross, the Savior Said
	338UM	Where He Leads Me
8:38	393LW	Jesus! Oh, How Could It Be True
9:2-8	129TH	Christ Upon the Mountain Peak
	133TH	O Light of Light, Love Given Birth
	136TH	O Wondrous Type! O Vision Fair
	433HB	Songs of Thankfulness and Praise (St.4)
	73TH	Swiftly Pass the Clouds of Glory
9:2-6	89LW	How Good, Lord, to Be Here
9:14-29	567TH	Thine Arm, O Lord, in Days of Old
9:14-27	266UM	Heal Us, Emmanuel, Hear Our Prayer
9:24	42SFGP	Jesus, Help My Unbelief
9:35	301HB	O Master, Let Me Walk With Thee
9:40-41	433PH	There's a Spirit in the Air
9:41	303HB	Where Cross the Crowded Ways of Life
10:2-9	350TH	O God of Love, to Thee We Bow
	352TH	O God, to Those Who Here Profess
10:13-16	226LW	Dearest Jesus, We Are Here
	475LW	Gracious Savior, Gentle Shepherd
	312MH	See Israel's Gentle Shepherd Stand
	277UM	Tell Me the Stories of Jesus
	480TH	When Jesus Left His Father's Throne
10:13-14	123HB	Jesus Loves Me!
10:14-16	228LW	Our Children Jesus Calls
10:14	473LW	You Parents, Hear What Jesus Taught
10:17-31	304HB	O Jesus, I Have Promised
10:27	135HB	A Mighty Fortress

10:28	251MH	Jesus, I My Cross Have Taken
10:33-34	468HB	The Strife Is O'er, the Battle Done
10:35-40	530UM	Are Ye Able
	231TH	By All Your Saints Still Striving
	276TH	For Thy Blest Saints, a Noble Throng
10:43-45	301HB	O Master, Let Me Walk With Thee
10:46-52	48HB	O For a Thousand Tongues to Sing
	567TH	Thine Arm, O Lord, in Days of Old
	633TH	Word of God, Come Down on Earth
11:1-11	486TH	Hosanna to the Living Lord
11:1-10	424HB	A Stable Lamp Is Lighted (St.2)
	447HB	All Glory, Laud and Honor
	74TH	Blest Be the King Whose Coming
	395HB	Hark! the Glad Sound! the Savior Comes (St.4)
	448HB	Hosanna, Loud Hosanna
	442HB	My Song Is Love Unknown
	65TH	Prepare the Way, O Zion
	449HB	Ride On! Ride On in Majesty
	50TH	This Is the Day the Lord Hath Made (Sts.3-5)
	480TH	When Jesus Left His Father's Throne
11:8-10	447HB	All Glory, Laud and Honor
	279UM	Filled With Excitement
	277UM	Tell Me the Stories of Jesus
11:9	568PH	Holy, Holy, Holy Lord
11:17	51TH	We the Lord's People, Heart and Voice Uniting
11:20-25	650UM	Give Me the Faith Which Can Remove
11:22	431HT	Have Faith in God, My Heart
11:24	145HB	Christ Is Made the Sure Foundation
	711TH	Seek Ye First the Kingdom of God
11:25-26	674TH	Forgive Our Sins as We Forgive
11:25	581TH	Where Charity and Love Prevail
12:29-31	172HB	Rise Up, Ye Saints of God
	581TH	Where Charity and Love Prevail
12:35-37	42HB	All Hail the Power of Jesus' Name

13:1-2	598TH	Lord Christ, When First Thou Cam'st to Earth (St.2)
13:13	304HB	O Jesus, I Have Promised
13:24-29	454TH	Jesus Came, Adored by Angels
13:24-27	393HB	Lo! He Comes, With Clouds Descending
13:26-27	16LW	Hosanna Now Through Advent
13:32-37	394HB	"Sleepers, Wake!" A Voice Astounds Us
	68TH	Rejoice! Rejoice, Believers
13:33	355HT	Christian Seek Not Yet Repose
14:15-25	305TH	Come, Risen Lord, and Deign to Be Our Guest
14:22-25	174TH	At the Lamb's High Feast We Sing
	326HB	Bread of the World
	340TH	For the Bread Which You Have Broken
	341HB	Now, My Tongue, the Mystery Telling
	213HU	This Do Remembering Me
	51TH	We the Lord's People, Heart and Voice Uniting
	322TH	When Jesus Died to Save Us
	249LW	Your Table I Approach
	320TH	Zion, Praise Thy Savior, Singing
14:24-25	528TH	Lord, You Give the Great Commission (St.3)
14:26	449LW	When in Our Music God Is Glorified
14:32-42	431MH	'Tis Midnight, and on Olive's Brow
	451HB	Go to Dark Gethsemane (St.1)
14:36	170HU	Have Thine Own Way, Lord
	167MH	My Jesus, As Thou Wilt
14:50	443HB	Ah, Holy Jesus, How Hast Thou Offended
	454HB	Alone Thou Goest Forth, O Lord
14:53-15:20	451HB	Go to Dark Gethsemane (St.2)
14:53-72	443HB	Ah, Holy Jesus, How Hast Thou Offended
14:62	454TH	Jesus Came, Adored by Angels
	393HB	Lo! He Comes, With Clouds Descending
14:66-72	231TH	By All Your Saints Still Striving
15:1	451HB	Go to Dark Gethsemane
15:6-15	443HB	Ah, Holy Jesus, How Hast Thou Offended
	442HB	My Song Is Love Unknown

15:16-39	452HB	O Sacred Head, Sore Wounded
15:16-20	598TH	Lord Christ, When First Thou Cam'st to Earth
	170TH	To Mock Your Reign, O Dearest Lord
15:21-39	451HB	Go to Dark Gethsemane (St.3)
	446HB	Sing, My Tongue, the Glorious Battle
15:22-47	172TH	Were You There When They Crucified My Lord
15:22-28	101HB	There Is a Green Hill Far Away
15:25	12TH	The Golden Sun Lights up the Sky
15:29-30	90LW	Jesus, Refuge of the Weary
15:33-36	18TH	As Now the Sun Shines Down at Noon
15:33	16TH	Now Let Us Sing Our Praise to God
	163TH	Sunset to Sunrise Changes Now
	23TH	The Fleeting Day Is Nearly Gone
15:34	605WB	Throned Upon the Awful Tree
15:42-47	442HB	My Song Is Love Unknown
	173TH	O Sorrow Deep
16:1-11	231TH	By All Your Saints Still Striving
	183TH	Christians, to the Paschal Victim
	184TH	Christ the Lord Is Risen Again
	464HB	Come, Ye Faithful, Raise the Strain
	469HB	Good Christians All, Rejoice and Sing
	180TH	He Is Risen, He Is Risen
	465HB	Jesus Christ Is Risen Today
	190TH	Lift Your Voice Rejoicing, Mary
	196TH	Look There! the Christ, Our Brother, Comes
	467HB	O Sons and Daughters, Let Us Sing
	201TH	On Earth Has Dawned This Day of Days
	374HB	The Day of Resurrection
	673TH	The First One Ever, Oh Ever, to Know (St.3)
	468HB	The Strife Is O'er, the Battle Done
16:1-8	107PH	Celebrate with Joy and Singing
16:2-9	452TH	Glorious Day When Christ Was Born
	48TH	O Day of Radiant Gladness
	373HB	On This Day, the First of Days
	52TH	This Day at Thy Creating Word

16:2-9	50TH	This Is the Day the Lord Hath Made
	51TH	We the Lord's People, Heart and Voice Uniting
16:5-7	284TH	O Ye Immortal Throng (St.6)
16:6	713TH	Christ Is Arisen
	466HB	Christ the Lord Is Risen Today
16:15-16	297TH	Descend, O Spirit, Purging Flame
	139TH	When Jesus Went to Jordan's Stream (St.3)
16:15	34SFGP	Alleluia, Alleluia, Give Thanks
16:16	225LW	All Who Believe and Are Baptized
16:19	217TH	A Hymn of Glory Let Us Sing
	49HB	Alleluia! Sing to Jesus
	477HB	Hail the Day That Sees Him Rise
	194TH	Jesus Lives! Thy Terrors Now
	220TH	O Lord Most High, Eternal King
	215TH	See the Conqueror Mounts in Triumph
	219TH	The Lord Ascendeth Up on High

Luke

1:1-4	285TH	What Thanks and Praise to Thee We Owe
1:5-25, 57-80	231TH	By All Your Saints Still Striving
	271TH	The Great Forerunner of the Morn
1:5-38	282TH	Christ, the Fair Glory of the Holy Angels (St.3)
1:26-56	265TH	The Angel Gabriel From Heaven Came
	268TH	Ye Who Claim the Faith of Jesus
	7HB	Ye Watchers and Ye Holy Ones
1:26-38	231TH	By All Your Saints Still Striving
	396HB	Creator of the Stars of Night
	403HB	From East to West, From Shore to Shore (Sts.1-3)
	270TH	Gabriel's Message Does Away
	252TH	Jesus! Name of Wondrous Love
	81TH	Lo, How a Rose E'er Blooming
	266TH	Nova, Nova
	429HB	Of the Father's Love Begotten (St.2)
	267TH	Praise We the Lord This Day
	55TH	Redeemer of the Nations, Come

1:26-38	54TH	Saviour of the Nations, Come
	126SFGP	She Flies On (St.3)
	278TH	Sing We of the Blessed Mother
	673TH	The First One Ever, Oh, Ever to Know (St.1)
	263TH	The Word Whom Earth and Sea and Sky
	215UM	To a Maid Engaged to Joseph
	248TH	To the Name of Our Salvation
	258TH	Virgin-born, We Bow Before Thee
1:31	39HB	At the Name of Jesus
1:41	187LW	When All the World Was Cursed
1:44	187LW	When All the World Was Cursed
1:45	276UM	The First One Ever
1:46-55	374HU	My Soul Doth Magnify the Lord
	198UM	My Soul Gives Glory to My God
	211LW	My Soul Now Magnifies the Lord
	600PH	Song of Mary
	495HB	Tell Out, My Soul, the Greatness of the Lord
1:67-75	389HB	Come, O Long-Expected Jesus
1:68-79	444TH	Blessed Be the God of Israel
	446HB	Sing, My Tongue
	601PH	Song of Zechariah
1:70	314LW	O Christ, Our Light, O Radiance True
1:78-79	362HB	Christ, Whose Glory Fills the Skies
	390HB	O Come, O Come, Emmanuel
1:79	703TH	Lead Us, O Father, in the Paths of Peace
	314LW	O Christ, Our Light, O Radiance True
2:1-20	412HB	'Twas in the Moon of Wintertime
	103TH	A Child Is Born in Bethlehem
	51LW	A Great and Mighty Wonder
	424HB	A Stable Lamp Is Lighted
	279WB	Ah, Dearest Jesus, Holy Child
	210LW	All Glory Be to God Alone
	215LW	All Glory Be to God on High
	21PH	All My Heart Today Rejoices
	111HU	All My Heart This Night
	417HB	All Poor Men and Humble
	408HB	Angels from the Realms of Glory

2:1-20

90HU	Angels We Have Heard on High
96TH	Angels We Have Heard on High
110HU	As Ancient Sunlight
419HB	Away in a Manger, No Crib For His Bed
30PH	Born in the Night, Mary's Child
402HB	Break Forth, O Beauteous Heavenly Light
82UM	Canticle of God's Glory (Gloria in Excelsis)
106TH	Christians, Awake, Salute the Happy Morn
336TH	Come With Us, O Blessed Jesus
48LW	Come, Your Hearts and Voices Raising
97TH	Dost Thou in a Manger Lie
428HB	Every Star Shall Sing
66LW	Every Year the Christ Child
403HB	From East to West, From Shore to Shore
54PH	From Heaven Above
37LW	From Heaven Above to Earth I Come
52LW	From Heaven Came the Angels Bright
71LW	From Shepherding of Stars
420HB	Gentle Mary Laid Her Child
576PH	Gloria, Gloria
452TH	Glorious the Day When Christ Was Born
71UM	Glory Be to the Father
566PH	Glory to God in the Highest
99TH	Go Tell It on the Mountain
380WB	God Has Spoken--by His Prophets
105TH	God Rest You Merry, Gentlemen
469HB	Good Christian Friends, Rejoice and Sing
400HB	Good Christian Men, Rejoice
407HB	Hark! the Herald Angels Sing
54LW	He Whom Shepherds Once Came Praising
171LW	Holy God, We Praise Your Name
33PH	Holy Night, Blessed Night
56LW	I Am So Glad When Christmas Comes
34PH	In Bethlehem a Babe Was Born
418HB	In the Bleak Midwinter
229UM	Infant Holy, Infant Lowly
427HB	It Came Upon the Midnight Clear
401HB	Joy to the World!
44LW	Let All Together Praise Our God

2:1-20	128SFGP	Let There Be Peace on Earth
	324HB	Lord, Enthroned in Heavenly Splendor
	65PH	Midnight Stars Make Bright the Sky
	47LW	Now Sing We, Now Rejoice
	415HB	O Come, All Ye Faithful
	83LW	O God of God, O Light of Light
	421HB	O Little Town of Bethlehem
	308PH	O Sing a Song of Bethlehem
	284TH	O Ye Immortal Throng (St.2)
	429HB	Of the Father's Love Begotten
	40LW	Oh, Rejoice, All Christians, Loudly
	65LW	On Christmas Night All Christians Sing
	391HB	On Jordan's Bank
	92TH	On This Day Earth Shall Ring
	39LW	Once Again My Heart Rejoices
	112HB	Once in Royal David's City
	520LW	Rejoice! Rejoice This Happy Morn
	50PH	Rise up, Shepherd, and Follow
	14PH	Savior of the Nations, Come
	414HB	See Amid the Winter's Snow
	52PH	Sheep Fast Asleep
	416HB	Silent Night, Holy Night
	237UM	Sing We Now of Christmas
	426TH	Songs of Praise the Angels Sang (St.2)
	47PH	Still, Still, Still
	241UM	The Boy-Child of Mary
	410HB	The First Nowell
	227UM	The Friendly Beasts
	110TH	The Snow Lay on the Ground
	98TH	Unto Us a Boy Is Born
	38LW	Welcome to Earth, O Noble Guest
	53PH	What Child Is This
	232UM	When Christmas Morn Is Dawning
	491TH	Where Is This Stupendous Stranger
	405HB	While Shepherds Watched
	63LW	Who Are These That Earnest Knock
2:21	39HB	At the Name of Jesus
	252TH	Jesus! Name of Wondrous Love
	250TH	Now Greet the Swiftly Changing Year (St.2)

3:4-5	65TH	Prepare the Way, O Zion
3:16	245HB	Come, Holy Ghost, Our Souls Inspire
	500TH	Creator Spirit, By Whose Aid
	513TH	Like the Murmur of the Dove's Song
	501TH	O Holy Spirit, By Whose Breath
	239HB	O Thou Who Camest From Above
	60HB	Spirit Divine, Attend Our Prayers
3:21-22	116TH	"I Come," the Great Redeemer Cries
	121TH	Christ, When For Us You Were Baptized
	265HB	Come, Gracious Spirit, Heavenly Dove
	244HB	Come, Holy Spirit, Heavenly Dove
	513TH	Like the Murmur of the Dove's Song
	71PH	Lord, When You Came to Jordan
	100HB	O Love, How Deep, How Broad, How High
	604UM	Praise and Thanksgiving Be to God
	126SFGP	She Flies On (St.4)
	433HB	Songs of Thankfulness and Praise (St.2)
	60HB	Spirit Divine, Attend Our Prayers
	120TH	The Sinless One to Jordan Came
	223LW	To Jordan Came the Christ, Our Lord
	131TH	When Christ's Appearing Was Made Known (St.3)
	252UM	When Jesus Came to Jordan
	139TH	When Jesus Went to Jordan's Stream
4:1-15	120TH	The Sinless One to Jordan Came (St.4)
4:1-13	438HB	Forty Days and Forty Nights
	443TH	From God Christ's Deity Came Forth
	146TH	Now Let Us All With One Accord
	92LW	O Lord, Throughout These Forty Days
	100HB	O Love, How Deep, How Broad How High
	126SFGP	She Flies On (St.4)
	143TH	The Glory of These Forty Days
4:4	343TH	Shepherd of Souls, Refresh and Bless
4:16-21	395HB	Hark! the Glad Sound! the Savior Comes
4:16-20	332PH	Live Into Hope
4:17-19	166LW	Holy Spirit, Light Divine
	30LW	Once He Came in Blessing

4:18-19	24SFGP	I Am the Light of the World (St.2,3)
	539TH	O Zion, Haste, Thy Mission High Fulfilling
	115SFGP	The Spirit of the Lord
4:18	395HB	Hark, the Glad Sound
4:31-37	264UM	Silence, Frenzied, Unclean Spirit
4:31-34	567TH	Thine Arm, O Lord, in Days of Old
4:34	421TH	All Glory Be to God on High
5:1-11	276TH	For Thy Blest Saints, a Noble Throng (St.2)
	377PH	Lord, You Have Come to the Lakeshore
	661TH	They Cast Their Nets in Galilee
5:11	249HB	Dear Lord and Father of Mankind (St.2)
	386LW	Jesus, Still Lead On
5:12-26	567TH	Thine Arm, O Lord, in Days of Old
5:13	367UM	He Touched Me
5:17-26	433HB	Songs of Thankfulness and Praise (St.3)
5:27-32	706TH	In Your Mercy, Lord You Called Me
5:27-28	231TH	By All Your Saints Still Striving
	281TH	He Sat to Watch O'er Customs Paid
6:6-11	567TH	Thine Arm, O Lord, in Days of Old
6:12	249HB	Dear Lord and Father of Mankind (St.3)
6:20	73SFGP	Jesus the Christ Said (St.2)
6:43-45	392TH	Come, We That Love the Lord
	308HB	Lord, Dismiss Us With Thy Blessing
6:46-48	174HU	We Would Be Building
6:46-49	379PH	My Hope Is Built on Nothing Less
6:47-49	139HB	How Firm a Foundation, Ye Saints of the Lord
7:1-23	567TH	Thine Arm, O Lord, in Days of Old
7:1-17	48HB	O For a Thousand Tongues to Sing
7:13-35	271TH	The Great Forerunner of the Morn (St.4)
7:18-23	442HB	My Song Is Love Unknown
	139TH	When Jesus Went to Jordan's Stream (St.2)
7:26-35	643TH	My God, How Wonderful Thou Art

8:1-3	231TH	By All Your Saints Still Striving
8:2	567TH	Thine Arm, O Lord, in Days of Old
8:4-15	588TH	Almighty God, Your Word Is Cast
	541TH	Come, Labor On
	259LW	Preach You the Word
8:8	536TH	God Has Spoken to His People
8:22-25	221HB	Eternal Father, Strong to Save
	509UM	Jesus, Savior, Pilot Me
	373PH	Lonely the Boat
	512UM	Stand by Me
8:26-56	567TH	Thine Arm, O Lord, in Days of Old
8:39	247LW	Sent Forth by God's Blessing
8:40-56	48HB	O For a Thousand Tongues to Sing
8:43-48	266UM	Heal Us, Emmanuel, Hear Our Prayer
9:2	528TH	Lord, You Give the Great Commission
9:11	193LW	By All Your Saints in Warfare
9:18-22	254TH	You Are the Christ, O Lord
9:23-25	572TH	Weary of All Trumpeting (St.3)
9:23-24	176HB	Take Up Thy Cross
9:23-26	174HB	Stand Up, Stand Up for Jesus
9:23	76SFGP	We Have This Ministry (St.3)
9:28-36	129TH	Christ Upon the Mountain Peak
	89LW	How Good, Lord to Be Here
	133TH	O Light of Light, Love Given Birth
	87LW	Oh, Wondrous Type! Oh, Vision Fair
	433HB	Songs of Thankfulness and Praise (St.4)
	73PH	Swiftly Pass the Clouds of Glory
9:37-43	567TH	Thine Arm, O Lord, in Days of Old
9:51	268HB	Lead Us, Heavenly Father, Lead Us
9:57	304HB	O Jesus, I Have Promised
9:58	442HB	My Song Is Love Unknown
9:62	564TH	He Who Would Valiant Be
	304HB	O Jesus, I Have Promised
10:1-2	316LW	Send Now, O Lord, to Every Place
10:2	540TH	Awake, Thou Spirit of the Watchmen
	541TH	Come, Labor On
	318LW	Hark, the Voice of Jesus Calling
	260LW	Lord of the Living Harvest

12:35-40	68TH	Rejoice! Rejoice, Believers
12:49	541UM	See How Great a Flame Aspires
12:51-53	661TH	They Cast Their Nets in Galilee
13:6-9	392TH	Come, We That Love the Lord
	308HB	Lord, Dismiss Us With Thy Blessing
13:10-17	567TH	Thine Arm, O Lord, in Days of Old
13:18-21	366HB	The Day Thou Gavest, Lord, Is Ended
13:29	149HB	In Christ There Is No East or West
	217HU	One Table Spread
13:34-35	590TH	O Jesus Christ, May Grateful Hymns Be Rising
14:1-6	567TH	Thine Arm, O Lord, in Days of Old
14:15-24	333HB	Deck Thyself, My Soul, With Gladness
14:16-24	339UM	Come, Sinners, to the Gospel Feast
14:27	113HB	In the Cross of Christ
	484TH	Praise the Lord Through Every Nation
	176HB	Take Up Your Cross, the Savior Said
15:2-4	229LW	Jesus Sinners Will Receive
15:3-7	132HB	The King of Love My Shepherd Is
15:11-32	343UM	Come Back Quickly to the Lord
	48SFGP	Now the Silence, Now the Peace
15:20-24	347LW	Today Your Mercy Calls Us
15:24,32	49SFGP	Amazing Grace (St.1)
	44SFGP	Part of the Family
16:19-31	354TH	Into Paradise May the Angels Lead You
	356TH	May Choirs of Angels Lead You
17:3-4	674TH	"Forgive Our Sins as We Forgive"
17:5	142MH	O For a Faith that Will Not Shrink
17:11-19	567TH	Thine Arm, O Lord, in Days of Old
17:13	208LW	Lamb of God, Pure and Sinless
18:9-14	390PH	O Savior, in This Quiet Place
18:13	93LW	Savior, When in Dust to You
	234LW	To You, Omniscient Lord of All
18:15-17	227LW	This Child We Now Present to You

18:15-17	480TH	When Jesus Left His Father's Throne
18:15-16	123HB	Jesus Loves Me!
18:16	501WB	O God, This Child from You Did Come
18:18-30	304HB	O Jesus, I Have Promised
18:31-34	109LW	Jesus, I Will Ponder Now
18:31-33	468HB	The Strife Is O'er, the Battle Done
18:33	464HB	Come, You Faithful, Raise the Strain
18:35-43	48HB	O For a Thousand Tongues to Sing
	567TH	Thine Arm, O Lord, in Days of Old
	633TH	Word of God, Come Down to Earth
19:5-9	219HB	Our Father, By Whose Name
19:29-46	486TH	Hosanna to the Living Lord
19:29-40	424HB	A Stable Lamp Is Lighted (St.2)
19:29-39	447HB	All Glory, Laud, and Honor
	74TH	Blest Be the King Whose Coming
	395HB	Hark! the Glad Sound! The Savior Comes (St.4)
	442HB	My Song Is Love Unknown
	65TH	Prepare the Way, O Zion
	449HB	Ride On! Ride on in Majesty
	50TH	This Is the Day the Lord Hath Made (Sts.3-5)
	480TH	When Jesus Left His Father's Throne
19:36-38	447HB	All Glory, Laud, and Honor
	279UM	Filled With Excitement
19:37-38	20LW	O Bride of Christ, Rejoice
	460LW	When Morning Gilds the Skies
19:37-40	210LW	All Glory Be to God Alone
19:38	448HB	Hosanna, Loud Hosanna
19:39-40	424HB	A Stable Lamp Is Lighted
19:41-42	590TH	O Jesus Christ, May Grateful Hymns Be Rising
	303HB	Where Cross the Crowded Ways of Life
19:41	168HB	All Who Love and Serve Your City
	390LW	For Jerusalem You're Weeping
	437PH	Our Cities Cry to You, O God
	636WB	When Jesus Wept
19:43-44	598TH	Lord Christ, When First Thou Cam'st to Earth (St.2)

19:46	51TH	We the Lord's People, Heart and Voice Uniting
20:41-44	42HB	All Hail the Power of Jesus' Name
21:6	598TH	Lord Christ, When First Thou Cam'st to Earth (St.2)
21:19	53TH	Once He Came in Blessing
21:25-36	462LW	The Day Is Surely Drawing Near
21:25-28	454TH	Jesus Came, Adored by Angels
	393HB	Lo! He Comes With Clouds Descending
21:36	434LW	Christians, While on Earth Abiding
	463LW	The Clouds of Judgment Gather
21:38	637WB	When Morning Gilds the Skies
22:7-20	305TH	Come, Risen Lord, and Deign to Be Our Guest
22:14-20	174TH	At the Lamb's High Feast We Sing
	340TH	For the Bread Which You Have Broken
	528TH	Lord, You Give the Great Commission (St.3)
	341HB	Now My Tongue, the Mystery Telling
	515PH	Now to Your Table Spread
	51TH	We the Lord's People, Heart and Voice Uniting
	322TH	When Jesus Died to Save Us
	320TH	Zion, Praise Thy Savior, Singing
22:19-20	326HB	Bread of the World in Mercy Broken
22:19	316MH	According to Thy Gracious Word
	342TH	O Bread of Life, For Sinners Broken
22:26-27	301HB	O Master, Let Me Walk With Thee
22:30-31	474HB	That Easter Day With Joy Was Bright
22:31-32	511LW	In the Hour of Trial
22:39-46	451HB	Go to Dark Gethsemane (St.1)
22:39-43	284TH	O Ye Immortal Throng (St.4)
22:40b	301PH	Lord Jesus, Think on Me
22:54-23:25	451HB	Go to Dark Gethsemane (St.2)
22:54-62	443HB	Ah, Holy Jesus, How Hast Thou Offended
	231TH	By All Your Saints Still Striving
22:61	511LW	In the Hour of Trial

23:11	598TH	Lord Christ, When First Thou Cam'st to Earth
	452HB	O Sacred Head, Sore Wounded
	170TH	To Mock Your Reign, O Dearest Lord
23:13-25	442HB	My Song Is Love Unknown
23:18-25	443HB	Ah, Holy Jesus, How Hast Thou Offended
23:20-24	443HB	Ah, Holy Jesus, How Have You Offended
	119LW	O Dearest Jesus, What Law Have You Broken
23:26-49	451HB	Go to Dark Gethsemane (St.3)
	452HB	O Sacred Head, Sore Wounded
	446HB	Sing, My Tongue, the Glorious Battle
23:33-56	460HB	Were You There When They Crucified My Lord
23:33-34	240TH	Harken to the Anthem Glorious (St.3)
23:33	101HB	There Is a Green Hill Far Away
23:34	112LW	Jesus, in Your Dying Woes
	528TH	Lord, You Give the Great Commission (St.4)
23:38	100LW	On My Heart Imprint Your Image
23:39-43	354TH	Into Paradise May the Angels Lead You
	356TH	May Choirs of Angels Lead You
23:41-44	371UM	I Stand Amazed in the Presence
23:42	527UM	Do, Lord, Remember Me
	599PH	Jesus, Remember Me
	491UM	Remember Me
	560TH	Remember Your Servants, Lord
23:43	112LW	Jesus, in Your Dying Woes
23:44-46	97LW	Alas! and Did My Savior Bleed
	18TH	As Now the Sun Shines Down at Noon
23:44	16TH	Now Let Us Sing Our Praise to God
	23TH	The Fleeting Day Is Nearly Gone
	163TH	Sunset to Sunrise Changes Now
23:46	112LW	Jesus, in Your Dying Woes
	406PH	Why Has God Forsaken Me?
23:50-56	442HB	My Song Is Love Unknown
23:53	505LW	Were You There
24:1-11	276UM	The First One Ever
24:1-9	107PH	Celebrate With Joy and Singing

24:29	287LW	Abide With Us, Our Savior
	344LW	Lord Jesus Christ, Will You Not Stay
	488LW	Sun of My Soul, O Savior Dear
24:30	340WB	Come, Risen Lord, and Deign to Be Our Guest
24:30-35	505PH	Be Known to Us in Breaking Bread
24:34	133HU	Joy Dawned Again
24:36-43	474HB	That Easter Day With Joy Was Bright
24:46-47	34SFGP	Alleluia, Alleluia, Give Thanks (St.2)
24:47	322LW	From Greenland's Icy Mountains
24:47-48	321LW	Spread the Reign of God the Lord
24:47-53	247LW	Sent Forth by God's Blessing
24:50-51	217TH	A Hymn of Glory Let Us Sing
	49HB	Alleluia! Sing to Jesus (St.2)
	477HB	Hail the Day That Sees Him Rise
	194TH	Jesus Lives! Thy Terrors Now
	220TH	O Lord Most High, Eternal King
	222TH	Rejoice, the Lord of Life Ascends
	215TH	See the Conqueror Mounts in Triumph
	219TH	The Lord Ascendeth Up On High

John

1:1-18	421TH	All Glory Be to God on High
	443TH	From God Christ's Deity Came Forth
	452TH	Glorious the Day When Christ Was Born
	407HB	Hark! the Herald Angels Sing (Sts.2 & 3)
	415HB	O Come, All Ye Faithful (St.2)
	100HB	O Love, How Deep, How Broad, How High
	85TH	O Savior of Our Fallen Race
	429HB	Of the Father's Love Begotten
	112HB	Once in Royal David's City
	88TH	Sing, O Sing, This Blessed Morn (St.2)
	630TH	Thanks to God Whose Word Was Spoken
	489TH	The Great Creator of the Worlds
	381TH	Thy Strong Word Did Cleave the Darkness
	491TH	Where Is This Stupendous Stranger
	633TH	Word of God, Come Down on Earth

1:1-14	22SFGP	O Christ, the Word Incarnate (St.1)
	55TH	Redeemer of the Nations, Come
	54TH	Savior of the Nations, Come
	235HB	Thou, Whose Almighty Word
	69HT	When Things Began to Happen
1:1,14	197HU	O Word of God Incarnate
1:1-9	549PH	O Gladsome Light!
	14HU	O Splendor of God's Glory (St.1)
1:1-8	598WB	The True Light That Enlightens Man
1:1-7	319LW	O God, O Lord of Heaven and Earth
1:1-5	428HB	Every Star Shall Sing
1:1-4	45LW	O Savior of Our Fallen Race
	39HB	At the Name of Jesus
	38TH	Jesus, Redeemer of the World
	213LW	We All Believe in One True God, Maker
1:1-3	103SFGP	Morning Has Broken
1:4-5	115HB	I Heard the Voice of Jesus Say (St.3)
	649TH	O Jesus, Joy of Loving Hearts
1:5	402HB	Break Forth, O Beauteous Heavenly Light
	480WB	Now, on Land and Sea Descending
1:6-8	143TH	The Glory of These Forty Days (St.3)
1:9	542TH	Christ Is the World's True Light
	115HB	I Heard the Voice of Jesus Say (St.3)
	104SFGP	Many Are the Lightbeams (St.1)
	486LW	O Gladsome Light, O Grace
	101SFGP	O Laughing Light (St.3)
	110SFGP	O Love That Wilt Not Let Me Go (St.2)
1:12	506WB	O How Shall We Receive You
1:14-17	37TH	O Brightness of the Immortal Father's Face
1:14	62HB	Come, O Almighty King
	279HB	Father Eternal, Ruler of Creation
	74LW	From God the Father, Virgin-Born
	235HB	God, Whose Almighty Word
	407HB	Hark! The Herald Angels Sing
	481LW	O Splendor of the Father's Light
	335LW	O Word of God Incarnate
	429HB	Of the Father's Love Begotten
	331PH	Thanks to God Whose Word Was Written
	213LW	We All Believe in One True God, Maker

1:14	35LW	We Praise, O Christ, Your Holy Name
1:15-28	103HB	Herald, Sound the Note of Judgment
	391HB	On Jordan's Bank the Baptist's Cry
	69TH	What Is the Crying at Jordan
1:15-17	187LW	When All the World Was Cursed
1:19-36	59TH	Hark! a Thrilling Voice Is Sounding
1:19-23	67TH	Comfort, Comfort Ye My People
	153HB	There's a Voice in the Wilderness Crying
1:23	65TH	Prepare Ye the Way, O Zion
1:29-36	421TH	All Glory Be to God on High
	324HB	Lord, Enthroned in Heavenly Splendor
1:29-35	478HB	Hail, Thou Once Despised Jesus
1:29-34	116TH	"I Come," the Great Redeemer Cries
	121TH	Christ, When For Us You Were Baptized
	314PH	Like the Murmur of the Dove's Song
	100HB	O Love, How Deep, How Broad, How High
	433HB	Songs of Thankfulness and Praise (St.2)
	120TH	The Sinless One to Jordan Came
	131TH	When Christ's Appearing Was Made Known
	139TH	When Jesus Went to Jordan's Stream
1:29-30	391HB	On Jordan's Bank the Baptist's Cry
1:29,35-36	117HU	Behold the Lamb
	366HU	O Christ, Thou Lamb of God
1:29	111LW	A Lamb Alone Bears Willingly
	133PH	All Glory Be to God on High
	82UM	Canticle of God's Glory (Gloria in Excelsis)
	466HB	Christ the Lord Is Risen Today
	64SFGP	Christus Paradox (St.1)
	366LW	I Lay My Sins on Jesus
	213HT	Jesus, the Name High Over All
	284HB	Just as I am, Without One Plea
	208LW	Lamb of God, Pure and Sinless
	378LW	My Faith Looks Trustingly
	285HB	My Faith Looks Up to Thee
	82PH	O Lamb of God Most Holy!
	187LW	When All the World Was Cursed
1:32	265HB	Come, Gracious Spirit, Heavenly Dove

1:32	244HB	Come, Holy Spirit, Heavenly Dove
	513TH	Like the Murmur of the Dove's Song
	60HB	Spirit Divine, Attend Our Prayers
1:35-42	231TH	By All Your Saints Still Striving
	166HB	Jesus Calls Us; O'er the Tumult
1:35-36	18LW	Hark! A Thrilling Voice Is Sounding
	208LW	Lamb of God, Pure and Sinless
1:40-51	193LW	By All Your Saints in Warfare
1:40-42	276TH	For Thy Blest Saints, a Noble Throng (St.2)
1:43-46	231TH	By All Your Saints Still Striving
2:1-11	138TH	All Praise to You, O Lord
	642UM	As Man and Woman We Were Made
	443TH	From God Christ's Deity Came Forth
	109HT	Jesus, Come, For We Invite You
	302HT	Jesus, Lord We Pray
	297HT	Lord Jesus Christ, Invited Guest and Savior
	252LW	Lord, When You Came as Welcome Guest
	433HB	Songs of Thankfulness and Praise (St.2)
	81LW	When Christ's Appearing Was Made Known
3:1-8	297TH	Descend, O Spirit, Purging Flame
	295TH	Sing Praise to Our Creator
	296TH	We Know That Christ Is Raised and Dies No More
3:3-8	605UM	Wash, O God, Our Sons and Daughters
3:5	493PH	Dearest Jesus, We Are Here
	62SFGP	Now There Is No Male or Female (St.3)
3:8	314PH	Like the Murmur of the Dove's Song
	30SFGP	There's a Spirit in the Air (Sts.1,7)
3:14-15	321HB	Lift High the Cross
	603TH	When Christ Was Lifted From the Earth
3:15	340PH	Eternal Light, Shine in My Heart
3:16-17	489TH	The Great Creator of the Worlds (St.6)
3:16	421TH	All Glory Be to God on High
	53HU	God Is Love
	352LW	God Loved the World So That He Gave

3:16	54HU	I Sing the Praise of Love
	530TH	Spread, O Spread, Thou Mighty Word
	330LW	The Gospel Shows the Father's Grace
	485PH	To God Be the Glory
3:21	8SFGP	Help Us Accept Each Other (St.3)
3:30	27SFGP	O Jesus Christ, Grow Thou in Me (St.1)
4:1-42	673TH	The First One Ever, Oh, Ever to Know (St.2)
4:5-15	641UM	Fill My Cup, Lord
4:6	18TH	As Now the Sun Shines Down at Noon
4:7-26	276UM	The First One Ever
4:7-15	327TH	Draw Nigh and Take the Body of the Lord
	144HB	Glorious Things of Thee Are Spoken
4:13-14	90SFGP	Come, Let Us Sing (St.2)
	115HB	I Heard the Voice of Jesus Say
	649TH	O Jesus, Joy of Loving Hearts
	700TH	O Love That Casts Out Fear
4:14	77HB	Jesus, Lover of My Soul
4:35	540TH	Awake, Thou Spirit of the Watchmen
	541TH	Come, Labor On
	318LW	Hark, the Voice of Jesus Calling
4:37-38	289TH	Our Father, By Whose Servants
4:46-54	48HB	O For a Thousand Tongues to Sing
	567TH	Thine Arm, O Lord, in Days of Old
4:53	219HB	Our Father, by Whose Name
5:1-18	48HB	O For a Thousand Tongues to Sing
	433HB	Songs of Thankfulness and Praise (St.3)
	567TH	Thine Arm, O Lord, in Days of Old
5:43	65TH	Prepare the Way, O Zion
	50TH	This Is the Day the Lord Hath Made
6:16-21	221HB	Eternal Father, Strong to Save
6:25-69	326HB	Bread of the World, in Mercy Broken
	633TH	Word of God, Come Down to Earth
6:25-59	49HB	Alleluia! Sing to Jesus (St.3)
	323TH	Bread of Heaven, On Thee We Feed
	327TH	Draw Nigh, and Take the Body of the Lord

6:25-59	302TH	Father, We Thank Thee Who Has Planted
	269HB	Guide Me, O Thou Great Jehovah
	318TH	Here, O My Lord, I See Thee Face to Face
	472TH	Hope of the World, Thou Christ of Great Compassion
	116HB	How Sweet the Name of Jesus Sounds
	314TH	Humbly I Adore Thee, Verity Unseen
	335TH	I Am the Bread of Life
	324HB	Lord, Enthroned in Heavenly Splendor
	342TH	O Bread of Life, For Sinners Broken
	308TH	O Food to Pilgrims Given
	322HB	O God, Unseen Yet Ever Near
	649TH	O Jesus, Joy of Loving Hearts
	343TH	Shepherd of Souls, Refresh and Bless
	320TH	Zion, Praise Thy Savior, Singing
6:27	306HB	Forth in Your Name, O Lord, I Go
6:32-59	185TH	Christ Jesus Lay in Death's Strong Bands (St.4)
6:32-35	86SFGP	Break Now the Bread of Life (St.3)
	248LW	Lord Jesus Christ, Life-Giving Bread
6:33	220LW	Guide Me Ever, Great Redeemer
6:34	629UM	You Satisfy the Hungry Heart
6:35-58	630UM	Become to Us the Living Bread
	326HB	Bread of the World
	332HB	Let All Mortal Flesh Keep Silence
	631UM	O Food to Pilgrims Given
	627UM	O the Depth of Love Divine
6:35	333HB	Deck Thyself, My Soul, With Gladness
	628UM	Eat This Bread
	641UM	Fill My Cup, Lord
	243LW	Here, O My Lord, I See You Face to Face
	115HB	I Heard the Voice of Jesus Say
	343HB	Jesus, Thou Joy of Loving Hearts
	244LW	O Living Bread From Heaven
	239LW	Soul, Adorn Yourself With Gladness
6:37	345LW	Come Unto Me, Ye Weary
	77HB	Jesus, Lover of My Soul
	284HB	Just as I Am, Without One Plea
	93SFGP	Shepherd, Like a Shepherd Lead Us (St.3)

6:38-39	72LW	The Only Son From Heaven
6:41-48	501PH	Bread of Heaven, on Thee We Feed
6:44-45	153LW	Draw Us to You
6:48-51	209HU	Broken Bread and Outpoured
	73SFGP	Jesus the Christ Said (St.1)
	66SFGP	There's a Quiet Understanding
6:48	248LW	Lord Jesus Christ, Life-Giving Bread
6:50-57	236LW	Jesus Christ, Our Blessed Savior
6:51	326HB	Bread of the World
	68SFGP	O Bread of Life
6:53-58	15SFGP	Jesus, to Your Table Led (St.1)
6:54,68	340PH	Eternal Light, Shine in My Heart
6:55	398HT	Bread of Heaven, on You We Feed
	411HT	In the Quiet Consecration
6:63-68	202LW	Dearest Jesus, at Your Word
6:63	47SFGP	Rise Up, O Saints of God (St.5)
6:68-69	358LW	Seek Where You May to Find a Way
6:69	421TH	All Glory Be to God on High
7:37-38	327TH	Draw Nigh and Take the Body of the Lord
	115HB	I Heard the Voice of Jesus Say (St.2)
	649TH	O Jesus, Joy of Living Hearts
	347LW	Today Your Mercy Calls Us
7:42	443TH	From God Christ's Deity Came Forth
8:12	402HB	Break Forth, O Beauteous
	365LW	Christ Be My Leader
	542TH	Christ Is the World's True Light
	119HB	Christ Is the World's Light
	362HB	Christ, Whose Glory Fills the Skies
	S10HT	Come, Let Us Worship Christ
	206LW	God Himself Is Present
	24SFGP	I Am the Light of the World
	115HB	I Heard the Voice of Jesus Say (St.3)
	490TH	I Want to Walk as a Child of the Light
	104SFGP	Many Are the Lightbeams (St.1)
	314LW	O Christ, Our Light, O Radiance True
	101SFGP	O Laughing Light (St.3)
	481LW	O Splendor of the Father's Light
	14HU	O Splendor of God's Glory

8:12	672TH	O Very God of Very God
8:31	334LW	Lord, Keep Us Steadfast in Your Word
8:31b-32	202LW	Dearest Jesus, at Your Word
8:32	86SFGP	Break Now the Bread of Life (St.3)
	84SFGP	God of All Being, Throned Afar (Sts.3,4)
	392PH	Take Thou Our Minds, Dear Lord
8:44-46	446LW	Jehovah, Let Me Now Adore You
8:58	401TH	The God of Abraham Praise
	439TH	What Wondrous Love Is This
9:1-41	48HB	O For a Thousand Tongues to Sing
	567TH	Thine Arm, O Lord in Days of Old
	235HB	Thou, Whose Almighty Word
	633TH	Word of God, Come Down to Earth
9:2-3	280PH	Amazing Grace, How Sweet the Sound
9:4	168HB	All Who Love and Serve Your City
	192HU	Lord God of Hosts
9:5	115HB	I Heard the Voice of Jesus Say (St.3)
9:25	49SFGP	Amazing Grace, How Sweet the Sound (St.1)
	437HT	Lord, I Was Blind; I Could Not See
10:1-30	478TH	Jesus, Our Mighty Lord
	132HB	The King of Love My Shepherd Is
10:1-18	708TH	Savior, Like a Shepherd Lead Us
10:1-5	629UM	You Satisfy the Hungry Heart
10:9	S10HT	Come, Let Us Worship Christ
	73SFGP	Jesus the Christ Said (St.2)
	44LW	Let All Together Praise Our God
10:10	23SFGP	For the Healing of the Nations (St.3)
10:11-30	305HT	Loving Shepherd of Your Sheep
10:11	443HB	Ah, Holy Jesus, How Have You Offended
	64SFGP	Christus Paradox (St.1)
	73SFGP	Jesus the Christ Said (St.2)
	119LW	O Dearest Jesus, What Law Have You Broken
	93SFGP	Saviour, Like a Shepherd Lead Us
	131HB	The Lord's My Shepherd
10:14-16	334TH	Praise the Lord, Rise Up Rejoicing
10:14	292LW	In Adam We Have All Been One

10:15	469HB	Good Christians All, Rejoice and Sing (St.4)
10:28	527PH	Near to the Heart of God
11:1-44	48HB	O For a Thousand Tongues to Sing
11:16	381LW	Let Us Ever Walk With Jesus
11:25-27	335TH	I Am the Bread of Life
	212LW	We All Believe in One True God, Father
11:25	145LW	I Am Content! My Jesus Ever Lives
	73SFGP	Jesus the Christ Said (St.4)
11:35	715TH	When Jesus Wept, the Falling Tear
	406PH	Why Has God Forsaken Me?
12:12-19	486TH	Hosanna to the Living Lord
12:12-15	424HB	A Stable Lamp Is Lighted (St.2)
	447HB	All Glory, Laud and Honor
	74TH	Blest Be the King Whose Coming
	395HB	Hark! the Glad Sound! The Savior Comes (St.4)
	442HB	My Song Is Love Unknown
	65TH	Prepare the Way, O Zion
	449HB	Ride On! Ride On in Majesty
	50TH	This Is the Day the Lord Hath Made
	480TH	When Jesus Left His Father's Throne
12:12-13	279UM	Filled With Excitement
	448HB	Hosanna, Loud Hosanna
12:13	568PH	Holy, Holy, Holy Lord
	277UM	Tell Me the Stories of Jesus
12:20-22	193LW	By All Your Saints in Warfare
12:24-25	47SFGP	Rise Up, O Saints of God (St.5)
12:24	100SFGP	Now the Green Blade Riseth
12:26	304HB	O Jesus, I Have Promised
12:32-36	321HB	Lift High the Cross
	603TH	When Christ Was Lifted From the Earth
12:32	153LW	Draw Us to You
	356LW	Drawn to the Cross, Which You Have Blessed
12:35-36,46	490TH	I Want to Walk as a Child of the Light
12:35-36	115HB	I Heard the Voice of Jesus Say (St.3)
12:46	362HB	Christ, Whose Glory Fills the Skies
	115HB	I Heard the Voice of Jesus Say (St.3)

12:46	672TH	O Very God of Very God
13:1-17	69SFGP	Jesu, Jesu, Fill Us With Your Love
13:3-5	94PH	An Upper Room Did Our Lord Prepare
13:7	159HB	God Moves in a Mysterious Way
13:34-35	526HT	The New Commandment
14:1-3	194TH	Jesus Lives! Thy Terrors Now
14:2-3	1TH	Father, We Praise Thee, Now the Night Is Over
	112HB	Once in Royal David's City
	48TH	Praise the Lord Through Every Nation
14:2	264LW	I Know That My Redeemer Lives
14:3	150LW	On Christ's Ascension I Now Build
14:5-9	490TH	I Want to Walk as a Child of the Light (St.2)
14:6	487TH	Come, My Way, My Truth, My Life
	413WB	He Is the Way
	465PH	Here, O Lord, Your Servants Gather
	116HB	How Sweet the Name of Jesus Sounds
	457PH	I Greet Thee, Who My Sure Redeemer Art
	478TH	Jesus, Our Mighty Lord
	73SFGP	Jesus the Christ Said (St.2)
	703TH	Lead Us, O Father, in the Paths of Peace
	76MH	Thou Art the Way: To Thee Alone
	485PH	To God Be the Glory
	283LW	You Are the Way; to You Alone
14:9-11	149LW	A Hymn of Glory Let Us Sing
14:13-14	145HB	Christ Is Made the Sure Foundation
	433LW	Come, My Soul, With Every Care
	711TH	Seek Ye First the Kingdom of God
	248TH	To the Name of Our Salvation
14:15-21	241HB	Love Divine, All Loves Excelling
14:15	280LW	Jesus, Your Boundless Love So True
14:16-18	412WB	He Did Not Want to Be Far
14:16	215LW	All Glory Be to God on High
	67HB	Come Down, O Love Divine
	500TH	Creator Spirit, By Whose Aid
	228TH	Holy Spirit, Font of Light

14:16	514TH	To Thee, O Comforter Divine
14:17	321PH	Holy Spirit, Truth Divine
14:18	398PH	There's a Sweet, Sweet Spirit
14:23,26	67HB	Come Down, O Love Divine
14:23	375LW	You Will I Love, My Strength
14:26	454PH	Blessed Jesus, at Your Word
	245HB	Come, Holy Ghost, Our Souls Inspire
	422WB	Holy Spirit, Truth Divine
14:27	350UM	Come, All of You
14:35	510HT	Come, Let Us Worship Christ
15:1-11	513TH	Like the Murmur of the Dove's Song
	76SFGP	We Have This Ministry (St.2)
15:1-8,16	308HB	Lord, Dismiss Us With Thy Blessing
15:1-6	323TH	Bread of Heaven, On Thee We Feed
	198TH	Thou Hallowed Chosen Morn of Praise
15:1-5	273LW	Amid the World's Bleak Wilderness
	418PH	God, Bless Your Church With Strength
15:5	194LW	By All Your Saints in Warfare
	397UM	I Need Thee Every Hour
	314PH	Like the Murmur of the Dove's Song
	104SFGP	Many Are the Lightbeams (St.2)
	44SFGP	Part of the Family (St.3)
15:7	145HB	Christ Is Made the Sure Foundation
15:12-17	343PH	Called as Partners in Christ's Service
	60SFGP	I Come With Joy
15:12-13	367PH	Jesu, Jesu, Fills Us With Your Love
15:12	560UM	Help Us Accept Each Other
15:13	480HB	Crown Him With Many Crowns (St.4)
	442HB	My Song Is Love Unknown
	319TH	You, Lord, We Praise in Songs of Celebration
15:14-16	348TH	Lord, We Have Come at Your Own Invitation
	114HB	What a Friend We Have in Jesus
15:14-15	659UM	Jesus Our Friend and Brother
15:15	38SFGP	Come, Children, Join to Sing (St.2)
15:16	706TH	In Your Mercy, Lord, You Called Me
	107HT	My Lord, I Did Not Choose You
15:16b	145HB	Christ Is Made the Sure Foundation

15:19	507WB	O I Know the Lord
15:26-27	150HU	O Spirit of the Living God
	514TH	To Thee, O Comforter Divine
15:26	62HB	Come, Thou Almighty King
16:13-15	265HB	Come, Gracious Spirit, Heavenly Dove
	156LW	Creator Spirit, Heavenly Dove
16:13-14	265HB	Come, Gracious Spirit, Heavenly Dove
16:13	154LW	Come, Holy Ghost, God and Lord
	79SFGP	God, We Praise You For the Morning (St.4)
	419WB	Holy Spirit, Dispel Our Sadness
	166LW	Holy Spirit, Light Divine
	155LW	To God the Holy Spirit Let Us Pray
16:22	442LW	In You Is Gladness
16:23	446LW	Jehovah, Let Me Now Adore You
	711TH	Seek Ye First the Kingdom of God
17:1-26	315TH	Thou, Who at Thy First Eucharist Didst Pray
17:8	354LW	I Know My Faith Is Founded
17:9-11	420HT	O Christ, at Your First Eucharist
17:17	86SFGP	Break Now the Bread of Life (St.3)
17:20-23	305TH	Come, Risen Lord, and Deign to Be Our Guest
17:23	163HU	Lord, Bless Our Homes
	382HB	Sing to the Lord of Harvest
18:12-19:16	451HB	Go to Dark Gethsemane (St.2)
18:15-27	443HB	Ah, Holy Jesus, How Hast Thou Offended
	231TH	By All Your Saints Still Striving
18:28-19:16	442HB	My Song Is Love Unknown
18:39-40	443HB	Ah, Holy Jesus, How Hast Thou Offended
19:2-5	598TH	Lord Christ, When First Thou Cam'st to Earth
	452HB	O Sacred Head, Sore Wounded
	170TH	To Mock Your Reign, O Dearest Lord
19:17-42	172TH	Were You There When They Crucified My Lord

20:1-18	673TH	The First One Ever, Oh, Ever to Know (St.3)
	468HB	The Strife Is O'er, the Battle Done
20:1	452TH	Glorious the Day When Christ Was Born
	48TH	O Day of Radiant Gladness
	373HB	On This Day, the First of Days
	52TH	This Day at Thy Creating Word
	50TH	This Is the Day the Lord Hath Made
	51TH	We the Lord's People, Heart and Voice Uniting
20:11-18	314UM	In the Garden (I Come to the Garden Alone)
	134UM	O Mary, Don't You Weep
20:19-31	212TH	Awake, Arise, Lift Up Your Voice
	467HB	O Sons and Daughters, Let Us Sing
	474HB	That Easter Day With Joy Was Bright
	209TH	We Walk by Faith, and Not by Sight
	39SFGP	Jesus, Stand Among Us
20:19-23	68SFGP	O Bread of Life
	6SFGP	Where Charity and Love Prevail (St.4)
20:19	370HB	Saviour, Again to Your Dear Name
20:21-23	235LW	As Surely as I Live, God Said
	258LW	God of the Prophets, Bless the Prophets' Sons
	263LW	Send, O Lord, Your Holy Spirit
20:22-23	511TH	Holy Spirit, Ever Living
20:22	240HB	Breathe on Me, Breath of God
	503UM	Let it Breathe on Me
	543UM	O Breath of Life
20:24-29	231TH	By All Your Saints Still Striving
	125SFGP	God, When I Stand (St.4)
	242TH	How Oft, O Lord, Thy Face Hath Shone
	393HB	Lo! He Comes, With Clouds Descending
	399PH	We Walk by Faith and Not by Sight
20:24	130LW	O Sons and Daughters of the King
20:26-29	130LW	O Sons and Daughters of the King
20:26-28	193LW	By All Your Saints in Warfare
21:15-17	231TH	By All Your Saints Still Striving
	472HT	Christian, Do You Hear the Lord?

21:15	517LW	I am Jesus' Little Lamb
	81SFGP	More Love to Thee, O Christ
21:15-17	192LW	By All Your Saints in Warfare
21:19-24	387LW	Praise and Thanks and Adoration
21:24	231TH	By All Your Saints Still Striving
	245TH	Praise God for John, Evangelist

Acts

1:1-14	586WB	The Friends of Christ Together
1:1-11	217TH	A Hymn of Glory Let Us Sing
	49HB	Alleluia! Sing to Jesus (St.2)
	477HB	Hail the Day That Sees Him Rise
	220TH	O Lord Most High, Eternal King
	222TH	Rejoice, the Lord of Life Ascends
	215TH	See the Conqueror Mounts in Triumph
	219TH	The Lord Ascendeth Up on High
1:1-3	285TH	What Thanks and Praise to Thee We Owe
1:5	461WB	Lord Jesus Christ, Our Lord Most Dear
1:8	67HB	Come Down, O Love Divine
	513TH	Like the Murmur of the Dove's Song
	501TH	O Holy Spirit, By Whose Breath
	531TH	O Spirit of the Living God
	539TH	O Zion, Haste, Thy Mission High Fulfil-ling
	506TH	Praise the Spirit in Creation
	521TH	Put Forth, O God, Thy Spirit's Might
1:9-11	149LW	A Hymn of Glory Let Us Sing
	152LW	Up Through the Endless Ranks of Angels
1:9	461HB	Hail Thee, Festival Day (Easter)
	476HB	Hail Thee, Festival Day (Ascension)
	481HB	Hail Thee, Festival Day (Pentecost)
	194TH	Jesus Lives! Thy Terrors Now
1:10-11	284TH	O Ye Immortal Throng (St.7)
1:11	388HB	All Beautiful the March of Days
	39HB	At the Name of Jesus
1:12-14	193LW	By All Your Saints in Warfare
	278TH	Sing We of the Blessed Mother
1:15-26	231TH	By All Your Saints Still Striving

2	229HT	Christians Lift Up Your Hearts
	537UM	Filled With the Spirit's Power
	240HT	Praise for the Spirit
	577HT	Spirit Divine, Inspire Our Prayers
2:1-42	230TH	A Mighty Sound From Heaven
	297TH	Descend, O Spirit, Purging Flame
	481HB	Hail Thee, Festival Day (Pentecost)
	223TH	Hail This Joyful Day's Return
	299TH	Spirit of God, Unleashed on Earth
	229TH	Spirit of Mercy, Truth, and Love
2:1-21	583WB	The Day of Pentecost Arrived
2:1-13	131PH	Wind Who Makes All Winds That Blow
2:1-11	128PH	On Pentecost They Gathered
	506TH	Praise the Spirit in Creation
2:1-4	129PH	Come, O Spirit, Dwell Among Us
	127PH	Come, O Spirit
	163LW	O Day Full of Grace
	203LW	O Day of Rest and Gladness
	531TH	O Spirit of the Living God
	126SFGP	She Flies On (St.5)
	108SFGP	Spirit, Spirit of Gentleness (St.3)
	611WB	Upon Your Great Church Universal
2:1-3	245HB	Come, Holy Ghost, Our Souls Inspire
	226TH	Come, Thou Holy Spirit Bright
	500TH	Creator Spirit, By Whose Aid
	228TH	Holy Spirit, Font of Light
	524PH	Holy Spirit, Lord of Love
	513TH	Like the Murmur of the Dove's Song
	197HB	Now Thank We All Our God
	501TH	O Holy Spirit, By Whose Breath
	239HB	O Thou Who Camest From Above
	60HB	Spirit Divine, Attend Our Prayers
2:1-2	579TH	Almighty Father, Strong to Save
2:1	48TH	O Day of Radiant Gladness
	373HB	On This Day, the First of Days
	52TH	This Day at Thy Creating Word
	51TH	We the Lord's People, Heart and Voice Uniting
2:3-4	353WB	Descend, O Spirit, Purging Flame
2:4	154LW	Come, Holy Ghost, God and Lord

2:4	322PH	Spirit of the Living God
2:15	12TH	The Golden Sun Lights Up the Sky
2:16-21	108SFGP	Spirit, Spirit of Gentleness (St.4)
2:17-18	223HB	God of Grace and God of Glory
2:21-36	271LW	Christ Is the World's Redeemer
2:21	39HB	At the Name of Jesus
	252TH	Jesus! Name of Wondrous Love
	248TH	To the Name of Our Salvation
2:22-36	184TH	Christ the Lord Is Risen Again
	455TH	O Love of God, How Strong and True
	215TH	See the Conqueror Mounts in Triumph
	492TH	Sing, Ye Faithful, Sing With Gladness
	471HB	This Joyful Eastertide
2:23-36	144LW	Triumphant from the Grace
2:24	123LW	Christ Jesus Lay in Death's Strong Bands
2:28	516WB	O Lord, Whose Gracious Presence Shone
2:29-32	466HB	Christ the Lord Is Risen Today
2:31-33	461HB	Hail Thee, Festival Day (Easter)
	476HB	Hail Thee, Festival Day (Ascension)
	481HB	Hail Thee, Festival Day (Pentecost)
2:32-33	421TH	All Glory Be to God on High
	366TH	Holy God, We Praise Thy Name
	364TH	O God, We Praise Thee, and Confess
2:33	64SFGP'	Christus Paradox (St.3)
2:36	108HB	The Head That Once Was Crowned With Thorns
2:38	408LW	I Am Trusting You, Lord Jesus
2:39	501WB	O God, This Child from You Did Come
3:1-10	23TH	The Fleeting Day Is Nearly Gone
3:12-26	492TH	Sing, Ye Faithful, Sing With Gladness
3:13	623WB	We Come Unto Our Fathers' God
3:14-15	442HB	My Song Is Love Unknown
3:15	122LW	O Darkest Woe
3:24-26	33LW	Let the Earth Now Praise the Lord
3:25	398WB	God of the Prophets! Bless the Prophets' Sons
4:7-12	252TH	Jesus! Name of Wondrous Love
	248TH	To the Name of Our Salvation

4:10-12	428WB	I Sing as I Arise Today
4:11-12	145HB	Christ Is Made the Sure Foundation
	379PH	My Hope Is Built on Nothing Less
	146HB	The Church's One Foundation
4:11	129PH	Come, O Spirit, Dwell Among Us
4:12	39HB	At the Name of Jesus
	457PH	I Greet Thee, Who My Sure Redeemer Art
	48HB	Oh, for a Thousand Tongues to Sing
	358LW	Seek Where You May to Find a Way
4:24-30	17LW	O Lord of Light, Who Made the Stars
4:33	469HB	Good Christians All, Rejoice and Sing!
4:36-37	231TH	By All Your Saints Still Striving
5:30-31	421TH	All Glory Be to God on High
	366TH	Holy God, We Praise Thy Name
	364TH	O God, We Praise Thee, and Confess
	108HB	The Head That Once Was Crowned With Thorns
	462HB	Welcome, Happy Morning
6:1-8:2	243TH	When Stephen, Full of Power and Grace
7:32	187HB	Faith of Our Fathers
	401TH	The God of Abraham Praise
7:54-60	231TH	By All Your Saints Still Striving
	237TH	Let Us Now Our Voices Raise (St.2)
	577HT	The Son of God Rides Out to War
7:55-56	421TH	All Glory Be to God on High
	366TH	Holy God, We Praise Thy Name
	364TH	O God, We Praise Thee, and Confess
7:59-60	240TH	Harken to the Anthem Glorious (St.2)
8:26-40	297TH	Descend, O Spirit, Purging Flame
9:1-22	256TH	A Light From Heaven Shone Round
	231TH	By All Your Saints Still Striving
	255TH	We Sing the Glorious Conquest
9:3-8	18TH	As Now the Sun Shines Down at Noon
9:6	374LW	Savior, Thy Dying Love

10:9	18TH	As Now the Sun Shines Down at Noon
10:37	391HB	On Jordan's Bank
10:39-40	462HB	"Welcome, Happy Morning!" Age to Age Shall Say
	476HB	Hail Thee, Festival Day (Ascension)
	461HB	Hail Thee, Festival Day (Easter)
10:42	421TH	All Glory Be to God on High
	366TH	Holy God, We Praise Thy Name
	364TH	O God, We Praise Thee, and Confess
	63TH	O Heavenly Word, Eternal Light
10:43	382WB	God Has Spoken--by His Prophets
10:44-48	297TH	Descend, O Spirit, Purging Flame
11:15	322PH	Spirit of the Living God
11:24	263LW	Send, O Lord, Your Holy Spirit
12:1-5	304LW	The Son of God Goes Forth to War
12:1-2	193LW	By All Your Saints in Warfare
	276TH	For Thy Blest Saints, a Noble Throng
12:25	231TH	By All Your Saints Still Striving
13:32-33	469HB	Good Christian Men, Rejoice and Sing
	33LW	Let the Earth Now Praise the Lord
13:52	515TH	Holy Ghost, Dispel Our Sadness
14:15	404WB	God, Who Made the Earth and Heaven
14:17	480PH	Praise Our God Above
15:34	231TH	By All Your Saints Still Striving
15:36-40	213TH	By All Your Saints Still Striving
16:9	322LW	From Greenland's Icy Mountains
16:26	527MH	And Can It Be That I Should Gain
16:32-34	219HB	Our Father, by Whose Name
17:6	506TH	Praise the Spirit in Creation
17:24	291LW	Built on the Rock
17:24-31	546HT	Lord, You Need No House
17:24-25	457WB	Lord, by Whose Breath All Souls and Seeds

17:26	465WB	Lord of All Nations, Grant Me Peace
	87SFGP	Praise Our Maker (St.1)
18:10	437PH	Our Cities Cry to You, O God
20:28	402LW	Lord of Glory, You Have Bought Us
	40TH	O Christ, You Are Both Light and Day
	146HB	The Church's One Foundation
	599WB	Thee We Adore, O Hidden Savior, Thee
20:30	540PH	God Be With You Till We Meet Again
20:35	402LW	Lord of Glory, You Have Bought Us
22:1-16	256TH	A Light From Heaven Shone Around
	231TH	By All Your Saints Still Striving
	255TH	We Sing the Glorious Conquest
22:6	18TH	As Now the Sun Shines Down at Noon
24:25	349LW	Delay Not, Delay Not, O Sinner, Draw Near
26:9-21	256TH	A Light from Heaven Shone Around
	231TH	By All Your Saints Still Striving
	255TH	We Sing the Glorious Conquest
26:13	18TH	As Now the Sun Shines Down at Noon
26:18	322LW	From Greenland's Icy Mountains
26:22	29HU	Great God, We Sing That Mighty Hand

Romans

2:16	63TH	O Heavenly Word, Eternal Light
3:5	355LW	Salvation Unto Us Has Come
3:10-26	151TH	From Deepest Woe I Cry to Thee
3:12	363LW	All Mankind Fell in Adam's Fall
3:23-25a	478HB	Hail, Thou Once Despised Jesus
3:23-24	671TH	Amazing Grace! How Sweet the Sound
	686TH	Come, Thou Fount of Every Blessing
3:25	357LW	I Trust, O Christ, in You Alone
3:25-26	368LW	My Hope Is Built on Nothing Less
3:28	353LW	Dear Christians, One and All

6:4	68HB	I Bind Unto Myself Today
	374HB	The Day of Resurrection
6:6-11	697TH	My God, Accept My Heart This Day
6:9-10	183TH	Christians, to the Paschal Victim
	469HB	Good Christians All, Rejoice and Sing (St.4)
6:9	466HB	Christ the Lord Is Risen Today
6:15-23	252TH	Jesus! Name of Wondrous Love (St.5)
6:16-23	396HB	Creator of the Stars of Night
	270TH	Gabriel's Message Does Away
6:16	257LW	Let Me Be Yours Forever
6:22	341PH	Blessed Assurance, Jesus in Mine!
8	225HT	Born by the Holy Spirit's Breath
	457HT	He Lives in Us, The Christ of God
8:2	225HU	Jesus, I Live to Thee
8:4	163HU	Lord, Bless Our Homes
8:6	566WB	Send Down Your Truth, O God
8:9	167LW	Creator Spirit, by Whose Aid
8:9-11	336WB	Come, Holy Spirit, God and Lord!
8:11	139LW	Jesus Lives! The Victory's Won
8:14-17	149HB	In Christ There Is No East or West
8:14-16	446LW	Jehovah, Let Me Now Adore You
8:14	213LW	We All Believe in One True God, Maker
8:15-17	404UM	Every Time I Feel the Spirit
8:15-16	219HB	Our Father, by Whose Name
8:15	165LW	Come, Oh, Come, O Quickening Spirit
8:18-25	46HU	Creation's Lord, We Give Thee
8:18-23	279HB	Father Eternal, Ruler of Creation
	23SFGP	For the Healing of the Nations (St.4)
	47SFGP	Rise Up, O Saints of God (St.4)
8:18-21	52HU	From the Slave Pens
8:18	621TH	Light's Abode, Celestial Salem
	186HB	O What Their Joy and Their Glory Must Be
8:19-23	396HB	Creator of the Stars of Night
8:19-21	180HB	Abide With Me
8:26-27	67HB	Come Down, O Love Divine
	146HU	Come, Holy Ghost, Our Souls
	148HU	Creator Spirit, Come to Us

8:26-27	698TH	Eternal Spirit of the Living Christ
	513TH	Like the Murmur of the Dove's Song
8:26	406UM	Canticle of Prayer
	77SFGP	Holy Spirit, Hear Us (St.2)
	576WB	Spirit of God, Man's Hope in All the Ages
	338WB	Come, O Come, Great Quickening Spirit
	432LW	Eternal Spirit of the Living Christ
	212LW	We All Believe in One True God, Father
8:27	79SFGP	God, We Praise You For the Morning
8:28	455HT	Father, Although I Cannot See
	368WB	Father, Whose Will Is Life and Good
	159HB	God Moves in a Mysterious Way
	429LW	I Leave All Things to God's Direction
	422LW	What God Ordains Is Always Good
8:29	100LW	On My Heart Imprint Your Image
8:31-32	415LW	All Depends on Our Possessing
8:31-39	407LW	If God Himself Be for Me
8:32	371WB	For Perfect Love So Freely Spent
	50SFGP	How Great Thou Art (St.3)
	321LW	Spread the Reign of God the Lord
	530TH	Spread, O Spread, Thou Mighty Word
8:32-33	69LW	Let Our Gladness Have No End
8:34-39	194TH	Jesus Lives! Thy Terrors Now
	447TH	The Christ Who Died But Rose Again
8:34	421TH	All Glory Be to God on High
	49HB	Alleluia! Sing to Jesus (St.3)
	478HB	Hail, Thou Once Despised Jesus
	366TH	Holy God, We Praise Thy Name
	364TH	O God, We Praise Thee, and Confess
8:35-39	384PH	O Love That Wilt Not Let Me Go
	369LW	Through Jesus' Blood and Merit
8:37	316LW	Send Now, O Lord, to Every Place
	171HB	Soldiers of Christ, Arise
8:37-39	485WB	O Christ, Whose Love Has Sought Us Out
8:38-39	284HB	Just as I Am, Without One Plea
8:38	442LW	In You Is Gladness
9:20-21	170HU	Have Thine Own Way, Lord
10:3-4	193HU	Where Restless Crowds

10:8-13	39HB	At the Name of Jesus
	252TH	Jesus! Name of Wondrous Love
	248TH	To the Name of Our Salvation
10:12-13	465PH	Here, O Lord, Your Servants Gather
10:14-17	507HT	How Shall They Hear the Word of God?
10:14-15	160HU	Lord, We Thank Thee
10:15	577WB	Spread, O Spread the Mighty Word
	321LW	Spread the Reign of God the Lord
11:17-21	153HU	The Church of Christ Is One
11:25-28	206HU	O Zion, Haste
11:33-36	159HB	God Moves in a Mysterious Way
11:33-35	76HB	There's a Wideness in God's Mercy
12:1-21	610TH	Lord, Whose Love Through Humble Service
12:1-2	414PH	As Those of Old Their Firstfruits Brought
	402HT	Father Almighty, We Your Humble Servants
	404LW	Take My Life, O Lord, Renew
	134SFGP	To Show by Touch and Word (St.2)
	116SFGP	Worship the Lord (St.5)
12:1	97LW	Alas! and Did My Saviour Bleed
	294HB	Take My Life, and Let It Be
12:3-8	104SFGP	Many Are the Lightbeams (Sts.3-5)
	76SFGP	We Have This Ministry (St.2)
12:4-8	513TH	Like the Murmurs of the Dove's Song
12:4-5	295LW	Blest Be the Tie That Binds
	576TH	God Is Love, and Where True Love Is
	581TH	Where Charity and Love Prevail
	606TH	Where True Charity and Love Dwell
12:6-8	228TH	Holy Spirit, Font of Life
	501TH	O Holy Spirit, by Whose Breath
12:9-21	593TH	Lord, Make Us Servants of Your Peace
12:15	133SFGP	The Servant Song (St.4)
12:17	347TH	Go Forth for God: Go to the World in Peace
13:1-7	497LW	God Bless Our Native Land
	502LW	Lord, While for Humankind We Pray

13:8-10	134SFGP	To Show by Touch and Word (St.3)
13:10-11	463WB	Lord of All Being, Throned Afar
13:11-14	547TH	Awake, O Sleeper, Rise from Death
13:11-12	394HB	"Sleepers, Wake!" A Voice Astounds Us
	365WB	Father, We Praise You
	18LW	Hark! A Thrilling Voice Is Sounding
13:12	613WB	Veiled in Darkness Judah Lay
14:7	302HB	Lord, Speak to Me
14:8	225HU	Jesus, I Live to Thee
	400PH	When We Are Living
14:9	480HB	Crown Him With Many Crowns
	478TH	Jesus, Our Mighty Lord
14:11	396HB	Creator of the Stars of Night
	252TH	Jesus! Name of Wondrous Love
	509WB	O Jesus Christ, to You May Hymns Be Rising
14:17	302HB	Lord, Speak to Me
	333HT	The Kingdom of God Is Justice and Joy
15:4	631TH	Book of Books, Our People's Strength
	628TH	Help Us, O Lord, To Learn
	22SFGP	O Christ, the Word Incarnate
	630TH	Thanks to God Whose Word Was Spoken
15:7	8SFGP	Help Us Accept Each Other (St.1)
	603TH	When Christ Was Lifted From the Earth
15:13	472TH	Hope of the World, Thou Christ of Great Compassion
	308HB	Lord, Dismiss Us With Thy Blessing
16:17	214HB	O God of Earth and Altar
16:25-26	62HU	God of the Prophets

1 Corinthians

1:10	576TH	God Is Love, and Where True Love Is
	581TH	Where Charity and Love Prevail
	606TH	Where True Charity and Love Dwell
1:18-25	446HB	Sing, My Tongue, the Glorious Battle

5:7b	324HB	Lord, Enthroned in Heavenly Splendor
6:11	295TH	Sing Praise to Our Creator
6:19-20	158HU	An Ancient Dwelling
	58HB	Blest Are the Pure in Heart
6:19	67HB	Come Down, O Love Divine
	500TH	Creator Spirit, By Whose Aid
9:24-27	422TH	Not Far Beyond the Sea, Nor High (St.3)
9:24-26	175HB	Fight the Good Fight With All Thy Might
9:24-25	357HB	Awake, My Soul, Stretch Every Nerve
9:24	27TH	O Blest Creator, Source of Light
10:1-4	149TH	Eternal Lord of Love, Behold Your Church
	144HB	Glorious Things of Thee Are Spoken
	269HB	Guide Me, O Thou Great Jehovah
	343TH	Shepherd of Souls, Refresh and Bless
	187TH	Through the Red Sea Brought at Last
10:1-2	78SFGP	Out of Deep Unordered Water (St.3)
10:3-4	324HB	Lord, Enthroned in Heavenly Splendor
	308TH	O Food to Pilgrims Given
	322HB	O God, Unseen Yet Ever Near
	79HB	Rock of Ages, Cleft For Me
10:12-13	438HB	Forty Days and Forty Nights
	142TH	Lord, Who Throughout These Forty Days
	146TH	Now Let Us All With One Accord
	143TH	The Glory of These Forty Days
10:16-17	305TH	Come, Risen Lord, and Deign to Be Our Guest
	304TH	I Come With Joy to Meet My Lord
	250LW	Lord Jesus Christ, We Humbly Pray
	620UM	One Bread, One Body
	44SFGP	Part of the Family (St.3)
	315TH	Thou, Who at Thy First Eucharist Didst Pray
	70SFGP	What Is the Place
	521PH	You Satisfy the Hungry Heart
10:16	240LW	Draw Near and Take the Body of the Lord
	247LW	Sent Forth by God's Blessing

10:17	146HB	The Church's One Foundation (St.2)
10:31	357HB	Awake, My Soul, and With the Stars
	626TH	Lord, Be Thy Word My Rule
11:23-29	236LW	Jesus Christ, Our Blessed Savior
11:23-26	174TH	At the Lamb's High Feast We Sing
	326HB	Bread of the World in Mercy Broken
	305TH	Come, Risen Lord, and Deign to Be Our Guest
	340TH	For the Bread Which You Have Broken
	220HU	Here, O My Lord
	246LW	Lord Jesus Christ, You Have Prepared
	528TH	Lord, You Give the Great Commission (St.3)
	341HB	Now, My Tongue, the Mystery Telling
	515PH	Now to Your Table Spread
	68SFGP	O Bread of Life
	51TH	We the Lord's People, Heart and Voice Uniting
	70SFGP	What Is the Place
	322TH	When Jesus Died to Save Us
	320TH	Zion, Praise Thy Savior, Singing
11:24	S6HT	Broken For Me
	342TH	O Bread of Life, For Sinners Broken
11:27-32	333HB	Deck Thyself, My Soul, With Gladness
11:27-28	325HB	Let Us Break Bread Together
11:28	242LW	I Come, O Savior, to Your Table
12	620UM	One Bread, One Body
12:3	S17HT	Jesus Is Lord! Creation's Voice Proclaims It
	218HT	Name of All Majesty
	505TH	O Spirit of Life, O Spirit of God
	506TH	Praise the Spirit in Creation
12:4-31	550UM	Christ, From Whom All Blessings Flow
12:4-13	104SFGP	Many Are the Lightbeams (Sts.3-5)
12:4-11	125PH	Come, Holy Spirit, Our Souls Inspire
	228TH	Holy Spirit, Font of Light
	501TH	O Holy Spirit, by Whose Breath
12:12-31	295TH	Sing Praise to Our Creator

12:12-31	296TH	We Know That Christ Is Raised and Dies No More
12:12-17	513TH	Like the Murmur of the Dove's Song
12:12-13,27	576TH	God Is Love, and Where True Love Is
	581TH	Where Charity and Love Prevail
	606TH	Where True Charity and Love Dwell
13	256HB	Gracious Spirit, Holy Ghost
	474HT	Holy Spirit, Gracious Guest
	531PH	Not for Tongues of Heaven's Angels
	335PH	Though I May Speak
13:1-3	408UM	The Gift of Love
13:4-7	13SFGP	Morning Glory, Starlit Sky (Sts.2-3)
13:12	525UM	We'll Understand It Better By and By
13:14	219HB	Our Father, by Whose Name
15	313UM	Christ Is Risen
	468HB	The Strife Is O'er
15:1-6	598PH	This Is the Good News
15:1-4	162HT	These Are the Facts as We Have Received Them
15:3-4, 35-36	204TH	Now the Green Blade Riseth
15:3-8	452TH	Glorious the Day When Christ Was Born
15:3-4	465HB	Jesus Christ Is Risen Today
15:3	355PH	Hear the Good News of Salvation
15:7	231TH	By All Your Saints Still Striving
15:10	671TH	Amazing Grace! How Sweet the Sound
	686TH	Come, Thou Fount of Every Blessing
15:12-23	109PH	Christ Is Risen
15:16-20	471HB	This Joyful Eastertide
15:17-20	124LW	Christ Is Arisen
15:19	360PH	Hope of the World
15:20,42	134HU	Alleluia! Hearts to Heaven
15:20-23, 35-50	191TH	Alleluia, Alleluia! Hearts and Voices Heavenward Raise
15:20	465HB	Jesus Christ Is Risen Today
	702UM	Sing With All the Saints in Glory
15:20-26	144LW	Triumphant From the Grave

15:20-22	464HB	Come, Ye Faithful, Raise the Strain
15:21-22	445TH	Praise to the Holiest in the Height
15:22	636UM	Christian People, Raise Your Song
	459HT	In Christ Shall All Be Made Alive
15:24-28	492TH	Sing, Ye Faithful, Sing With Gladness
15:25	44HB	Rejoice, the Lord Is King
	174HB	Stand Up, Stand Up for Jesus
15:26-28	110PH	Christ Jesus Lay in Death's Strong Bonds
15:30-58	621TH	Light's Abode, Celestial Salem
15:35ff	266LW	Jesus Christ, My Sure Defense
15:51-57	471HB	This Joyful Eastertide
15:51-54	468HB	Alleluia! The Strife Is O'er
15:51-52	719UM	My Lord, What a Morning
	704UM	Steal Away to Jesus
	44HB	Rejoice, the Lord Is King
15:54-57	188TH	Love's Redeeming Work Is Done
	468HB	The Strife Is O'er, the Battle Done
	220TH	O Lord Most High, Eternal King
	358TH	Christ the Victorious, Give to Your Servants
15:55-57	466HB	Christ the Lord Is Risen Today
	366TH	Holy God, We Praise Thy Name
	472TH	Hope of the World, Thou Christ of Great Compassion
	132LW	Make Songs of Joy
	364TH	O God, We Praise Thee, and Confess
	144LW	Triumphant From the Grave
15:55	180HB	Abide With Me: Fast Falls the Eventide
	123LW	Christ Jesus Lay in Death's Strong Bands
	138LW	He's Risen, He's Risen
15:57	377LW	Hope of the World
	520LW	Rejoice, Rejoice This Happy Morn
15:58	306HB	Forth in Your Name, O Lord, I Go
16:1-4	9TH	Not Here for High and Holy Things
	705TH	As Those of Old Their First Fruits Brought
16:13	511UM	Am I a Soldier of the Cross
	174HB	Stand Up, Stand Up For Jesus
	463LW	The Clouds of Judgment Gather

| 16:13 | 203HU | We Are Living |
| 16:14 | 134SFGP | To Show by Touch and Word (St.3) |

2 Corinthians

1:8-10	265LW	In the Very Midst of Life
1:20-22	697TH	My God, Accept My Heart This Day
1:21-22	686TH	Come, Thou Fount of Every Blessing
3:6	505TH	O Spirit of Life, O Spirit of God
3:17	388UM	O Come and Dwell in Me
3:18	52SFGP	Come, Thou Fount of Every Blessing (St.3)
	23SFGP	For the Healing of the Nations (St.4)
	307HB	From Glory to Glory Advancing, We Praise Thee, O Lord
	620TH	Jerusalem, My Happy Home
	241HB	Love Divine, All Loves Excelling
	133TH	O Light of Light, Love Given Birth (St.3)
	136TH	O Wondrous Type! O Vision Fair (St.5)
	373LW	Renew Me, O Eternal Light
4:1-12	76SFGP	We Have This Ministry
4:1-2	203HU	We Are Living
4:3-7	48HU	O Grant Us Light
4:4	287HU	Lighten the Darkness
4:6	362HB	Christ, Whose Glory Fills the Skies
	465TH	Eternal Light, Shine in My Heart
	274HB	Let There Be Light
	419TH	Lord of All Being, Throned Afar
	486LW	O Gladsome Light, O Grace
	5TH	O Splendor of God's Glory Bright
	481LW	O Splendor of the Father's Light (St.1)
	447HT	Out of Darkness, Let Light Shine
	328LW	Thy Strong Word
4:7-18	16HU	Strong Son of God
4:13	213LW	We All Believe in One True God, Maker
4:14	194TH	Jesus Lives! Thy Terrors Now
4:15	3HU	We Praise Thee, O God

8:8-15	292TH	O Jesus, Crowned With All Renown
8:9	42LW	Let Us All With Gladsome Voice
	63HT	Lord, You Were Rich Beyond All Splendour
	13SFGP	Morning Glory, Starlit Sky (St.4)
	40LW	Oh, Rejoice, All Christians, Loudly
9:1-15	705TH	As Those of Old Their First Fruits Brought
	9TH	Not Here for High and Holy Things
9:8	280PH	Amazing Grace, How Sweet the Sound
9:10-12	384HB	Come, Ye Thankful People, Come
9:15	245LW	O Jesus, Blessed Lord, My Praise
	364LW	Oh, How Great Is Your Compassion
11:2	146HB	The Church's One Foundation
12:7-10	124SFGP	God, You Meet Us (St.1)
	27SFGP	O Jesus Christ, Grow Thou in Me (St.2)
12:9	139HB	How Firm a Foundation, Ye Saints of the Lord
	171HB	Soldiers of Christ, Arise
13:14	351TH	May the Grace of Christ Our Savior

Galatians

1:1	461HB	Hail Thee, Festival Day (Easter)
	476HB	Hail Thee, Festival Day (Ascension)
	481HB	Hail Thee, Festival Day (Pentecost)
1:11-24	256TH	A Light From Heaven Shone Around
	231TH	By All Your Saints Still Striving
	255TH	We Sing the Glorious Conquest
1:18-19	231TH	By All Your Saints Still Striving
2:1-10	231TH	By All Your Saints Still Striving
2:20	34SFGP	Alleluia, Alleluia! Give Thanks (St.3)
	280LW	Jesus, Your Boundless Love So True
	697TH	My God, Accept My Heart This Day

2:20	414UM	Thou Hidden Love of God
3:7-9	6HU	The God of Abraham Praise
3:10-14	270TH	Gabriel's Message Does Away
3:16-21	355LW	Salvation Unto Us Has Come
3:23-4:7	294TH	Baptized in Water
	47SFGP	Rise Up, O Saints of God (St.2)
	295TH	Sing Praise to Our Creator
3:27-28	550UM	Christ, From Whom All Blessings Flow
	149HB	In Christ There Is No East or West
3:27	122SFGP	You Have Put on Christ
3:28	62SFGP	Now There Is No Male or Female (St.1)
	620UM	One Bread, One Body
	581TH	Where Charity and Love Prevail
4:4-5	407HB	Hark the Herald Angels Sing
4:6	446LW	Jehovah, Let Me Now Adore You
5:1	544HT	Freedom of Life Are Ours
	62SFGP	Now There Is No Male or Female (St.1)
	32SFGP	Walls That Divide
5:13	301HB	O Master, Let Me Walk With Thee
	133SFGP	The Servant Song
5:22-23	236HT	May We O Holy Spirit Bear Your Fruit
5:22	58SFGP	For the Fruit of All Creation (St.3)
	513TH	Like the Murmur of the Dove's Song
	57SFGP	Love, Joy and Peace
5:24	697TH	My God, Accept My Heart This Day
5:25-26	279HB	Father Eternal, Ruler of Creation
	163HU	Lord, Bless Our Homes
5:25	326PH	Spirit of God, Descend Upon My Heart
6:2	180HU	Am I My Brother's Keeper
	9SFGP	Blest Be the Tie That Binds (St.3)
	343PH	Called as Partners in Christ's Service
	133SFGP	The Servant Song
	76SFGP	We Have This Ministry (St.2)
	184HU	When I Needed a Neighbor
6:7-8	374PH	Lord, Make Us Servants of Your Peace
6:8	58SFGP	For the Fruit of All Creation (St.3)

6:14	163UM	Ask Me What Great Thing I Know
	440HB	Beneath the Cross of Jesus
	113HB	In the Cross of Christ I Glory
	178TH	Jesus Is Lord of All the Earth (St.3)
	697TH	My God, Accept My Heart This Day
	434TH	Nature With Open Volume Stands
	446HB	Sing, My Tongue
	108HB	The Head That Once Was Crowned With Thorns
	118LW	We Sing the Praise of Him Who Died
	109HB	When I Survey the Wondrous Cross
6:15	176TH	Over the Chaos of the Empty Waters
	296TH	We Know That Christ Is Raised and Dies No More

Ephesians

1:3-4	706TH	In Your Mercy, Lord, You Called Me
1:3-8	370LW	Blest the Children of Our God
1:4-6	295TH	Sing Praise to Our Creator
1:5-8	671TH	Amazing Grace! How Sweet the Sound
	686TH	Come, Thou Fount of Every Blessing
1:7-14	465PH	Here, O Lord, Your Servants Gather
1:7-8	76HB	There's a Wideness in God's Mercy
1:7	478HB	Hail, Thou Once Despised Jesus
	38TH	Jesus, Redeemer of the World
	434TH	Nature With Open Volume Stands
1:9-11	57HU	God Is Working His Purpose Out
1:9	159HB	God Moves in a Mysterious Way
1:10	492TH	Sing, Ye Faithful, Sing With Gladness
1:12-14	32SFGP	Walls That Divide (St.4)
1:13-14	294TH	Baptized in Water
	686TH	Come, Thou Fount of Every Blessing
	697TH	My God, Accept My Heart This Day
	514TH	To Thee, O Comforter Divine
1:17-19a	324PH	Open My Eyes That I May See
1:19-23	302HU	Holy God, We Praise Thy Name
	136LW	Today in Triumph Christ Arose
1:20-22	64SFGP	Christus Paradox (St.3)
1:20	421TH	All Glory Be to God on High

1:20	366TH	Holy God, We Praise Thy Name
	3364TH	O God, Be Praise Thee, and Confess
1:22-23	145HB	Christ Is Made the Sure Foundation
	293LW	Lord Jesus Christ, the Church's Head
2:4-10	671TH	Amazing Grace! How Sweet the Sound
	686TH	Come, Thou Fount of Every Blessing
	706TH	In Your Mercy, Lord, You Called Me
2:8-10	385UM	Let Us Plead For Faith Alone
2:8-9	351LW	By Grace I'm Saved
	151TH	From Deepest Woe I Cry to Thee
2:8	233HU	Amazing Grace
	44SFGP	Part of the Family
	79HB	Rock of Ages, Cleft for Me
2:11-22	471PH	O Praise the Gracious Power
2:13-17	160HU	Lord, We Thank Thee
2:13-16	284HB	Just as I Am, Without One Plea
2:14-17	64SFGP	Christus Paradox (St.1)
	32SFGP	Walls That Divide
2:14-16	478HB	Hail, Thou Once Despised Jesus
2:15-22	343PH	Called as Partners in Christ's Service
2:19-22	291LW	Built on the Rock
	145HB	Christ Is Made the Sure Foundation
	235TH	Come Sing, Ye Choirs Exultant (St.3)
	67HU	Not Alone For Mighty Empire
	146HB	The Church's One Foundation
2:20-22	422LW	What God Ordains Is Always Good
3:1	242HB	Make Me a Captive, Lord
3:7-9	164LW	Holy Spirit, Ever Dwelling
3:12	378LW	My Faith Looks Trustingly
3:14-15	219HB	Our Father, By Whose Name
3:14-21	357HT	Father and God, From Whom Our World Derives
3:14-19	284HB	Just as I Am, Without One Plea
	422TH	Not Far Beyond the Sea, Nor High (St.2)
3:16-17	16LW	Hosanna Now Through Advent
3:16-21	280LW	Jesus, Your Boundless Love So True
3:17-21	100HB	Oh, Love, How Deep
3:17-19	366PH	Jesus, Thy Boundless Love to Me

3:17-19	455TH	O Love of God, How Strong and True
3:18-19	547TH	Awake, O Sleeper, Rise From Death (St.1)
4:1-16	521TH	Put Forth, O God, Thy Spirit's Might
4:3-6	9SFGP	Blest Be the Tie That Binds
4:3-5	547TH	Awake, O Sleeper, Rise From Death (Sts.2-3)
4:4-7	5HU	We Believe in One True God
4:4-6	305TH	Come, Risen Lord, and Deign to Be Our Guest
	252HB	Eternal Ruler of the Ceaseless Round
	178HB	Onward, Christian Soldiers
	527TH	Singing Songs of Expectation
	146HB	The Church's One Foundation (St.2)
4:4-5	152HB	Your Hand, O God, Has Guided
4:8-10	220TH	O Lord Most High, Eternal King
	492TH	Sing, Ye Faithful, Sing With Gladness
4:15	8SFGP	Help Us Accept Each Other (St.3)
4:22	12LW	The Advent of Our God
4:25	576TH	God Is Love, and Where True Love Is
	581TH	Where Charity and Love Prevail
	606TH	Where True Charity and Love Dwell
4:30	294TH	Baptized in Water
	514TH	To Thee, O Comforter Divine
4:31-32	576TH	God Is Love, and Where True Love Is
	581TH	Where Charity and Love Prevail
	606TH	Where True Charity and Love Dwell
4:32	547TH	Awake, O Sleeper, Rise From Death (St.4)
5:1-2	299HB	O Brother Man
5:2,14	547TH	Awake, O Sleeper, Rise From Death (St.4)
5:2	296LW	I Love Your Kingdom, Lord
	376LW	Love in Christ Is Strong and Living
5:8-14	490TH	I Want to Walk as a Child of the Light
5:15-20	490PH	With Glad, Exuberant Carolings
5:18-20	30SFGP	There's a Spirit in the Air
5:19-20	439LW	I Will Sing My Maker's Praises
	403LW	Praise and Thanksgiving
5:19	426TH	Songs of Praise the Angels Sang
	420TH	When in Our Music God Is Glorified

5:23-32	519TH	Blessed City, Heavenly Salem
	524TH	I Love Thy Kingdom, Lord
	146HB	The Church's One Foundation
5:24-33	351HB	O Perfect Love
5:30	576TH	God Is Love, and Where True Love Is
	581TH	Where Charity and Love Prevail
	606TH	Where True Charity and Love Dwell
5:31	350TH	O God of Love, to Thee We Bow
	352TH	O God, to Those Who Here Profess
6:10-18	303LW	Rise! To Arms! With Prayer Employ You
	171HB	Soldiers of Christ, Arise
6:10-17	252HB	Eternal Ruler of the Ceaseless Round
	171HB	Soldiers of Christ, Arise
	174HB	Stand Up, Stand Up for Jesus
6:10-12	135HB	A Mighty Fortress
6:11	534HT	Soldiers of the Cross, Arise
6:14-17	374UM	Standing on the Promises
6:24	404LW	Take My Life, O Lord, Renew

Philippians

1:9-11	392TH	Come, We That Love the Lord
	308HB	Lord, Dismiss Us With Thy Blessing
1:9	359PH	More Love to Thee, O Christ
1:21	195LW	For All Your Saints, O Lord
	267LW	For Me to Live Is Jesus
	268LW	Oh, How Blest Are You
1:27	153HU	The Church of Christ Is One
2:4	163HU	Lord, Bless Our Homes
2:5-11	42HB	All Hail the Power of Jesus' Name
	204HT	All Praise to Christ, My Lord and King Divine
	477TH	All Praise to Thee, For Thou, O King Divine
	39HB	At the Name of Jesus
	271LW	Christ Is the World's Redeemer
	64SFGP	Christus Paradox (St.1)

Colossians

2:12-14	373HB	On This Day, the First of Days
2:15	128LW	Awake, My Heart, With Gladness
3:1-4,15-17	346PH	Christ, You Are the Fullness
3:1	149LW	A Hymn of Glory Let Us Sing
	366TH	Holy God, We Praise Thy Name
	364TH	O God, We Praise Thee, and Confess
3:1-4	415LW	All Depends on Our Possessing
	150LW	On Christ's Ascension I Now Build
3:1-10	373LW	Renew Me, O Eternal Light
3:11	542TH	Christ Is the World's True Light
	149HB	In Christ There Is No East or West
	581TH	Where Charity and Love Prevail
3:12-15	576TH	God Is Love, and Where True Love Is
	593TH	Lord, Make Us Servants of Your Peace
	581TH	Where Charity and Love Prevail
	606TH	Where True Charity and Love Dwell
3:13-14	376LW	Love in Christ Is Strong and Living
3:13	674TH	Forgive Our Sins as We Forgive
3:16	349HU	Let Thy Word Abide
	426TH	Songs of Praise the Angels Sang
	420TH	When in Our Music God Is Glorified
3:17	661TH	Christ the Worker
	306HB	Forth in Your Name, O Lord, I Go
	261HB	Teach Me, My God and King
	483LW	With the Lord Begin Your Task
4:14	231TH	By All Your Saints Still Striving

1 Thessalonians

1:2-10	99SFGP	This Is the Threefold Truth
1:10	236LW	Jesus Christ, Our Blessed Savior
2:19-20	46HB	Fairest Lord Jesus
3:11-13	63TH	O Heavenly Word, Eternal Light
4:13-17	194TH	Jesus Lives! Thy Terrors Now
	471HB	This Joyful Eastertide

4:16-17	393HB	Lo! He Comes, With Clouds Descending
5,6	547TH	Awake, O Sleeper, Rise From Death
5	490HT	As Sons of the Day and Daughters of Light
5:5-9	302LW	Rise, My Soul, to Watch and Pray
5:8	252HB	Eternal Ruler of the Ceaseless Round
	171HB	Soldiers of Christ, Arise
	174HB	Stand Up, Stand Up For Jesus
5:14-21	347TH	Go Forth For God; Go to the World in Peace
5:17	114HB	What a Friend We Have in Jesus
5:23-24	540PH	God Be With You Till We Meet Again
5:23	166LW	Holy Spirit, Light Divine

2 Thessalonians

1:7-10	393HB	Lo! He Comes, With Clouds Descending
2:13	295TH	Sing Praise to Our Creator
3:1	315LW	Awake, Thou Spirit of the Watchman
3:3	421LW	In God, My Faithful God
3:6-15	357HB	Awake, My Soul, and With the Sun
	9TH	Not Here For High and Holy Things
3:16	219LW	Grant Peace, We Pray, in Mercy, Lord
	370HB	Savior, Again to Thy Dear Name We Raise

1 Timothy

1:1	472TH	Hope of the World, Thou Christ of Great Compassion
	368LW	My Hope Is Built on Nothing Less
1:6	263LW	Send, O Lord, Your Holy Spirit
1:17	26HB	Immortal, Invisible, God Only Wise
2:1-3	499LW	Christ, by Heavenly Hosts Adored

2:5-6	368TH	Holy Father, Great Creator
2:6	34LW	Come, O Precious Ransom
3:16	408HB	Angels From the Realms of Glory
	39LW	Once Again My Heart Rejoices
6:12	187HB	Faith of Our Fathers
	175HB	Fight the Good Fight
	304LW	The Son of God Goes Forth to War
6:14-16	169LW	Come, O Almighty King
	480HB	Crown Him With Many Crowns
6:15-16	153PH	He Is King of Kings
	26HB	Immortal, Invisible, God Only Wise
6:17	134HB	All My Hope on God Is Founded

2 Timothy

1:6-7	239HB	O Thou Who Camest From Above
1:7	166LW	Holy Spirit, Light Divine
1:8-10	151TH	From Deepest Woe I Cry to Thee
1:10	123LW	Christ Jesus Lay in Death's Strong Bands
1:12	354LW	I Know My Faith Is Founded
	714UM	I Know Whom I Have Believed
	448HT	I'm Not Ashamed to Name My Lord
2:2	302HB	Lord, Speak to Me That I May Speak
2:3-4	174HB	Stand Up, Stand Up For Jesus
2:3	178HB	Onward, Christian Soldiers
	171HB	Soldiers of Christ, Arise
2:11-12	108HB	The Head That Once Was Crowned With Thorns
2:13	277PH	O God, Our Faithful God
2:19	139HB	How Firm a Foundation
2:21	294HB	Take My Life, and Let It Be
2:22	58HB	Blest Are the Pure in Heart
3:14-17	631TH	Book of Books, Our People's Strength
	628TH	Help Us, O Lord to Learn
	627TH	Lamp of Our Feet, Whereby We Trace

3:14-17	630TH	Thanks to God Whose Word Was Spoken
3:16-17	252HT	Powerful in Making Us Wise to Salvation
4:1	421TH	All Glory Be to God on High
	366TH	Holy God, We Praise Thy Name
	364TH	O God, We Praise Thee, and Confess
	63TH	O Heavenly Word, Eternal Light
4:2	375PH	Lord of All Good
4:3-4	187HB	Faith of Our Fathers
	214HB	O God of Earth and Altar
4:7-8	231TH	By All Your Saints Still Striving
	175HB	Fight the Good Fight With All Thy Might
	501HB	For All the Saints, Who From Their Labors Rest
	173HB	Lead On, O King Eternal
	174HB	Stand Up, Stand Up For Jesus
	286TH	Who Are These Like Stars Appearing
4:11	231TH	By All Your Saints Still Striving
	285TH	What Thanks and Praise to Thee We Owe
4:18	139HB	How Firm a Foundation, Ye Saints of the Lord

Titus

3:4-7	294TH	Baptized in Water
	151TH	From Deepest Woe I Cry to Thee
	209LW	Kyrie, God Father
	364LW	Oh, How Great Is Your Compassion
	295TH	Sing Praise to Our Creator
	296TH	We Know That Christ Is Raised and Dies No More

Hebrews

1	221HT	The Brightness of God's Glory
1:1-10,25	478HB	Hail, Thou Once Despised Jesus
1:1-2:18	489TH	The Great Creator of the Worlds

1:1-14	100HB	O Love, How Deep, How Broad, How High
	491TH	Where Is This Stupendous Stranger
1:1-13	630TH	Thanks to God Whose Word Was Spoken
1:1-12	97TH	Dost Thou in a Manger Lie
	108TH	Now Yield We Thanks and Praise
	415HB	O Come, All Ye Faithful (St.2)
1:1-8	212LW	We All Believe in One True God, Father
1:1-2	343LW	God Has Spoken by His Prophets
1:2	151LW	O Christ, Our Hope
1:3-7	46HB	Fairest Lord Jesus
1:3	421TH	All Glory Be to God on High
	64SFGP	Christus Paradox (St.3)
	366TH	Holy God, We Praise Thy Name
	364TH	O God, We Praise Thee, and Confess
	474PH	O Splendor of God's Glory Bright
	44HB	Rejoice, the Lord Is King
1:6	408HB	Angels, From the Realms of Glory
1:14	189LW	Lord God, to You We All Give Praise
	190LW	Stars of the Morning, So Gloriously Bright
2:1-18	452TH	Glorious the Day When Christ Was Born
	100HB	O Love, How Deep, How Broad, How High
2:5-9	42HB	All Hail the Power of Jesus' Name
2:9	480HB	Crown Him With Many Crowns
	442HB	My Song Is Love Unknown
	455TH	O Love of God, How Strong and True
	108HB	The Head That Once Was Crowned With Thorns
2:9-10	275LW	Oh, Love, How Deep
	108HB	The Head That Once Was Crowned
2:14-18	438HB	Forty Days and Forty Nights
	142TH	Lord, Who Throughout These Forty Days
	275LW	Oh, Love, How Deep
2:15	285HB	My Faith Looks Up to Thee
2:17-10:25	49HB	Alleluia! Sing to Jesus (St.4)
	327TH	Draw Nigh and Take the Body of the Lord
	310TH	O Saving Victim, Opening Tide
2:17-18	421LW	In God, My Faithful God

2:18	268HB	Lead Us, Heavenly Father, Lead Us
3:7-14	349LW	Delay Not, Delay Not, O Sinner Draw Near
3:12-13	697TH	My God, Accept My Heart This Day
4:9-11	48TH	O Day of Radiant Gladness
4:9	515LW	I'm But a Stranger Here
	386LW	Jesus, Still Lead On
4:12-13	249HT	How Sure the Scriptures Are!
4:14-16	219TH	The Lord Ascendeth Upon High
	184HT	Where High the Heavenly Temple Stands
4:15	268HB	Lead Us, Heavenly Father, Lead Us
	492TH	Sing, Ye Faithful, Sing With Gladness
5:1-10	443TH	From God Christ's Deity Came Forth
	219TH	The Lord Ascendeth Up on High
5:7-9	455TH	O Love of God, How Strong and True
5:7	108LW	From Calvary's Cross I Heard Christ Say
6:19	379PH	My Hope Is Built on Nothing Less
7:1-10:25	443TH	From God Christ's Deity Came Forth
7:11-28	174TH	At the Lamb's High Feast We Sing
7:25	264LW	I Know That My Redeemer Lives
	394LW	Son of God, Eternal Savior
7:26-8:26	219TH	The Lord Ascendeth Up on High
8:1	421TH	All Glory Be to God on High
	366TH	Holy God, We Praise Thy Name
	364TH	O God, We Praise Thee, and Confess
9:10	439HT	What Offering Shall We Give?
9:11-10:39	337TH	And Now, O Father, Mindful of the Love
	338TH	Where, O Father, We Thy Humble Servants
9:11-28	686TH	Come, Thou Fount of Every Blessing
	160TH	Cross of Jesus, Cross of Sorrow
	219TH	The Lord Ascendeth Up on High
9:14	207LW	To Your Temple, Lord, I Come

9:15	368TH	Holy Father, Great Creator
9:23-26	324HB	Lord, Enthroned in Heavenly Splendor
9:26	134HU	Alleluia! Hearts to Heaven
9:28	120LW	Upon the Cross Extended
10:1-22	324HB	Lord, Enthroned in Heavenly Splendor
10:4	99LW	Not All the Blood of Beasts
10:10-22	174TH	At the Lamb's High Feast We Sing
	202TH	The Lamb's High Banquet Called to Share
10:12-14	134HU	Alleluia! Hearts to Heaven
10:12	236LW	Jesus Christ, Our Blessed Savior
10:14	367LW	When Over Sin I Sorrow
10:19-25	686TH	Come, Thou Fount of Every Blessing
	219TH	The Lord Ascendeth Up on High
10:22	419UM	I Am Thine, O Lord
10:30-39	53TH	Once He Came in Blessing
11	324LW	As Moses, Lost in Sinai's Wilderness
	508UM	Faith, While Trees Are Still in Blossom
	187HB	Faith of Our Fathers
	419PH	How Clear Is Our Vocation, Lord
11:5	388UM	O Come and Dwell in Me
11:8-40	393TH	Praise Our Great and Gracious Lord
11:13-16	383LW	All Who Would Valiant Be
	515LW	I'm But a Stranger Here
	186HB	O What Their Joy and Their Glory Must Be
	423LW	When I Suffer Pains and Losses
11:13	269HB	Guide Me, O Thou Great Jehovah
11:23-29	363TH	Ancient of Days, Who Sittest Throned in Glory
11:29	425TH	Sing Now With Joy Unto the Lord
	187TH	Through the Red Sea Brought at Last
11:33-40	383LW	All Who Would Valiant Be
12:1-3	545TH	Lo! What a Cloud of Witnesses
	192HU	Lord God of Hosts
12:1-2	546TH	Awake, My Soul, Stretch Every Nerve
	253TH	Give Us the Wings of Faith to Rise
12:1	175HB	Fight the Good Fight With All Thy Might

12:1	501HB	For All the Saints
	354PH	Guide My Feet
	364PH	I Sing a Song of the Saints of God
	490TH	I Want to Walk as a Child of the Light (St.3)
12:2	421TH	All Glory Be to God on High
	478HB	Hail, Thou Once Despised Jesus
	366TH	Holy God, We Praise Thy Name
	378LW	My Faith Looks Trustingly
	364TH	O God, We Praise Thee, and Confess
	108HB	The Head That Once Was Crowned With Thorns
12:3-11	574TH	Before Thy Throne, O God, We Kneel
	152TH	Kind Maker of the World, O Hear
	142TH	Lord, Who Throughout These Forty Days
12:5-11	139HB	How Firm a Foundation, Ye Saints of the Lord
12:12-14	230HU	I Know Not Where the Road
12:14	265HB	Come, Gracious Spirit, Heavenly Dove (St.3)
12:18-24	310LW	Look Toward the Mountains
12:24	368TH	Holy Father, Great Creator
	362LW	Jesus, Your Blood and Righteousness
13:1-3	184HU	When I Needed a Neighbor
13:5-6	304HB	O Jesus, I Have Promised
13:5	139HB	How Firm a Foundation, Ye Saints of the Lord
	420LW	If You But Trust in God to Guide You
13:6	279HU	My Shepherd Will Supply My Need
13:7-9	614TH	Christ Is the King! O Friends Upraise
13:7	193LW	By All Your Saints in Warfare
13:8	263HT	O Christ, the Same, Through All Our Story's Pages
	523UM	Refuge
13:10-12	219TH	The Lord Ascendeth Up on High
13:12-15	321HB	Lift High the Cross
13:12	101HB	There Is a Green Hill Far Away
13:15	134HB	All My Hope on God Is Founded
13:20-21	478TH	Jesus, Our Mighty Lord

| 13:20-31 | 708TH | Savior, Like a Shepherd Lead Us |

James

1:2-12	139HB	How Firm a Foundation, Ye Saints of the Lord
1:12	174HB	Stand Up, Stand Up For Jesus
1:17-18	56SFGP	God, Whose Giving Knows No Ending (St.1)
	57SFGP	Love, Joy and Peace (St.2)
1:17	199HB	For the Beauty of the Earth
	81HB	I Sing the Mighty Power of God
	68HU	O Beautiful For Spacious Skies
	371LW	O God, My Faithful God
	383HB	We Plow the Fields, and Scatter
1:22-27	628TH	Help Us, O Lord, to Learn
	610TH	Lord, Whose Love Through Humble Service
1:27	299HB	O Brother Man
	296HB	We Give Thee But Thine Own
2:1-13	568TH	Father All Loving, Who Rulest in Majesty
2:1-9	602TH	Jesu, Jesu, Fill Us With Your Love
	603TH	When Christ Was Lifted From the Earth
2:1	149HB	In Christ There Is No East or West
2:14-26	628TH	Help Us, O Lord, to Learn
2:14-17	610TH	Lord, Whose Love Through Humble Service
	592UM	When the Church of Jesus
3:1-5:6	574TH	Before Thy Throne, O God, We Kneel
4:6-10	58HB	Blest Are the Pure in Heart
4:7-10	301PH	Lord Jesus, Think on Me
4:8	527PH	Near to the Heart of God
5:1-6	160HB	O Holy City, Seen of John

1 Peter

1:2	68HB	I Bind Unto Myself Today
1:3-5	99SFGP	This Is the Threefold Truth
	136LW	Today in Triumph Christ Arose
1:3	472TH	Hope of the World, Thou Christ of Great Compassion
1:5-7	337LW	Preserve Your Word, O Savior
1:6-9	442LW	In You Is Gladness
	423LW	When I Suffer Pains and Losses
1:8	42LW	Let Us All With Gladsome Voice
	282LW	O Savior, Precious Savior
1:10-12	62HU	God of the Prophets
	33LW	Let the Earth Now Praise the Lord
1:16	395UM	Take Time to Be Holy
1:18-21	59TH	Hark! a Thrilling Voice Is Sounding
1:18-19	524TH	I Love Thy Kingdom, Lord
	270LW	Jesus, Priceless Treasure
	208LW	Lamb of God, Pure and Sinless
	138HT	No Weight of Gold or Silver
	146HB	The Church's One Foundation
1:19-21	82PH	O Lamb of God Most Holy!
1:19	98LW	Glory Be to Jesus
	276HB	Thy Kingdom Come, O God
1:20	433HB	Songs of Thankfulness and Praise
1:22	299HB	O Brother Man
1:20-23	394LW	Son of God, Eternal Savior
1:23-25	204TH	Now the Green Blade Riseth
	341LW	O God, Our Lord, Your Holy Word
2:4-9	290LW	Christ Is Our Cornerstone
2:4-8	145HB	Christ Is Made the Sure Foundation
	146HB	The Church's One Foundation
2:6-7	129PH	Come, O Spirit, Dwell Among Us
2:7	121HB	O Jesus, King Most Wonderful
2:9-11	504HT	Church of God, Elect and Glorious
2:9-10	536TH	God Has Spoken to His People
	59TH	Hark! a Thrilling Voice Is Sounding
	51TH	We the Lord's People, Heart and Voice Uniting
2:9	459LW	Forth in the Peace of Christ

2:21-25	52SFGP	Come, Thou Fount of Every Blessing (St.2)
	379LW	"Come, Follow Me" Said Christ, the Lord
	103PH	Deep Were His Wounds, and Red
	336LW	Grant, Holy Ghost, That We Behold
	120LW	Upon the Cross Extended
	478TH	Jesus, Our Mighty Lord
	13SFGP	Morning Glory, Starlit Sky (St.5)
2:21-24	468HB	The Strife Is O'er, the Battle Done
2:21	381LW	Let Us Ever Walk With Jesus
	387LW	Praise and Thanks and Adoration
2:24-25	443HB	Ah, Holy Jesus, How Hast Thou Offended
2:24	97LW	Alas! and Did My Savior Bleed
	95LW	Grant, Lord Jesus, That My Healing
	357LW	I Trust, O Christ, in You Alone
	151LW	O Christ, Our Hope
3:7	534PH	The Grace of Life Is Theirs
3:18-4:6	455TH	O Love of God, How Strong and True
3:18-22	502UM	Thy Holy Wings, O Savior
3:18-20	462HB	"Welcome Happy Morning!" Age to Age Shall Say
3:18	442HB	My Song Is Love Unknown
3:22	44HB	Rejoice, the Lord Is King
4:5	421TH	All Glory Be to God on High
	366TH	Holy God, We Praise Thy Name
	364TH	O God, We Praise Thee, and Confess
	63TH	O Heavenly Word, Eternal Light
4:8	134SFGP	To Show by Touch and Word (St.3)
4:11	171HB	Soldiers of Christ, Arise
5:7	1HB	All Creatures of Our God and King
	175HB	Fight the Good Fight (St.3)
5:8	391LW	I Walk in Danger All the Way
	463LW	The Clouds of Judgment Gather
5:10	254LW	May God the Father of Our Lord

2 Peter

1	538HT	Come, Praise the Name of Jesus
1:17-18	129TH	Christ Upon the Mountain Peak
	133TH	O Light of Light, Love Given Birth
	136TH	O Wondrous Type! O Vision Fair
	433HB	Songs of Thankfulness and Praise
1:19	542TH	Christ Is the World's True Light
	362HB	Christ, Whose Glory Fills the Skies
	22SFGP	O Christ, the Word Incarnate (St. 1)
	40TH	O Christ, You Are Both Light and Day
	69PH	O Morning Star, How Fair and Bright
	340LW	We Have a Sure Prophetic Word
3:18	298TH	All Who Believe and Are Baptized

1 John

1:1-2	78LW	Jesus Has Come and Brings Pleasure
1:5-7	143HU	Christ Is the World's True Light
	490TH	I Want to Walk as a Child of the Light
1:7-10	77HB	Jesus, Lover of My Soul
1:7-9	284HB	Just as I Am, Without One Plea
1:7	243LW	Here, O My Lord, I See You Face to Face
	362LW	Jesus, Your Blood and Righteousness
	368LW	My Hope Is Built on Nothing Less
	48HB	Oh, for a Thousand Tongues to Sing
	467UM	Trust and Obey
2:6	381LW	Let Us Ever Walk With Jesus
2:15-17	418LW	What Is the World to Me
3:2	372PH	Lord, I Want to Be a Christian
3:5	492TH	Sing, Ye Faithful, Sing With Gladness
3:14-18	279HB	Father Eternal, Ruler of Creation
3:16-18	610TH	Lord, Whose Love Through Humble Service
3:16	304TH	I Come With Joy to Meet My Lord
	603TH	When Christ Was Lifted From the Earth
	319TH	You, Lord, We Praise in Songs of Celebration

3:17-18	180HU	Am I My Brother's Keeper
	296HB	We Give Thee But Thine Own
3:20-21a	321PH	Holy Spirit, Truth Divine
3:23	476LW	I Pray You, Dear Lord Jesus
3:24	225HU	Jesus, I Live to Thee
4:7-21	6SFGP	Where Charity and Love Prevail
4:7-12	84TH	Love Came Down at Christmas
4:7-17	241HB	Love Divine, All Loves Excelling
4:7-8	155HU	God Is Love, and Where True Love
4:7	468HT	Beloved, Let Us Love; For Love Is of God
4:8-16	379TH	God Is Love, Let Heaven Adore Him
	471TH	We Sing the Praise of Him Who Died
4:8,16	57SFGP	Love, Joy and Peace (St.2)
	43SFGP	Love, Love, Love Your God
4:9	69LW	Let Our Gladness Have No End
	72LW	The Only Son From Heaven
	439TH	What Wondrous Love Is This
4:9-10	122LW	O Darkest Woe
	330LW	The Gospel Shows the Father's Grace
4:9-21	46LW	Love Came Down at Christmas
4:11-21	279HB	Father Eternal, Ruler of Creation
4:12,16	576TH	God Is Love, and Where True Love Is
	581TH	Where Charity and Love Prevail
	606TH	Where True Charity and Love Dwell
4:13-16	20LW	O Bride of Christ, Rejoice
4:14	74LW	From God the Father, Virgin-Born
	69LW	Let Our Gladness Have No End
4:16	376LW	Love in Christ Is Strong and Living
	549UM	Where Charity and Love Prevail
4:18	527PH	Near to the Heart of God
	700TH	O Love That Casts Out Fear
	28SFGP	Would You Bless Our Homes and Families
	353TH	Your Love, O God, Has Called Us Here
4:19	689TH	I Sought the Lord, and Afterward I Knew
	706TH	In Your Mercy, Lord, You Called Me
4:20-21	180HU	Am I My Brother's Keeper
5:4-9	215LW	All Glory Be to God on High

5:6	139TH	When Jesus Went to Jordan's Stream (St.3)
5:14-16	145HB	Christ Is Made the Sure Foundation
	711TH	Seek Ye First the Kingdom of God
5:20-21	408TH	Sing Praise to God Who Reigns Above (St.3)

Jude

8-9	282TH	Christ, the Fair Glory of the Holy Angels (St.2)
20-21	337LW	Preserve Your Word, O Savior
21	69PH	O Morning Star, How Fair and Bright
25	173LW	Glory Be to God the Father

Revelation

1:1-3	231TH	By All Your Saints Still Striving
1:3	536TH	God Has Spoken to His People
1:4-7	332HB	Let All Mortal Flesh Keep Silence (St.2)
1:5-6	173LW	Glory Be to God the Father
	465HB	Jesus Christ Is Risen Today
	324HB	Lord, Enthroned in Heavenly Splendor
1:5	215HT	Let Us Love and Sing and Wonder
1:7	393HB	Jesus Comes With Clouds Descending
	393HB	Lo, He Comes With Clouds Descending
1:8	62HB	Come, Thou Almighty King
	327TH	Draw Nigh and Take the Body of the Lord
	429HB	Of the Father's Love Begotten
1:9-20	22SFGP	O Christ, the Word Incarnate
1:9-10	193LW	By All Your Saints in Warfare
1:12-18	177HT	He Walks Among the Golden Lamps
	500HT	Risen Lord, Whose Name We Cherish
1:13-15	156PH	You, Living Christ, Our Eyes Behold
1:18	465HB	Jesus Christ Is Risen Today

1:18	194TH	Jesus Lives! Thy Terrors Now
	44HB	Rejoice, the Lord Is King
1:20	335LW	O Word of God Incarnate
2:7	536TH	God Has Spoken to His People
2:10	501HB	For All the Saints
	160LW	O Holy Spirit, Enter In
2:10b	174HB	Stand Up, Stand Up for Jesus
2:11,17	536TH	God Has Spoken to His People
2:17	66SFGP	There's a Quiet Understanding
2:28	362HB	Christ, Whose Glory Fills the Skies
	40TH	O Christ, You Are Both Light and Day
2:29	536TH	God Has Spoken to His People
3:1-6	547TH	Awake, O Sleeper, Rise From Death
3:4-5	356TH	May Choirs of Angels Lead You
3:6	536TH	God Has Spoken to His People
3:7	390HB	O Come, O Come, Emmanuel
	82SFGP	Open My Eyes That I May See (St.1)
3:8	347LW	Today Your Mercy Calls Us
3:13	536TH	God Has Spoken to His People
3:17	284HB	Just as I Am, Without One Plea
3:20	382PH	Somebody's Knocking at Your Door
3:21	324HB	Lord, Enthroned in Heavenly Splendor
3:22	536TH	God Has Spoken to His People
4-5	191HT	Come and See the Shining Hope
	570HT	Heavenly Hosts in Ceaseless Worship
4:2-11	478HB	Hail, Thou Once Despised Jesus
4:6-11	235TH	Come Sing, Ye Choirs Exultant (St.2)
	88SFGP	Holy God, We Praise Your Name (St.2)
	364TH	O God, We Praise Thee, and Confess
	367TH	Round the Lord in Glory Seated
	401TH	The God of Abraham Praise
4:6	49HB	Alleluia! Sing to Jesus (St.3)
4:7-8	643TH	My God, How Wonderful Thou Art
4:8-11	460PH	Holy God, We Praise Your Name
	50HB	Holy, Holy, Holy
	332HB	Let All Mortal Flesh Keep Silence
	241HB	Love Divine, All Loves Excelling

4:8	169LW	Come, O Almighty King
	140PH	Holy, Holy
	48TH	O Day of Radiant Gladness
4:11	302TH	Father, We Thank Thee Who Hast Planted
	284LW	Hail, O Once Rejected Jesus
	18LW	Hark! A Thrilling Voice Is Sounding
	37TH	O Brightness of the Immortal Father's Face
	36TH	O Gladsome Light, O Grace
	25TH	O Gracious Light, Lord Jesus Christ
	429HB	Of the Father's Love Begotten
	S30HT	You Are Worthy
5	206HT	Come Let Us Join Our Cheerful Songs
5:5	146LW	Lo, Judah's Lion Wins the Strife
5:6-14	49HB	Alleluia! Sing to Jesus
	213TH	Come Away to the Skies (St.5)
	374TH	Come, Let Us Join Our Cheerful Songs
	480HB	Crown Him With Many Crowns
	478HB	Hail, Thou Once Despised Jesus
	324HB	Lord, Enthroned in Heavenly Splendor
	434TH	Nature With Open Volume Stands
	14SFGP	This Is the Feast
	439TH	What Wondrous Love Is This
	46SFGP	When Morning Gilds the Skies
	94SFGP	Ye Servants of God (Sts.3,4)
5:6	64SFGP	Christus Paradox (St.1)
5:9	34LW	Come, O Precious Ransom
5:10	459LW	Forth in the Peace of Christ
5:11-14	674UM	See the Morning Sun Ascending
5:12-14	594PH	This Is the Feast of Victory
5:12-13	147PH	Blessing and Honor
	30HB	Ye Servants of God, Your Master Proclaim
5:12	64SFGP	Christus Paradox (St.4)
	83LW	O God of God, O Light of Light
5:13	131LW	Now All the Vault of Heaven Resounds
5:9-14	210LW	All Glory Be to God Alone
5:9-16	42HB	All Hail the Power of Jesus' Name
5:11-13	126LW	At the Lamb's High Feast We Sing

5:11-13	48HB	Oh, for a Thousand Tongues to Sing
5:12	204LW	Come, Let Us Join Our Cheerful Songs
	173LW	Glory Be to God the Father
	118LW	We Sing the Praise of Him Who Died
5:13	190LW	Stars of the Morning, So Gloriously Bright
6:9-11	240TH	Harken to the Anthems Glorious
6:11	655UM	Fix Me, Jesus
6:12-17	719UM	My Lord, What a Morning
7:3	686TH	Come, Thou Fount of Every Blessing
	321HB	Lift High the Cross
	697TH	My God, Accept My Heart This Day
7:9-17	421TH	All Glory Be to God on High
	231TH	By All Your Saints Still Striving
	275TH	Hark! the Sound of Holy Voices
	240H	Harken to the Anthem Glorious
	571HT	Here From All Nations
	572HT	How Bright These Glorious Spirits Shine
	184HB	Jerusalem the Golden
	324HB	Lord, Enthroned in Heavenly Splendor
	284TH	O Ye Immortal Throng (Sts.7 & 8)
	619TH	Sing Alleluia Forth in Duteous Praise
	6HB	Ye Holy Angels Bright
	7HB	Ye Watchers and Ye Holy Ones
7:9-14	366TH	Holy God, We Praise Thy Name
	364TH	O God, We Praise Thee, and Confess
	199LW	We Worship You, O God of Might
	112PH	Christ the Lord Is Risen Again
7:9-12	480HB	Crown Him With Many Crowns
	306LW	Jerusalem, O City Fair and High
	643TH	My God, How Wonderful Thou Art
	434TH	Nature With Open Volume Stands
	112HB	Once in Royal David's City
	94SFGP	Ye Servants of God (Sts.3,4)
7:9-11	42HB	All Hail the Power of Jesus' Name
7:10-12	173LW	Glory Be to God the Father
7:11-12	131LW	Now All the Vault of Heaven Resounds
	674UM	See the Morning Sun Ascending
7:12-14	301HU	Blessing and Honor

7:13-17	192LW	Behold a Host Arrayed in White
	195LW	For All Your Saints, O Lord
	356TH	May Choirs of Angels Lead You
	286TH	Who Are These Like Stars Appearing
7:13-14	362LW	Jesus, Your Blood and Righteousness
7:14-17	144HB	Glorious Things of Thee Are Spoken
7:14	341PH	Blessed Assurance, Jesus Is Mine!
	173LW	Glory Be to God the Father
	366LW	I Lay My Sins on Jesus
	285HB	My Faith Looks Up to Thee
7:15	241HB	Love Divine, All Love Excelling
11:15-18	480HB	Crown Him With Many Crowns
11:15	289PH	God of Every Nation
	18LW	Hark! A Thrilling Voice Is Sounding
11:19	18LW	Hark! A Thrilling Voice Is Sounding
12:7-10	446HB	Sing, My Tongue
12:7-8	282TH	Christ, the Fair Glory of the Holy Angels (St.2)
13:9	536TH	God Has Spoken to His People
14:1-5	434TH	Nature With Open Volume Stands
	439TH	What Wondrous Love Is This
14:4	188LW	Sweet Flowerets of the Martyr Band
14:6-7	341LW	O God, Our Lord, Your Holy Word
14:13	358TH	Christ the Victorious, Give to Your Servants
	501HB	For All the Saints
	357TH	Jesus, Son of Mary
	268LW	Oh, How Blest Are You
15:3-4	181TH	Awake and Sing the Song
	50HB	Holy, Holy, Holy! Lord God Almighty!
	532TH	How Wondrous and Great Thy Works, God of Praise
17:14	213HB	Judge Eternal, Throned in Splendor

21:1-4	300HU	I Want to Be Ready
21:2-22:5	184HB	Jerusalem the Golden
	621TH	Light's Abode, Celestial Salem
	160HB	O Holy City, Seen of John
	186HB	O What Their Joy and Their Glory Must Be
21:2-27	519TH	Blessed City, Heavenly Salem
	145HB	Christ Is Made the Sure Foundation
	354TH	Into Paradise May the Angels Lead You
	356TH	May Choirs of Angels Lead You
21:2-3	144HB	Glorious Things of Thee Are Spoken
	306LW	Jerusalem, O City Fair and High
21:3-4	706UM	Soon and Very Soon
21:4	566TH	From Thee All Skill and Science Flow
	285HB	My Faith Looks Up to Thee (St.3)
	378LW	My Faith Looks Trustingly
	268LW	Oh, How Blest Are You
21:5	383UM	This Is a Day of New Beginnings
21:6	429HB	Of the Father's Love Begotten
21:10-12	307LW	Jerusalem, My Happy Home
21:18-23	184HB	Jerusalem the Golden
21:19-27	394HB	"Sleepers, Wake!" A Voice Astounds Us
21:21	501HB	For All the Saints
21:21-22	177LW	Wake, Awake, For Night Is Flying
21:22-27	366TH	Holy God, We Praise Thy Name
21:23-26	435HB	As With Gladness Men of Old (Sts.4 & 5)
21:23-25	452TH	Glorious the Day When Christ Was Born
21:23	490TH	I Want to Walk as a Child of the Light
	672TH	O Very God of Very God
21:24	463LW	The Clouds of Judgment Gather
22	160HB	O Holy City, Seen of John
	431PH	O Lord, You Gave Your Servant John
22:1-5,17	275TH	Hark! the Sound of Holy Voices
22:1-5	723UM	Shall We Gather at the River
22:1-2	78SFGP	Out of Deep Unordered Water
22:1	49HB	Alleluia! Sing to Jesus (St.3)
	244TH	Come, Pure Hearts, in Joyful Measure (St.2)
22:2	23SFGP	For the Healing of the Nations

22:3-5	240TH	Harken to the Anthem Glorious
22:3	30HB	Ye Servants of God, Your Master Proclaim
22:5	362HB	Christ, Whose Glory Fills the Skies
	452TH	Glorious the Day When Christ Was Born
	501LW	God of Our Fathers
22:13	429HB	Of the Father's Love Begotten
	598PH	This Is the Good News
22:16	542TH	Christ Is the World's True Light
	362HB	Christ, Whose Glory Fills the Skies
	117HB	How Bright Appears the Morning Star
	40TH	O Christ, You Are Both Light and Day
	73LW	O Morning Star, How Fair and Bright
	72LW	The Only Son From Heaven
	276HB	Thy Kingdom Come, O God
22:17	350UM	Come, All of You
	347LW	Today Your Mercy Calls Us
22:20	26LW	The King Shall Come

III. AN INDEX OF
HYMN PRELUDES

Introduction

Organists seeking preludes, interludes and postludes based on hymn tunes can choose from a considerable repertory representing the entire history of music for the instrument. In the absence of a general index, locating a prelude on a particular hymn-tune, however, can be a daunting experience. The problem is compounded by the fact that many hymn-tunes bear more than one name and, what is more, a given name often refers to more than one tune. The purpose of this index is to provide access to the literature of hymn preludes. It includes chorale preludes only when the tune appears in hymnals commonly in use in North America.

No attempt has been made to correlate hymn tunes and hymn texts since the association of particular tunes with particular texts varies widely from church to church. Once a particular tune has been decided on for a given hymn, this index will help organists to locate preludes based on that tune. I have deliberately restricted myself to a rather small selection of published material containing hymn preludes, generally in the form of collections.

The index comprises three parts:

1. The Index proper

The entry for each hymn prelude gives the name of the tune, the name of the composer, and the location of the work by volume and page or number of the work in the volume. J.S. Bach is identified simply as Bach except where other members of the Bach family have composed preludes on the same tune. Occasionally a work consisting of several variations will appear only partially in another edition. In this case, the complete version is listed first, followed by partial versions, e.g.

Lobt Gott, ihr Christen, allzugleich   Walther (WBM 19, 8 vars.; WO
                                        80, vars.1-7;HP 4:30, var.1; PO
                                        5:30, var.2; GG 1:42, var.6; PO
                                        I:94; PO 2:42, var.8; GT 2:149,
                                        vars. 1,2,3,6,7)

The full eight variations appear only in WBM, with partial versions in
a number of other editions.

   The Parish Organist series, published by Concordia, and abbrevi-
ated as PO in this index, includes two versions of volumes 1 through
4: the four individual volumes and a single volume containing all four.
The individual volumes are represented in this index as PO 1, PO 2,
PO 3, and PO 4, the inclusive volume as PO I.

   A single * indicates that the tune in question is represented by
another name in this index. The cross-reference is given to the right;
a complete list of cross-references is given in the List of Equivalent
Tune Names.

   A double * indicates that there are two tunes bearing the same
name, differentiated in this index by roman numerals I and II. A musical index of these tunes is given in the List of Melodic Incipits.

   2. List of Equivalent Tune Names

   The names of hymn tunes, unlike the names of horses, are not
recorded at a central registry. The confusion that results from single
hymn tunes bearing multiple names may be relieved, at least in part,
by consulting the list of equivalent tune names.

   3. List of Melodic Incipits

   No less confusing than a melody bearing more than one name is a
name referring to more than one melody. The list of melodic incipits
may allow the user to sort out these multiple tunes.

Index of Hymn Preludes

A Rouen Melody	Willan (WH 3:31)
A solis ortus cardine	Peeters (PG 2:12)
	Proulx (PPS 2:16)
	Scheidt (HP 2:28)
	[See also Christum wir sollen]
A va de	Cherwien (CI 3:16)
	Skaalen (HP 16:43)
Abbot's Leigh	Patterson (HP 19:10)
Abends	Peeters (PH 23:10)
Aberystwyth	Held (HP 19:7)
	Janson (HP 7:8)
	Peeters (PH 18:1)
	Thalben-Ball (TB 1)
	Willan (WH 1:39)
Abide with Me*	[See Eventide]
Abridge	Thalben-Ball (TB 2)
Ach bleib bei uns	Bach (BSC 95)
	Dupré (D 1)
	Wente (HP 19:14)
Ach bleib mit deiner Gnade*	[See Christus der ist mein Leben]
Ach Gott und Herr	Bach (BU 3)
	Buxtehude (BC 2)
	Dupré (D 2)
	Hessenberg (OB 168)
	Walther (WO 2, 3 vars.; PO I:5; PO 1:11, var.3)
	Walther (PO 8:28; GG 1:3)
	Walther (HP 12:8)
Ach Gott vom Himmelreiche	Bobb (HP 16:46)
	Johns (HP 14:7)

Ach Gott vom Himmelreiche	Peeters (PH 5:5)
	Scheidt (EK 1:1)
Ach Jesu, dessen treu*	[*See* O Gott, du frommer Gott I]
Ach, was soll ich Sünder machen	Bach (BP 104)
	Marpurg (MC 10)
	Pachelbel (PA 4:38, 6 vars.)
	Walther (WO 7-11, 5 vars.)
	Walther (HP 19:16)
Ack, bliv hos oss*	[*See* Pax]
Ack, saliga stunder	Rohlig (HP 19:22)
Ack, vad är dock livet här	Bender (HP 7:10)
Ad perennis	Peeters (PH 21:7)
Adeste fideles	Cherwien (CI 2:4)
	Adams (GRV 1)
	Callahan, Partita on Adeste fideles (Concordia)
	Demessieux (DT 4)
	Dickinson, Postlude on Adeste fideles (Novello 336)
	Hofland (PO I:8, PO 1:14)
	Moser (PO 6:7)
	Purvis (PL 46)
	Thiman (FVC 15)
	Sensmeier (HP 3:30)
Adoro te devote	Casner (PO 11:5)
	Cherwien (CI 3:6)
	Kalbfleisch (HP 16:50)
	Peeters (PG 2:3)
	Pelz (HP 19:21)
	Purvis (PF 2)
Aeterna Christi munera	Peeters (PH 5:4; PG 2:8)
	Willan (WF 1)
Af himlens	Bouman (HP 19:25)
	Cherwien (CI 2:14)
Agincourt Hymn*	[*See* Deo Gracias]
Agnus Dei*	[*See* Christe, du Lamm Gottes]
Ainsi que la biche ree	Peeters (PH 1:2)

Ajalon*	[See Gethsemane]
All Saints	Peeters (PH 19:4)
All Saints New	Crane (PO 11:6)
	Engel (HP 13:33)
	Ferguson (HP 19:32)
	Peeters (PH 20:8)
	Willan (WP 3:2)
All Things Bright and Beautiful	Smith (CPE 20)
All' Ehr' und Lob	Lenel (PO 8:42)
	Miles (PO I:10, PO 1:16)
	Peeters (PH 14:6)
	Rohlig (HP 12:20)
	Schack (HP 19:29)
Alle Jahre wieder	Beck (HP 3:32)
Alle Menschen müssen	
sterben I**	Bach, J.C. (HP 8:10)
	Bach, J.S. (PO I:78, PO 2:26)
	Bach, J.S. (BO 74)
	Bach, J.S. (BN 62)
	Krebs (GT 1:16)
	Schultz (PO 12:40)
	Zachau (PO 7:24; 80:46; GG 1:5)
Alle Menschen müssen	
sterben II**	Bach, J.C. (HP 8:10)
	Bach, J.S. (BN 62)
	Bender (BK 3:4)
	Dupré (D 5)
	Pachelbel (PA 4:12: 8 vars.; HP 6:28: var.3; GG 1:4: var.3; HP 38:12)
Allein Gott in der Höh sei Ehr	Armstorff (GT 1:22; GRV 8)
	Bach (GT 1:24; 45:8)
	Bach (BCL 30)
	Bach (BCL 33)
	Bach (BCL 41)
	Bach (BU 8)
	Bach (BU 11)
	Bach (BU 14)
	Bach (B18 67)

Allein Gott in der Höh sei Ehr	Bach (B18 72)
	Bach (B18 79)
	Bender (BK 1:1)
	Böhm (BS 26)
	Dupré (D 4)
	Marpurg (20)
	Pachelbel (PA 2:24, 2 vars.; PO I:1;
	PO 1:7, var.1; GT 1:29, var.2)
	Peeters (PC 2:7)
	Reger (RC 1:1)
	Sweelinck (HP 14:30-32)
	Vetter (80:5, HP 13:20-22)
	Walther (WO 12; GT 1:34, 2 vars.)
	Walther (EK 1:2)
	Walther (80:6; GG 1:6)
	Walther (GG 1:8)
	Walther (HP 19:34)
	Wenzel (OB 130)
	Zachau (80:4; GG 1:6)
Allein zu dir, Herr Jesu Christ	Bach (BN 24)
	Erich (45:14; EK 1:4)
	Pachelbel (PA 3:13; GT 1:41, 2
	vars.; GG 2:88, var.2)
	Peeters (PH 13:4)
	Siedel (OB 166)
	Sweelinck (2:23)
	Walther (WO 16)
	Walther (GG 2:89)
	Zachau (HP 19:37)
Alles ist an Gottes segen	Bender (BK 3:5)
	Cherwien (CI 4:14)
	Karg-Elert (GG 3:171)
	Pelz (HP 16:52)
	Polley (HP 19:40)
	Reger (EK 1:7; RC 1:2)
	Wenzel (OB 215)
	Wolfgrum (GG 3:172)
	Wood (PPS 3:4)
Allgütiger, mein Preisgesang*	[See Erfurt]

Almsgiving	Peeters (PH 17:3)
Altdorf*	[See Nun freut euch]
Alta trinita beata	Peeters (PH 5:7)
Amazing Grace*	[See New Britain]
Amens sjunge hvarje tunga	Schultz (HP 19:42)
America	Ives, Variations on "America" for Organ (Mercury Music Corp.)
	Peeters (PH 24:1)
American Hymn	Wienhorst (HP 19:44)
An Wasserflüssen Babylon	Ahle (EK 1:42)
	Bach (B18: 22)
	Bach (GT 1:47)
	Bender (BK 2:14)
	Dupré (D 6)
	Pachelbel (PA 3:50; PO 7:8)
	Walther (WO 26; GT 1:50)
	Zachau (GG 1:9)
	Zipp (HP 7:12)
Angelic Songs*	[See Tidings]
Angel's Song*	[See Song 34]
Angel's Story	Krapf (HP 19:46)
	Willan (PO 12:60)
Angelus	Johnson (HP 7:14)
	Peeters (PH 1:6)
Anthem*	[See Lift Every Voice and Sing]
Anthes	Hildner (PO I:12, PO 1:18)
	Kloppers (HP 20:10)
Antioch	Cherwien (CI 3:8)
	Gehrke (PO I:14, PO 1:20, HP 3:35)
Ar hyd y nos	Bobb (HP 20:13)
Arden	Thalben-Ball (TB 4)
Argyle*	[See Ewing]
Arnsberg*	[See Wunderbarer König or Seelenbräutigam]
Ascended Triumph	Polley (HP 12:24)
Ascension	Willan (FVW 1)
Ash Grove*	[See The Ash Grove]
Atkinson	Powell (HP 20:16)

Auf, auf, mein Herz,
    mit Freuden

    Bender (BK 2:3)
    Haase (HP 10:8)
    Held (HE 12)
    Marpurg (MC 45)
    Moser (PO I:16, PO 1:22)
    Moser (PO 8:7)
    Peeters (PC 3:26)
    Weismann (EK 1:8)
    Wolfrum (GG 3:174)

Auf, ihr Hirten   Schroeder (SO 6)
Auf meinen lieben Gott*   [See Wo soll ich fliehen hin]
Aughton*   [See He Leadeth Me]
Aurelia   Bunjes (PO I:18)
    Cherwien (CI 5:2)
    Johns (HP 16:57)
    Lovelace (HP 20:20)
    Peeters (PH 10:5)

Aus der Tiefe*   [See Heinlein]
Aus meines Herzens Grunde   Bach, J.C. (PO I:20)
    Bach, J.S. (PO 5:18)
    Reger (RC 1:4)
    Walther (GG 1:10; GT 1:59)
    Wenzel (EK 1:12)
    Zipp (HP 1:7)

Aus tiefer Not I**   Bach (BCL 74)
    Bach (BCL 78; GT 1:64)
    Dupré (D 8)
    Hannebeck, Wagner (OB 195 I)
    Mendelssohn (Sonata III)
    Peeters (PC 2:25)
    Ramin (EK 1:13)
    Reger (RC 1:3)
    Scheidt (80:14; GT 1:63)
    Zachau (GG 2:90; 80:15; HP
      20:25)

Aus tiefer Not II**   Bach (BN 22)
    Bender (BK 2:45)
    Bieske (OB 195 II)

Christ lag in
  Todesbanden   Zachau (80:18)
Christ unser Herr
  zum Jordan kam   Bach (BCL 68)
                                Bach (BCL 73)
                                Bender (HP 5:32)
                                Bornefeld (OB 146)
                                Buxtehude (BC 6; 45:12)
                                Dupré (D 13)
                                Engel (HP 16:7)
                                Pachelbel (PA 3:10)
                                Zachau (GG 2:99)
Christe, der du bist
  Tag und Licht   Bach (BN 16)
                                Böhm (BS 40; GT 1:105)
                                Krieger (GG 2:92)
                                Scheidt (HP 22:36)
Christe, du Lamm Gottes   Bach (BO 36; GT 1:109)
                                Bender (BK 2:43)
                                Dupré (D 10)
                                Gerike (HP 7:22)
                                Kauffmann (GG 2:92)
                                Lenel (LF)
                                Mueller (PO 7:18)
                                Wenzel (OB 136)
Christe Redemptor   Held (HP 3:19)
                                Parry (PC 1:6)
                                Peeters (PH 23:2; PG 1:7)
                                Purvis (PM 2)
                                Willan (WF 2)
Christe sanctorum   Engel (HP 21:13)
                                Krapf (WS 4:29)
                                Lovelace (HP 16:10, 2 vars.)
                                Wienhorst (HP 13:23)
Christmas   Barlow (PO 11:12)
Christmas Dawn*   [See Wir hatten gebauet]
Christmas Eve*   [See Jeg er saa glad]
Christum wir sollen
  loben schon   Bach (BO 20)

Christum wir sollen
    loben schon

        Bach (BU 23)
        Böhm (BS 54)
        Dupré (D 14)
        Lenel (LF)
        Praetorius (PRC 1)
        Walther (WO 18, 3 vars.; HP 3:10, var. 1)
        Willan (WC 2:5)

Christus, der ist
    mein Leben

        Bach (BN 52)
        Bender (BK 3:8)
        Cherwien (CI 1:10)
        Hellmann (EK 1:25)
        Koch (OB 208)
        Marpurg (MC 16; GT 1:110)
        Pachelbel (PA 4:4, 12 vars.; PO I:41; 1:47, var. 7)
        Peeters (PH 12:7)
        Reger (RC 1:5)
        Walther (WO 22; GT 1:111; GG 1:13: 2 vars.)
        Walther (80:20; GG 1:14)
        Walther (HP 21:38)

Church Triumphant   Thalben-Ball (TB 18)
City of God   Schalk (HP 21:40)
Cleansing Fountain*   [*See* Cowper]
Coena Domini   Busarow (HP 17:13)
Collingwood   Thalben-Ball (TB 19)
Commandments*   [*See* Wenn wir in höchsten Nöten sein]

Communion*   [*See* Rockingham Old]
Complainer   Rotermund (HP 21:25)
Conditor alme siderum   Johnson (HP 1:12)
        Peeters (PG 1:3)
        Rowley (FVA 11)
        Zimmer (HP 21:42)
        [*See* also Lob sei dem allmächtigen Gott]

Da Jesus an dem
    Kreuze stund   Scheidt (GT 1:116; 45:34, 2 vars.)
                       Scheidt (HP 7:24)
Dana*   [See Amen sjunge hvarje tunga]
Dank sei Gott in der Höhe   Bialas (GG 4:260)
                       Peeters (PH 11:8)
Darmstadt*   [See Meinen Jesum lass' ich nicht I]
Darwall*   [See Darwall's 148th]
Darwall's 148th   Barlow (HP 22:11)
                       Darke (DC 2)
                       Lovelace (HP 14:10)
                       Miles (PO I:28, PO 1:34)
                       Peeters (PH 11:3)
                       Thalben-Ball (TB 22)
                       Whitlock (WT1)
                       Willan (WP 1:8)
Das neugeborne Kindelein   Peeters (PH 9:7)
                       Rohlig (HP 17:17)
Das walt Gott Vater   Beck (HP 14:36)
                       Peeters (PH 5:6)
De profundis*   [See Aus tiefer Not I]
Dejlig er den Himmel blaa   Cassler (HP 5:27)
                       Johnson (PPS 2:11)
Den Blomstertid nu kommer   Krapf (HP 22:24)
                       Peeters (PH 22:2)
Den die Hirten lobeten sehre* [See Quem pastores]
Den signede Dag   Gehrke (HP 12:22)
                       Patterson (HP 22:26)
Den store hvide flok   Hillert (HP 14:39)
                       Schack (HP 22:28)
Denfield*   [See Azmon]
Dennis   Cherwien (CI 5:4)
Dennis   Ferguson (HP 22:30)
Deo Gracias   Hillert (HP 5:34)
                       Mackie (HP 22:32)
                       Peeters (PH 4:1)
                       Whitlock (WT1)
                       Willan (WS 2:14)
Der am Kreuz*   [See Werde munter mein Gemüte]

Down Ampney	Schulz (HP 23:27)
Dretzel*	[See O dass ich tausend Zungen hätte I]
Drumclog*	[See Martyrdom]
Du keusche Seele du	Peeters (PH 4:4)
Du Lebensbrot, Herr Jesu Christ	Bender (BK 3:14)
	Marx (OB 236)
	Mudde (PO 11:24)
	Münch (HP 17:23)
	Raphel (HP 17:26)
	Wiemer (GG 4:274)
Du meiner Seelen*	[See Angelus]
Du som gaar ud	Zimmer (HP 23:30)
Duke Street	Cherwien (CI 3:22)
	Held (PPS 1:6)
	Schack (HP 23:32)
	Wienhorst (PO I:34, PO 1:40)
Dulce carmen	Manz (PO 11:44)
Dundee	Lang (HP 23:34)
	Parry (PC 1:1)
	Peeters (PH 12:9)
	Ridout (RT 1)
	Thalben-Ball (TB 24)
	Unkel (PO I:36, PO 1:42)
	Willan (WP 1:10)
Dunfermline	Bevan, Metrical Psalm-Prelude on Dunfermline (Waterloo)
	Thalben-Ball (TB 25)
Dunstan	Bouman (HP 29:16)
	Cherwien (CI 1:20)
	Gotsch (HP 23:42)
Durham	Parry (PC 1:3)
	Sensmeier (HP 23:36)
	Willan (WP 2:5)
Durrow	Wienhorst (HP 23:38)
Earth and All Stars	Cherwien (CI 3:19)
	Held (HP 23:40)

Erschienen ist der
    herrliche Tag

                    Bach (BO 55)
                    Bender (BK 2:16)
                    Beyer (HP 10:19)
                    Dupré (D 24)
                    Kauffmann (HP 24:24)
                    Reger (RC 1:8)
                    Scheidt, Kickstat (WS 2:22)
                    Walther (WO 32, 5 vars.; EK 1:47,
                        var.1)
                    Walther (GG 1:18; PO 8:30)

Erstanden ist der
    heil'ge Christ

                    Bach (BO 54; GG 2:108)
                    Dupré (D 25)
                    Gehrke (WS 2:29)

Es ist das Heil uns
    kommen her

                    Anonymous (GT 1:154; 80:27)
                    Bach (BO 66; EK 1:49)
                    Bender (BK 1:6)
                    Buxtehude (BC 19)
                    Cherwien (CI 6:14)
                    Dupré (D 26)
                    Kauffmann (HP 16:13)
                    Kloppers (HP 24:26)
                    Marx (OB 242 II)
                    Peeters (PH 9:2)
                    Reda (OB 242 I)
                    Reger (RC 1:10)
                    Sweelinck (SA 29)
                    Walther (GG 1:19)
                    Zachau (GT 1:156)

Es ist ein' Ros' entsprungen   Brahms (BE 26)
                    Mueller (PO I:44, PO 1:50)
                    Peeters (PH 1:4)
                    Pröger (GG 3:191)
                    Raphael (EK 1:50)
                    Thate (PO 5:23)
                    Vogel (HP 3:22)
Es ist genug   Held (HP 10:20)

Forest Green

Gieschen (HP 3:38)
Lovelace (PPS 2:25)
Purvis (PT 12)

Fortunatus   Ore (HP 10:23)
Fortunatus New   Johns (HP 7:31)
                           Schalk (WS 2:8)
Foundation   Owens (HP 25:22)
Fountain*   [See Cowper]
Framingham*   [See Hursley]
Franconia   Hillert (PO 11:30)
                           Lang (HP 1:16, HP 6:8 different
                               key)
                           Mackie (HP 16:20)
                           Peeters (PH 18:5)
                           Thalben-Ball (TB 30)
Frankfort   [See Wie schön leuchtet or Dir, dir,
                               Jehovah]
Franzen   Busarow (HP 34:44)
                           Peeters (PH 9:9)
Fred til bod   Cassler (HP 10:26)
                           Cherwien (CI 5:17)
                           Goode (HP 25:15)
                           Peeters (PH 12:2)
Fredericktown   Johns (HP 25:34)
French Tune*   [See Dundee]
Freu' dich Erd' und
    Sternenzelt   Schroeder (SO 4)
Freu dich sehr, o meine
    Seele   Bach (BN 68)
                           Bender (BK 1:10)
                           Böhm (BS 58; GT 1:159: 12 parti-
                               tas; PO 5:12)
                           Kickstat (HP 25:24)
                           Oley (GT 1:169)
                           Pachelbel (PA 4:48, 4 vars.; GG
                               1:24, vars.2,4; HP 1:18, var.2)
                           Reger (RC 1:11)
                           Schultz (HP 25:26)
                           Walther (WO 40; GT 1:170)

Freuen wir uns all in ein	Bouman (HP 1:20)
Freuet euch, ihr Christen alle	Beck (HP 3:24)
	Gerike (HP 6:10)
	Krenek (GG 4:282)
	Pepping (PK 9)
	Wiemer (GG 4:280)
Freylinghausen*	[See Macht hoch die Tür I]
Friend*	[See Converse]
Fröhlich soll mein Herze springen	Bender (BK 2:20)
	Busarow (HP 3:28, 2 vars.)
	Hessenberg (GG 4:283)
	Moser (PO 5:26)
	Oechsler (GG 3:192)
	Pepping (PK 8)
	Raasted (GG 3:194)
	Raphael (EK 1:62)
From heaven high*	[See Vom Himmel hoch]
Fulda	Thalben-Ball (TB 31)
Galilean	Dahl (HP 25:28)
	Hofland (PO I:51, PO 1:57)
Galilee	Gotsch (HP 25:30)
Garelochside	Gieschen (HP 6:12)
Gartan	Krapf (HP 3:34)
Gaston*	[See Azmon]
Gaude, regina gloriae	Peeters (PH 12:5)
Gaudeamus pariter	Beck (HP 10:28)
	Cherwien (CI 5:22)
	Held (HE 9)
	Hillert (HP 16:22)
	Krapf, Schroeder (WS 2:24)
Gelobet seist du, Jesu Christ	Bach (BO 10; EK 1:65; GT 2:1)
	Bach (BU 31)
	Bach (BU 32)
	Bender (BK 1:12)
	Böhm (BS 69)
	Böhm (BS 72; WBM 10: 5 vars.)

Gelobet seist du, Jesu
    Christ

Gelobt sei Gott im
    höchsten Thron

Geneva
Geneva 24*
Germany*
Gethsemane

Gevaert
Giardini*
Gibbons*
Gibbons' "Song 22"
Gladness*
Gloria

Go Tell It
God of Our Fathers
God Rest You Merry,
    Gentlemen
God Save the Queen (King)*
Godesberg*
Gonfalon Royal

Buttstedt (80:33)
Buxtehude (BC 23)
Buxtehude (BC 31)
Dupre (D 27)
Kirnberger (AWK 13)
Pachelbel (PA 2:12; PO 5:28)
Scheidt (80:32; GT 2:2; PO 6:12;
    HP 3:36)
Walther (GG 2:112; GT 2:4)

Baumann (GG 4:285)
Bender (PO 8:16)
Krapf (HP 10:32)
Peeters (PH 2:6)
Thalben-Ball (TB 104)
Wenzel, Kickstat (WS 2:20)
Willan (NT 14, WC 1:4)
Owens (HP 25:32)
[See Freu dich sehr]
[See Walton]
Lang (HP 7:43)
Lenel (PO 7:28)
Powell (PO I:54, PO 1:60)
Rotermund (HP 25:37)
Purvis (PM 6)
[See Italian Hymn]
[See Light Divine]
Willan (WH 3:19)
[See Cas radosti]
Gehrke (PO 6:32, HP 4:8, different
    key)
Hillert (HP 4:10)
Peeters (PH 24:2)

Rutter (CPE 4)
[See National Anthem]
[See Gott des Himmels]
Cundick (HP 25:40)

Goodwin*   [See Webb]
Gopsal   Thalben-Ball (TB 32)
Gordon   Peeters (PH 22:3)
Gospel Banner*   [See Missionary Hymn]
Gott der Vater wohn uns bei   Busarow (HP 25:42)
                                    Buxtehude (BC 32; EK 1:70)
                                    Micheelsen (HP 13:4)
                                    Pachelbel (PA 2:60)
                                    Scheidt (80:34; GT 2:5)
                                    Walther (GG 2:113)

Gott des Himmels und der
    Erden   Heaton (HP 25:46)
                                    Marpurg (MC 29)
                                    Peeters (PH 7:4)
                                    Reger (RC 1:12)
                                    Walther (GG 1:26; 80:30; GT 2:7)

Gott, durch deine Güte*   [See Gottes Sohn ist kommen]
Gott ist gegenwartig*   [See Wunderbarer König]
Gott sei Dank   Garske (HP 26:8)
                                    Gieseke (HP 14:44)
                                    Lenel (PO I:53, PO 1:59)
                                    Peeters (PH 8:8)
                                    Thalben-Ball (TB 35)

Gott sei gelobet und
    gebenedeiet   Hennig (HP 17:34)
                                    Poser (OB 163)
                                    Scheidemann (GG 2:120; 80:36)
Gott will's machen   Thalben-Ball (TB 34)
Gottes Sohn ist kommen   Bach (PO 5:13)
                                    Bach (BO 4)
                                    Bach (BU 33)
                                    Bach (BU 34)
                                    Bobb (HP 26:10)
                                    Buttstedt (GT 2:9)
                                    Dupré (D 28)
                                    Kauffmann (GG 2: 116; EK 1:72)
                                    Petzold (HP 1:22)
                                    Walther (WO 42; GT 2:10)
                                    Walther (GG 2:118)

Gottlob, es geht nunmehr
  zu Ende Schalk (HP 7:34)
Grace Church Krapf (HP 17:37)
Grace Church, Gananoque Lovelace (HP 26:12)
Gräfenberg Bender (BK 1:32; HP 34:8)
  Hark (PO I:110; PO 2:58)
  Held (HPP 16)
  Peters (PH 12:6)
  Petzold (EK 2:164)
  Raasted (GG 3:223)
  Schultz (HP 37:42)
  Schwarz (OB 231)
  Wolfrum (GG 3:222)
Granton Hillert (HP 26:14)
Great God, Our Source Haan (HP 26:20)
Great White Host* [See Den store hvide flok]
Greensleeves Cherwien (CI 2:10)
  Gehrke (PO 5:34, HP 4:14)
  Gehring (PPS 2:30)
  Purvis (PL 2)
  Vaughan Williams, A Vaughan
  Williams Organ Album (Oxford)
  Woodman, Noël anglais
    [Greensleeves] (E.C.Schirmer)

Grosser Gott, du liebst
  Erbarmen Baur (OB 180)
  Beck (HP 27:32)
  Callahan (HP 26:22)
  Cherwien (CI 6:24)
  Fleischer (PO I:56, PO 1:62)
  Grabner (WS 3:5)
  Held (HPP 22)
  Högner (GG 3:198)
  Johns (HP 13:27)
  Peeters (PC 3:36)
Gud er Gud Busarow (HP 26:17)
Gud skal alting Mage Held (HP 26:24)
Guds Menighed, syng Held (HP 26:26)
  Peeters (PH 11:6)

Hermas

Herongate

Herr Christ, der einig
    Gottes Sohn

Herr Gott, dich loben alle wir*

Herr, ich habe misgehandelt

Herr Jesu Christ, dich
    zu uns wend

Herr Jesu Christ, du hast
    bereit*

Herr Jesu Christ, mein's*

Ferguson (HP 26:42)

Thalben-Ball (TB 38)

Bach (BU 35)
Bach (BO 6; GG 2:122)
Buxtehude (BC 34, 2 vars.)
Dupré (D 30)
Pachelbel (PA 2:8)
Scheidemann (HP 6:14)
Sweelinck (SA 32; EK 1:75)
Walther (WO 43; 80:37)
Walther (GG 2:124)
Walther (HP 26:44)

[See Old 100th]

Gieseke (HP 13:30)
Marpurg (MC 67)
Patterson (HP 26:46)

Bach (BO 59; GT 2:24)
Bach (BU 43)
Bach (BU 45)
Bach (B18: 31)
Bender (BK 1:14)
Böhm (BS 76; GT 2:26, 6 vars.; EK
    1:79, var.6)
    Driessler (OB 126)
Dupré (D 32)
Peeters (PH 6:1)
Reger (RC 1:9)
Rotermund (HP 27:7)
Walther (PO I:59; PO 2:7; GG 1:27)
Walter (HP 17:40)
Walther (WO 46, 5 vars.)
Walther (GT 2:34, 7 vars.)

[See Du Lebensbrot, Herr Jesu
    Christ]

[See O Jesu Christ, mein's Lebens
    Licht II]

Herr Jesu Christ, wahr
   Mensch   Bach, J.S. (BO 42)
                               Bach, W.F. (45:7)
                               Birk (OB 161)
                               Buxtehude (BC 148)
                               Dupré (D 76)
                               Gieschen (HP 7:38)
                               Hessenberg (GG 4:378)
Herr, wie du willst*   [See Aus tiefer Not II]
Herre Jesu Krist   Peeters (PH 13:7)
Herrnhut   Peeters (PH 13:5)
Herzlich lieb hab' ich
   dich, o Herr   Alberti (GT 2:51; 80:40)
                                 Bach (GT 2:58, arr. from Cantata
                                   19)
                               Bach (BN 58)
                               Bender (BK 2:22)
                               Engel (HP 27:17)
                               Kauffmann (GG 2:129)
                               Krebs (GT 2:52)
                               Schmid (EK 1:83)
                               Wagner (OB 247)
                               Walther (GT 2:54; WO 52)
                               Walther (GT 2:65; GG 2:130)
Herzlich tut mich erfreuen   Brahms (BE 15)
                               Kalbfleisch (HP 10:35)
                               Koch (WS 2:28, 2 vars.)
                               Kropfreiter (GG 4:295)
Herzlich tut mich verlangen* [See Passion Chorale]
Herzliebster Jesu   Bender (BK 1:18)
                                 Brahms (PO 7:10; BE 10)
                               Cherwien (CI 5:18)
                               Haase (HP 8:7)
                               Henderson, Meditation on Herzlieb-
                                   ster Jesu (Jaymar)
                               Kauffmann (GG 2:132)
                               Oley (PO I:65, PO 2:13)
                               Peeters (PC 3:17)
                               Pepping (PK 14)

Ich singe dir

Bender (BK 2:26)
Hofland (PO I:84; PO 2:32; HP
12: 14)
Polley (HP 27:40)

Ich steh' an diener
Krippen hier

Klebe (GG 4:303)
Thate (PO 6:13)
Weyrauch (EK 2:92)

Ich sterbe täglich

Gehrke (HPC 1:25)
Kretzschmar (PO I:72; PO 2:20)
Schultz (HP 17:43)

Ich will dich lieben,
meine Stärke

Baur (OB 254)
Cherwien (CI 6:10)
Kickstat (HP 27:45)
Landmann (GG 3:204)
Peeters (PH 16:8)
Pröger (GG 3:205)
Reger (RC 2:17)

Illsley

Thalben-Ball (TB 41)

In Babilone

Barlow (WS 3:17)
Cherwien (CI 4:22)
Haan (HP 28:8)
Held (HPP 9)
Peeters (PH 3:2)
Purvis (PT 26)
Weiss (PO 11:38)
Wienhorst (HP 12:30)

In dich hab ich
gehoffet, Herr I**

Bach, J.S. (BO 70; GG 2:136; GT
2:89)
Dupré (D 38)
Koch (OB 179)

In dich hab ich
gehoffet, Herr II**

Bach, J.C. (80:43)
Bach, J.M. (HP 28:15)
Bach, J.S. (BU:48)
Bender (BK 1:30)
Pachelbel (PA 3:43; GG 1:31)
Raphael (EK 2:99; EK 2:153)

Invocation	Powell (HP 28:23)
Irby	Cherwien (CI 5:8)
	Johns (HP 4:18)
	Thalben-Ball (TB 42)
Irish	Peeters (PH 14:5)
	Willan (WP 2:16)
Island	Peeters (PH 8:6)
	Rotermund (HP 35:36)
Islesworth	Mackie (HP 28:29)
	Peeters (PH 17:2)
Ist Gott für mich	Kickstat (HP 28:34)
Iste Confessor	Koch (WS 4:12, 2 vars.)
	Peeters (PG 1:28)
	Petrich (HP 28:32)
	Willan (WH 3:10)
It Is Well	Gotsch (HP 28:46)
Italian Hymn	Cherwien (CI 7:6)
	Pearce (HP 28:36)
	Peeters (PH 8:9)
	Stellhorn (PO I:74; PO 2:22)
	Thalben-Ball (TB 65)
	Wente (HP 13:32)
	Willan (PO 8:44)
Jam lucis	Arnatt (WS 4:32)
	Barlow (HP 28:40)
	Peeters (PG 2:10)
Jefferson	Cherwien (CI 4:18)
	Cherwien (CI 7:10)
	Johnson (HP 2:4)
	Powell (HP 1:28)
Jeg er saa glad	Ore (HP 4:21)
Jeg vil mig Herren love*	[See Copenhagen]
Jerusalem, du	
hochgebaute Stadt	Flugel (GG 3:207)
	Kickstat (HP 28:44)
	Reger (RC 2:18)
	Thomas (EK 2:106)
Jervaulx Abbey	Peeters (PH 5:2)

Jesus Christus, unser
    Heiland I**   Buxtehude (BC 54; GG 2:138)
                                Distler (OB 154 II; GG 4:322)
                                Dupré (D 43)
                                Koch (OB 154 I)
                                Pachelbel (PA 2:52)
                                Peeters (PH 9:5)
                                Walther (EK 2:114)

Jesus Christus, unser
    Heiland II**   Bach (B18: 87)
                                Bach (B18: 91)
                                Bach (BCL 81)
                                Bach (BCL 89)
                                Dupré (D 44)
                                Hennig (HP 17:52)
                                Pachelbel (PA 3:24)
                                Peeters (PH 10:10)
                                Tunder (45:37)

Jesus ist kommen   Bender (BK 3:23)
                                Brod (HP 6:18)
                                Pröger (GG 3:211)
                                Raphel (EK 2:115)
                                Reger (GG 3:210, RC 3:51)

Jesus, meine Zuversicht   Bach (PO I:80, PO 2:28)
                                Bach (BU 58)
                                Dupré (D 45)
                                Lang (HP 36:16)
                                Lovelace (HP 29:13)
                                Metzger (PO 12:10)
                                Micheelsen (HP 10:48)
                                Peeters (PH 7:2)
                                Raasted (EK 2:118)
                                Reger (RC 2:20)
                                Thalben-Ball (TB 75)
                                Walther (WO 72; GG 1:35; GT
                                    2:120, 3 vars.; PO 8:23, var.2)

Joanna*   [See St. Denio]
Judas Maccabaeus   Johns (HP 10:40)
Just as I Am   Bouman (HP 29:18)

Just as I Am — Cherwien (CI 1:20)

Kedron — Gieseke (HP 29:20)
Kentucky 93rd — Zimmer (HP 29:31)
King's Lynn — Coleman, Rhapsody on King's Lynn
    (Bosworth & Co)
Rohlig (WS 3:20)
Schack (ST7)
Schalk (HP 15:8)
Thalben-Ball (TB 43)
Whitlock (WT2)
King's Weston — Cherwien (CI 6:2)
Johnson (HP 14:14)
Speller (SP 1:8)
Wienhorst (WS 2:36; HP 15:10)
Kingdom — Schalk (HP 17:54)
Kingly Love — Hillert (WS 3:22; HP 29:22)
Kingsfold — Johns (HP 29:24)
Kirken* — [*See* Kirken den er et gammelt hus]
Kirken den er et
    gammelt hus — Cherwien (CI 7:24)
Hoelty-Nickel (PO I:82, PO 2:30)
Peeters (PH 4:6)
Peeters (PH 10:1)
Powell (HP 29:26)
Knickerbocker — Barlow (HP 17:56)
Wood (PPS 3:14)
Komm, Gott Schöpfer — Bach (BO 58)
Bach (B18: 94)
Cook (FVW 4)
Demessieux (DT 22)
Dupré (D 46)
Engel (HP 13:12)
Held (HPP 3)
Metzler (HP 15:19)
Pachelbel (PA 2:58)
Peeters (PC 2:28; PG 1:26)
Schack (HP 29:34)
Schack (HP 40:24)

Komm, Gott Schöpfer

Sowerby (SW 6)
Titelouze (PO 8:36)
Walther (EK 2:119; GT 2:123)
Walther (GG 2:140)
Zachau (HP 12:32)

Komm, Heiliger Geist,
    Herre Gott

Armsdorf (80:48)
Bach (B18: 3)
Bach (B18: 13)
Bender (BK 2:25)
Buxtehude (BC 55; EK 2:120; GT
    2:126)
Buxtehude (BC 58)
Dupré (D 47)
Kauffmann (GG 2:142)
Pachelbel (PA 2:57)
Peeters (PH 3:3)
Telemann (PO I:85, PO 2:33)
Telemann (HP 12:38)
Walther (GG 2:143)
Weckmann (PO 8:33)
Zachau (80:49; GT 2:128; 45:45)

Komm, o komm, du Geist
    des Lebens

Drews (HP 29:36)
Hasse (GG 3:212)
Kirnberg (GG 3:214)
Klotz (HP 12:34)
Peeters (PC 2:31)
Petzold (EK 2:123)
Raphael (PO 8:31)
Reger (RC 2:22)
Thalben-Ball (TB 86)

Komm, süsser Tod

Peeters (PH 21:3)

Kommst du nun, Jesu*

[See Lobe den Herren]

Kommt her zu mir

Buxtehude (BC 60)
Gerike (HP 29:38)
Peeters (PH 10:3)
Peeters (PH 23:9)
Siedel (OB 245)

Kommt her zu mir

Von Bruck (EK 2:125)
Walther (WO 75, 2 vars.)
Walther (GG 1:38)

König*

[*See* O dass ich tausend Zungen hätte
II]

Kremser

Engel (HP 29:42)
Peeters (PH 22:7)
Willan (PO I:88, PO 2:36)

Kuortane

Held (HP 29:44)
Peeters (PH 18:8)

Kyrie, Gott Vater in
Ewigkeit

Bach (BCL 16)
Bach (BCL 27)
Dupré (D 49)
Krapf (HP 13:34)
Wente (HP 29:46)
Wenzel (OB 130)
Wolfrum (GG 3:214)
Wolfrum (GG 3:215)

Ladywell
Lakewood
Lancashire

Thalben-Ball (TB 44)
Bobb (HP 30:8)
Arnatt (PO 11:42)
Gerike (HP 30:12)
Peeters (PH 20:5)

Land of Rest

Gieschen (HP 30:14)
Speller (SP 1:3)

Langham
Lasset uns mit Jesu ziehen

Wienhorst (HP 30:16)
Kretzschmar (PO I:90, PO 2:38)
Peeters (PH 16:3)
Rotermund (HP 30:22)

Lasst uns alle

Held (HP 4:24)
Metzger (PO 5:46)
Willan (WC 1:2)

Lasst uns erfreuen

Bender (HP 10:42, 2 vars.)
Cabena, Sonata da Chiesa, 3rd
Movement (Jaymar)
Cherwien (CI 5:20)
Ferguson (HP 30:18)

Lasst uns erfreuen	Gieschen (HP 12:16)
	Johnson (HP 15:12, 2 vars.)
	Moser (PO I:92, PO 2:40)
	Peeters (PH 3:1)
	Peeters (PH 21:8)
	Peeters (FVE 17)
	Reichel (PO 8:26)
	Slater, An Easter Alleluia (Oxford)
	Speller (SP 1:6)
	Thalben-Ball (TB 46)
Lauda anima	Adam (PO 11:45)
	Thalben-Ball (TB 74)
	Wienhorst (HP 36:10)
Laudes Domini	Wyble (HP 30:32)
Laurel	Schalk (HP 30:28)
Laus Deo	Gilbert (FVW 19)
	Thalben-Ball (TB 45)
Laus Regis	Schack (HP 14:28)
Le Cantique de Simeon*	[See Nunc dimittis]
Le Jeune	Peeters (PH 17:8)
Leominster	Johns (HP 30:30)
Leoni	Lubrich (PO 11:48; HP 42:46)
	Peeters (PH 6:11)
Les Anges dans nos campagnes*	[See Gloria]
Les Commandements de Dieu	Thalben-Ball (TB 47)
Let Us Break Bread*	[See Break Bread Together]
Leupold	Schalk (HP 30:11)
Lewis-Town	Fedak (HP 30:25)
Liebster Immanuel	Peeters (PH 1:8)
	Peeters (PH 24:3)
Liebster Jesu, wir sind hier	Bach, J.S. (PO I:102, PO 2:50)
	Bach (BO 60)
	Bach (BU 60; GT 2:135)
	Bach (BU 61; GT 2:136)
	Bach (BU 59, GG 1:39)
	Bender (HP 16:26; BK 1:24)
	Birk (OB 127)

Lobe den Herren

Reger (EK 2:131; NT 20; RC 2:24)
Walther (GG 1:40; EK 2:129;
    80:51, GT 2:145; NT 22)
Zipp (PO 12:5)

Lobe den Herren, o
   meine Seele

Beck (HP 31:12)

Lobt Gott den Herrn,
   ihr Heiden all

Chemin-Petit (HP 31:25)
Klebe (GG 4:333)
Marx (OB 189)
Wenzel (EK 2:136)

Lobt Gott, ihr Christen,
   allzugleich

Bach, J.C. (GT 2:147)
Bach, J.S. (BO 18)
Bach, J.S. (BU 64; EK 2:138; GT
   2:148)
Bender (BK 2:32)
Buxtehude (BC 62; GG 1:41; GT
   2:149)
Dupré (D 54)
Lübeck (ADW 8)
Reger (RC 2:23)
Walther (WBM 19, 8 vars.; WO 80,
   vars.1-7; HP 4:30, var.1; PO
   5:30, var.2; GG 1:42, var.6; PO
   I:94; PO 2:42, var.8; GT 2:149,
   vars. 1, 2, 3, 6, 7)
Walther (HP 31:14)
Willan (WC 2:4)

London New

Peeters (PH 21:11)
Thalben-Ball (TB 50)
Willan (WP 2:18)

Lord, Revive Us

Lenel (WS 3:14)
Pelz (HP 31:16)

Lost in the Night

Haan (HP 31:18)

Love Divine

Thalben-Ball (TB 51)

Love Unknown

Arnatt (WS 2:4)
Held (HP 8:12)

Lovely*

[See Rhosymedre]

Meinen Jesum lass' ich
    nicht II***

       Raphael (HP 32:14)
       Reger (GG 3:221; RC 2:26)

Meinen Jesum lass' ich
    nicht III**

       Marpurg (MC 12)

Meinen Jesum lass' ich
    nicht IV**

       Walther (GT 2:166, 6 vars.)

Meinigen*   [*See* Munich]

Melcombe   Canning (PO 11:60; HP 32:18)
       Parry (PC 1:5)
       Peeters (PH 8:7)
       Thalben-Ball (TB 57)
       Willan (WH 1:26)

Melita   Kalbfleisch (HP 32:20)
       Peeters (PH 13:8)

Mendelssohn   Gehrke (PO I:100; PO 2:48)
       Schack (HP 4:32)

Mendip   Thalben-Ball (TB 58)

Mendon   Gehrke (PO 11:62; HP 32:22)
       Peeters (PH 11:2)

Meribah   Bender (HP 32:24)

Merrial   Gieschen (HP 32:26)

Messiah*   [*See* Bereden väg för Herran *or*
         Antioch]

Metzler's Redhead   Thalben-Ball (TB 60)

Meyer   Thalben-Ball (TB 61)

Michael   Bouman (HP 32:28)

Midden in de Dood   Bouman (HP 17:58)

Miles Lane   Johnson (HP 32:32)
       Peeters (PH 6:5)
       Thalben-Ball (TB 62)
       Willan (WP 1:1)

Milwaukee*   [*See* Macht hoch die Tür II]

Mission   Hillert (WS 3:28)

Missionary Hymn   Peeters (PH 14:7)
       Schultz (HP 32:34)
       Stelzer (PO I:103; PO 2:51)

Mit Ernst, o Menschenkinder*   [*See* Von Gott will ich nicht
         lassen]

Mit Freuden zart	Abel (WS 2:16)
	Bender (BK 2:36)
	Distler (GG 4:338)
	Haase (PO 11:61)
	Hellmann (EK 2: 158)
	Micheelsen (HP 11:7)
	Pearce (HP 32:38)
	Schack (18)
Mit Fried und Freud ich fahr dahin	Bach, J.C. (80:55)
	Bach, J.S. (BO 30; GT 2:172)
	Buxtehude (BC 77; PO 6:49)
	Dupré (D 56)
	Hennig (HP 15:22)
	Peeters (PH 4:2)
	Willan (WC 2:3)
	Zachau (HP 32:40)
Mit meinem Gott geh ich zur Ruh*	[See In dich hab ich gehoffet, Herr II]
Mitten wir im Leben sind	Peeters (PH 21:2)
	Scheidt (GT 2:174; 80:56)
	Walther (GG 1:46)
	Weyrauch (EK 2:156; HP 32:42)
Monkland	Peeters (PH 6:10)
	Statham (FVH 7)
	Thalben-Ball (TB 63)
Monks Gate	Patterson (HP 32:44)
	Thalben-Ball (TB 59)
Morecambe	Pearce (HP 32:37)
Morestead	Schalk (HP 32:46)
Morgenglanz der Ewigkeit	Bender (BK 1:31)
	Crane (PO 11:64)
	Peeters (PH 7:3)
	Reger (EK 2:159; GG 2:222)
Morgenlied	Busarow (HP 11:8)
Morning Hymn	Bobb (HP 33:8)
	Peeters (PH 7:1)
	Thalben-Ball (TB 64)

Morning Light*   [*See* Webb]
Morning Song*   [*See* Consolation]
Morning Star   Bender (PO 11:66, HP 6:20 different key)

Moscow*   [*See* Italian Hymn]
Moville   Beck (HP 33:10)
Müde bin ich   Beck (HP 33:12)
Mueller*   [*See* Away in a Manger]
Munich*   [*See* O Gott du frommer Gott II]
My Country 'Tis of Thee*   [*See* America]

Naar mit Oie*   [*See* Consolation]
*Name of Jesus   Cherwien (CI 2:6)
                                    Krapf (HP 33:20)
Naomi   Peeters (PH 9:6)
Narenza   Thalben-Ball (TB 66)
Narodil se Kristus Pan   Beck (HP 4:34)
                                    Cherwien (CI 4:6)
National Anthem   Barlow (HP 33:26)
National Hymn*   [*See* America *or* God of our Fathers]

Nativity   Thalben-Ball (TB 67)
Navarre*   [*See* Rendez à Dieu]
Neander   Beck (HP 15:38)
                                    Bender (BK 3:30)
                                    Cherwien (CI 2:23)
                                    Fleischer (PO I:106; PO 2:54)
                                    Hessenberg (EK 3:215)
                                    Hillert (HP 40:16)
                                    Hiltscher (PO 8:24)
                                    Peeters (PH 6:3)
                                    Schneider (GG 3:235)
                                    Thalben-Ball (TB 68)
                                    Thate (OB 129)
Netherlands*   [*See* Kremser]
Nettleton   Lovelace (HP 33:30)
Neumark*   [*See* Wer nur den lieben Gott]
New Britain   Cherwien (CI 4:8)
                                    Folkening (HP 33:32)

New Britain   Held (PPS 1:10)
                                Langlais (LO 4)
New Malden   Johns (HP 33:34)
Newbury   Willan (WH 3:23)
Newington*   [See St. Stephen]
Nicaea   Busarow (HP 13:43)
                                Canning (PO I:108; PO 2:56)
                                Cherwien (CI 4:2)
                                Griffiths (FVW 14)
                                Hurford (CPE 15)
                                Willan (WP 1:14)
Nilsson   Gerike (HP 33:36)
Noël nouvelet   Cherwien (CI 2:12)
                                Schalk (HP 11:12)
Noel pour l'amour de Marie   Daquin (PO 6:36)
Noormarkku   Wienhorst (HP 33:38)
Nottingham*   [See St. Magnus]
Nous allons   Powell (HP 33:42)
Now   Busarow (HP 18:8)
                                Schalk (WS 4:9)
Nun bitten wir den
    Heiligen Geist   Bender (BK 2:38)
                                Böhm (BS 94)
                                Buxtehude (BC 88)
                                Buxtehude (BC 90; GG 2:146; GT
                                    3:1)
                                Kickstat (HP 33:40)
                                Pepping (HP 12:36)
                                Scheidemann (PO 8:39)
                                Scheidt, Kickstat (WS 3:15)
                                Schroeder (SV 10)
                                Walther (WO 96; 80:57)
                                Walther (GG 2:148)
                                Weyrauch (EK 2:160)
Nun danket all*   [See Gräfenberg]
Nun danket alle Gott   Bach (B18: 46)
                                Bach (NT 27: arr. from Cantata
                                    79)
                                Dupré (D 57)

Nun danket alle Gott	Haase (HP 34:10)
	Hillert (HP 13:46)
	Jackson (FVH 15)
	Karg-Elert
	Kauffmann (GG 2:150; PO I:112; PO 2:60; NT 30)
	Kickstat (HP 34:12)
	Oley (NT 26)
	Peeters (PC 2:3)
	Peeters (PH 23:7)
	Purvis (PF 4)
	Raphael (EK 2:162)
	Reger (NT 32; RC 2:27)
	Wagner (OB 228)
Nun freut euch I**	Bach (BU 70; GT 3:4; EK 1:53)
	Bach (GG 1:22; 80:28)
	Bender (BK 1:8)
	Dupré (D 58)
	Hessenberg (EK 1:56)
	Kauffmann (HP 24:28)
	Krebs (GT 3:6)
	Krebs (80:29)
	Micheelsen (HP 34:14)
	Pachelbel (PA 2:54; GT 3:6; GG 1:21)
	Pepping (PK 28)
	Praetorius (PO I:46, PO 1:52)
	Praetorius (PRC 32: 4 stanzas)
	Reger (RC 2:28)
Nun freut euch II**	Bender (BK 1:34)
	Bieske (HP 12:18; OB 239)
	Buxtehude (BC 92)
	Praetorius (PO I:114; PO 2:62)
	Weckmann (GG 1:48; EK 3:169; GT 3:9; 80:59)
Nun komm, der Heiden Heiland	
	Bach (B18 55; GT 3:12)
	Bach (B18 59, trio)
	Bach (B18 62, organo pleno)
	Bach (BO 3; EK 3:169)

Nun komm, der Heiden
    Heiland   Bach (BU 73, fughetta)
                               Bender (BK 1:36)
                               Bruhns (BR 25)
                               Buttstedt (AWK 15; PO I:120; PO
                                   3:10)
                               Buxtehude (BC 105)
                               Distler (PO 5: 14, from his Parti-
                                 ta)
                               Dupré (D 59)
                               Kauffmann (AWK 9; WBM 5: 4
                                 vars.; HP 2:8,var.4)
                               Pachelbel (PA 2:4; GT 3:15)
                               Reger (RC 2:29)
                               Speller (SP 2:2)
                               Walther (WO 98, 3 vars.; AWK
                                 6, var.1)
                               Zachau (GG 1:50; ADW 6)

Nun lasst uns all mit
    Innigkeit   Peeters (PH 12:5)
Nun lasst uns den Leib
    begraben   Bach (BN 50)
                               Bieske (OB 174)
                               Engel (HP 34:16)
                               Zipp (WS 2:14)

Nun lasst uns Gott dem
    Herren   Fussan (EK 3:170)
                               Lübeck (LS 60; GT 3:18, 6 vars.)
                               Pachelbel (PA 3:38; GG 1:51;
                                 80:61)
                               Walther (WO 102, 4 vars.; HP
                                 15:24, var.3)
                               Wenzel (OB 227)
                               Willan (WH 3:37)
                               Zachau (GG 1:52)

Nun lob, mein Seel, den
    Herren   Abel (HP 34:18)
                               Bach, J.C. (PO I:117; PO 3:7)
                               Bender (BK 2:40)
                               Buxtehude (BC 106)

O Durchbrecher alle Bande	Schmidt (OB 262)
O filii et filiae	Dandrieu (PO 8:20)
	Demessieux (DT 17)
	Farnum (Toccata, Theodore Presser)
	Held (HP 11:14)
	LeBegue (LC 200)
	Peeters (PH 2:7)
	Schroeder (WS 2:17, 2 vars.)
	Sowerby (SW 5)
	Willan (WH 1:34)
O Gott, du frommer Gott I**	Bach (BP 122; GT 3:34, partita 9 only)
	Bender (BK 2:42)
	Brahms (BE 22)
	Dupré (D 60)
	Hessenberg (GG 4:354)
	Reger (GG 3:226; RC 2:30)
O Gott, du frommer Gott II**	Peeters (PH 8:4)
	Sensmeier (HP 33:)
	Walther (PO I:128; PO 3:18; GG 1:58; EK 3:185; HP 34:32)
	Walther (GG 1:56; GT 3:36)
O grosser Gott	Schalk (HP 6:24)
	Schalk (HP 34:34)
O Haupt voll Blut und Wunden*	[See Passion Chorale]
O Heiland, reiss die Himmel auf	Bouman (HP 34:36)
	Schneider (GG 3:227)
	Weihrauch (EK 3:186)
	Zipp (HP 2:10)
O heilige Dreifaltigkeit	Barbe (HP 39:8)
	Bender (PO I: 132; PO 3:22; HP 34:38)
	Peeters (PH 11:7)

O Lamm Gottes, unschuldig	Pachelbel (PA 2:44; GT 3: 40; GG 1:59; EK 3:191; PO 7:14)
	Peeters (PC 3:19)
	Reger (RC 2:32)
O lux beata trinitas	Albert (45:1)
	Peeters (PH 3:5)
	Sweelinck (SA 46)
O mein Jesu, ich muss sterbern	
	Schroeder (PO 7:23)
	Wienhorst (HP 8:30)
O Perfect Love*	[See Sandringham]
O quanta qualia	Cherwien (CI 7:3)
	Hillert (PO 11:68; HP 35:10)
	Peeters (PH 21:13)
	Wente (HP 15:28)
O Sanctissima*	[See Sicilian Mariners]
O Seigneur	Barlow (WS 4:30)
	Wienhorst (HP 35:12)
O Store Gud	Held (PPS 1:14)
	Johns (HP 35:16)
O Traurigkeit, o Herzeleid	Bender (BK 1:41)
	Engel (HP 8:32)
	Raasted (EK 3:200)
	Thalben-Ball (TB 71)
	Weismann (PO 7:31)
	Willan (WC 2:2)
	Wolfrum (GG 3:227)
O Welt, ich muss dich lassen	
	Anonymous (GG 1:60)
	Bach, J.S. (PO I:136)
	Bender (BK 1:37)
	Brahms (BE 12)
	Brahms (BE 34; PO 6:42)
	Genzmer (HP 35:18)
	Isaac (HP 8:34)
	Kauffmann (HP 18:21)
	Ochsenkuhn (HP 6:22)

O Welt, ich muss dich
    lassen

                Peeters (PH 7:11)
                Raphael (EK 3:202)
                Reger (RC 2:33)
                Walther (GG 1:60; PO 7:34; GT
                    3:51)

O Welt, sieh hier   Krapf (HP 8:27)
                Pepping (PK 12)

O wie selig seid ich doch   Bouman (HP 35:20)
                Brahms (BE 20; GG 3:228)
                Peeters (PH 21:12)
                Reger (RC 3:52)
                Willan (WC 1:6)

Oakley   Sensmeier (HP 8:36)

Ohne Raste und unverweilt*   [*See* Vienna]

Oi Herra, jos mä
    matkamies maan   Krapf (HP 35:22)

Old 100th   J.C.Bach (PO I:117; PO 3:7)
                Blow (HP 18:15)
                Micheelsen (HP 35:24)
                Pachelbel (80:38; GT 2:13; NT
                    18)
                Peeters (PH 24:10)
                Petrich (HP 35:24)
                Purcell (The Organ Works, 16
                    [Novello])
                Thalben-Ball (TB 69)
                Walther (GT 2:15)
                Walther (GT 2:16; EK 1:77; GG
                    2:126; NT 16)
                Willan (WH 1:28)

Old 104th   Parry (PC 1:4)
                Thalben-Ball (TB 72)
                Willan (WH 2:25)

Old 107th   Busarow (HP 35:27)

Old 112th*   [*See* Vater unser]

Old 120th   Willan (WP 1:16)

Old 124th   Moser (PO I:138; PO 3:28)
                Peeters (PH 10:7)

Quem pastores

Kickstat (PO 6:22)
Kousemaker (HP 4:36)
Schwarz (GG 4:262)
Willan (WC 1:1)

Rathburn

Engel (HP 9:7)
Lubrich (PO 12:8)

Ratisbon*   [See Jesu, meine Zuversicht]
Ravenna*   [See Vienna]
Reading*   [See Erhalt uns, Herr]
Red wing seminary   Peeters (PH 12:4)
Redemption*   [See New Britain]
Redhead*   [See Gethsemane]
Redhead No.76*   [See Gethsemane]
Redhead 46*   [See Laus Deo]
Regent Square   Lang (HP 4:38)

Peeters (PH 11:4)
Thalben-Ball (TB 76)
Unkel (PO I:146; PO 3:36)
Videro (HP 36:18)

Regnator orbis*   [See O quanta qualia]
Regwal   Gieschen (HP 36:20)
Rendez à Dieu   Beyer (PO 12:11)

Cherwien (CI 6:18)

Resignation   Schalk (HP 36:22)
Resonet in laudibus   Hoegner (PO 6:30)

Purvis (PM 3)

Rest   Haan (HP 36:24)

Hulse (PO I:96; PO 2:44)

Restoration   Held (PPS 1:12)
Reuter   Bender (HP 36:26)
Rex Gloriae   Gieseke (HP 36:28)

Niblock (PO 12:12)

Rhosymedre   Beck (HP 36:30)

Powell (HP 9:8, 2 vars.)
Schultz (WS 4:25)
Vaughan Williams (VW 6)

Rhuddlan   Johns (HP 36:32)
Richmond*   [See Chesterfield]

St. Bride   Willan (WP 2:20)
St. Catherine   Callahan (HP 37:14)
St. Cecilia   Boda (PO 12:18)
St. Christopher   Schalk (HP 9:14)
St. Clement   Cherwien (CI 4:12)
    Halter (HP 37:16)
    Thalben-Ball (TB 81)
St. Columba   Cherwien (CI 3:18)
    Krapf (PO 12:20)
    Lang (HP 37:18)
    Leighton (LH 4)
    Ley (HV)
    Peeters (PH 23:5)
    Willan (WH 1:32)
St. Crispin   Bender (HP 37:22)
    Bouman (PO I:152; PO 3:42)
    Willan (WP 3:8)
St. Cross   Parry (PC 2:6)
    Willan (WP 3:10)
St. Cuthbert   Willan (WP 3:12)
St. Denio   Gehrke (WS 4:8)
    Powell (HP 37:20)
    Rohlig (PO 12:22)
    Rohlig (PO 12:24)
    Thalben-Ball (TB 78)
    Whitlock (WT2)
St. Dunstan's   Boda (PO 12:26)
    Petrich (HP 37:25)
St. Elizabeth*   [See Schönster Herr Jesu]
St. Etheldreda   Thalben-Ball (TB 82)
St. Ethelwald*   [See Energy]
St. Flavian   Canning (PO 12:28)
    Lang (HP 37:28)
    Peeters (PH 24:5)
    Willan (WH 1:17)
St. Francis*   [See Lasst uns erfreuen]
St. Fulbert   Slater (FVE 6)
St. Gabriel   Peeters (PH 7:10)
    Willan (WP 3:14)

St. George	Engel (HP 6:26)
	Gehrke (PO I:154; PO 3:44; HP 37: 30)
	Griffiths (FVH 1)
	Peeters (PH 22:1)
St. George's, Windsor*	[See St. George]
St. Gertrude	Haan (HP 37:33)
St. Hugh	Thalben-Ball (TB 83)
St. James	Krapf (PO 12:30)
	Thalben-Ball (TB 85)
	Willan (WP 3:16)
St. Leonard*	[See Komm, o komm, du Geist des Lebens]
St. Louis	Cherwien (CI 6:12)
	Lovelace (PPS 2:24)
	Schalk (HP 5:8)
St. Luke	Peeters (PH 13:3)
	Rotermund (HP 37:36)
St. Magnus	Barlow (PO 12:32)
	Busarow (HP 14:25)
	Jackson (JF 1)
	Thalben-Ball (TB 88)
	Wienhorst (HP 16:36)
	Willan (WP 1:22)
St. Margaret	Held (HP 37:40)
St. Mary Magdalene*	[See Gräfenberg]
St. Matthew	Peeters (PH 8:5)
	Thalben-Ball (TB 87)
St. Michael	Barlow (HP 37:45)
	Bender (PO I:131; PO 3:21)
	Peeters (PH 10:8)
	Rotermund (HP 18:29)
	Thalben-Ball (TB 89)
St. Patrick	Fetler (PO 12:34)
St. Patrick's Breastplate	Held (WS 3:6, HP 13:40)
	Krapf (HP 16:38)
	Peeters (PH 3:6)
	Stanford, Sonata Celtica, last movement (Stainer & Bell)

Santa Barbara
Savannah
Savoy*
Schmücke dich, o liebe
    Seele

Schönster Herr Jesu

Schumann*
Schwing dich auf zu
    deinem Gott
Seelenbräutigam

Sei Lob und Ehr'*
Septum verba
Sheldonian
Shepherding
Shrubsole*
Sicilian Mariners

Polley (HP 38:16)
Bouman (PO 12:42)
[*See* Old 100th]

Bach (B18 26; GT 3:56)
Bach (GT 3:59, arr. from Cantata
    180)
Brahms (BE 18; PO I:162; PO
    3:52)
Busarow (HPC 1:4)
Cherwien (CI 6:5)
Dupré (D 64)
Hessenberg (HP 18:32; OB 157)
Marpurg (MC 59)
Peeters (PH 9:4)
Reger (RC 2:34)
Telemann (HP 38:20)
Walther (WO 122; GT 3:61, 3
    vars.; GG 1:62, var.2)
Arbatsky (PO I:160; PO 3:50)
Cherwien (CI 3:10)
Engel (HP 38:22)
Peeters (PH 6:6)
[*See* Heath]

Landmann (GG 3:229)
Reichel (PO 8:14)
Bach, J.S. (PO I:165, PO 3:55)
Cherwien (CI 3:1)
Kickstat (HP 38:26)
Peeters (PH 23:1)
Reger (RC 2:35)
[*See* Es ist das Heil]
Gehrke (HP 9:16)
Patterson (HP 13:8)
Hillert (HP 5:7)
[*See* Miles Lane]
Hahn (HP 38:28)
Johnson (PO 12:44)

Sieh, hier bin ich

Silent Night*
Silver Street
Sine nomine

Slane

Sleepers Wake*
So nimm denn meine Hände
Soldau*
Solid Rock*
Sollt ich meinem Gott
    nicht singen

Solon*
Solothurn
Song 1

Song 13

Song 20

Peeters (PH 15:8)
Schalk (HP 38:30)
[See Stille nacht]
Peeters (PH 20:7)
Bouman (HP 15:32)
Gehrke (PO 12:46)
Jackson (JF 5)
Peeters (PH 5:1)
Peeters (PH 21:9)
Arnatt (PO 12:48)
France (SC 3)
Gerike (HP 38:32)
[See Wachet auf]
Wienhorst (HP 38:34)
[See Nun bitten wir]
[See The Solid Rock]

Bender (BK 1:42)
Fussen (EK 3:205)
Hogner (GG 3:232)
Karg-Elert (GG 3:230)
Marx (OB 232)
Pepping (PK 31)
Reger (RC 3:36)
Wente (HP 38:36)
[See New Britain]
Janson (HP 15:34)
Gieschen (HP 18:36)
Lovelace (HP 38:42)
Peeters (PH 21:7)
Willan (WP 2:24)
Coleman (HP 13:10; HP 38:44)
Noehren (PO 8:32)
Vaughan Williams, Prelude on
    Song 13 (Oxford University
    Press)
Whitlock (WT1)
Willan (WC 1:3)
Gehring (WS 3:30, 2 vars.)

Song 22*	[*See* Gibbons' "Song 22"]
Song 24	Willan (WH 1:3)
Song 34	Casner (WS 4:16)
	Pelz (HP 38:39)
	Thalben-Ball (TB 3)
	Willan (WS 1:2)
Song 67	Bouman (WS 4:19)
	Garske (HP 38:46)
	Peeters (PH 19:3)
	Thalben-Ball (TB 93)
	Willan (WP 3:2)
Sonne der Gerechtigkeit	Beck (HPC 1:8)
	Bender (WS 2:15)
	Bender (BK 3:32; HP 18:38)
	Borris (OB 218)
	Eben (GG 4:360)
	Gehrke (HP 11:28)
	Hellmann (EK 3:208)
	Pepping (PK 26)
	Schack (ST 14)
Southwell	Beck (HP 9:20)
	Canning (PO I:168; PO 3:58)
	Miles (PO 7:30; HP 39:27)
	Peeters (PH 13:1)
	Willan (WP 3:22)
Spanish Chant	Bunjes (PO I:166; PO 3:56)
Speak Forth Thy Word	Beck (WS 3:27)
Spires*	[*See* Erhalt uns, Herr]
Splendor paternae	Hillert (HP 39:10)
Sporh	Peeters (PH 19:1)
Stabat Mater	Bobb (HP 9:22)
	Demessieux (DT 10)
Star-Spangled Banner	Peeters (PH 24:6)
Steht auf, ihr lieben Kinderlein*	[*See* O heilige Dreifaltigkeit]
Stephanos	Lenel (PO I:169; PO 3:59)
	Pearce (HP 39:12)
Stille Nacht	Barber, Choral Prelude on Silent Night (G. Schirmer)

Tallis' Canon	Peeters (PH 7:8)
	Purvis (PT 20)
Tallis' Ordinal	Darke (DC 3)
	Peeters (PH 10:4)
	Rohlig (PO 12:50)
	Thalben-Ball (TB 98)
	Willan (WH 2:11)
Tandandei	Ferguson (HP 39:24)
Te Deum*	[See Grosser Gott]
Tempus adest floridum	Eben, Variations on "Good King Wenceslas" (Theodore Presser)
	Johns (HP 5:14)
Tender Thought	Janson (HP 18:40)
Ter Sanctus	Peeters (PH 6:4)
	Schroeder (WS 4:10, 2 vars.)
Terra Patris	Mackie (HP 39:28)
Teshiniens	Peeters (PH 2:4)
Thatcher	Peeters (PH 24:4)
The Ash Grove	Cherwien (CI 2:12)
	Cundick (HP 39:31)
	Schack (HP 18:44)
	Wood (PPS 3:6)
The Call	Heaton (HP 39:34)
The Eighth Tune*	[See Tallis' Canon]
The First Nowell	Gehrke (PO 5:47, HP 5:18)
The King's Banner	Lenel (WS 2:10)
The King's Majesty	Bender (WS 2:6)
	Drews (HP 9:24)
	Schack (ST 6)
The Saints' Delight	Beck (HP 39:36)
	Cherwien (CI 2:18)
	Gehring (WS 3:26)
	Schack (ST 12)
	Speller (SP 1:3)
The Solid Rock	Kohrs (HP 39:38)
They'll Know We Are Christians	Held (PPS 1:8)
Third Mode Melody	Krapf (HP 39:42)

Vom Himmel hoch, da komm
    ich her

    Reger (RC 3:40)

    Walther (WO 125, 2 vars.; PO
       I:180; PO 4:12, var.2; HP
       5:22, var.2; GG 1:64, var.2;
       GT 3:88, var.2)

    Zachau (GG 1:65; AWK 32;
       WBM 15, 3 vars.; PO 5:16,
       var.3)

Vom Himmel hoch, o Englein   Moser (PO 5: 35)

    Peter (EK 3:222, 6 vars.)

Von Gott will ich nicht
    lassen

    Bach, J.M. (GG 1:68; 45:4)

    Bach, J.S. (B18 51; GT 3:96)

    Buxtehude (BC 136, 2 vars.)

    Cherwien (CI 2:8)

    Daquin (Noel XI)

    Dupré (D 70)

    Hanff (HS 14)

    Le Begue (LC 214; PO 6:35)

    Krebs (GT 3:100)

    Marpurg (MC 37)

    Peeters (PH 16:1)

    Reger (RC 3:42)

    Schalk (HP 5:17)

    Walther (WO 128; GT 3:103, 2
       vars.; EK 3:230, var.1; GG
       1:69, var.1)

    Walther (HP 40:32)

Vor deinen Thron tret' ich*   [See Wenn wir in höchsten Nöten
    sein]

Vruechten   Bouman (WS 2:34)

    Schack (ST 20)

    Thalben-Ball (TB 105)

    Weber (HP 11:41)

Vulpius*   [See Gelobt sei Gott]

W zlobie lezy   Bobb (HP 5:24)

Was frag ich nach der Welt* [*See* Meinen Jesum lass' ich nicht
I]

Was Gott tut, das ist
wohlgetan   Bach (BN 60)
Bender (BK 1:50)
Cherwien (CI 6:18)
Kellner (GT 3:122; 45:22)
Krebs (GT 3:126)
Marpurg (MC 55)
Micheelsen (HP 41:21)
Pachelbel (PA 4:30, 9 vars.)
Peeters (PH 21:4)
Raphael (EK 3:235)
Reger (RC 3:44)
Walther (WO 129; GG 1:75; GT
3:119, 2 vars.)
Was mein Gott will   Bach, W.F. (GT 3:129; 45:6)
Grabner (HP 41:22)
Kindermann (80:74)
Marpurg (MC 51)
Mendelssohn (Sonata I)
Pachelbel (PA 3:40)
Walther (EK 3:236; GG 1:76)
Zachau (HP 41:18)
Watermouth*   [*See* Angel's Story]
We Are the Lord's   Weber (HP 41:24)
We Lift Our Hearts   Schalk (WS 4:23)
Webb   Arbatsky (PO I:186; PO 4:18)
Peeters (PH 14:9)
Schack (HP 41:27)
Wedlock   Sensmeier (HP 41:30)
Weil ich Jesu Schäflein bin Patterson (HP 41:33)
Weimar*   [*See* Jesu Kreuz, Leiden und Pein]
Wellington Square   Bender (HP 41:36)
Wem in Leidenstagen   Cassler (HP 9:36)
Powell (PO I:192; PO 4:24)
Thalben-Ball (TB 17)

Wenn wir in höchsten Nöten
sein   Bach, J.C. (GT 3:136; 80:76)

Werde munter, mein Gemüte	Reger (RC 3:47)
	Walther (WO 134; GT 3:156, 3 vars.; HP 17:45, var.1; GG 1:77, var.3)
	Whitlock (WT2)
Were You There	Goode (HP 42:8)
	Hancock (HP 9:38)
	Purvis (PL 7)
Westminster	Thalben-Ball (TB 108)
Westminster Abbey	Henderson, Toccata on Westminster Abbey (Jaymar)
	Schultz (HP 15:44)
Westminster Carol*	[See Gloria]
Weyse*	[See Den signede Dag]
What a Friend*	[See Converse]
While Shepherds Watched	Schack (HP 5:28)
Wie lieblich ist der Maien	Bender (WS 4:35)
	Bialas (GG 4:372)
	Hennig (HP 42:14)
Wie nach einer Wasserquelle*	[See Freu dich sehr]
Wie schön leuchtet	Armsdorff (GT 3:171)
	Bach (GT 3:160, arr. from Cantata 37)
	Bender (HP 13:18; BK 1:52)
	Buxtehude (BC 142; GT 3:165, chorale fantasy; GG 1:82, 83, first two sections)
	Cherwien (CI 5:14)
	David (EK 3:243)
	Dupré (D 74)
	Gehring (PPS 2:32)
	Gottschick (OB 173)
	Lenel (LF)
	Miles (PO 6:46)
	Pachelbel (PA 3:78; GT 3:163)
	Petzold (HP 11:48)
	Praetorius (PO I:194; PO 4:26)
	Reda (HP 42:11)

Wie schön leuchtet	Reger (RC 3:49)
	Scheidt (WBM 27, 7 vars.)
	Telemann (HP 5:38)
	Wente (HP 6:36)
Wie soll ich dich empfangen	Hessenberg (GG 4:374)
	Patterson (HP 3:22)
	Raphael (EK 3:245)
Wigtown	Peeters (PH 13:2)
	Thalben-Ball (TB 109)
Wiltshire	Thalben-Ball (TB 110)
William's*	[See St. Thomas]
Williams Bay	Nicholson (HP 42:16*)
Winchester New	Lang (FVA 8)
	Metzger (PO I:30; PO 1:36)
Winchester Old	Bichsel (PO I:200; PO 4:32)
	Bouman (HP 42:18)
	Langstroth (FVC 11)
	Peeters (PH 15:5)
Windham	Gotsch (HP 9:42)
	Schalk (HP 42:22)
Windsor	Coleman (HP 9:44)
	Thalben-Ball (TB 111)
	Willan (PO 12:62)
	Willan (WH 3:7)
Winterton	Rotermund (HP 42:24)
Wir danken dir, Herr Jesu Christ*	[See Herr Jesu Christ, wahr Mensch und Gott]
Wir dienen, Herr	Rogers (HP 18:50)
Wir glauben all an Einen Gott	Bach, J.C. (GT 3:177)
	Bach, J.S. (BCL 52; GT 3:178)
	Bach, J.S. (BCL 57)
	Bach, J.S. (BN 20)
	Dupre (D 77)
	Pachelbel (PA 3:4)
	Scheidt (80:80)
	Walther (HP 42:32)
	Wenzel (OB 132)

Wir glauben all an Einen
Gott
    Zachau (HP 42:26; GG 2:165; PO
    8:46)
Wir hatten gebauet
    Gieseke (HP 5:30)
Wir pflügen
    Langstroth (FVH 22)
    Peeters (PH 22:6)
    Wyble (HP 42:34)
Wir treten zum beten*
    [See Kremser]
Witt*
    [See Meinen Jesum lass' ich nicht]
Wittenburg*
    [See Jesus Christus, unser Heiland
    I or Nun danket alle Gott]
Wittenburg New
    Bender (WS 3:24)
    Busarow (HP 42:29)
    Cherwien (CI 7:15)
Wo Gott zum Haus
    Bach, J.C. (PO I:196; PO 4:28)
    Bauer (OB 194)
    Distler (HP 6:39)
    Pachelbel (PA 3:35, 2 vars.; PO
    6:44, var.1; HP 42:36)
    Peeters (PC 3:14)
    Peeters (PH 23:8)
Wo soll ich fliehen hin
    Bach (BSC 90)
    Bach (BU 103)
    Bohm (BS 28)
    Buxtehude (80:10, 2 vars.)
    Dupré (D 79)
    Hanff (HS 6; GT 1:57; 45:16)
    Krebs (EK 1:10)
    Kuhnau (45:26)
    Pachelbel (PA 3:88)
    Walther (HP 3:25)
    Zachau (GG 1:10; HP 20:18)
Wojtkiewiecz
    Dahl (HP 42:38)
Wolder*
    [See Aus meines Herzens Grunde]
Wolvercote
    Thalben-Ball (TB 112)
Wondrous Love
    Barber, Wondrous Love: Vari-
    ations on a Shapenote Melody
    (G.Schirmer)
    Folkening (HP 42:40)

Woodbird	Diercks (PO 12:64)
Woodlands	Thalben-Ball (TB 113)
Woodworth	Coe (HP 42:42)
Worcester	Engel (HP 13:38)
Worgan*	[See Easter Hymn]
Wunderbarer König	Bender (BK 3:36)
	Cherwien (CI 1:16)
	Hanebeck (OB 128)
	Hasse (GG 3:238)
	Köhler (GG 3:240)
	Metzger (PO I:198)
	Muntschick (HP 42:44)
	Peeters (PH 6:7)
	Weyrauch (EK 3:250)
Würtemburg	Ratcliffe (FVE 13)
Yattendon 46	Peeters (PH 17:4)
Yigdal*	[See Leoni]
Yorkshire*	[See Stockport]
Zeuch ein zu deinen Toren	Bender (BK 3:39)
	Finkelbeiner (EK 3:251)
	Marx (WS 2:37)
	Peter (EK 3:254)
	Wolfrum (GG 3:241)
Známe to, Pane Boze nás	Beck (HP 9:46)
Zpivejmez vsickni vesele	Wienhorst (HP 11:50)

List of Equivalent Tune Names

(Tune names used in this index are given in the right-hand column)

Ach, bleib mit deiner Gnade	Christus, der ist mein Leben
Ach Herr, mich armen Sünder	Passion Chorale
Ach Jesu, dessen treu	O Gott, du frommer Gott I
Ack, bliv hos oss	Pax
Agincourt Hymn	Deo Gracias
Agnus Dei	Christe, du Lamm Gottes
Ajalon	Gethsemane
Angelic Songs	Tidings
Angel's Song	Song 34
Arnsberg	Wunderbarer König *or* Seelenbräutigam
Aus der Tiefe	Heinlein
Ave Maria Klarer und Lichter Morgenstern	Ellacombe
Avon	Martyrdom
Batty	Ringe recht
Behold a Host	Den store hvide flok
Bemerton	Wem in Leidenstagen
Berlin	Gott sei Dank
Bis hier her hat Gott mich gebracht	Du Lebensbrot, Herr Jesu Christ
Bohemian Brethren	Mit Freuden zart
Bourgeois	Freu dich sehr *or* Wenn wir in höchsten Nöten sein

Canterbury	Song 13
Carinthia	Gott sei Dank
Cassel	O du Liebe
Caswall	Wem in Leidenstagen
Celestia	Deilig er den Himmel blaa
Chartres	Or nous dites Marie
Cherubic Hymn	St. Petersburg
Christ Church	St. Peter
Christ Is My Life	Christus, der ist mein Leben
Christmas Dawn	Wir hatten gehauet
Christmas Eve	Jeg er saa glad
Commandments	Wenn wir in höchsten Nöten sein
Corde natus est parentis	Divinum mysterium
Cutler	All Saints New
Darmstadt	Meinen Jesus lass ich nicht I
Der am Kreuz ist meine Liebe	Werde munter mein Gemüte
Der Mange skal komme	Stockholm
Der Tag der ist so freudenreich	Dies est laetitiae
Dessau	Liebster Jesu, wir sind hier
Dover	Durham
Dretzel	O dass ich tausen Zunge hätte I
Drumgclog	Martyrdom
Easter Glory	Fred til Bod
Ein Kind geborn zu Bethleham	Puer natus in Bethlehem
Ein Lämmlein geht	An Wasserflüssen Babylon
Elbing	Du Lebensbrot, Herr Jesu Christ
Elton	Rest
Emmanuel	Det kimer nu til Julefest
Ephesus	Neander

Erfurt	Jesus Christus, unser Heiland II
Erie	Converse
Es ist gewisslich an der Zeit	Nun freut euch, lieben Christen gmein
Es ist kein Tag	Meyer
Fairest Lord Jesus	Schönster Herr Jesu
Fatherland	Heaven Is My Home
Fenwick	Martyrdom
Fountain	Cowper
Frankfort	Wie schön leuchtet *or* Dir, dir Jehovah
French Tune	Dundee
Freylinghausen	Macht hoch die Tür I
Friend	Converse
From Heaven High	Vom Himmel hoch
Gardner	Walton
Gaston	Azmon
Gaude, regina gloriae	Nun lasst uns mit Innigkeit
Geneva 24	Freu dich sehr
Germany	Walton
Giardini	Italian Hymn
Gibbons	Light Divine
Gladness	Cas radosti
God Save the Queen (King)	National Anthem
Godesberg	Gott des Himmels
Goodwin	Webb
Gospel Banner	Missionary Hymn
Gott ist gegenwartig	Wunderbarer König
Great White Host	Den store hvide flok
Hampton	Durham
Harmony Grove	New Britain
Hauge	Im Himmelen, Im Himmelen
Heber	Missionary Hymn

Herman	Lobt Gott, ihr Christen
Herr Jesu Christ, du hasst bereit	Du Lebensbrot, Herr Jesu Christ
Herr Jesu Christ, meins	O Jesu Christ, mein Lebens Licht
Herr, wie du willst	Aus tiefer Not II
Herzlich tut mich	Passion Chorale
Höchster Priester	Savannah
Hoff	Guds menighed, syng
Holy Mountain	Naar mit Oie
Hostis Herodes Himpie	Wo Gott zum Haus
I Love to Tell the Story	Hankey
In Gottes Namen fahren wir	Dies sind die heil'gen zehn Gebot
Innsbruck	O Welt, ich muss dich lassen
Jeg will mig Herren love	Copenhagen
Jesu, der du meine Seele	Alle Menschen müssen sterben II
Jesu, der du warest Todt	Jesu Kreuz, Leiden und Pein
Jesu, geh voran	Seelenbräutigam
Jesu, Joy of Man's Desiring	Werde munter
Jesu Leiden, Pein und Tod	Jesu Kreuz, Leiden und Pein
Jesu, meines Lebens Leben I	Alles Menschen müssen sterben I
Jesu Redemptor	Christe Redemptor
Jesus Bids Us Shine	Lumetto
Joanna	St. Denio
Just As I Am	Dunstan
König	O dass ich tausend Zunge hätte II
Le Cantique de Simeon	Nunc dimittis
Les anges dan nos campagnes	Gloria
Let Us Break Bread	Break Bread Together

Light Divine	Song 13
Lindeman	Gud skal alting mage
Lob Gott getrost mit Singen	Ich danke dir, lieber Herr
Love Divine	Le Jeune
Lovely	Rhosymedre
Lübeck	Gott sei Dank
Lucerne	O du Liebe
Luise	Jesus, meine Zuversicht
Luther	Nun freut euch
Luther's 130th	Aus tiefer Not I
Lyrica Davidica	Easter Hymn
Mache dich, mein Geist, bereit	Straf mich nicht
Magdeburg	Neander
Mainz	Stabat Mater
Meinigen	O Gott du frommer Gott II
Messiah	Bereden väg för Herran
Milwaukee	Macht hoch die Tür II
Min själog aand	Island
Mit Ernst, o Menschenkinder	Von Gott will ich nicht lassen
Morning Light	Webb
Morning Song	Consolation
Moscow	Italian Hymn
Mueller	Away in a Manger
Munich	O Gott du Frommer Gott II
Navarre	Rendez à Dieu
Netherlands	Kremser
Neumark	Wer nur den lieben Gott
New Britain	Amazing Grace
Newington	St. Stephen
Nottingham	St. Magnus
Nun danket all	Gräfenburg
Nun ruhen alle Wälder	O Welt, ich muss dich lassen
Nun singet und seid froh	In dulci jubilo
Nyland	Kuortane

O du Fröhliche	Sicilian Mariners
O Haupt von Blut und Wunden	Passion Choral
O Jesu än de dina	Franzen
O Jesulein süss	O heiliger Geist, O heiliger Gott *or* Komm, heiliger geist, mit deiner genad
O sanctissima	Sicilian Mariners
Ohne Rast und unverweilt	Vienna
Om Himmeriges Rige	Island
Old 112th	Vater unser
Old 134th	St. Michael
Our Lady, Trondhjem	Her vil ties
Oxford	St. Peter
Paedia	Her kommer dine arme smaa
Palestrina	Victory
Paris	Hursley
Pascal	Hursley
Passion Chorale	Herzlich tut mich
Pax	Ack, bliv hos oss
Perfect Love	O Perfect Love
Petra	Gethsemane
Praetorius	Puer nobis
Praise	Af himlens
Praise My Soul	Lauda anima
Preserve Us Lord	Erhalt uns, Herr
Psalm 12	Donne Secours
Psalm 42	Freu dich sehr
Psalm 140	Wenn wir in höchsten Nöten sein
Quebec	Hesperus
Ratisbon	Jesu meine Zuversicht
Ravenna	Vienna
Reading	Erhalt uns, Herr
Redemption	New Britain

Redhead	Gethsemane
Redhead 46	Laus Deo
Redhead No. 76	Gethsemane
Regnator orbis	O quanta qualia
Rest	Magdalen
Richmond	Chesterfield
Riddarhold	Upp, min tunga
Rochelle	Seelenbräutigam
Rock of Ages	Toplady
Rockingham	Rockingham Old
Rosa mystica	Es ist ein Ros
Rouen	Iste Confessor *or* St. Venantius
St. Boniface	Vienna
St. Elizabeth	Schönster Herr Jesu
St. Francis	Lasst uns erfreuen
St. George's, Windsor	St. George
St. Mary Magdalene	Gräfenberg
St. Paul	Es ist das Heil
St. Petersburg	Cherubic Hymn
St. Theodulph	Valet will ich dir geben
Saints' Delight	The Saints' Delight
Salvator natus	Narodil se Kristus Pan
Salzburg	Alle Menschen müssen sterben II
Sandringham	O perfect love
Savoy	Old 100th
Schumann	Heath
Sei Lob und Ehr' dem höchsten Gut	Es ist das Heil uns kommen her
Shrubsole	Miles Lane
Sleepers Wake	Wachet auf
Soldau	Nun bitten wir
Solid Rock	The Solid Rock
Solon	New Britain
Spires	Erhalt uns, Herr
Steht auf, ihr lieben Kinderlein	O heilige Dreifaltigkeit
Stillorgan	Hursley

Susanni	Vom Himmel hoch, O Englein
Swedish Litany	Ach, vad är dock livet här
Symphony	New Britain
Te Deum	Grosser Gott
The Eighth Tune	Tallis' Canon
Thou Man of Griefs	Kedron
To God on High	Allein Gott in der Höh sei Ehr
Ton-y-Botel	Ebenezer
Toulon	Old 124th, abbr.
Treuer Heiland	Dix
Trinity	Italian Hymn
Tut mir auf die schönste Pforte	Neander
Ulrich	Meinen Jesus lass ich nicht II
Veni creator	Komm, Gott Schöpfer
Veni, Redemptor gentium	Nun komm, der Heiden Heiland
Vigil	Haf trones lampe färdig
Vigiles et Sancti	Lasst uns erfreuen
Von Gott will ich nicht lassen	Une vierge pucelle
Vulpius	Gelobt sei Gott
Wade	St. Thomas
Was frag ich nach der Welt	O Gott du frommer Gott I
Watermouth	Angel's Story
Weimar	Jesu Kreuz, Leiden und Pein
Westminster Carol	Gloria
Weyse	Den signede Dag
What a Friend	Converse
Williams	St. Thomas
Wir danken dir, Herr Jesu Christ	Herr Jesu Christ, wahr Mensch und Gott

Wir treten zum beten	Kremser
Witt	Meinen Jesum lass' ich nicht
Wittenberg	Jesus Christus, unser Heiland I *or* Nun danket alle Gott
Wolder	Aus meines Herzens Grunde
Worgan	Easter Hymn
Wunderbarer König	Arnsberg
Yigdal	Leoni
Yorkshire	Stockport

List of Melodic Incipits

Considerable confusion results from hymn tunes with multiple names, or worse, names referring to multiple tunes. The following list of melodic incipits may help to alleviate the problem.

Alle Menschen müssen sterben I (Jesu meines Lebens Leben I)

Alle Menschen müssen sterben II (Jesu, der du meine Seele; Salzburg)

Jesu meines Lebens Leben II

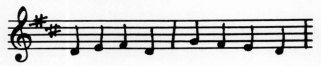

Aus tiefer Not I

Aus tiefer Not II

Christe, der du bist Tag und Licht

In dich hab ich gehoffet, Herr I

In dich hab ich gehoffet, Herr II (Mit meinem Gott geh ich zur Ruh;
Mein schönste Zier und Kleinod bist)

Jesus Christus, unser Heiland I (der den Tod)

Jesus Christus, unser Heiland II (der von uns; Erfurt)

Macht hoch die Tür I (Freylinghausen)

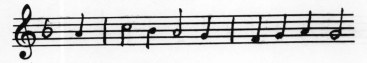

Macht hoch die Tür II (Milwaukee)

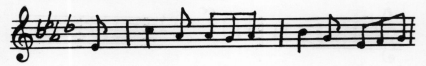

Meinen Jesum lass' ich nicht I (Darmstadt)

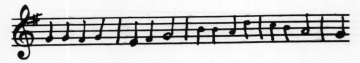

Meinen Jesum lass' ich nicht II (Ulich)

Meinen Jesum lass' ich nicht III

Meinen Jesum lass' ich nicht IV

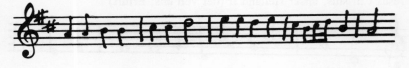

Nun freut euch I (Es ist gewisslich an der Zeit; Was kann uns kommen an für Not)

Nun freut euch II

O dass ich tausen Zungen hätte (Dretzel)

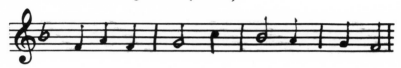

O dass ich tausen Zungen hätte (König)

O Gott du frommer Gott I (Ach Jesu, dessen treu)

O Gott du frommer Gott II (Munich)

O Jesu Christ, mein's Lebens Licht I

O Jesu Christ, meins Lebens Licht II (Herr Jesu Christ, mein's)

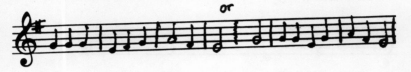

IV. A SCRIPTURAL INDEX OF ANTHEMS

Introduction

The material presented here represents a compilation of choral libraries from several churches and is obviously highly selective, with an aim toward maintaining musical and liturgical standards.

This index includes both anthems originally composed on an English-language text, and works in other languages for which an English translation has been provided in the score. No effort has been made in this index to address the issue of inclusive language, since an editor can only compile available materials. Those concerned with this question must, for the time being, make decisions on a case by case basis.

No indication is given for the instrumentation of individual works, which are most likely to be accompanied by organ in any event. Choir directors should note that even works designated as *a cappella* by the publisher may often be reasonably performed with a discreet organ accompaniment.

The index comprises three parts:

1. Scriptural Index of Anthems

The books of the Bible are listed in scriptural order followed by the chapters and verses set to music in a given anthem, the composer, the title, the distribution, the publisher and catalogue number (or page number for an anthem found in a collection), and the hymn-tune on which the anthem is based, if any. Books of the Bible for which no anthems have been found are listed in square brackets.

The distribution of voices uses the standard abbreviations: SATB for Soprano, Alto, Tenor, Bass. "SB" is used for a two-part anthem set for women and men; "U w/d" refers to an anthem for unison voices with a descant.

No publisher is given for Handel's *Messiah*, which appears in various editions in most church music libraries.

2. Seasonal Index of Anthems

Seasons or special uses are listed in alphabetical order, followed by the composer, the title, etc. as described above. The categories include Advent, All Saints, Ascension, Christmas, Church, Communion, Confirmation, Easter, Epiphany, Evening, Funeral, General, Good Friday, Lent, Morning, New Year, Palm Sunday, Passion, Pentecost, Presentation, Thanksgiving, Transfiguration, Trinity, Unity and Wedding.

When an anthem has been selected for Part I of this volume, the date is given at the end of the entry. Thus 26 Jun: B signifies the Sunday following June 26 in Year B.

3. Index of Hymn Tunes

The Index to Hymn Tunes is designed to locate anthems based on particular hymn tunes. It may also be used to find so-called congregational anthems, involving choirs, congregation and optional instrumentalists. Hymn tunes are listed alphabetically followed by the page numbers of this index containing anthems based on these tunes.

Choir directors seeking additional material are referred to James Laster's *Catalogue of Choral Music Arranged in Biblical Order* (Metuchen, N.J.: The Scarecrow Press, 2nd ed., 1994).

Scriptural Index of Anthems

Scripture	Composer	Title, Distribution and Publisher
Genesis		
6:9-20	Bartholomew, M.	De Animals a-Comin' [SATB] (G.Schirmer 9775)
32:22-30	Hopson, H.	Come, O Thou Traveler Unknown [SATB] (Carl Fischer CM8254) {Vernon}
Exodus		
1-14	Hopson, H.	Moses and the Freedom Fanatics [U] (Choristers Guild CGCA-210)
[Leviticus]		
Numbers		
4:24-26	Lutkin, P.C.	The Lord Bless You and Keep You [SATB] (CH1 12)
24:5,6	Ouseley, F.A.G.	How Goodly Are Thy Tents [SATB] (AC1 70)
24:17	Mendelssohn, F.	Behold a Star From Jacob Shining [SATB] ("Christus") (E.C.Schirmer 1683)
Deuteronomy		
4:29	Mendelssohn/Davis	If With All Your Hearts [SA] (GH 41)
[Joshua]		

444

[Judges]

[Ruth]

[1 Samuel]

2 Samuel
1:17	Tomkins, T.	Then David Mourned [SSATB] (C.F.Peters 6069) 26 Jun:B
23:3,4	Thompson, R.	The Last Words of David [SATB] (E.C.Schirmer 2294)

1 Kings
8:28-30	Tallis, T.	Hear the Voice and Prayer [SATB] (H.W.Gray 2968) 21 Aug:B
8:28,30	Wesley, S.S.	O Lord, My God [SATB] (CAB 341)

[2 Kings]

[1 Chronicles]

[2 Chronicles]

[Ezra]

[Nehemiah]

[Esther]

Job
7:1-7	Mendelssohn, F.	Lord, My God, Hear Now My Pleading [SATB] (Hope Publishing Co. A-479)
14:1-3	Wesley, S.S.	Man That Is Born of Woman [SATB] (CAB 292)

19:25-27	Bach, J.M.	I Know That My Redeemer Lives [SATBB] (CAB 166; SMB 69) 6 Nov: C
23:3,8-9	Bennett, W.S.	O That I Knew Where I Might Find Him! (CAB 358)
38:1-11	V.Williams, R.	The Voice Out of the Whirlwind [SATB] (Oxford 40.012)
40:7-10,14	V.Williams, R.	The Voice Out of the Whirlwind [SATB] (Oxford 40.012)

Psalms

1	Lekberg, S.	Blessed Is the Man [SATB] (Galaxy 1.2255.1) Easter 7:B
	Schütz, H.	Psalm 1 [SATB] (Mercury Music 352-00143)
		Blessed Is He [SA] (Concordia 98-1920) 10 Sep:B
1:1-2	Hassler, H.L.	Blest Be the Man [SATB] (Alexander Broude A.B.157-10)
2:3	Handel, G.F.	Let Us Break Their Bonds Asunder [SATB] ("Messiah")
4	Arcadelt, J.	Give Ear Unto My Prayer [SATB] (Novello 29 0304 00)
	Schütz, H.	Oh, Hear Me When I Cry to Thee [SATB] (BP2 5)
4:1	Schütz, H.	Give Ear Oh Lord [2 equal voices] (Mercury Music 352-00013)
4:9	Wesley, S.S.	Lead Me, Lord [SATB] (H.W.Gray S.A.61-3; CAB 240; AC1:78)
	Willan, H.	I Will Lay Me Down in Peace [SATB] (Concordia 98-1231)
5	Handel/Hopson	O Lord, Have Mercy [SAB] (HC 46)
5:2	Schütz, H.	Give Ear Oh Lord [2 equal voices] (Mercury Music 352-00013) 12 Jun:C

5:3	Schütz, H.	Now Behold, to Thee I Cry, O Lord [SATB] (G.Schirmer 11967)
	Tomkins, T.	My Voice Shalt Thou Hear [TTBB] (AM2 46)
5:8	Wesley, S.S.	Lead Me, Lord [SATB] (H.W.Gray S.A.61-3; CAB 240; AC1:78)
6	Schütz, H.	O Lord, My God, Rebuke Me Not [SATB] (BP1 3) Psalm 6 [SATB] (SP 4)
6:1-4	Locke, M.	Lord, Rebuke Me Not [TTB] (AM2 68)
8:1	Handel, G.F.	How Excellent Thy Name, O Lord [SATB] ("Saul") (E.C.Schirmer 1699) Trinity:A
	Marcello, B.	O Lord, Our Governor [U] (Concordia 98-1045) 2 OCT:B
	Telemann, G.P.	O Lord, Our Master, How Glorious Is Thy Name [U] (MS2 40)
9	Baker, R.C.	I Will Praise Thee, O Lord [SATB] (Frederick Harris HC 4083)
9:2,1	Willan, H.	I Have Trusted in Thy Mercy [U] (WP1 54)
9:9-11	Diemer, E.L.	Sing Praises to the Lord [SATB] (Hinshaw HMC-895)
12	Praetorius, M.	O God, From Heaven Look Below [TTB] (AM2 58) {Ach Gott, vom Himmel}
	Schütz, H.	O Lord, Look Down From Heaven [SATB] (BP1 4)
13:5	Willan, H.	I Have Trusted in Thy Mercy [U] (WP1 54) 26 Jun:A
13:6	Marcello, B.	And With Songs I Will Celebrate [SA or TB] (Concordia 98-1047)

17	Marcello, B.	Give Ear Unto Me [SS] (MS2 5; Novello 29 0320 02) 31 Jul:A
17:5,6	Marcello, B.	Oh, Hold Thou Me Up [SA or TB] (MS1 7; Concordia 98-1046)
19	Beethoven, L.	The Heavens Are Telling [SATB] (E.C.Schirmer 303) 20 Oct:A
	Boyce, William	The Heavens Declare the Glory of God [SATB] (Harmonia-Uitgave HU 2969)
	Marcello/Hopson	Psalm 19 [SATB] (Agape HH3912) 11 Sep:B
	Marcello/McAfee	The Heavens Declare the Glory of God [SATB] (Bourne B205468-358)
19:1-4	Haydn, F.J.	The Heavens Are Telling [SATB] ("The Creation") (E.C.Schirmer 1188) Lent 3:B
19:14	Purcell, H.	Let the Words of My Mouth [TTB] (AM2 72) 25 SEP:B
20	Schütz, H.	Psalm XX [SATB] (FP 2) 12 Jun:B
20:5-7	Croft, W.	We Will Rejoice [SATB] (Broude Brothers MGC 9)
22	Schütz, H.	My God, My God, O Lord, My God [SATB] (BP1 5) Lent 2:B
22:1-3	Blow, J.	My God, My God, Look Upon Me [SATB] (Broude Bros. BB903)
22:2	Reynolds, J.	O My God, I Cry in the Daytime [SA] (AC2 70)
22:8	Handel, G.F.	He Trusted in God [SATB] ("Messiah")
23	Beck, T.	My Shepherd Will Supply My Need [SA] (AT1 10) {Resignation}

23	Beck, T.	My Shepherd Will Supply My Need [SSA] (AT1 12) {St. Columba}
	Dvorak, A.	God Is My Shepherd [U] (MS2 11)
	Gibbs, C.A.	Brother James's Air [SAB] (Oxford OCS2005) {Marosa}
	Jacob, G.	Brother James's Air [SATB] (Oxford OCS 763) {Marosa} Lent 4:A
	Lenel, L.	Loving Shepherd of the Sheep [SS] (MS1 71)
	Rutter, J.	The Lord Is My Shepherd [SATB] (Oxford 94.216) Easter 4:A
	Schalk, C.	My Shepherd Will Supply My Need [SB] (CR2 20) {Resignation}
	Schubert, F.	The Lord Is My Shepherd [SA] (Novello 29 0328 08)
	Schütz, H.	The Lord Is Now My Shepherd True [SATB] (BP1 6)
	Trew, A.	Brother James's Air [U] (Oxford OCS 1139) {Marosa}
	V.Williams, arr.	The Twenty-Third Psalm [SATB] ("The Pilgrim's Progress") (Oxford) 17 Jun:B
	Wesley, S.S.	The Lord Is My Shepherd [SATB] (CAB 412)
	Willan, H.	The Lord's My Shepherd [SA] (CS 39) {Marosa} Easter 4:B
23:1-3	Greene, M.	The Lord Is My Shepherd [SS] (AC2 63)
24	Bissell, K.	Lift Up Your Heads, O Ye Gates [SA] (OC 53) 10 Jul:B
	Vulpius, M.	Lift up Your Heads, Ye Mighty Gates! [SATB] (E.C.Schirmer 2435)
	Willan, H.	Lift up Your Heads [SATB] (Concordia 98-2003) {Macht hoch die Tür}

24:7-10	Handel, G.F.	Lift up Your Heads, O Ye Gates [SATB] ("Messiah")
	Mathias, W.	Lift Up Your Heads, O Ye Gates [SATB] (AC1 81; Oxford University Press A304)
	Willan, H.	Lift Up Your Heads, O Ye Gates [SSA] (WP2 44)
24:7-8	Hammerschmidt, A.	Lift Up Your Heads, Ye Gates [SSATBB] (Theodore Presser 312-41080)
25	Arcadelt, J.	O Lord, I Cry to Thee [SATB] (CH1 8)
		O Lord, My God, to Thee [SATB] (CAB 344)
25:1	Marcello, B.	To Thee, O Lord My God [TB] (AM2 86)
	Rachmaninov, S.	To Thee, O Lord [SATB] (AC1 203)
25:3	Mendelssohn, F.	Cast Thy Burden Upon the Lord [SATB] ("Elijah") (CAB 55; CH1 18) 10 Jul:C
25:5,6	Farrant, R.	Call to Remembrance, O Lord [SATB] (CAB 49) Lent 1:B
25:15-17,19	Boyce, W.	Turn Thee Unto Me [SSATB] (CAB 467)
25:16,17	Boyce, W.	The Sorrows of My Heart [SS] (AC2 73)
26	Arcadelt, J.	O Lord, My God, to Thee [SATB] (CAB 344)
		O Lord, I Cry to Thee [SATB] (CH1 8) 28 Aug: A
26:8,9,12	Tomkins, T.	O Lord, I Have Loved [SAATB] (C.F.Peters 6068)
27:1	Schütz/Wagner	The Lord Is My Light and My Strength [SB] (McAfee Music DMC 1208)
27:9	Farrant, R.	Hide Not Thou Thy Face [SATB] (Oxford TCM 60A; Morning Star MSM-50-3403; CAB 152) Lent 2:C

29:1-2	Schütz, H.	Give to Jehovah [U] (MS2 74) Epiphany 1: B
31:1-2	Handel/Hilton	In Thee, O Lord, Have I Trusted [SAB] (Mercury Music 342-00439)
	Schütz, H.	Lord, in Thee Do I Put My Trust [SATB] (G.Schirmer 11971; Plymouth SC-117) Epiphany 9: A
32	Schütz, H.	Psalm 32 [SATB] (SP 6)
33:1	Steffani, A.	Rejoice in the Lord [SAB] (Concordia 98-2217)
33:1-11	V.Williams, R.	A Choral Flourish [SATB] (Oxford 43.934)
	Viadana/Razey	Rejoice in the Lord [SAB] (Carl Fischer CM 8083)
33:1-3	Viadana, L.	Triumph and Rejoice in the Lord [SATB] (Walton Music Corp.) 4 Jun: A
33:11,12	Willan, H.	Great Is the Lord [SATB] (Gordon Thompson G-590)
34	Handel, G.F.	I Will at All Times Praise the Lord (St.Paul) [SATB] (HC 11)
34:1	King, C.	I Will Alway Give Thanks [SS] (AC2 52) 7 Aug: B
34:1-3	King, R.	I Will Alway Give Thanks [SAB] (SJ 46)
34:8	V.Williams, R.	O Taste and See [SATB] (AC4 86; FMB 11; OEA 106; Oxford University Press 43 P 909) 23 Oct: A
36:5-7,9	Marcello, B.	Thy Mercy, Jehovah [TB] (AM2 74)
37:5	Liebhold	Commit Your Life to the Lord [SATB] (SMB 88) Epiphany 7: C
38	Schütz, H.	Psalm 38 [SATB] (SP 8)
38:19	Lasso, O.	Lord, My Foes Are Yet Among the Living [SATB] (RS 44)

39	Bissell, K.	Hear Thou My Prayer, O Lord [SATB] (G.V.Thompson VG-544)
	Goudimel, C.	Psalm XXXIX [SATB] (G.Schirmer 9415)
	Wesley, S.S.	Thou Wilt Keep Him in Perfect Peace [SATTB] (CAB 457)
39:5-8, 13,15	Greene, M.	Lord, Let Me Know Mine End [SATB] (Oxford University Press; RSCM)
40:1	Mendelssohn, F.	I Waited For the Lord [SS] ("Hymn of Praise") (Novello 10 0094 10)
40:1-12	Mendelssohn, F.	I Waited for the Lord [SATB] ("Hymn of Praise") (Carl Fischer CM6250)
41:7	Victoria, T.L.	I Was Like a Lamb in Innocence [SATB] (RS 129)
42	Mendelssohn, F.	As the Hart Pants (Sacred Cantata) [SATB] (G.Schirmer 5185)
42:1	Palestrina, G.P.	As the Hart Is Athirst [SATB] (RS 94)
42:1-2	Willan, H.	Like as the Hart [SATB] (Concordia 98-1230; PCB 67) 19 Jun: C
42:1-3	Howells, H.	Like as the Hart [SATB] (AC4 158)
43	Mendelssohn, F.	Judge Me, O God [SSAATTBB] (CAB 225)
43:3,4	Willan, H.	Oh, Send Out Thy Light [SA] (WP2 11) 30 Oct: A
45:2,8	Nanino, G.B.	Molded in Grace Are Thy Lips [SATB] (RS 62) 20 Aug: B
46	Marcello, B.	Heart's Adoration [SA] (Oxford E122)
	Praetorius, M.	A Safe Stronghold Our God Is Still [TTB] (AM2 56) {Ein' feste Burg}

46	Schütz, H.	A Mighty Fortress Is Our God [SATB] (BP2 6)
	Tunder, F.	A Mighty Fortress Is Our God [U] (MS2 20) {Ein' feste Burg}
	Tunder & Bach	A Mighty Fortress Is Our God [SATB] (CH2 32) {Ein' feste Burg} 20 Nov: C
	Wolff, S.D.	A Mighty Fortress Is Our God [SATB, Cong.] (Concordia 98-2606) {Ein' feste Burg}
46:1	Mozart, W.A.	God Is Our Refuge [SATB] (MA1 4) 29 May: A
46:4	Marcello, B.	There Is a River [U] (E.C.Schirmer 1894)
47	Finzi, G.	God Is Gone Up [SATB] (Boosey & Hawkes 17140)
	M. Greene	O Clap Your Hands [SSATB] (Novello)
	Rorem, N.	God Is Gone Up [SATB] (Boosey & Hawkes 6446)
	Schütz, H.	Oh Clap Your Hands, Ye People All [SATB] (BP2 8)
	V.Williams, R.	O Clap Your Hands [SATB, div.] (Galaxy 1.5000)
	Willan, H.	God Is Gone up With a Shout [SATB] (Concordia 98-1543) Easter 7: C
47:1-7	Rutter, J.	O Clap Your Hands [SATB] (AC4 53; Oxford A307)
47:4-7	Howells, H.	One Thing Have I Desired [SATB] (Novello 29 0406 03)
47:5-7	Croft, W.	God Is Gone up With a Merry Noise [SSAATB soli, SATB choir] (Novello 20225; Leeds Music Canada)
47:5	Handl, J.	Ascendit Deus [SATBB] (Associated A-83)
48	Schütz, H.	Great Is the Lord, and Greatly Praised [SATB] (BP2 9)

48:1	Willan, H.	Great Is the Lord [SATB] (Gordon Thompson G-590)
50	Le Jeune, C.	Psalm 50 [SAB] (TP 14) 7 Aug: C
50:1-6	Haydn, F.J.	The Lord, th'Almighty Monarch, Spake [SATB] (Broude Bros. CR14)
50:1,3,4	Marcello, B.	The Mighty God [SAB] (Concordia 98-2314) Transfiguration: B
51	Allegri, G.	Miserere [SSATB] (Novello 29 0291 05)
	Lotti, A.	Miserere Mei [SATB] (Boosey & Hawkes OCTB1938) 11 Sep: C
	Purcell/Hopson	O God, Have Mercy [SB] (Sacred Music Press S-5774-2) 31 Jul: B
	Schütz, H.	Psalm 51 [SATB] (SP 10)
51:1	Tomkins, T.	Have Mercy Upon Me, O Lord [TBB] (AM2 44)
51:2	Handel, G.F.	Wash Me Throughly [SS] (AC2 40)
51:2-3	Wesley, S.S.	Wash Me Throughly From My Wickedness [SATB] (CAB 487; E.C.Schirmer 321; SMB 58)
51:9-11	Attwood, T.	Turn Thy Face From My Sins [SATB] (CAB 483; Novello 29 0221 04)
51:10-12	Schalk, C.	Create in Me a Clean Heart, O God [SB] (CR2 31)
	Willan, H.	Create in Me a Clean Heart, O God [U] (MS2 50)
		Create in Me a Clean Heart, O God [SATB] (CH1 5)
51:12-14	Brahms, J.	Make Thou in Me, God [SATBB] (C.F. Peters 66134)
53:4,5	Handel, G.F.	Surely He Hath Borne Our Griefs [SATB] ("Messiah")

55	Mendelssohn, F.	Hear My Prayer [SATB] (Novello 29 0117 10)
55:22	Mendelssohn, F.	Cast Thy Burden Upon the Lord [SATB] ("Elijah") (CAB 55; CH1 18)
58:11	Handel, G.F.	The Lord Gave the Word [SATB] ("Messiah")
62:1,2,7a	Willan, H.	Truly My Soul Waiteth Upon God [SS] (WP1 52) Epiphany 3: B
63:1-5,8	Purcell, H.	O God, Thou Art My God [SATB] (Novello 46 0005 03) Lent 3: C
63:1,3,4	Handel, G.F.	Blest Are They Whose Spirits Long ("Israel in Egypt") [SB] (HC 19)
65	Bissell, K.	Laudate Dominum [SSA] (OC 25) Laudate Dominum [SATB] (Waterloo) Thanksgiving: A
	Greene, M.	Thou Visitest the Earth [SATB] (CAB 453)
	Hare, I.	Thou, O God, Art Praised in Sion [SATB] (AC4 94)
	Haydn/Hopson	Thanks Be to God Forever [SATB] (Harold Flammer A-6642)
65:9-11	Greene, M.	Thou Visitest the Earth [SA] (MS1 21) 10 Jul: A
66	Schütz, H.	Praise God, Ye Lands [SATB] (BP1 7)
66:14,17	Greene, M.	O Come Hither [SS] (AC2 58)
67	Mathias, W.	Let the People Praise Thee, O God [SATB] (Oxford A331) Easter 2: C
	Scheidemann, D.	A Mighty Fortress Is Our God [SATB] (CH1 16)
	Schütz, H.	God, Be Merciful Unto Us [SATB] (G.Schirmer 11969)
	Tye, C.	O God Be Merciful Unto Us [SATB] (Oxford University Press TCM 73a)

67	Willan, H.	God Be Merciful Unto Us and Bless Us [SSA] (WP2 16) 14 Aug: A
		God of Mercy [SATB] (C.F.Peters 6989) {Heathlands}
67:3,4,5	Willan, H.	Let the People Praise Thee, O God [SS] (WP1 56)
67:4-7	Hammerschmidt, A.	Let the People Praise Thee, O God [U] (Concordia 98-1826)
70:1-4	Batten, A.	Haste Thee, O God [SATB] (AC1 64)
74:12	Willan, H.	O Praise the Lord [SATB] (C.F.Peters 6464)
76:2	Handl, J.	See, Now, How Doth the Righteous Man Perish [SATB] (RS 17)
81:1-4	Batten, A.	O Sing Joyfully [SATB] (RSCM)
81:1-3	Symons, C.	Sing We Merrily [SS] (AC2 100) Epiphany 9: B
81:16	Mozart, W.A.	He Fed Them Also With Finest Meal [SATB] (MA1 18)
82:8	Tallis, T.	Rise, God! Judge Thou the Earth in Might [SATB] (G.Schirmer 10480)
84	Brahms, J.	How Lovely Is Thy Dwelling-Place [SATB] (Carl Fischer CM632)
		We Love the Place [SATB] (Requiem) (CAB 494)
	Fauré/Hopson	Psalm 84: Cantique de Jean Racine [SATB] (Carl Fischer CM 8042)
	Schütz, H.	How Lovely Is Thy Dwelling [SATB] (BP1 8)
		Psalm LXXXIV [SATB] (FP 4)
	V.Williams, R.	O How Amiable [SATB] (AC4 152, OEA 181, Oxford University Press 42.056)

84	Willan, H.	Oh, How Amiable Are Thy Dwellings [SS] (WP1 62)
84:4	Willan, H.	O Praise the Lord [SATB] (C.F.Peters 6464)
		Great Is the Lord [SATB] (Gordon Thompson G-590)
84:9-10	Howells, H.	Behold, O God Our Defender [SATB] (Novello 29 0439 10)
84:11	Bach, J.S.	God Is Ever Sun and Shield [U] (MS3 25)
85	Byrd, W.	Drop Down, Ye Heavens [SAATB] (Oxford University Press TCM 31)
	Crotch, W.	Comfort, O Lord, the Soul of Thy Servant [SATB] (CAB 77)
85:10-11	Statham, H.	Drop Down, Ye Heavens [SS] (OEA 172)
85:10,11	Tallis, T.	Rise, God! Judge Thou the Earth in Might [SATB] (G.Schirmer 10480)
85:11	Banchieri, A.	Truth Has Risen [SATB] (Music 70 M70-101)
86	Arensky/Davis	Bow Down Thine Ear, O Lord [SA] (GH 14)
	Bach, J.S.	Bow Down Your Ear [SATB] (Theodore Presser 392-41595)
	Des Pres, J.	Thou Art Great [SATB] (Tetra TC1129)
	Holst, G.	Psalm 86 [SATB] (Galaxy 15353)
86:1,3,5	Arensky, A.S.	Bow Down Thine Ear, O Lord [SATB] (CAB 46)
86:4	Crotch/Davis	Comfort, O Lord, the Soul of Thy Servant [SA] (GH 21; E.C.Schirmer 412)
86:5,6	Willan, H.	Give Ear, O Lord, Unto My Prayer [SSA] (WP1 35)
86:9,10,12	Tallis, T.	Rise, God! Judge Thou the Earth in Might [SATB] (G.Schirmer 10480)

88	Bach/Cornelius	Why Hast Thou Hidden Thy Face [SATB] (Hänssler-Verlag)
89:1	Mendelssohn/Young	I Will Sing of Thy Mercies [2-part] ("St.Paul") (Agape AG7228)
89:19	Willan, H.	Great Is the Lord [SATB] (Gordon Thompson G-590)
90	Lekberg, S.	Lord, Thou Hast Been Our Dwelling Place [SATB] (N.A.Kjos ED 5174)
	V.Williams, R.	Lord, Thou Hast Been Our Refuge [SATB, SATB div] (G.Schirmer 9720)
		O How Amiable [SATB] (AC4 152, OEA 181, Oxford University Press 42.056)
90:1-2	Mendelssohn, F.	Thou, Lord, Our Refuge [SATB] (CAB 450)
90:13	Attwood, T.	Turn Thee, Again, O Lord [SATB] (CAB 463; E.C.Schirmer 1721) 23 Oct: A
91:9-13	Britten, B.	Whoso Dwelleth Under the Defence of the Most High [SATB div] (Faber)
92	McAfee, D.	Psalm Ninety-Two [SATB] (Walton W2804)
95	Bissell, K.	O Come Let Us Sing [SA] (OC 2) Lent 3: A
95:1-2	Handel/Hopson	Oh, Sing to God Your Joyful Praise [SATB] (Concordia 982872) Lent 3: A
95	Le Jeune, C.	Psalm 95 [SAB] (TP 8)
	Mendelssohn, arr.	For the Lord Is a Mighty God [SB] (Mark Foster MF 233)
	Schütz, H.	Psalm 95 [SATB] (PP 4)
96	Handel, G.F.	O Sing Unto the Lord [SAB] (Concordia 98-2200)
	Handel/Hines	Let the Whole Earth Stand in Awe [SAB] (Concordia 98-2473)

96	Schütz, H.	Sing to the Lord Now, All the Earth [SATB] (BP2 12)
96:1-3	Hassler, H.L.	Sing Ye Unto the Lord [SATB] (RS 32; E.C.Schirmer ECS 1262) 29 May: C
96:1-4	Hassler, H.L.	Sing Unto the Lord a New Song [SSATB] (Schott 5950)
96:3-10	Purcell, H.	Declare His Honour [SATB] (CAB 88)
96:3-4	Handel, G.F.	Declare His Honor [SAB] (GB 7)
96:6,10	Purcell/Davis	Glory and Worship Are Before Him [SA] (GH 24)
97	Schütz, H.	The Lord Is Ruler Over All [SATB] (BP1 9)
		Psalm XCVII [SATB] (FP 6)
98	Archer, V.	Sing a New Song to the Lord [SATB] (Waterloo) 13 Nov: C
	Schütz, H.	Psalm 98 [SATB] (PP 6)
	Willan, H.	O Sing Unto the Lord a New Song [SATB] (C.F.Peters 6016)
98:1,2	Willan, H.	Oh, Sing Unto the Lord a New Song [SSA] (WP2 40) Easter 6: B
100	Agazzari, A.	Make a Joyful Noise to God [SAB] (GB 65)
	Britten, B.	O Be Joyful in the Lord [SATB] (AC4 140)
	Caldara, A.	Serve the Lord With Gladness [SATB] (Plymouth Music SC-120)
	Couperin, F.	Make a Joyful Noise [SAB] (SJ 4)
	Handel, G.F.	Serve the Lord With Gladness [SA] (Augsburg 11-4630)
	Holst, G.	All People That on Earth Do Dwell [SATB] (Galaxy 1.5031) {Old 100th}

100	Lasso, O.	Make a Joyful Noise Unto the Lord [SATB] (Boosey & Hawkes B5490)
		O Be Joyful [SATB] (Carl Fischer CM8300)
	Le Jeune, C.	Psalm 100 [SAB] (TP 11)
	Mathias, W.	Make a Joyful Noise Unto the Lord [SATB] (AC4 134)
	Mendelssohn, F.	The Hundredth Psalm [SATB] (Concordia 98-2215)
	Nyquist, K.	Psalm 100 [SATB] (Walton WH-196)
	Rutter, J.	O Be Joyful in the Lord [SATB] (Oxford A346)
	Schütz, H.	Make Joyful Sound Unto the Lord [SATB] (BP1 11)
	Schütz, H.	Psalm 100 (Echo) [SATB SATB] (Theodore Presser 312-40084)
		Psalm 100 [SATB] (PP 8)
	Tallis, T.	All People That on Earth Do Dwell [SATB] (E.C.Schirmer 1012; C.Fischer CM7579)
	Tomblings, P.	All From the Sun's Uprise [SATB] (OEA 129)
	V.Williams, R.	The Old Hundredth Psalm Tune [SATB, Cong.] (Oxford 49.953) {Old 100th} Thanksgiving: A
		The Hundredth Psalm [SATB] (Galaxy 1.5022) 12 Jun: A
	Willan, H.	Make a Joyful Noise Unto the Lord [SA] (WP2 5)
		O Be Joyful [SATB] (G.V.Thompson G-591)
	Wolff, S.D.	Before Jehovah's Awesome Throne [SATB, Cong.] (Concordia 98-2689) {Old 100th}
102	Schütz, H.	Psalm 102 [SATB] (SP 14)

102:1	Purcell, H.	Hear My Prayer, O Lord [SSAATTBB] (Novello AP29; A.Broude 221-8)
103	Schütz, H.	My Soul, Now Bless Thy Maker [SATB] (BP2 10)
103:1-13	Ippolitof-Ivanof, M.	Bless Ye the Lord [SATB] (Carl Fischer CM936)
103:1-2	Tomkins, T.	Praise the Lord, O My Soul [SATB] (Oxford TCM 49)
103:1-4	Ippolitof-Ivanof, M.	O Praise the Lord, My Soul [SATB] (E.C.Schirmer 1743) 21 Aug: C
103:1-6	Distler, H.	Praise Ye the Lord [SATB] (Bärenreiter BA 134; FMB 5) {Lobe den Herren}
103:13	Cherubini/Lovelace	Like as a Father [Children,SB] (Choristers Guild A-156)
104	Gibbs, C.A.	Bless the Lord, O My Soul [SB] (OEA 90)
	Handel/Hopson	Bless the Lord, O My Soul [SAB] (HC 25)
	Raminsh, Imant	I Will Sing Unto the Lord [U and SATB] (Boosey & Hawkes OCTB6641)
104:25, 31-34	Schalk, C.	I Will Sing to the Lord [U] (AI 22)
105	Schütz, H.	Psalm 105 [SATB] (PP 10)
105:1-2	Croft, W.	O Give Thanks Unto the Lord [SAB] (Concordia 98-1788) 24 Jul: A
108:4	Mendelssohn, F.	Cast Thy Burden Upon the Lord [SATB] ("Elijah") (CAB 55; CHI 18)
109	Le Jeune, C.	Psalm 109 [SAB] (TP 5)
111:10	Schütz, H.	Fear the Almighty [2-part] (Concordia 98-1854) 14 Aug: B
112	Purcell, H.	O Happy Man [SATB] (Novello PSR 12) 28 Aug: C

113	Tallis/Roesch	Praise God, Ye Servants of the Lord [SATB] (Harold Flammer A-5682)
	Tye, C.	Sing to the Lord [SATB] (Novello 29 0306 07) 18 Sep: C
113:1-4	Tye, C.	Praise Ye the Lord, Ye Children [SATB] (Oxford TCM 58)
113:1,2	Blow, J.	Praise the Lord, Ye Servants [SATB] (AC1 174)
114	Kodály, Z.	Psalm 114 [SATB] (Boosey & Hawkes 5328) 4 Sep: A
115:1	Byrd, W.	Not Unto Us, O Lord [SAB] (FMB 14)
	Haydn, F.J.	We Seek Not, God, Our Lord, For Glory [SATB] (Concordia 98-1515)
	Walmisley, T.A.	Not Unto Us, O Lord [SATB] (AC1 107)
115:1a	Schalk, C.	Not Unto Us, O Lord [SA or TB] (CR3 33)
116	Purcell, H.	Since God So Tender a Regard [TTB] (AM2 74)
117	Schütz, H.	Oh, Praise Our God [SATB] (BP1 12)
		Praise God With Sound [SATB] (Broude Brothers 4067)
	Vivaldi, A.	Give Praise Unto the Lord [SATB] (Augsburg 11-1870)
		O Praise the Lord, All Nations [SATB] (SMB 29)
		Sing Praise Unto the Lord [SATB] (Theodore Presser 312-41364)
	Willan, H.	O Praise the Lord [SATB] (C.F.Peters 6464)
		Oh, Praise the Lord, All Ye Nations [SSA] (WP1 58)
		Arise, Shine, For Thy Light Is Come [SATB] (Concordia 98-1508)

117:1	Praetorius, M.	Praise Ye the Lord [SATB] (Theodore Presser 312-41067)
118:1-2	Victoria, T.L.	Blessed Are the Undefiled [SATB] (Walton Music W6020)
118:24	Handl, J.	This Is the Day [SATB SATB] (Concordia 98-1702)
	Lekberg, S.	This Is the Day Which the Lord Hath Made [SATB] (G.Schirmer 12064)
	Palestrina, G.P.	This Is the Day Which the Lord Has Made [SATB] (Alexander Broude A.B.752)
119:1,2,33	Willan, H.	Blessed Are the Undefiled [SA] (WP1 59) Epiphany 6: A
119:33	Attwood, T.	Teach Me, O Lord [SATB] (AC1 196; Novello 29 0225 07PCB 76) Epiphany 7: A
	Attwood/Davis	Teach Me, O Lord [SA] (E.C.Schirmer 1576; GH 79)
119:97	Croft, W.	Lord, What Love Have I [SS] (AC2 36)
119:105-108	Purcell, H.	Thy Word Is a Lantern [SATB] (Novello 29 0148)
119:175	Wesley, S.S.	Thou Wilt Keep Him in Perfect Peace [SATTB] (CAB 457)
121	Archer, V.	I Will Lift Up Mine Eyes [SATB] (Waterloo)
	Mendelssohn, arr.	I to the Hills Will Lift My Eyes [SA] (Agape HH3910)
	Schütz, H.	Psalm CXXI [SATB] (FP 8) I Lift My Longing Eyes With Love [SATB] (BP2 13)
121:1-4,8	Willan, H.	I Will Lift Up Mine Eyes [SATB] (Concordia MS 1017)
121:1-3	Mendelssohn, F.	Lift Thine Eyes to the Mountains [SSA] ("Elijah") (E.C.Schirmer 1017)

121:4	Mendelssohn, F.	He, Watching Over Israel [SATB] ("Elijah") (E.C.Schirmer 2786) 16 Oct: C
122	Bissell, K.	I Was Glad When They Said Unto Me [SATB] (Waterloo)
122:1-3, 6,7	Parry, C.H.H.	I Was Glad When They Said Unto Me [SATB] (Novello 29 0122 06)
122:1,2, 4-7	Boyce, W.	I Was Glad [SATB] (Novello 29 0454 03)
122:1,4-7	Purcell, H.	I Was Glad [SSATB] (Novello 29 0446)
122:1,2,7	Willan, H.	I Was Glad [SSA] (WP2 54)
122:6	Tomkins, T.	O Pray For the Peace of Jerusalem [SATB] (Broude Brothers 901; Theodore Presser 312-41111; Oxford University Press TCM 11)
122:6-7	Howells, H.	O Pray For the Peace of Jerusalem [SATB] (Oxford University Press A107)
122:6-8	Goss, J.	O Pray For the Peace of Jerusalem [SATB] (AC1 146)
122:6-9	Blow, J.	O Pray For the Peace of Jerusalem [SATB] (Novello 29 0145 05)
123:3-4	Palestrina, G.P.	Show Thy Mercy on Us [SATB] (RS 72)
125:12	Mendelssohn, F.	But the Lord Is Mindful of His Own [SATB] (G.Schirmer 4431)
126:5-6	Brahms, J.	Blessed Are They That Mourn [SATB] (CAB 19) Epiphany 4: A
128	Gibbons, O.	Blessed Are All They [SAATB] (Stainer & Bell 5553)
130	Bach, J.S.	Out of the Depth I Cry to Thee [SATB] (BC1 17)

130	Mendelssohn, F.	In Deep Despair I Call to Thee [SATB] (Concordia 97-4857) Lent 5: A
	Morley, T.	Out of the Deep [SAATB] (A. Broude)
	Mozart, W.A.	From the Depths Have I Called Unto Thee [SATB] (FMB 38) 4 Jun: B
		From the Depths of Despair [SATB] (MA1 10)
	Schütz, H.	Out of the Depths We Cry, Lord [SATB] (Augsburg 11-1546)
		From Depths of Woe I Cry to Thee [SATB] (BP2 14)
		Psalm 130 [SATB] (SP 16)
133	Clarke-Whitfeld, J.	Behold, How Good and Joyful [SATB] (AC1 38)
134	Le Jeune, C.	Psalm 134 [SAB] (TP 3)
135	Arkhangelsky, A.	Praise Ye the Name of the Lord [SATB] (Shawnee A-345)
	Bissell, K.	I Was Glad When They Said Unto Me [SATB] (Waterloo)
135:1-3	Willan, H.	O Praise the Lord [SATB] (C.F.Peters 6464)
139:1,6, 8-11	Willan, H.	Lord, Thou Hast Searched Me Out [SATB] (Harold Flammer A-5062) 4 Sep: C
139:23-24	Nares, J.	Search Me, O God [SATB] (CH2 28)
141	Arcadelt, J.	O Lord, I Cry to Thee [SATB] (CH1 8)
143	Schütz, H.	Psalm 143 [SATB] (SP 18)
144:9	Dvorak, A.	I Will Sing New Songs of Gladness [U] (MS3 33)
145	Greene, M.	I Will Magnify Thee, O God, My King [SATB] (Walton WM-135)

145:1,3, 8,21	Amner, J.	O God My King [SATB] (AC1 130) 18 Sep: A
145:3-4	Schütz, H.	Great Is Our Lord [2-part] (Mercury Music 352-00017)
145:18,19	Willan, H.	O Praise the Lord [SATB] (C.F.Peters 6464)
148	Holst, G.	Psalm 148 [SATB, div.] (Galaxy 1.5015) {Lasst uns erfreuen} Christmas 1: A
	Pitoni, G.	Come Ye With Joyfulness [SATB] (AC1 44)
149	Anerio, G.F.	O Sing Unto the Lord [SATB] (G.Schirmer 11273)
	Pitoni, G.	Sing to the Lord [SATB] (McLaughlin & Reilly 795)
	Sweelinck, J.P.	Sing to the Lord [SATB] (Concordia 98-2222) 4 Sep: A
149:1-2	Pitoni, G.	Sing to the Lord a New Song [SATB] (FMB 63) All Saints: C
149:1	Schütz, H.	O Sing Ye to the Lord [SATB] (Concordia 98-1974)
150	Franck, C.	Psalm 150 [SATB] (E.C.Schirmer 314; Oliver Ditson 332- 14082) Easter 2: C
	Gibbs, C.A.	O, Praise God in His Holiness [SB] (OEA 112)
	Handel/Hopson	Sing Forth, O Praise the Lord [SAB] (HC 34)
	Pitoni, G.	Praise Ye the Lord [SATB] (SMB 94)
	Rutter, J.	Praise Ye the Lord [SATB] (AC1 184)
	Schütz, H.	Praise God, the Lord, Ye People All [SATB] (BP2 16) Psalm 150 [SATB] (PP 12)
	Shaw, G.	Praise God in His Holiness [SSB] (G. Schirmer 8574)

| 150:1-4,6 | Weldon, J. | O Praise God in His Holiness [SAB] (SJ 12) |

Proverbs

| 8:22-31 | V.Williams, R. | My Soul, Praise the Lord [SATB] (Oxford 44.710) |

[Ecclesiastes]

Song of Solomon

1:10	Tomkins, T.	My Beloved Spake Unto Me [SSAB soli, SATB choir] (Schott 6147)
2:1-5, 7-8,10-11	Billings, W.	I Am the Rose of Sharon [SATB] (Broude Brothers)
2:3,4	Bairstow, E.C.	I Sat Down Under His Shadow [SATB] (AC1 74)
2:10-13	Hadley, P.	My Beloved Spake [SATB] (Curwen 61345)
2:10-12	Willan, H.	Rise Up, My Love, My Fair One [SATB] (Oxford University Press)
5:1-2,6	Billings, W.	I Am Come Into My Garden [SATB] (Broude Brothers)
5:8-11	Billings, W.	I Charge You, O Ye Daughters of Jerusalem [SATB] (Broude Brothers)
8:6	Walton, W.	Set Me as a Seal Upon Thy Heart [SATB] (Oxford University Press A86)

Isaiah

| 6:1-4 | Stainer, J. | I Saw the Lord [SATB SATB] (Novello) |
| 6:3 | Bach, C.P.E. | Holy Is God [SATB] (Concordia 97-6223) Trinity: B |

6:3	Cimarosa, D.	Holy, Holy, Holy [SATB] (Morning Star MSM-50-3006) Epiphany 5: C
	Mendelssohn, F.	Holy, Holy, Holy [SATB SATB] (Hinshaw HMC 1135)
7:10-14	Sweelinck, J.P.	Behold, A Virgin Shall Conceive [SSATB] (Concordia 98-2347) Advent 4: A
9:2-7	Bach/Davis	Break Forth, O Beautiful Heav'nly Light [SA] (GH 15) {Schop}
	Bach, J.S.	Break Forth, O Beauteous Heavenly Light [SATB] (Augsburg 11-1044) {Schop}
		Break Forth, O Beauteous Heavenly Light [SATB] (CH1 30) {Schop} Epiphany 3: A
9:6	Bissell, K.	Gloria in Excelsis [SSA] (OC 20) Epiphany 3: A
	Willan, H.	Unto Us a Child Is Born [SSA] (WP1 21)
9:6,7	Schütz, H.	To Us a Child Is Born [SSATBB] (Theodore Presser 312-41365)
11:1-10	Distler, H.	Lo! How a Rose E'er Blooming [SATB] (Concordia 98-1925) {Es ist ein' ros'} Advent 2: A
12	Jacob, G.	O Lord, I Will Praise Thee [SATB] (OEA 123)
12:2	Palestrina, G.P.	God Is My Strong Salvation [SATB] (Shawnee A-5902)
12:6	Nystedt, K.	Shout With Joy and Singing [SATB] (FL 4)
26:3	Wesley, S.S.	Thou Wilt Keep Him in Perfect Peace [SATTB] (CAB 457; Hinshaw HMC-506)
35:1-10	Wesley, S.S.	The Wilderness [SATB] (Novello 29 0599)
35:4	Lasso, O.	Be Ye Comforted [SATB] (Concordia 98-2422) Advent 3: A

40:1-2	Goudimel, C.	Comfort, Comfort Ye My People [SATB] (FMB 23) {Freu dich sehr}
40:4	Guerrero, F.	Sound Ye the Trumpet [SATB] (Concordia 98-2549)
40:5	Handel, G.F.	And the Glory of the Lord [SATB] ("Messiah") Advent 2: B
40:6	Handel, G.F.	For Unto Us a Child Is Born [SATB] ("Messiah") Advent 2: B
40:9;60:1	Handel, G.F.	O Thou That Tellest Good Tidings to Zion [SATB] ("Messiah")
40:9-11	Handel/Hopson	O Zion, Herald of Good News [SATB] (HC 51)
40:31	Handel, G.F.	Blest Are They Whose Spirits Long (Israel in Egypt) [SB] (HC 19) Epiphany 5: B
45:8	Byrd, W.	Drop Down, Ye Heavens [SAATB] (Oxford University Press TCM 31)
	Stratham, H.	Drop Down, Ye Heavens [SS] (OEA 172)
48:20	Shaw, M.	With a Voice of Singing [SA] (G.Schirmer 10227)
52:2-5	Palestrina, G.P.	Now Do We Behold Him [SATB] (Tetra TC-1135)
52:7,9	Handel, G.F.	How Beautiful Are the Feet [SATB] ("Messiah")
53:3-6	Mendelssohn	Surely His Stripes Have Made Us Whole [SATB] (Harold Flammer A-6095)
53:4	Handel, G.F.	Surely He Hath Borne Our Griefs [SATB] ("Messiah") Good Friday: B
	Lotti, A.	Surely He Has Borne Our Griefs [SAB] (GIA G-2807) Good Friday: C
53:4-5	Leo, L.	Surely He Has Borne Our Griefs [SA] (MS2 52)

53:4-5	Willan, H.	Behold the Lamb of God [SB] (Concordia 98-1509)
53:4-6	Willan/Wood	Surely He Has Borne Our Griefs [SATB] (Concordia 98-2520)
53:4,5	Hillert, R.	Surely He Has Borne Our Griefs [SATB] (FMB 52)
	Willan, H.	Behold the Lamb of God [SATB] (SJ 38)
53:4,5,6	Willan, H.	Surely He Hath Borne Our Griefs [SA] (WP2 36)
53:5	Handel, G.F.	And With His Stripes We Are Healed [SATB] ("Messiah") Good Friday: B
53:6	Handel, G.F.	All We Like Sheep Have Gone Astray [SATB] ("Messiah") 16 Oct: B
56:7	Howells, H.	Coventry Antiphon [SATB] (Novello 29 0506 10)
57:1-2	Handl, J.	See, Now, How Doth the Righteous Man Perish [SATB] (RS 17)
58:15	Battishill, J.	O Lord, Look Down From Heaven [SATB] (Novello NECM 1)
59:20	Beck, T.	Oh, Come, Oh, Come, Emmanuel [SA] (AT2 4) {Veni Emmanuel}
60:1	Willan, H.	Arise, Shine, For Thy Light Is Come [SATB] (Concordia 98-1508)
60:1,3	Bender, M.	Arise, Shine; For Your Light Has Come [SB] (Concordia 98-2707)
60:19	Greene, M.	The Sun Shall Be No More Thy Light [U] (MS3 20)
61:1-3,11	Elgar, E.	The Spirit of the Lord Is Upon Me [SATB] (Novello 29 0216)
62:11	Nystedt, K.	Your Savior Comes [SATB] (FL 10)

Jeremiah

| 11:19 | Victoria, T.L. | I Was Like a Lamb in Innocence [SATB] (RS 129) |
| 29:13 | Mendelssohn, F. | If With All Your Hearts [SATB] ("Elijah") (G.Schirmer 10019) |

Lamentations

1:12	Casals, P.	O Ye People [SATB] (Tetra/Continuo TC 1103)
	Correa, C.	O My People [SATB] (AC1 163)
	Ouseley, F.A.G.	Is It Nothing to You? [SATB] (CAB 183)
	Victoria, T.L.	O Ye People That Pass By [SATB] (RS 148)

[Ezekiel]

[Daniel]

[Hosea]

Joel

| 2:1 | Guerrero, F. | Sound Ye the Trumpet [SATB] (Concordia 98-2549) |

[Amos]

[Obadiah]

[Jonah]

[Micah]

[Nahum]

Habakkuk

| 2:14;3:18 | Willan, H. | O Praise the Lord [SATB] (C.F.Peters 6464) |

[Zephaniah]

Haggai
2:7   Howells, H.   Coventry Antiphon [SATB]
                                  (Novello 29 0506 10)

[Zechariah]

Malachi
1:11   Ouseley, F.A.G.   From the Rising of the Sun
                                  [SATB] (AC1 49; Banks &
                                  Son)
3:3   Handel, G.F.   And He Shall Purify [SATB]
                                  ("Messiah") Advent 2: C

Matthew
2   Cornelius/Atkins   The Three Kings [SATB] (Oxford
                                  OCS1502) Epiphany 1: A
2:1,2   Mendelssohn, F.   When Jesus Our Lord [STBB]
                                  (Christus) (CAB 511)
2:2,5   Hammerschmidt, A.   Where Is the Newborn King?
                                  [SSATB] (Concordia 97-
                                  5038)
2:9,10   Willan, H.   Lo, the Star Which They Saw
                                  [SSA] (WP2 28)
4:10   Bender, J.   Begone, Satan [U] (MS3 69) Lent
                                  1: A
5:4   Brahms, J.   Blessed Are They That Mourn
                                  [SATB] (CAB 19) Epiphany
                                  4: A
6:9-13   Praetorius, M.   Our Father, Thron'd in Heaven
                                  High [SA] (E.C.Schirmer
                                  1967) {Vater unser} 24 Jul: C
             Schütz, H.   Our Father [SATB] (Plymouth
                                  Music SC-58; Broude Bros.
                                  131)
6:33   Mozart, W.A.   Seek Ye First God's Own
                                  Kingdom [SATB] (MA1 23)
                                  Epiphany 8: A

11:10	Willan, H.	Behold, I Send My Messenger [SA] (WP2 14) Advent 3: A
11:28-30	Willan, H.	Come Unto Me, All Ye That Labor [U] (Concordia 98-2359; MS3 75) 3 Jul: A
11:30	Handel, G.F.	His Yoke Is Easy, and His Burden is Light [SATB] ("Messiah")
13:3-9	McAfee, D.	Parable of the Sower [SATB] (General Music)
13:39	Willan, H.	I Looked, and Behold a White Cloud [SATB] (Leslie Music 4125)
17:5	Nystedt, K.	This Is My Beloved Son [SAB] (SJ 10) Transfiguration: A
21:9	Bissell, K.	Hosanna to the Son of David [SSA] (OC 32)
	Cimarosa, D.	Holy, Holy, Holy [SATB] (Morning Star MSM-50-3006)
	Gesius, B.	Hosanna to the Son of David [SATB] (PCB 45)
	Gibbons, O.	Hosanna to the Son of David [SSAATB] (E.C.Schirmer 1189) Palm Sunday: B
	Gumpeltzhaimer, A.	Blessed Is He That Cometh [SS] (MS2 80)
	Mendelssohn, F.	Holy, Holy, Holy [SATB SATB] (Hinshaw HMC-1135)
	Monteverdi, C.	Holy, Holy, Holy [SATB] (Walton Music Corp. WW1142)
	Mozart, W.A.	He Is Blessed That Cometh [SATB] (CAB 131)
	Victoria, T.L.	Hosanna to the Son of David [SATB] (Concordia 98-1993; FMB 48) Lent 6: A
	Weelkes, T.	Hosanna to the Son of David [SSATBB] (Oxford University Press)
	Willan, H.	Hosanna to the Son of David [SA or SSA] (WP1 36)

22:20-21	Franck, M.	Jesus and the Pharisees [SATB] (Concordia 98-2093) 16 Oct: A
24:13	Mendelssohn, F.	He that Shall Endure to the End [SATB] ("Elijah") (CAB 144; G.Schirmer 10713)
25:1-13	Praetorius, M.	Rejoice, Rejoice, Believers [SATB] (CH1 28) 6 Nov: A
25:6	Mendelssohn, F.	Sleepers, Wake! [SATB] (AC1 192) {Wachet auf} 6 Nov: A
25:32-33	Nystedt, K.	Before Him [U] (MS3 40)
27:46	Haydn, M.	Dark Was the Earth With Clouds [SATB] (E.C.Schirmer 1691)
28:1-7	Gabrieli, A.	Scarce Had the Daystar Risen [SATB] (Broude Brothers MGC 5)
28:2-7	Anerio, F.	God, the Lord, Sent a Messenger [SATB] (Broude Brothers MGC 12)
28:2,5-8	Anerio, F.	And the Third Day God's Angel Came [SATB] (RS 3)
28:19	Gumpeltzhaimer, A.	Go Ye Into All the World [SA] (MS1 79)

Mark

1:1-8	Laster, J.H.	Prepare the Royal Highway [SATB] (Concordia 98-2852) {Bereden väg för herran}
7:37	Bender, J.	He Hath Done All Things Well [SATB] (FMB 20) 4 Sep: B
11:1	Gibbons, O.	Hosanna to the Son of David [SSAATB] (E.C.Schirmer 1189) Palm Sunday: B
11:9	Mendelssohn, F.	Holy, Holy, Holy [SATB SATB] (Hinshaw HMC-1135)
13:33-37	Schütz, H.	O Blessed Lord Our God [2-part] (E.C.Schirmer 2787) Advent 1: B
16:1-7	Hammerschmidt, A.	Who Rolls Away the Stone [SSATB] (Concordia 97-5166)

Luke

1:26-38	Schroeder, H.	A Dove Flew Down From Heaven [SATB] (Concordia 98-2061)
1:38	Hassler, H.L.	And Mary Said to the Angel [SATB] (Concordia 98-1960)
1:39-55	Eccard, J.	Over the Hills Young Mary Hastes [SSATB] (Concordia 98-2693) Advent 3: B
1:46-56	Duke, J.	Magnificat [U] (Valley Press) Advent 4: C
	Willan, H.	The Magnificat [SSA] (WP2 19) Magnificat [SATB] (Oxford S534)
1:78-89	Nystedt, K.	As the Dawn of Day [SATB] (FM 8)
2	Bissell, K.	And There Were Shepherds [SA] (OC 11)
2:1-14	Mayer, M.	The Christmas Gospel [SA] (MS3 47)
2:1-20	Hammerschmidt, A.	O Beloved Shepherds [SATB] (Concordia 97-6332)
	Rutter, J.	Angel's Carol [SATB] (Hinshaw HMC-1002)
2:8-16	Charpentier, M-A.	Song of the Birth of Our Lord Jesus Christ [SATB] (Concordia 97-6307)
2:10-11,14	Corelli/Stone	Glory to God in the Highest [SAB] (Boston Music 13895)
2:10-12	Smith, G.	Fear Not Good Shepherds [SSA] (SN 17)
2:11,15	Willan, H.	The Seed Is the Word of God [U] (WP2 30)
2:14	Bach, J.S.	Glory to God in the Highest [SSATB] (FMB 27)
	Handel, G.F.	Glory to God [SATB] ("Messiah") Christmas: A
	Pergolesi, G.B.	Glory to God in the Highest [SATB] (E.C.Schirmer ECS 370) Christmas: B
	Telfer, N.	Christmas Fanfare [SATB] (Stuart Beaudoin SAC-1)

2:14	Vierdanck, J.	Glory to God in the Highest [SA or TB] (MS1 39)
2:29-32	Willan, H.	The Nunc Dimittis [SSA] (WP2 52)
		Nunc Dimittis [SATB] (Oxford S534) Christmas 1: B
7:1-10	Victoria, T.L.	I, O Lord, Am Not Worthy [SATB] (GIA G-1957) Epiphany 9: C
15:4-7	Nystedt, K.	The Parable of the Good Shepherd [SATB] (Walton) 11 Sep: C
17:10-11	Schütz, H.	The Pharisee and the Publican [SATB] (G.Schirmer 7473)
18:10-14	Schütz, H.	Two Men Betook Themselves to Pray in the Temple [SATB] (Concordia 98-1569) 23 Oct: C
19:38	Dedekind, C.C.	Hosanna! Blessed Is He Who Comes [SAB] (GB 16)
	Gibbons, O.	Hosanna to the Son of David [SSAATB] (E.C.Schirmer 1189; Oxford Unversity Press TCM 39) Palm Sunday: B
23:28-30	Mendelssohn, F.	Daughters of Zion [SATB] ("Christus") (CAB 82)

John

1:1-14	Reger, M.	The Word Was Made Flesh [SATB] (Concordia 98-2389) Christmas 2: A
1:14	Hassler, H.L.	Thus the Word Was Made as Flesh [SSATTB] (Alexander Broude A.B.140-9)
	Mauersberger, E.	We Saw His Glory [SA] (MS2 41)
		We Saw His Glory [SATB] (CH2 59) Transfiguration: C
	Willan, H.	The Word Was Made Flesh [SSA] (WP2 26)

1:19-23	Gibbons, O.	This Is the Record of John [SAATB] (Oxford TCM 42; Novello 29 0147 01)
1:29	Beck, T.	Lamb of God, Pure and Holy [SSA] (AT2 15) {O Lamm Gottes, unschuldig}
		O Christ, Thou Lamb of God [SAA] (AT2 16) {Christe, du Lamm Gottes}
	Bouman, P.	Behold the Lamb of God [SA] (MS1 63)
	Handel, G.F.	Behold the Lamb of God [SATB] ("Messiah") Epiphany 2: A
	Willan, H.	Behold the Lamb of God [SB] (Concordia 98-1509)
		Behold the Lamb of God [SATB] (SJ 38)
3:16	Bissell, K.	God So Loved the World [U] (OC 24)
	Bruckner, A.	God So Loved the World [SATB] (GIA G-1438)
	Distler, H.	For God So Loved the World [SAB] (Concordia 98-2239) Lent 4: B
	Gibbons, O.	So God Loved the World [SAATB] (Novello 88 0015 04) Lent 2: A
	Schütz, H.	For God So Loved the World [SATTB] (SMB 43)
	Telemann, G.P.	God So Loved the World [SAB] (GB 23)
	Vulpius, M.	God Loved the World [SATB] (CH2 63) {Die helle Sonne leuchte}
3:16,17	Goss, J.	God So Loved the World [SATB] (CAB 118)
3:16-17	Haydn/Lovelace	God So Loved the World [SATB] (Augsburg 11-2147)
4:23,24	Bennett, W.S.	God Is a Spirit [SATB] (CAB 115)

4:35,36	Willan, H.	I Looked, and Behold a White Cloud [SATB] (Leslie Music 4125)
6:53-56	Tallis, T.	Verily, Verily I Say Unto You [SATB] (AC1 208)
8:12	Bouman, P.	I Am the Light of the World [U] (AI 12)
9:24	Kopylov/Davis	God Is a Spirit [SA] (GH 29)
10:14	Wetzler, R.	I Am the Good Shepherd [U] (AI 18)
11:25,26	Willan, H.	I Am the Resurrection and the Life [SA] (WP2 9)
12:13	Mendelssohn, F.	Holy, Holy, Holy [SATB SATB] (Hinshaw HMC-1135)
14	Willan, H.	If Ye Love Me [SSA] (WP1 44)
14:15-17	Tallis, T.	If Ye Love Me [SATB] (CAB 179; E.C.Schirmer 2992; G.Schirmer 10234; Oxford University Press TCM 69) Easter 6: A
14:18	Willan, H.	I Will Not Leave You Comfortless [SA] (WP2:48)
14:18-20	Byrd, W.	I Will Not Leave You Comfortless [SSATB] (Novello 29 0123 04)
16:23,24	Willan, H.	Verily, Verily, I Say Unto You [U] (WP2 42)
18:33-37	Handel/Liebergen	How Excellent Thy Name [SATB] ("Saul") (Alfred Publishing Co. 7810) 20 Nov: B
20:1-18	Hammerschmidt, A.	Who Rolls Away the Stone [SSATB] (Concordia 97-5166)
20:13	Morley, T.	Alas, They Have Taken the Lord [SATB] (Stainer & Bell W65)
20:19-20	Handl, J.	There Came Jesus [SATB] (GIA G-2460) Pentecost: A
20:29	Bennett, W.S.	O That I Knew Where I Might Find Him! [SATB] (CAB 358)

| 20:29 | Marenzio, L. | Because You Have Seen Me, Thomas [SATB] (Concordia 98-2617) Easter 2: B |

Acts

1:1-14	Tye, C.	The Parting Word the Savior Spoke [SATB] (EMA 28) Easter 7: A
1:15-26	Tye, C.	The Chosen Twelve, Now Lacking One [SATB] (EMB 20)
2:14a,22-32	Tye, C.	The One Who Died by Sinners' Hands [SATB] (EMA 5) Easter 2: A
2:14a,36-47	Tye, C.	The Man We Crucified [SATB] (EMA 9) Easter 3: A
3:13-15	Tye, C.	God's Power Still Indwelling Him [SATB] (EMB 5) Easter 3: B
4:8-12	Tye, C.	The Courts of Evil Still Condemn [SATB] (EMB 7)
4:23-33	Tye, C.	As Christ, Their Master, Once Condemned [SATB] (EMB 10)
5:12,17-32	Tye, C.	How Futile of the Grave [SATB] (EMC 5)
6:1-9,51-60	Tye, C.	The Kingdom, Like a Mustard Seed [SATB] (EMA 14)
8:26-40	Tye, C.	Not for Jerusalem and Jew Alone [SATB] (EMB 13)
9:1-20	Tye, C.	Saul Heard the Cry We All Must Hear [SATB] (EMC 8)
11:19-30	Tye, C.	The Blood of Martyrs Is Not Shed in Vain [SATB] (EMB 16)
13:15-16	Tye, C.	God's Promises Have Never Failed [SATB] (EMC 12)
13:44-52	Tye, C.	The Gospel, Like a Passing Cloud [SATB] (EMC 16)
14:8-18	Tye, C.	How Like Two Gods the Apostles Seem [SATB] (EMC 19)

16:6-10	Tye, C.	A Voice From Macedonia Cries [SATB] (EMC 23)
17:1-15	Tye, C.	First to the Jews, and Then the Greeks [SATB] (EMA 18)
17:22-31	Tye, C.	All Have a God Whom They Revere [SATB] (EMA 23)

Romans

4:5	Anerio, F.	Alleluia! Christ Is Risen [SATB] (Broude Bros. MGC 43)
5:1-5	Gibbons, O.	Lord, Grant Grace, We Humbly Beseech Thee [SATB SATB] (Concordia 98-1970)
6:9	Bissell, K.	Christ Being Raised From the Dead [SSA] (OC 38)
		Christ Being Raised From the Dead [SATB] (G.V.Thompson 1537) 19 Jun: A
	Wetzler, R.	I Am the Good Shepherd [U] (AI 18)
	Willan, H.	O Sing Unto the Lord a New Song [SATB] (C.F.Peters 6016)
6:9,10	Willan, H.	Christ Being Raised From the Dead [SSA] (WP1 40)
8:31-34	Franck, M.	If God Be For Us [SATB] (GIA G-2201)
10:15	Mendelssohn, F.	How Lovely Are the Messengers [SATB] ("St.Paul") (E.C.Schirmer 1134) 7 Aug: A
10:18	Handel, G.F.	Their Sound Is Gone Out [SATB] ("Messiah")
12:1-2	Johnson, R.M.	A Living Sacrifice [U] (AI 20) 21 Aug: A
13:12	Willan, H.	Rejoice, O Jerusalem, Behold, Thy King Cometh [SATB] (Concordia 98-1506) Advent 1: A

| 13:12 | Willan, H. | Rejoice, O Jerusalem, Behold, Thy King Cometh [SATB] (WHD 23) |
| 14:17 | Mendelssohn/ Denton | Lord, Speak to Me [SATB] (Lorenz B411) |

1 Corinthians

2:9	Lasso, O.	Eye of Man Hath Not Seen [SA] (AC2 4) Epiphany 5: A
5:8	Anerio, F.	Alleluia! Christ Is Risen [SATB] (Broude Bros. MGC 43)
15:20	Billings, W.	Easter Anthem [SATB] (G.Schirmer 9949)
	Bissell, K.	Christ Is 'Risen From the Dead [SATB] (Waterloo)
15:21-22	Anerio, F.	Alleluia! Christ Is Risen [SATB] (Broude Bros. MGC 43)
	Handel, G.F.	Since by Man Came Death [SATB] ("Messiah") Easter: C
15:55-57	Handel, G.F.	But Thanks Be to God [SATB] ("Messiah") Epiphany 8: C

[2 Corinthians]

[Galatians]

Ephesians

| 5:8,9 | Willan, H. | Now Are Ye Light in the Lord [U] (WP2 31) Lent 4: A |

Philippians

2:8	Anerio, F.	Christ Became Obedient Even Unto Death [SATB] (GIA G-1967)
2:8,9	Bissell, K.	Christ Hath Humbled Himself [SA] (OC 30)
	Willan, H.	Christ Hath Humbled Himself [SA] (WP1 32)

2:10-11	Langlais, J.	At the Name of Jesus [SATB] (LA 4)
	Handl, J.	At the Name of Jesus [SATB] (Concordia 98-1051) 25 Sep: A
	V.Williams/Beck	At the Name of Jesus [SSA] (AT1 28) {King's Weston}
	Willan, H.	At the Name of Jesus [SA] (WP2 34)
4:4-7	Anonymous	Rejoice in the Lord Alway [SATB] (Oxford University Press TCM 55)
	Ley, H.G.	Rejoice in the Lord Alway [SS] (CAB 383)
	Purcell, H.	Rejoice in the Lord Alway [SATB] (CAB 388; Concordia 97-6344) Advent 3: C
	Redford, J.	Rejoice in the Lord Alway [SATB] (SMB 6) Oct 9: A
4:4,5	Willan, H.	Rejoice in the Lord Alway [SA] (WP2 12)
4:5	Mendelssohn, F.	But the Lord Is Mindful of His Own [SATB] (G.Schirmer 4431)

Colossians

3:1-2	Anonymous	If Ye Be Risen Again [TTBB] (AM2 18)
4:14,18	Goss, J.	If We Believe that Jesus Died [SATB] (CAB 171)
5:23	Beck, T.	Holy Ghost, With Light Divine [SA] (AT1 20) {Light Divine}

[2 Thessalonians]

[1 Timothy]

2 Timothy

2:19	Mendelssohn, F.	But the Lord Is Mindful of His Own [SATB] (G.Schirmer 4431)

[Titus]

[Philemon]

Hebrews

1:6	Handel, G.F.	Let All the Angels of God Worship Him [SATB] ("Messiah")

James

1:12	Mendelssohn, F.	Happy and Blest Are They [SATB] ("St.Paul") (E.C.Schirmer 1133)

1 Peter

1:3-5;15-17	Wesley, S.S.	Blessed Be the God and Father [SATB] (CAB 34; Novello 29 0102 01)

[2 Peter]

1 John

1:5	Wesley, S.S.	Thou Wilt Keep Him in Perfect Peace [SATTB] (CAB 457)
1:7 Us	Schütz, H.	The Blood of Jesus ... Cleanses From All Sin [SAB] (GB 23)
4:7-8,10	Langlais, J.	Beloved, Let Us Love One Another [U] (LA 2) Easter 5: B

[2 John]

[3 John]

[Jude]

Revelation

1:4-6	Langlais, J.	Grace to You [SATB] (LA 2)
1:4b-8	Handel/Liebergen	How Excellent Thy Name [SATB] ("Saul") (Alfred Publishing Co. 7810)
1:5,6	V.Williams, R.	Unto Him That Loved Us [U] (MS1 20)
2	V.Williams, R.	The Song of the Tree of Life [2-part] (Oxford 82.037)
4:11	Willan, H.	Worthy Art Thou, O Lord [SATB] (Concordia 98-1015)
5:12-13	Handel, G.F.	Worthy Is the Lamb That Was Slain [SATB] ("Messiah") Easter 3: C
	Weelkes, T.	Alleluia, I Heard a Voice [SATBB] (Oxford TCM45)
7:9-12	Croft, W.	Ye Servants of God [SATB] (Sam Fox Publishing Co. XPS 192)
7:12	Hasse, C.F.	Doxology: Amen, Praise Ye the Lord [SATB] (Carl Fischer CM7879)
7:13-17	Franck, M.	Revelation Motet [SATB] (Broude Bros. B.B.141) Easter 4: C
14:4,5	Goss, J.	These Are They Which Follow the Lamb [SATB] (AC1 200)
14:14,15	Willan, H.	I Looked, and Behold a White Cloud [SATB] (Leslie Music 4125)
19:6,16	Handel, G.F.	Hallelujah [SATB] ("Messiah")
21:1-4	Bainton, E.L.	And I Saw a New Heaven [SATB] (Novello 1155)
21:13	Nystedt, K.	God's Dwelling [SATB] (FL 6)
22:1,17	Copland, A.	At the River [SATB] (Boosey & Hawkes 5513)
24:13	Goss, J.	I Heard a Voice From Heaven [SATB] (CAB 163)

Seasonal Index of Anthems

Advent	[See also settings of "Hosanna to the Son of David" listed under Matthew 21:9, Mark 11:1 and Luke 19:38]
Bach, J.S.	Dearest Lord Jesus [SATB] (OEA 1)
	Savior of the Heathen, Come [SATB] (BC2 10) {Nun komm, der Heiden Heiland}
	Wake, Awake, For Night Is Flying [SATB] (BC1 3) {Wachet auf}
	Zion Hears the Watchmen Singing [SATB] (BC2 22) {Wachet auf}
Bairstow, E.C.	Let All Mortal Flesh Keep Silence [SATB] (Stainer & Bell 294)
Batten, A.	Two Short Anthems: Lord, We Beseech Thee *and* When the Lord Turned Again [SATB] (Oxford University Press TCM 76)
Brahms, J.	A Dove Flew Down From Heaven [SATB] (SMB 16)
Buck, P.C.	Into This World of Sorrow [SATB] (CAB 182)
Busarow, D.	Come, Thou Long-Expected Jesus [U] (AI 7) {Jefferson}
	On Jordan's Bank the Baptist's Cry [SATB, cong.] (Concordia 98-2639) {Puer nobis}
Buxtehude, D.	Arise, Sons of the Kingdom [U] (MS1 34)
Byrd, W.	Drop Down, Ye Heavens [SAATB] (Oxford University Press TCM 31)
Crüger & Bach	Savior of the Nations, Come [SATB] (SG 7) {Nun komm, der Heiden Heiland}

485

Davies, H.W.	Hark the Glad Sound! [SATB] (CAB 126)
Drischner, M.	A Ship With Cargo Precious [U] (MJ 12)
	Creator of the Stars of Night [U] (MJ 14) {O Heiland, reiss die himmel auf}
	O Lord, How Shall I Meet Thee [U] (MJ 13) {Wie soll ich dich empfangen}
	Rejoice, Rejoice, Believers [U] (MJ 8)
	Wake, Awake, For Night Is Flying [U] (MJ 10) {Wachet auf}
Handel, G.F.	Daughter of Zion [SA] ("Judas Maccabeus") (E.C.Schirmer 1956; MS1 31)
	Daughter of Zion [SATB] ("Judas Maccabeus") (CH1 27)
Hassler, H.L.	Blow Ye the Trumpet [SSATB] (Music 70 M70-573)
Hillert, R.	Come, Thou Long-Expected Jesus [SATB] (CH2 48; SG 11) {Jefferson}
Holst, G.	Let All Mortal Flesh Keep Silence [SATB] (Stainer & Bell) {Picardy}
Kodály, Z.	O Come, O Come, Emmanuel [SAB] (Boosey & Hawkes CCS 70) {Veni Emmanuel} Advent 1: C
Ley, H.G.	Come, Thou Long Expected Jesus [SATB] (OEA 1)
Metzger, H.	O Savior, Rend the Heavens Wide [SATB] (SG 12) {O Heiland, reiss die Himmel auf}
Nicholson, S.H.	Lo! He Comes With Clouds Descending [SATB] (SG 8) {Picardy}
Powell, R.J.	The Angel Gabriel [U] (RM 12)a
Reger, M.	Behold, the Days Come, Saith the Lord [SATB] (CH2 41)
Rorem, N.	Shout the Glad Tidings [SATB] (Boosey & Hawkes 6008)
Schalk, C.	Lo, He Comes With Clouds Descending [SB] (CR2 3) {Picardy}
	Oh, Come, Oh, Come, Emmanuel [SB] (CR3 3) {Veni Emmanuel}

Schalk, C.	Savior of the Nations, Come [SB] (CR1 3) {Nun komm, der Heiden Heiland} The King Shall Come When Morning Dawns [SB] (CR2 6) {Consolation}
Schroeter, L.	Hail to the Lord's Anointed [SATB] (PCB 24)
Stanton, W.K.	Christ Is the World's True Light [U w/d] (OEA 9)
Tallis/Scott	Almighty Word [SATB, cong.] (Oxford University Press)
Tunder, F.	Wake, Awake, for Night Is Flying [U] (MS1 28)
Von Burck, J.	Prepare the Way Before Him [SATB] (PCB 27)
Willan, H.	Come, Jesus, Holy Child [U w/d] (WP1 12) {Puer nobis}
	Creator of the Stars of Night [SATB] (SG 9) {Conditor alme siderum}
	Hosanna Now Through Advent [U w/d] (WP1 14) {Maria ist geboren}
	Lo, in the Time Appointed [SATB] (AC4 174; Oxford 94.310)
	Maria Walks Amid the Thorn [SA] (CS 12) {Maria durch den Dornwald ging}
	O Emmanuel, Come, Be Our Salvation [SATB] (CH2 46)
	Prepare the Way, O Zion [SS] (CS 10) {Bereden väg för herran}
Wood, C.	O Thou the Central Orb [SATB] (AC4 9)
Woodward, G.F.	Hark! A Thrilling Voice Is Sounding [SATB] (SG 10) {Freuen wir uns alle}
Zipp, F.	Wake, Awake, for Night Is Flying [SAB] (SJ 16) {Wachet auf}

All Saints

Bainton, E.L.	And I Saw a New Heaven [SATB] (Novello 1155)
Bairstow, E.C.	Blessed City, Heavenly Salem [SATB] (Banks & Son)

Bullock, E.	Give Us the Wings of Faith [SATB] (AC4 128)
Davies, H.W.	The Souls of the Righteous [SATB] (CAB 418)
Dering, R.	Souls of the Righteous [SS] (AC2 12)
Handel, G.F.	Their Bodies Are Buried in Peace [SATB] (CAB 430)
Harris, W.H.	Faire Is the Heaven [SATB SATB] (AC4 100)
	O What Their Joy and Their Glory Must Be [SATB] (CAB 367)
Ley, H.G.	Lo, Round the Throne a Glorious Band [SSATB] (CAB 248)
Marchant, S.	The Souls of the Righteous [SATB] (OEA 97)
Nares, J.	The Souls of the Righteous [SS] (AC2 80)
Ridout, A.	Let Saints on Earth in Concert Sing [U] (AC2 97)
Tomkins, T.	Great and Marvellous [SATB] (Oxford University Press TCM 98)
V.Williams, R.	Let Us Now Praise Famous Men [U] (CAB 245; G.Schirmer 8384) All Saints: A
	For All the Saints [SATB] (Oxford 40.002) {Sine nomine} All Saints: B
Wesley, S.S.	Thou Judge of Quick and Dead [SATB] (CAB 439)
Willan, H.	O How Glorious [SATB] (H.W.Gray GCMR 00713)
	O King All Glorious [SATB] (Oxford 94.308)
	O What Their Joy and Their Glory Must Be [SATB] (C.F.Peters 6066) {O quanta qualia}
Wolff, S.D.	For All the Saints [SATB, cong.] (Concordia 98-2637) {Sine nomine}

Ascension

	[*See also* Psalm 47]
Bach, J.S.	Draw Us to Thee [SATB] (BC1 7) {Zeuch uns nach dir}
Drischner, M.	Ascended Is Our God and Lord [U] (MJ 33)
	Dear Christians, One and All, Rejoice [U] (MJ 34) {Nun freut euch II}
Gibbons, O.	O God the King of Glory [SAATB] (Oxford TCM10)
Jackson, F.	Lift Up Your Heads [SATB] (AC4 43)
Klammer, T.P.	Ascended Is Our God and Lord [SSA] (MS1 74)
Ley, H.G.	A Choral Hymn [SATB] (OEA 68) {Montrose}
Lotti, A.	Sing, Joyous Christians [SATB] (CH1 57)
Mendelssohn, F.	Above All Praise and All Majesty [SATB] (OEA 74)
Mozart, W.A.	Alleluia [Canon] (MS1 74)
Palestrina, G.P.	King of Majesty [SATB] (RS 81)
Purcell, H.	O God, the King of Glory [SATB] (AC1 136; SMB 73)
Schalk, C.	We Thank Thee, Jesus, Dearest Friend [SB] (CR1 26) {Erschienen ist}
Shrubsole, W.	All Hail the Power of Jesus' Name [SATB] (CH1 63) {Miles Lane}
Tallis, T.	If Ye Love Me [SATB] (RS 113)
Vulpius, M.	To Heaven Ascended Christ, Our King [SATB] (CH2 75)
Willan, H.	Ascended Is Our God and Lord [SS] (CS 43) {Gen Himmel aufgefahren}
	The King Ascendeth Into Heaven [SA] (WP1 41)

Christmas

Adam, A.	O Holy Night [SATB] (Novello 29 0128 05)
Anonymous	Angels We Have Heard on High [SATB] (CH1 38) {Gloria}

Anonymous	O Come, All Ye Faithful [SATB] (SG 19) {Adeste fideles}
Bach & Osiander	The Only Son From Heaven [SATB] (SG 40) {Herr Christ, der einig Gottes Sohn}
Bach & Herman	Let All Together Praise Our God [SATB] (SG 22) {Lobt Gott, ihr Christen}
Bach/Davis	O Jesu, So Sweet [SA] (GH 62) {O Jesulein süss}
Bach, J.C.	Night of Wonder [SATB] (Tetra TCR 1160)
Bach, J.S.	A Child Is Born in Bethlehem [SATB] (BC2 8) {Puer natus}
	Beside Thy Manger Here I Stand [SA] (MS1 44)
	Beside Thy Manger Here I Stand [SAB] (SJ 30)
	From Heav'n Above [SATB] (BC1 22) {Vom Himmel hoch}
	Lord Jesus Christ, Thou Prince of Peace [SATB] (BC1 9) {Du Friedefürst}
	Praise God the Lord, Ye Sons of Men [SATB] (BC1 16) {Lobt Gott, ihr Christen}
	The Only Son From Heaven [SATB] (MS3 42) {Herr Christ, der einig Gottes Sohn}
Baker, A.E.	Whence Is That Goodly Fragrance? [U w/d] (CAB 522)
Barnes, E.S.	Angels We Have Heard on High [SATB] (SG 20) {Gloria}
Beck, T.	Oh, Come, Oh, Come, Emmanuel [SA] (AT2 4) {Veni Emmanuel}
	A Child Is Born, the Son of God [SSA] (AT2 8)
	The King Shall Come When Morning Dawns [SATB] (SG 13) {Consolation}
Bender, J.	From East to West, From Shore to Shore [SATB] (SG 16) {Christum wir sollen loben}

Billings, W.	A Virgin Unspotted [SATB] (Mercury Music 352-00064)
	The Shepherd's Carol [SATB] (Summy-Birchand B-366)
Bissell, K.	O My Dear Heart [SA] (OC 18)
Bodenschatz, E.	Joseph, Dearest Joseph Mine [SATB] (FMB 36) {Resonet in laudibus} Christmas Eve: C
Buck, P.C.	Now to the Earth in Mercy [SATB] (CAB 315)
Bunjes, P.G.	Who Are These That Earnest Knock [SATB] (SG 37) {Dies est laetitiae}
Byrd, W.	An Earthly Tree a Heavenly Fruit [SS] (Stainer & Bell CC246)
	Cradle Song [SATB] (Stainer & Bell CC477)
Byrd/Hopson	Sing, For Christ Is Born [SATB] (H.W.Gray GCMR03597)
Carol	Angels O'er the Fields Were Flying [SA] (GH 8)
Carol, arr.Davis	Sing We Noel [SA] (GH 74)
Daquin/DeCormier	Noel We Sing [SATB] (G. Schirmer 51436)
Darke, H.	In the Bleak Mid-Winter [SATB] (Stainer & Bell 842)
Davies, H.W.	O Little Town of Bethlehem [SATB] (Novello)
Davis, K.	Carol of the Drum [SATB] (Belwin Mills)
Distler, H.	Dear Christians, One and All Rejoice [SATB] (Concordia)
Drischner, M.	Christ the Lord to Us Is Born [U] (MJ 15) {Narodil se kristus pan}
	From Heaven Above, Ye Angels All [U] (MJ 20) {Vom Himmel hoch, o Englein}
	Joseph, Dearest Joseph Mine [U] (MJ 18) {Resonet in laudibus}
	O Jesus So Sweet, O Jesus So Mild [U] (MJ 16) {O Jesulein süss}

Ferguson, J.   Let Our Gladness Have No End [U] (AI
                      14) {Narodil se kristus pan}
Franck, C.   At the Cradle [SA] (E.C.Schirmer 1533)
                      Christmas Eve: A
Franck, J.W.   O Christians, Sing With Exultation
                      [SATB] (CH1 36)
Friedell, H.   Song of Mary [SATB] (H.W. Gray)
Gastoldi/Beck   In Thee Is Gladness [SSA] (AT1 24) {In
                      dir ist Freude}
Gastoldi, G.   In Thee Is Gladness [SATB] (CH1 42) {In
                      dir ist Freude} Christmas 1: C
Gaul, H.   Carol of the Russian Children [SATB]
                      (G.Schirmer 6770) Christmas Eve: C
Gibbons, O.   A Christmas Introit [SATB] (Roberton
                      Publications 85097)
                      See, See, the Word Is Incarnate [SAATB]
                      (Stainer & Bell W72)
                      Song 46 [SATB] (AC1 30)
Halter, C.   O Holy Child, We Welcome Thee [SATB]
                      (PCB 30)
Hassler, H.L.   Angel Hosts to the Shepherds Speaking
                      [SATB] (RS 23)
Haydn, F.J.   Gloria from the "Harmoniemesse" [SATB]
                      (Theodore Presser 312-41591)
                      Christmas Eve: B
                      Gloria from the "Heiligmesse" [SATB]
                      (Walton Music W031)
                      Gloria from the "Missa Brevis" [SATB]
                      (Theodore Presser 392-41544)
Haydn, M.   O Joyful Day [SATB] (G.Schirmer 11044)
Hoddinott, A.   Puer Natus (A Child Is Born in Bethlehem)
                      [SSAATTBB] (AC4 18)
Holman, D.   Make We Joy Now [SATB] (Novello)
Holst, G.   Christmas Day [SATB] (Novello 1011-33)
                      Christmas Day: C
                      Christmas Song (Personent Hodie) [U]
                      (G.Schirmer 8119) Christmas Eve: B
                      In the Bleak Mid-Winter [SATB] (HB 418)
                      {Cranham}

Holst, G.	Jesu, Thou the Virgin-Born [SATB] (CH2 54)
	Let All Mortal Flesh Keep Silence [SATB] (Galaxy 1.5019) {Picardy}
	The Savior of the World Is Born [SATB] (MS2 36)
	This Have I Done For My True Love [SATB] (Galaxy 1.5080)
Joubert, J.	There Is No Rose of Such Virtue [SATB] (Novello 29 0171)
Jungst, H.	While By My Sheep I Watched at Night [SATB] (CH1 33)
	Christmas Hymn [SS] (SN 3)
Kirk, T.	Sing Noel [SS] (SN 5)
Kodály, Z.	A Christmas Carol (All Men Draw Near) [SATB] (Oxford 89.091)
Koler, M.	Beside Thy Manger Here I Stand [U] (MS3 63)
Lasso, O.	On This Day Appeareth in Israel [SSA] (Concordia 98-2913)
Marshall, J.	Good News [SATB] (Carl Fischer 7758)
Marx & Bach	We Praise, O Christ, Your Holy Name [SATB] (SG 14) {Gelobet seist du, Jesu Christ}
Nanino, G.B.	Born For Us This Day [SATB] (RS 53)
	On This Day the King of Heaven [SATB] (SMB 22)
Niles, J.J.	Jesus, Jesus, Rest Your Head [SA] (SN 12)
Parker, A.	Fum, Fum, Fum [SATB] (Carl Fischer CM7842)
	Masters in This Hall [SATB] (Carl Fischer CM7838)
Parker & Shaw	Fum, Fum, Fum [SATB] (G.Schirmer 10182)
	My Dancing Day [SATB] (Lawson-Gould 731) Christmas Eve: A
Pearsall, R.L.	In Dulci Jubilo [SATB] (Novello 160041)

Peeters, F.	Christmas Hymn-Anthem (All My Heart Today Rejoices) [SATB] (C.F.Peters 107b)
Pelz, W.L.	Who Are These That Earnest Knock [SATB] (WHD 27)
Perle, G.	Christ Is Born Today [SATB] (Galaxy 1.3246)
Plainsong	Of the Father's Love Begotten [U] (SG 39) {Divinum mysterium}
Powell, R.J.	A Babe Is Born [SA] (RM 29)
	Christians, Awake [U] (RM 32) {Yorkshire}
	Let Christians All [SA] (RM 9)
	Mary Rocks the Holy Child [U] (RM 21)
	Rejoice and Be Merry [U] (RM 3)
	Shepherds Ran to Bethlehem [SA] (RM 24)
	Sing, O Sing [U] (RM 15)
Praetorius, M.	At the Birth of Christ the Lord [SATB] (RS 108)
	Behold Is Born Emmanuel [SATB] (RS 101)
	Lo, How a Rose E'er Blooming [SATB] (WHD 35) {Es ist ein' Ros'}
	The Quempas Celebration [SATB] (SG 34) {Quem pastores}
	The Quempas Carol [SATB] (Concordia 98-1518)
	To Us a Child of Hope Is Born [SATB] (PCB 33) {Lobt gott, ihr Christen}
	Today Is Born Emmanuel [SATB] (CH1 34)
Reger, M.	The Virgin's Slumber Song [SA] (G.Schirmer A-94)
Rorem, N.	Shout the Glad Tidings [SATB] (Boosey & Hawkes 6008)
Rowley, A.	Shepherds Loud Their Praises Singing [SATB] (OEA 15) {Quem pastores}
Rutter, J.	The Holly and the Ivy [SATB] (Oxford X271)

Rutter, J.	Mary's Lullaby [SATB] (Oxford University Press X272)
Saint-Saëns, C.	Sing to the Lord of Hosts [SATB] (Carl Fischer CM8346)
Schalk, C.	All My Heart This Night Rejoices [SB] (CR1 6) {Fröhlich soll mein Herze springen}
	The Great God of Heaven [SB] (CR2 8)
	We Praise, O Christ, Your Holy Name [SB] (CR3 7) {Gelobet seist du, Jesu Christ}
	Wake, Shepherds, Awake [SATB] (Concordia 98-2882) {Ihr Hirten, erwacht}
Scheidt, S.	Ah, Dearest Jesus, Holy Child [canon] (PCB 38)
Schein, J.H.	Praise God the Lord, Ye Sons of Men [SA] (MS2 32) {Lobt Gott, ihr christen}
	Let All Together Praise Our God [SATB] (CH2 49) {Lobt Gott, ihr Christen}
Schroeter, L.	Rejoice, Rejoice, O Christians [SATB] (CH2 56) {Freut euch, ihr Lieben}
Schultz, R.C.	To Thee My Heart I Offer [SATB] (CH1 39)
Shaw, M.	Fanfare for Christmas Day [SATB] (G.Schirmer 8745)
	Gentle Mary Laid Her Child [SATB] (SG 32) {Tempus adest floridum}
Stainer, J.	What Child Is This [SATB] (SG 36) {Greensleeves}
Stewart, H.C.	On This Day Earth Shall Ring [SATB] (AC4 24)
Telfer, N.	Christmas Fanfare [SATB] (Stuart D. Beaudoin SAC-1)
Tye, C.	A Sound of Angels [SATB] (AC1 7)
V.Williams, R.	O Little Town of Bethlehem [SATB] (SG 31) {Forest Green}
	Fantasia on Christmas Carols [SATB] (Galaxy 1.5026)

V.Williams, R.	God Rest You Merry [SA] (Oxford 44.088)
Vance, M.	Christmas Is ... [SA or SSA] (SN 21)
Vivaldi, A.	Gloria [SATB] (Kalmus 06497)
Vulpius, M.	This Little Babe So Few Days Old [SATB] (SG 33) {Das neugeborne Kindelein}
	Lo, How a Rose E'er Blooming [Canon] (WHD 34)
Walker, D.	A Spiritual Quodlibet for Christmas [U] (Concordia 98-2143)
	Mary Had a Baby [U] (Concordia 98-2140)
	O Mary, Where Is Your Baby? [U w/d] (Concordia 98-2142)
	Rise Up, Shepherd, and Follow [U] (Concordia 98-2141) Christmas Day: A
	Shepherds in Judea [U w/d] (Concordia 98-2078)
	The Little Cradle Rocks Tonight in Glory [U] (Concordia 98-2139)
Walther, J.	Joseph, Dearest Joseph Mild (SSATB] (Associated Music A-400)
Walther & Bach	In Dulci Jubilo [SATB] (SG 28) {In dulci jubilo}
Warlock, P.	Adam Lay Ybounden [U] (Oxford University Press OCS 10)
	What Cheer? Good cheer! [U] (Boosey & Hawkes OCUB5314)
Washburn, J.	The Golden Vase Carol [SATB] (G.V.Thompson G-5001)
Waters, C.F.	I Sing of a Maiden that Is Makeless [SATB] (OEA 21)
Weelkes, T.	Gloria in Excelsis [SSAATB] (Oxford 43.337)
Willan, H.	All My Heart Today Rejoices [SS] (CS 18) {Fröhlich soll mein Herze springen}
	Away in a Manger [SA] (CS 22) {Cradle Song} Christmas 1: A
	Child in the Manger [SA] (CS 24) {Bunessan}

Willan, H.

From Heaven High, I Come to Earth [SA] (CS 20) {Vom Himmel hoch}

Glory Be to God on High [U] (MS1 51)

Good Christian Men, Rejoice [SA] (CS 28) {In dulci jubilo}

He Whom Joyous Shepherds Praised [SS] (CS 26) {Quem pastores}

Jesous Ahatonhia [SATB] (Frederick Harris HC-5037)

Jesu, Good Above All Other [2-part] (C.F.Peters 6676) {Quem pastores}

Let All Mortal Flesh Keep Silence [SATB] (C.F.Peters 6262) {Picardy}

Love Came Down at Christmas [SA] (CS 29) {Gartan}

Missa Brevis No.4 [SATB] (Carl Fischer CM449) {Divinum mysterium}

O Little Town of Bethlehem [SA] (CS 16) {Forest Green}

Oh, Come, All Ye Faithful [SS] (CS 14) {Adeste fideles}

Shepherds Watched Their Flocks by Night [U] (CS 32)

Sing, Oh, Sing, This Blessed Morn [U w/d] (WP1 16) {Nun komm, der Heiden Heiland}

Snowy Flakes Are Falling Softly [U] (WP1 18)

Today Christ Is Born [SATB] (Carl Fischer CM469)

When the Herds Were Watching [SA] (WP2 23) {Chantons je vous prie}

Willcocks, D.

Of the Father's Heart Begotten [SATB] (AC1 166) {Divinum mysterium}

Wolff, S.D.

Sing With Joy, Glad Voices Lift [SS] (MS1 46)

Now Sing We, Now Rejoice [SAB] (SJ 24) {In dulci jubilo}

Wolff, S.D.	Good Christian Men, Rejoice [SATB, Cong.] (Concordia 98-2254) {Gelobt sei Gott}
	O Come, All Ye Faithful [SATB, Cong.] (Concordia 98-2228) {Adeste fideles}
	Joy to the World [SATB, Cong.] (Concordia 98-2509) {Antioch}
Young, D.M.	A Babe Is Born [SATB] (Concordia 98-2900)

Church   [*See also* Psalms 84, 90 *and* 122]

Bach, J.S.	To Thee, Jehovah, Will I Sing Praises [U or SS] (MS2 14)
Bender, J.	Built on the Rock the Church Doth Stand [SA] (MS1 26)
Bruckner, A.	Place of Refuge [SATB] (SMB 100)
Harris, W.H.	Behold, the Tabernacle of God [SATB] (RSCM)
Jackson, F.	Lo, God Is Here [SATB] (AC1 88)
Purcell, H.	Christ Is Made the Sure Foundation [SATB] (CH2 14)
Schalk, C.	We Worship Thee, Almighty Lord [SB] (CR2 23) {Ter sanctus}
Schütz, H.	One Thing I Pray to God For [SS] (AC2 16)
Willan, H.	Behold, the Tabernacle of God [SATB] (Carl Fischer CM427)

Communion   [*See also* Psalm 34]

Bach/Davis	Take My Life, and Let It Be [SA] (GH 77)
Bach, J.S.	Deck Thyself, My Soul, With Gladness [SATB] (BC2 11) {Schmücke dich}
Bairstow, E.C.	Jesu, the Very Thought of Thee [SATB] (Oxford University Press A5]
	Let All Mortal Flesh Keep Silence [SSAATTBB] (AC4 88)
Byrd, W.	Hail, True Body [SATB] (RS 9; Oxford University Press TCM 3)

Byrd, W.	Jesu, Lamb of God, Redeemer [SATB] (CAB 202)
Casciolini, C.	Lamb of God [SATB] (CH1 50)
Dowland, J.	My Spirit Longs for Thee [SATB] (OEA 102)
Franck, C.	O Saviour Offered For Mankind [SS] (AC2 85)
Franck/Davis	O Lord, Most Merciful [SA] (GH 64)
Franck, M.	O Holy Spirit, Grant Us Grace [SATB] (CH1 47)
Gritton, E.	Lord That Descendedst, Holy Child [SATB] (AC1 98)
Handel, G.F.	Lord, I Trust Thee [SATB] (AC1 95)
	Soul, Adorn Thyself with Gladness [SAB] (SJ 32)
Kodály, Z.	Communion [SATB] (Boosey & Hawkes 5574)
Lasso, O.	Agnus Dei [SATB] (Music 70 M70-589)
Mozart/Davis	Jesu, Holy Spirit [SA] (GH 47)
Mozart, W.A.	Jesu, Lamb of God, Redeemer [SATB] (CAB 209)
	Jesu, Word of God Incarnate [SATB] (Leslie Music HC 4014; MA2 46; SMB 50)
Palestrina, G.P.	O Holy Jesu [SATB] (OEA 104)
Schalk, C.	The Nunc Dimittis [SB] (CR1 37)
	Sent Forth By God's Blessing [SATB] (Concordia 98-2973) {The Ash Grove}
	Soul, Adorn Thyself With Gladness [SB] (CR1 33) {Schmücke dich}
Shephard, R.	Jesu! The Very Thought Is Sweet [SATB] (RSCM)
Tye, C.	Give Almes of Thy Goods [SATB] (AC1 54)
Victoria, T.L.	Given For Us, Born For Mankind [SATB] (RS 141)
Wagner, R.	O Christ, O Blessed Lord [SATB] (AC1 117)
Whitlock, P.W.	Be Still, My Soul [SATB] (Oxford University Press A43)

Whitlock, P.W.   Here, O My Lord, I See Thee Face to
                    Face [SATB] (Oxford University Press
                    A42)
                    O Living Bread, Who Once Didst Die
                    [SATB] (Oxford University Press
                    A41)
Willan, H.   O Sacred Feast [SATB] (H.W.Gray]
Wöldike, M.   O Thou Who at Thy Eucharist Didst Pray
                    [SATB] (OEA 99)

Confirmation
Brahms, J.   A Blessing for Confirmation [SATB] (PCB
                    74)

Easter   [*See also* Song of Solomon]
Amner, J.   Christ Rising Again [SATB] (Oxford
                    University Press)
Anonymous   Jesus Is Our Joy, Our Treasure [SATB]
                    (WHD 16)
Bach, J.S.   Jesu, Hope of Man's Despairing [SATB]
                    (OEA 35)
                    Up, Up! My Heart! With Gladness
                    [SATB] (AC1 206)
Batten, A.   When the Lord Turned Again [SATB]
                    (Oxford University Press TCM 76)
Beck, T.   The King Shall Come [SA] (AT2 3)
                    {Consolation}
                    With High Delight Let Us Unite [SA]
                    (AT1 17) {Mit Freuden zart}
                    This Joyful Eastertide [SSA] (AT2 17)
                    {Vruechten}
                    At the Lamb's High Feast We Sing [SSA]
                    (AT1 3) {Sonne der Gerechtigkeit}
Bender, J.   Come, Ye Thankful, Raise the Strain [SA]
                    (MS1 68)
Bissell, K.   Christ Is Risen [U] (OC 36)

Boyce/Hardwicke	Alleluia, Alleluia [SATB] (Plymouth SC-126)
Britten, B.	Festival Te Deum [SATB] (Boosey & Hawkes) Easter: C
Bullock, E.	Good Christian Men Rejoice and Sing [SATB] (OEA 38)
Buxtehude, D.	Instruments, Waken and Publish Your Gladness [SAB] (Concordia 98-1422; SJ 40) Easter: B
Carol	Awake, Thou Wintry Earth [SA] (GH 12) {Vruechten}
Cope, C.	He Is Risen [SB] (OEA 42)
Couperin, F.	To Christ Now Arisen [SS] (AC2 27)
Davies, H.W.	O Sons and Daughters, Let Us Sing˙ [SATB] (Novello) {O filii et filiae}
Dickinson, C.	In Joseph's Lovely Garden [SSAB] (H.W.Gray GSC 185)
Drischner, M.	Christ Jesus Is Arisen [U] (MJ 30)
	At the Lamb's High Feast We Sing [U] (MJ 29) {Sonne der Gerechtigkeit}
	Good Christian Men, Rejoice and Sing [U] (MJ 32) {Gelobt sei Gott}
Gaul, H.	Russian Easter Carol of the Trees [SATB] (Oliver Ditson 332-14551)
Gibbs, C.A.	Most Glorious Lord of Lyfe! [SATB] (CAB 296)
	The Strife Is O'er [SATB] (OEA 46)
Gibbons, O.	If Ye Be Risen [SATB] (Novello)
Goss, J.	If We Believe That Jesus Died [SATB, div.] (Alexander Broude; Banks & Son)
Gumpeltzhaimer, A.	Christ Is Arisen [canon] (PCB 38)
Hairston, J.	Amen [SAB] (Schumann Music Co.)
Handel, G.F.	Praise to God, Who Rules the Earth [SATB] (E.C.Schirmer 2622) Easter:A
Handl, J.	This Is the Day [SATB SATB] (Concordia)
Hanff, J.N.	Alleluia! [SAB] (GB 58)
Harris, W.H.	This Joyful Eastertide [SATB] (Novello 18652) {Vruechten}

Hassler, H.L.	Christ Is Arisen [SATB] (Belwin Mills MC26) {Christ ist erstanden}
Helder, B.	The Strife Is O'er [SATB] (PCB 52)
Hutchison, W.	O Sons and Daughters, Let Us Sing! [SATB] (Carl Fischer CM8312) {O filii et filiae}
Kihlken, H.	Resurrection Carol [SATB] (AMSI 502)
Leisring, V.	Ye Sons and Daughters of the King [SATB SATB] (E.C.Schirmer 2272) Easter: B
Lenel, L.	With High Delight [SA] (MS2 61) {Mit Freuden zart}
Lord, D.	Most Glorious Lord of Lyfe [SATB] (AC1 101)
Lotti, A.	Sing, Joyous Christians [SATB] (CH1 57) Joy Fills the Morning [SATB] (H.W.Gray 172)
Mudde, W.	At the Lamb's High Feast We Sing [SA] (MS2 67) {Sonne der Gerechtigkeit}
Peter, H.	Awake, My Heart, With Gladness [U] (MS3 81)
Praetorius, M.	Alleluia! The Strife Is O'er, the Battle Done [SATB] (CH2 69)
Reda, S.	Christ Jesus Lay in Death's Strong Bands [SSATB] (SMB 65) {Christ lag in Todesbanden}
Rhau, G.	The Day of Resurrection [SA] (MS2 66) {Herzlich tut mich erfreuen}
Riegel, F.	With High Delight [SATB] (WHD 44) {Mit Freuden zart}
Rutter, J.	Christ the Lord Is Risen Again [SSATB] (AC4 33; Oxford 42.362)
Schalk, C.	Make Songs of Joy [SB] (CR3 24) {Zpivejmez vsickni vesele}
	Triumphant From the Grave [SB] (CR3 20) {Triumph}
	Christ the Lord Is Risen Again [SB] (CR1 23) {Christus ist erstanden}
	That Easter Day with Joy Was Bright [SB] (CR1 26) {Erschienen ist}

Schalk, C.	Ye Sons and Daughters of the King [SB] (CR2 17) {vb O filii et filiae}
Schütz, H.	Sing Praise to Our Glorious Lord [SATB] (FMB 15)
	On Wings of Living Radiance [SATB] (CH1 62)
Shaw, M.	Easter Alleluia [SATB] (G.Schirmer 10052) {Orientis partibus}
Shepherd, H.	Christ Rising Again [TTBB] (AM2 5)
Stanford, C.V.	Ye Choirs of New Jerusalem [SATB] (AC1 215)
Stanton, W.K.	Alleluia! Hearts to Heaven [U w/d] (OEA 52)
Telemann, G.P.	Alleluia [U] (MS3 84)
Thatcher, R.S.	Come Ye Faithful [SATB] (OEA 58)
Thoburn, C.R.	Hilariter [SATB] (H.W.Gray GCMR03587)
Thompson, R.	Alleluia [SATB] (E.C.Schirmer 1786) Easter: A
V.Williams, R.	Easter [B solo, SATB] (Galaxy)
Vulpius/Davis	Praise We Our God [SA] (GH 72) {Vulpius}
Vulpius, M.	The Strife Is O'er [SATB] (CAB 421; CH1 60) {Vulpius}
Wagner, G.G.	All Praise to Him Who Came to Save [SATB] (CAB 10)
Willan, H.	Angels, Roll the Rock Away [SSA] (WP1 38) {Orientis partibus}
	Christ, Our Passover [SA] (WP2 38)
	Christ, Our Passover [SATB] (FMB 57) Easter 5: A
	Now Let the Heavens Be Joyful [SS] (CS 35)
	This Joyful Eastertide [SA] (CS 37) {Hae groot de vrugten zijn}
Williams, R.	Christ the Lord Is Risen Today; Alleluia! [SATB] (PCB 49) {Llanfair} Easter 5: C
Wolff, S.D.	Christ the Lord Is Risen! [SATB] (CH2 70)

Wolff, S.D.	This Joyful Eastertide [SATB, Cong.] (Concordia 98-2221) {Vruechten}
	This Joyful Eastertide [SAB] (Morning Star MSM-50-4401) {Vruechten}
	The Day of Resurrection [SATB] (Concordia 98-2575) {Wie lieblich ist der Maien}
	O Sons and Daughters of the King [SATB, Cong.] (Concordia 98-2583) {O filii et filiae}
Wood, C.	Hail, Gladdening Light [SATB SATB] (C.F.Birchand A11)
Epiphany	[*See also* Malachi]
Attwood, T.	O God, Who By the Leading of a Star [SATB] (AC1 123)
Bach, J.S.	How Bright Appears the Morning Star [SATB] (BC1 13) {Wie schön leuchtet}
Bach/Hopson	The Only Son From Heaven [SATB] (Augsburg 11-2569)
Bissell, K.	Christ Whose Glory Fills the Skies [SATB] (G.V. Thompson)
Busarow, D.	Farewell to Alleluia [SATB] (Concordia 98-2995) {Picardy}
Crotch, W.	Lo! Star-Led Chiefs [SATB] (CAB 255; Novello 687)
Drischner, M.	Now Let Us Come Before Him [U] (MJ 21) {Nun lasst uns Gott dem Herren}
	How Lovely Shines the Morning Star [U] (MJ 22) {Wie schön leuchtet}
Eccard, J.	When to the Temple Mary Went [SSATBB] (CAB 515)
Franck, J.W.	O Jesus, King of Glory [SATB] (CH1 46)
Gibbons, O.	Almighty and Everlasting God [SATB] (Oxford University Press TCM 36)
	O Thou, the Central Orb [SAATB] (Stainer & Bell 5553) Epiphany 4: B

Handl, J.	Out of the East Came Magi [SATB] (Concordia 98-2955) Epiphany 1: A
Hillert, R.	From Shepherding of Stars That Gaze [SATB] (SG 26) {Shepherding}
Hovland, E.	The Glory of the Father [SATB] (Walton W2973)
Howells, H.	Here Is the Little Door [SATB] (Galaxy 1.5227) Epiphany 3: C
Jewell, K.W.	To Jesus From the Ends of Earth [SATB] (WHD 36) {Jesous Ahatonhia}
Rorem, N.	Before the Morning Star Begotten [SATB] (Boosey & Hawkes 6443)
Schalk, C.	How Lovely Shines the Morning Star [SB] (CR1 9) {Wie schön leuchtet}
	Brightest and Best of the Stars of the Morning [SB] (CR3 10)
Schop, J.	How Lovely Shines the Morning Star [SS] (MS1 54)
Shaw, M.	Kings in Glory [SATB] (OEA 22)
Telfer, N.	Light for the Child [SATB] (Waterloo) Epiphany 4: C
Tye, C.	O Christ, Thou Bright and Morning Star [SATB] (CH1 44) Epiphany 2: B
Vance, M.	March of the Kings [SAB] (G.Schirmer 12333)
Warlock, P.	Bethlehem Down [SATB] (Boosey & Hawkes OC4B3246) Epiphany 1: C
Willan, H.	A Soft Light From the Stable Door [SATB] (G.V.Thompson EI1062)
	Here Are We in Bethlehem [SATB] (Oxford 94.313) Epiphany 2: C
	Oh, How Beautiful the Sky [SSA] (CS 30) {Deilig er den himmel blaa} Christmas 2: A
Willan, H.	What Star Is This, With Beams So Bright [SS] (CS 33) {Puer nobis} Epiphany 1: A
	From the Eastern Mountains [SA] (WP1 22) {Laud tibi, christe}

Willan, H.

From the Eastern Mountains [SATB]
(G.V.Thompson G-5011) {Montes
orientis}

The Three Kings [SSATBB] (Oxford OCS
718)

Evening

Bach/Davis

Now All the Woods Are Sleeping [SA]
(GH 56) {O Welt, ich muss dich
lassen}

Bach, J.S.

Since Now the Day Has Reached Its Close
[SATB] (BC2 12) {Nun sich der Tag
geendet}

Bennett, G.S.

Abide With Me [SATB] (CAB 1)

Besly, M.

O Lord, Support Us [SATB] (CAB 346)

Bissell, K.

Now God Be With Us [U] (OC 44)
{Christe sanctorum}

Byrd, W.

O Christ Who Art the Light and Day
[SSATB] (CAB 318)

O Christ Who Art the Light and Day
[SATBB] (Oxford University Press
TCM 7)

Drese, A.

Round Me Falls the Night [SATB] (CAB
397)

Gardiner, B.H.

Evening Hymn [SATB] (Novello 29 0133)

Goudimel, C.

O Gladsome Light, O Grace [SATB]
(CAB 325)

Dark'ning Night the Land Doth Cover
[SATB] (CAB 79)

Haydn, F.J.

Evensong to God [SATB] (Belwin Mills
OCT02562)

Joubert, J.

O Lorde, the Maker of Al Thing [SATB]
(Novello 29 0250)

Mundy, W.

O Lord, the Maker of All Things [SATB]
(CAB 348; Oxford University Press
TCM 38)

Purcell, H.

Now that the Sun Hath Veil'd His Light
[U] (CAB 309)

Evening Hymn [U] (AC2 30)

| Schalk, C. | O Gladsome Light, O Grace [SB] (CR2 28) {Nunc dimittis} |

Funeral

Bach, J.S.	In Peace and Joy I Now Depart [SATB] (BC2 9) {Mit Fried und Freud}
Croft, W.	Burial Sentences [SATB] (Oxford University Press)
Mozart, W.A.	Eyes Be Weeping [SATB] (MA1 26)
Neumark, G.	If Thou But Suffer God to Guide Thee [U or SS] (MS2 16) {Wer nur den lieben Gott}
Purcell, H.	Thou Knowest, Lord, the Secrets of Our Hearts [SATB] (Alexander Broude)
Tchaikovsky, P.I.	How Blest Are They [SSAATTBB] (E.C.Schirmer 1138)
Willan, H.	O Strength and Stay [SATB] (C.F.Peters 6126)

General

Amner, J.	I Will Sing Unto the Lord [SSATB] (Oxford University Press)
Anonymous	I Thank Thee [SATB] (Belwin Mills)
Arne, T.	Help Me, O Lord [SAB] (OEA 133)
Attwood, T.	O Lord, We Beseech Thee [SATB] (Broude Bros. MGC 44)
Bach, J.S.	Abide, O Dearest Jesus [SATB] (BC1 19) {Ach, bleib mit deiner Gnade}
	Awake Us, Lord, and Hasten [SATB] (AC1 34) {Herr Christ, der einig Gottes Sohn}
	Come, Sweetest Death [SATB] (OEA 134) {Komm, süsser tod}
	Dearest Lord Jesus, Oh, Why Dost Thou Tarry? [SATB] (BC1 8) {Liebster Herr Jesu}
	Flocks in Pastures Green Abiding [SATB] (OEA 136)
	Forget Me Not [SATB] (OEA 141)

Bach, J.S.

From God Shall Nought Divide Me
[SATB] (BC2 5) {Von Gott will ich
nicht lassen}

God Is Living, God Is Here! [SATB]
(AC1 212)

If God Himself Be For Me [SATB] (CH1
51) {Valet will ich dir geben}

If Thou But Suffer God to Guide Thee
[SATB] (BC1 10) {Wer nur den lieben
Gott}

Jesu, Joy of Man's Desiring [SATB]
(Belwin Mills 64027; CAB 195)
{Werde munter}

Jesu, Lead My Footsteps Ever [SATB]
(CAB 213)

Jesus, Who Didst Ever Love Me [SATB]
(BC1 21) {Jesu richte mein Beginnen}

Jesus I Will Never Leave [SATB] (BC2
21) {Meinen Jesum lass ich nicht}

Jesus, Lead Thou On [SATB] (BC2 16)
{Jesu, geh' voran}

Jesus, Refuge of the Weary [SA] (MS1 60)
Jesus Christ, My Sure Defense
[SATB] (BC2 19) {Jesus, meine
Zuversicht}

King of Glory, King of Peace [SATB]
(CAB 235; CH2 12) {Jesu, meines
Herzens Freud}

Let All the Multitudes of Light [SA] (MS1
66)

Lord Jesus Christ, With Us Abide [SATB]
(BC1 6) {Ach, bleib bei uns}

Lord Jesus Christ, Thou Prince of Peace
[U or SS] (MS2 44) {Du Friedefürst}

Lord Jesus Christ, Be Present Now
[SATB] (BC2 3) {Herr Jesu Christ,
dich zu uns wend}

My Inmost Heart Now Raises [SATB]
(BC2 2) {Aus meines Herzens
Grunde}

Bach, J.S.

My Soul, Now Bless Thy Maker [SATB]
(BC1 23) {Nun lob, mein Seel, den
Herren}

Now Rest Beneath Night's Shadow
[SATB] (BC1 11) {O Welt, ich muss
dich lassen}

O God, Thou Faithful God [SATB] (CAB
330)

Our Father, Thou in Heaven Above
[SATB] (BC2 1) {Vater unser}

Praise to the Lord, the Almighty [SATB]
(BC1 20) {Lobe den herren}

Rise, My Soul, to Watch and Pray [SATB]
(BC2 14) {Mache dich, mein Geist,
bereit}

Sing Praise to Christ [SATB] (WHD 4)

Subdue Us By Thy Goodness [SATB]
(CAB 399) {Herr Christ, der einig
Gottes Sohn}

The Only Son From Heaven [SA] (MS1
58)

To Thee, Jehovah, Will I Sing Praises
[SATB] (BC2 17) {Dir, dir, Jehovah}

What Is the World to Me [SATB] (BC2 4)
{Was frag' ich nach der Welt}

Whate'er God Ordains Is Good [SATB]
(BC2 6) {Was Gott tut, das ist
wohlgetan}

When O'er My Sins I Sorrow [SATB]
(BC2 20) {Wenn meine Sünd' mich
kränken}

Where'er I Go, Whate'er My Task
[SATB] (BC2 15) {In allen meinen
Taten}

Bach/Roper

Flocks in Pastures Green Abiding [SATB]
(Oxford A116)

Bairstow, E.C.

Jesu, the Very Thought of Thee [SATB]
(CAB 223)

Save Us, O Lord [SATB] (Novello 740)

Barcrofte, G.

O Almighty God [SATB] (AC1 112)

Bax, A.	Lord, Thou Hast Told Us [SATB] (AC4 28)
Beethoven, L.	Hallelujah Unto God's Almighty Son [SATB] ("Mount of Olives") (E.C.Schirmer 1602)
	The Heavens Declare the Creator's Glory [U] (CAB 410)
	Lord, Have Mercy Upon Us [SATB] (Plymouth Music Co. PCS-175)
Beobide/Davis	God Our Father, Lord of Heaven [SA] (GH 33)
Bergsma, W.	Praise [SATB] (Galaxy 1.2165)
Bissell, K.	Lord, Dismiss Us With Thy Blessing [SATB] (G.V.Thompson G-565)
	Worship the Lord [SA] (OC 8)
	Sing to the Lord [SSA] (OC 15)
Blow, J.	Let My Prayer [SATB] (AC1 86)
Bortniansky/Davis	Cherubim Song [SA] (E.C.Schirmer 1565)
	Lo, a Voice to Heaven Sounding [SA] (GH 50)
Bortniansky/arr.	Cherubim Song [SSA] (Ditson 332-14948)
Bourgeois, L.	O Strength and Stay [SATB] (AC1 156)
Brahms, J.	Ah, Thou Poor World [SATB] (AC1 10)
	O Jesu, Joy of Loving Hearts [U] (MS1 80)
	Let Nothing Ever Grieve Thee [SATB] (C.F.Peters 6093) Epiphany 6: B
Buck, P.C.	O Lord God [SSA] (CAB 334)
Bunjes, P.G.	Praise to the Lord, the Almighty [SATB] (Concordia 98-1473) {Lobe den Herren}
Busarow, D.	Rise, Shine, You People! [SATB, Cong.] (Concordia 98-2890) {Wojtkiewiecz}
Buxtehude, D.	Command Thine Angel That He Come [SATB] (Broude Brothers BB 120)
	In God, My Faithful God [U] (MS2 24) {Auf meinen lieben Gott}
	Let Shouts of Gladness Rise [U] (MS2 24) {Auf meinen lieben Gott}

Byrd, W.	Prevent Us, O Lord [SAATB] (Oxford TCM 15)
Campbell,S.S.,arr.	Praise to God in the Highest [SATB] (AC1 179)
Carter, S.	I Come Like a Beggar [U] (Stainer & Bell)
	One More Step [SSA] (Stainer & Bell)
Copland, A.	Simple Gifts [SA or TB] (Boosey & Hawkes OCFB1903) 25 Sep: C
Crotch, W.	Be Peace on Earth [SA] (OEA 147)
Davies, H.W.	Lord, It Belongs Not to My Care [SATB SATB] (CAB 266)
Davis, K.K.	Praise to the Lord, the Almighty [SA] (GH 68) {Lobe den Herren}
	Ye Watchers and Ye Holy Ones [SA] (GH 93) {Lasst uns erfreuen}
Davison, A.T.	Ye Watchers and Ye Holy Ones [SATB] (E.C.Schirmer 389) {Lasst uns erfreuen}
Dering, R.	Above Him Stood the Seraphim [SS] (OEA 155)
Dowland, J.	He That Is Down Needs Fear No Fall [SATB] (OEA 160)
Drischner, M.	Commit Whatever Grieves Thee [U] (MJ 36)
	God, Who Madest Earth and Heaven [U] (MJ 4)
	If God Himself Be For Me [U] (MJ 38) {Ist Gott für mich}
	Lord Jesus Christ, Be Present Now [U] (MJ 5) {Herr Jesu Christ, dich zu uns wend}
	Lord, as Thou Wilt, Deal Thou With Me [U] (MJ 6) {Aus tiefer Not II}
	Praise to the Lord, the Almighty [U] (MJ 3) {Lobe den Herren}
	Redeemed, Restored, Forgiven [U] (MJ 8)
	This Day at Thy Creating Word [U] (MJ 25)
Ellington, D.	Come Sunday [SATB] (G.Schirmer HL50481495)

Farmer, J.	The Lord's Prayer [SATB] (Hinrichsen 1506; Oxford A231a)
Farrant, R.	Lord, For Thy Tender Mercies' Sake [SATB] (Broude Brothers CR55) Epiphany 7: B
Farrar, E.	Almighty God, the Fountain of All Wisdom [SATB] (AT1 24)
Franck, C.	Welcome, Welcome, Dear Redeemer [SATB] (G.Schirmer 3284)
Frauenholz, J.C.	Praise the Almighty [SATB] (CH2 37)
Gibbons, O.	Ye That Do Your Master's Will [SATB] (CAB 527)
	Almighty and Everlasting God [SATB] (CAB 12; Oxford TCM 36) 29 May: B
Gretchaninoff, A.	Come, and Let Us Worship [SSAATTBB] (Boston Music 7299)
	Our Father [SATB] (Oliver Ditson 332-13000)
Handel/Davis	In Thee, O Lord, Have I Trust [SA] (GH 45)
Handel, G.F.	Alleluia from "Let Thy Hand Be Strengthened" [SATB] (Frederick Harris HC5007)
	Alleluia from "Sieg der Wahrheit und Zeit" [SATB] (E.C.Schirmer 2637)
	Father of Heaven [SATB] ("Judas Maccabeus") (E.C.Schirmer 1014)
	Hallelujah, Amen [SATB] ("Judas Maccabeus") (E.C.Schirmer 3040) 4 Jun: C
	Hallelujah from "Saul" [SATB] (E.C.Schirmer 1698)
	Let Their Celestial Concerts All Unite [SATB] ("Samson") (E.C.Schirmer 199) 19 Jun: B
	Lord, Hear Our Thanks [U] (HC 3)
	O Lovely Peace, With Plenty Crown'd ("Judas Maccabeus") [SA] (E.C.Schirmer 1039)

Handel, G.F.	Thanks Be to Thee [U] (E.C.Schirmer 959)
	The Smiling Dawn of Happy Days ("Jephtha") [U] (E.C.Schirmer 458)
	Sing Unto God [SATB] ("Judas Maccabeus") (Carl Fischer CM7414)
	Then Round About the Starry Throne [SATB] ("Samson") (E.C.Schirmer 907) 6 Nov: B
	Welcome as the Cheerful Light [SS] ("Jephtha") (E.C.Schirmer 1061) 14 Aug: C
	Where'er You Walk [U] (E.C.Schirmer 426) 3 Jul: C
Handel/Hopson	Rejoice, Give Thanks [SB] (HC 14)
Handel/Liebergen	Sing With Joy [SATB] (Carl Fischer CM8345)
Harris, W.H.	Tarry No Longer; Toward Thine Heritage [U] (OEA 167)
	Most Glorious Lord of Life [STB] (OEA 163)
Hassler, H.L.	Alleluia [SSATB] (Elkan-Vogel 362-03368)
	Dear Christians, One and All, Rejoice [SATB] (Concordia 98-1949) {Nun freut euch II}
	Glory [SATB] (Theodore Presser 312-41383)
Haydn, F.J.	Achieved Is the Glorious Work [SATB] ("The Creation") (G.Schirmer 2359; Walton W6001) 13 Nov: B
	'Tis Thou To Whom All Honor [SATB] (Mercury Music 352-00084)
Hobby, R.A.	O Christ, Our Light, Our Radiance True [SATB] (Concordia 98-2891) {O Jesu Christe, wahres Licht}
	Jesus, Thy Church With Longing Eyes [SATB] (Concordia 98-2891) {O Jesu Christe, wahres Licht}

Holst, G.	Eternal Father [SATB] (CAB 103; G.Schirmer 8510)
	Turn Back O Man [SATB] (Galaxy 2152) 13 Nov: A
Holst/Lefebvre	The Heart Worships [SATB] (Galaxy 1.5055)
Howells, H.	My Eyes for Beauty Pine [U; optional SATB] (OEA 169)
	All My Hope on God Is Founded [U w/d] (Novello 29 0301 06) {Michael}
	I Love All Beauteous Things [SATB] (Novello 29 0502 07)
	My Eyes for Beauty Pine [SATB] (Oxford A14)
Ives, C.	Lord God, Thy Sea Is Mighty [SATB] (Associated A-824)
Kitson, C.H.	Christ Is the World's Redeemer [SATB] (CH2 21) {Moville}
Lasso, O.	Blest Is the Man [SA] (AC2 2)
Lehman, R.	A Hymn of Praise [SAB] (Morning Star MSM-50-7201) {Christe sanctorum}
Lenel, L.	The King Shall Come When Morning Dawns [SA] (MS2 28) {Consolation}
	All Praise to God, Who Reigns Above [SS] (MS1 14)
Ley, H.G.	We Praise Thee, O God [U] (MS3 7)
Loosemore, W.	O Lord, Increase Our Faith [SATB] (Novello 88 0007 03)
Lord, D.	A Prayer for Peace [SATB] (AC4 172)
	Close in My Breast Thy Perfect Love [SS] (AC2 104)
Lovelace, A.C.	Glory, Love, and Praise and Honor [SAB] (Concordia 98-2885) {Bonn}
McKie, W.	We Wait For Thy Loving Kindness [SATB] (AC4 77)
Mendelssohn, arr.	Almighty God, Grant Us Thy Peace [SA] (Presser 312-41388)
	In Heavenly Love Abiding [SA] (Theodore Presser 312-41389)
Mendelssohn, F.	Grant Us Thy Peace [SATB] (CAB 120)

Mendelssohn, F.	Grant Peace, We Pray [SATB] (Concordia 98-2212) 31 Jul: C
Mozart, W.A.	Just Men Are Led by God [SATB] (MA1 34)
	Holy Redeemer [SATB] (MA2 24)
Mudd [Weelkes]	Let Thy Merciful Ears [SATB] (Morning Star MSM-50-9104)
Mueller, C.F.	Praise Ye the Lord, the Almighty [SATB] (Carl Fischer CM 6765) {Lobe den Herren}
Mundy, J.	Sing Joyfully [SAATB] (Oxford University Press TCM 92)
Nystedt, K.	Praise to God [SATB] (Associated Music Publishers)
Pachelbel, J.	What God Ordains Is Always Good [U] (MS1 18) {Was Gott tut, das ist wohlgetan} 17 Jul: C
	What God Ordains Is Always Good [SATB] (WHD 19) {Was Gott tut, das ist wohlgetan}
Palestrina, G.P.	Thee We Adore [SSAT] (CAB 426)
Parry, C.H.H.	My Soul, There Is a Country [SATB] (CAB 300)
Peek, R.	O Thou to Whose All-Searching Sight [SAB] (SJ 20)
Proulx, R.	O God, Beyond All Praising [SATB, Cong.] (GIA Publications G-3190) {Thaxted}
Purcell, H.	Let My Prayer Come Up [SSATB] (Mercury Music 352-00440) 25 Sep: B
	Thou Knowest, Lord [SATB] (CAB 448)
Purcell/Moffat	Sound the Trumpet [SA] (E.C.Schirmer 487)
Rutter, J.	All Things Bright and Beautiful [SS] (Hinshaw HCM-663)
	Be Thou My Vision [SATB] (Hinshaw HMC-1035)
	God Be in My Head [SATB] (Oxford 94.326)

Rutter, J.   Praise to the Lord, the Almighty [SATB]
                          (Hinshaw HCM-917) {Lobe den
                          Herren}
Schalk, C.   In God, My Faithful God [SB] (CR1 19)
                          {Auf meinen lieben Gott}
                          Let Me Be Thine Forever [SB] (CR1 29)
                          {Ich danke dir, lieber Herre}
                          Redeemed, Restored, Forgiven [SB] (CR1
                          29) {Ich danke dir, lieber Herre}
                          Lord, Keep Us Steadfast in Your Word
                          [SB] (CR3 35) {Erhalt uns, Herr}
Shave, E.   Teach Us, Good Lord [SATB] (Novello)
Schubert, F.   Great Is Jehovah the Lord [SATB]
                          (Novello)
                          Strike the Cymbal, Bow the String!
                          [SATB] (E.C.Schirmer) 25 Jun: C
Schütz, H.   Christ, Our Blessed Saviour [SATB]
                          (G.Schirmer 9657)
                          O Mighty God, Our Lord [2 equal voices]
                          (Mercury Music 352-00018)
                          O May the Eyes of All [SATB] (Theodore
                          Presser 312-41328)
Shaw, M.   Christ's Flock [SATB] (G.Schirmer
                          10584)
Somers, H.   Song of Praise [Two-part] (Gordon V.
                          Thompson)
Sowerby, L.   Benedictus Es Domine [U]
                          (H.T.Fitzsimons F2294)
Staden, J.   Awake, My Soul, Thy Voice Now Raise
                          [SATB] (CH1 10)
Stanford, C.V.   O For a Closer Walk [SATB] (AC1 142)
Steffani, A.   Come, Ye Children [SS] (AC2 22)
Stone, R.   The Lord's Prayer [SATB] (AC1 172)
Tallis, T.   All People That On Earth Do Dwell
                          [SATB] (AC1 18)
Tchaikovsky, P.I.   For Thou Art Worthy to be Praised
                          [SATB] (E.C.Schirmer 2624)
Tchesnokov, P.   Salvation Belongeth to Our God [SATB]
                          (E.C.Schirmer 2483)

Tchesnokov, P.	Salvation Is Created [SATTBB] (J.Fischer FEC04129; Plymouth SCR-125)
Telfer, N.	Break Forth Into Singing [SATB] (Waterloo)
	God Is the Light [SAB] (Stuart Beaudoin SAC-9)
Terry, R.R.	Richard de Castre's Prayer to Jesus [SATB] (OEA 175)
Tomkins, T.	O God, Wonderful Art Thou [SAATB] (Oxford University Press TCM 99)
Tye, C.	O God of Bethel [SATB] (CAB 327)
	O Come, Ye Servants of the Lord [SATB] (AC1 120)
	O Jesus, King Most Wonderful [SATB] (CH2 8; WHD 12)
V.Williams, arr.	Come Down, O Love Divine [SATB] (H.W.Gray GCMR03569) {Down Ampney}
V.Williams/Percival	The Call [SATB] (Galaxy 1.5245)
V.Williams, R.	All Hail the Power [SATB] (Oxford 42.230) {Miles Lane}
	Eternal Father, Who Hast Called Us [U] (MS2 23)
	The Song of the Tree of Life [U or 2-part] (AC2 92)
Victoria, T.L.	Jesu! The Very Thought Is Sweet [SATB] (CAB 217)
	Jesus, Thoughts of Thee We Find Sweet [SATB] (RS 137)
	Jesu, the Very Thought of Thee [SATB] (OEA 153)
	Sanctus and Hosanna [SATB] (Shawnee Press A-1645)
Viderö, F.	O Love of Whom Is Truth and Light [SATB] (OEA 144)
Walmisley, T.A.	From All That Dwell Below the Skies [SATB] (CAB 111)
Weelkes, T.	Let Thy Merciful Ears, O Lord [SATB] (E.C.Schirmer 1018)

White, L.J.	A Prayer of St. Richard of Chichester [U w/d] (OEA 177)
Whyte, R.	O Christ, Who Art the Light and Day [SATB] (AC1 118)
Willan, H.	A Spring Carol [SS] (CS 42) {Lasst uns erfreuen}
	Beautiful Savior [U] (CS 5) {Schönster Herr Jesu}
	Christ Hath a Garden [SATB] (Frederick Harris HC4056)
	Christ, Whose Glory Fills the Skies [SATB] (Concordia 98-2006) {Ratisbon}
	Fairest Lord Jesus [SA] (C.F.Peters 6233)
	Father of Heaven, Whose Love Profound [SATB] (Concordia 98-2005) {Angelus}
	Lead Us, Heavenly Father [SATB] (G.V.Thompson EI1064) {Mannheim}
	Let All the World in Every Corner Sing [SSA] (C.F.Peters 6677)
	Lord of All Hopefulness [SATB] (C.F.Peters 6985) {Slane} Epiphany 6: C
	Praise to the Lord [SATB] (C.F.Peters 6266) {Lobe den Herren}
	Rejoice, Ye Pure in Heart! [SATB] (C.F.Peters 6065) {Marion} 2 Oct: C
	Rejoice, O Land [SATB] (C.F.Peters 6986) {Wareham}
	Rise, Crowned With Light [SATB] (Concordia 98-2001) {Old 124th}
	The Lord's Prayer [U] (MS3 38)
	Ye Watchers and Ye Holy Ones [SATB] (C.F.Peters 6238) {Lasst uns erfreuen}
Wolff, S.D.	All Hail the Power of Jesus' Name [SATB, cong.] (Concordia 98-2576) {Miles Lane}

Wolff, S.D.	Crown Him With Many Crowns [SATB, Cong.] (Concordia 98-2332) {Diademata}
	God of Grace and God of Glory [SATB] (Concordia 98-2743) {Cwm Rhondda}
	Lord of Glory, You Have Bought Us [SATB, Cong.] (Concordia 98-2869) {Hyfrydol}
	Oh, Worship the King [SATB, Cong.] (Concordia 98-2323) {Hanover}
	Praise, My Soul, the King of Heaven [SATB, Cong.] (Concordia 98-2585) {Lauda anima}
	Rejoice, the Lord Is King [SATB, Cong.] (Concordia 98-2552) {Darwall's 148th}
	Rejoice, the Lord Is King [SATB] (Morning Star MSM-50-9023) {Gopsal}
	Ye Watchers and Ye Holy Ones [SATB, Cong.] (Concordia 98-1904) {Lasst uns erfreuen}
Wood, C.	Jesu! The Very Thought Is Sweet [SATB] (CAB 220)
Wood, D.	Now that the Daylight Fills the Sky [SA] (AI 10) {Laurel}

Good Friday

Anonymous	Darkness, Gross Darkness Did Cover the Earth [SATB] (CH1 52)
Bach, J.S.	Go to Dark Gethsemane [SATB] (CH2 68) {Nicht so traurig}
Bruckner, A.	Sing, My Tongue, the Glorious Battle [SATB] (CH2 66)
Mozart, W.A.	We Adore You, O Christ [SATB] (MA1 6)
Tallis, T.	That Virgin's Child [SATB] (G.Schirmer 9946)

Lent	[*See also* Psalm 51]
Amner, J.	Hear, O Lord [SSATB] (Oxford University Press)
Arcadelt/Davis	Hear Thou My Prayer, O Lord [SA] (GH 36)
Bach/Buszin	Jesus Is My Heart's Delight [SATB] (PCB 39)
Bach, J.S.	Beloved Jesus, What Law Hast Thou Broken [SATB] (BC2 18) {Herzliebster Jesu}
	God Is Our Hope and Strength [SATB] (AC1 59) {O Gott, du frommer Gott II}
	Jesus, I Will Ponder Now [SATB] (BC1 4) {Jesu, deine Passion}
	O Lamb of God Most Holy [SATB] (BC1 5) {O Lamm Gottes, unschuldig}
	O Sacred Head, Now Wounded [SATB] (BC1 2; PCB 48) {Passion Chorale}
	O Sinner, Come Thy Sin to Mourn [SATB] (BC1 18) {O Mensch, bewein}
	With Heavy Fetters Sin Had Bound Me [SAB] (GB 39)
Barber, S.	Let Down the Bars, O Death [SATB] (G.Schirmer 8907) Lent 4: C
Batten, A.	Hear My Prayer, O God [SSATB] (Oxford University Press)
	Two Short Anthems: Deliver Us, O Lord Our God; O Praise the Lord [SATB] (Oxford University Press TCM 56)
Battishill, J.	O Lord, Look Down From Heaven [SATB] (Novello NECM 1)
Beck, T.	Wondrous Love [SA] (AT2 12) {The Sacred Harp}
Beethoven/Davis	O God, Thy Goodness Reacheth Far [SA] (GH 60)
Bender, J.	O Christ, Thou Lamb of God [U] (MS1 62)

Berger, J.	O Lord Seek Us [SATB] (European American)
Bissell, K.	Ah, Holy Jesu [SA] (OC 49) {Herzliebster Jesu}
Busarow, D.	My Song Is Love Unknown [SAB] (Concordia 98-2336) {Love Unknown}
Buxtehude & Schein	O God, My Faithful God [SATB] (CH2 24) {Auf meinen lieben Gott}
Buxtehude, D.	Jesus, Priceless Treasure [SAB] (GB 35) {Jesu, meine Freude}
Byrd, W.	Bow Thine Ear, O Lord [SATTB] (Oxford University Press CMS 43)
	Jesu, Lamb of God, Redeemer [SATB] (CAB 202)
Casner, M.D.	O Jesus, I Have Promised [U w/d] (CH2 16) {Llanfyllin}
Crüger/Neumann	Ah, Holy Jesus, How Hast Thou Offended [SATB] (Music 70 M70-366) {Herzliebster Jesu}
David, J.N.	O Christ, Thou Lamb of God [SATB] (SMB 48) Lent 1: C
Davison/Davis	I Would We Lived as Angels Do [SA] (GH 40)
Drischner, M.	Lord Jesus, We Give Thanks to Thee [U] (MJ 28)
	O Lamb of God Most Holy [U] (MJ 26)
	When I Survey the Wondrous Cross [U] (MJ 25)
Eccard, J.	O Lamb of God Most Holy [SATTB] (G. Schirmer 11340)
Farrant/Davis	Hide Not Thou Thy Face From Us [SA] (GH 38)
Farrant, R.	Hide Not Thou Thy Face From Us; Call to Remembrance, O Lord [SATB] (Oxford University Press TCM 60)
Farrant, R.	Lord, For Thy Tender Mercy's Sake [SATB] (PCB 70) Epiphany 7: B
Franck, M.	Thou Goest to Jerusalem [SATB] (PCB 42)

Gibbons, O.	O Lord, Increase My Faith [SATB] (FMB 70) Lent 5: B
Goss, J.	O Saviour of the World [SATB] (CAB 352; Jackman 392-00737)
Greene, M.	Lord, Let Me Know Mine End [SATB] (Oxford University Press; RSCM)
Gumpeltzhaimer, A.	When My Last Hour Is Close at Hand [SATB] (FMB 74) Lent 5: C
	Jesus' Cross, the Death and Pain [SATB] (WHD 39)
Handel, G.F.	O Sacred Head Now Wounded [U] (MS2 56) {Passion Chorale}
Haydn, F.J.	O Lord, Give Ear to Me [SATB] (Tetra TC 1130)
Hilton, J.	Lord, For Thy Tender Mercy's Sake [SATB] (OEA 27)
Holst, G.	Turn Back O Man [SATB] (Stainer & Bell)
Jennings, C.	O Christ, Our King, Creator, Lord [U] (AI 16) {Oakley}
Kindermann, J.E.	O Jesus, My Lord, My God [SAB] (SJ 36)
Loosemore, W.	O Lord, Increase My Faith [SABT] (CAB 337) Lent 5: B
Marcello, B.	Give Ear Unto Me [SS] (AC2 46)
Mendelssohn F.	Lord, I Flee to Thee For Refuge [SATB] (CAB 271)
	Lord Jesus Christ, My Life, My Light [SATB] (WHD 42) {O Jesu Christ, mein's Lebens Leben}
Micheelsen, H.F.	A Lamb Goes Uncomplaining Forth [U] (MS3 78) {An Wasserflüssen Babylon}
Mozart, W.A.	Jesu, Lamb of God, Redeemer [SATB] (CAB 209)
Palestrina, G.P.	O Saviour of the World [SATB] (CAB 355)
Purcell, H.	Remember Not, Lord, Our Offences [SSATB] (E.C.Schirmer 993)
Schalk, C.	My Song Is Love Unknown [SB] (CR2 14) {Rhosymedre}

Schalk, C.	O Christ, Thou Lamb of God [SB] (CR1 16) {Christe, du Lamm Gottes}
	Sing, My Tongue [SAB] (CR3 16) {Fortunatus New}
	Lamb of God [SB] (CR3 31)
Schütz, H.	Praise to Thee, Lord Jesus [SATB] (Novello 29 0139 00)
Stainer, J.	God So Loved the World [SATB] (from The Crucifixion, Novello 8002)
Tchaikovsky/Davis	Christ, When a Child, a Garden Made [SA] (GH 17)
Tchaikovsky, P.I.	A Legend [SATB] (E.C.Schirmer 2200)
	Hear, Lord. Lord Make Haste to Help Us [SSAATTBB] (CAB 148)
Tye, C.	Lord, For Thy Tender Mercies' Sake [SATB] (CAB 264)
	To Our Redeemer's Glorious Name [SATB] (PCB 7)
Viadana, L.	Lord Jesus Christ [U] (MS3 72)
Walton, W.	A Litany (Drop, Drop, Slow Tears) [SATB] (AC4 29)
Weelkes, T.	Let Thy Merciful Ears, O Lord [SATB] (CAB 243) {O Gott, du frommer Gott II}
Willan, H.	O Savior of the World [SSA] (WP1 34)
	There Is a Green Hill Far Away [SSA] (WP1 27) {Horsley}
	Lamb of God, Pure and Holy [SA] (WP1 24) {O Lamm Gottes, unschuldig}
	O Christ, Thou Lamb of God [SA] (WP1 30) {Christe, du Lamm Gottes}
Wolff, S.D.	Jesus, Grant Me This, I Pray [SATB] (PCB 11)
Mary	[See also Magnificat settings listed under Luke 1:46-56]
Willan, H.	I Beheld Her, Beautiful as a Dove [SATB] (Oxford 94.315)

Morning

Armstrong, T.	Christ, Whose Glory Fills the Skies [SATB] (CAB 57)
Bairstow, E.C.	The Day Draws On With Golden Light [SATB] (CAB 405)
Bissell, K.	Christ Whose Glory Fills the Skies [U] (OC 46)
	Christ Whose Glory Fills the Skies [SATB] (G.V.Thompson G-556)
Ford/Davis	Almighty God, Who Hast Me Brought [SA] (GH 6)
Ford, T.	Almighty God, Who Hast Me Brought [SATB] (AC1 28; CAB 15; Novello 29 0307 05)

New Years

| Bach, J.S. | Now Let Us Come Before Him [SATB] (BC1 15) {Nun lasst uns Gott dem Herren} |
| Buxtehude, D. | To God the Anthem Raising [U] (MS1 34) |

Palm Sunday

[*See also* Hosanna to the Son of David, Matthew 21:9; Mark 11:1; Luke 19:38]

Bach/Davis	All Glory, Laud and Honor [SA] (GH 3) {Valet will ich dir geben}
Bach, J.S.	All Glory Laud and Honour [SATB] (CAB 5; CH1 56) {Valet will ich dir geben}
Berger, J.	Alleluia, from "Brazilian Psalm" [SATB div.] (G.Schirmer 9992) Palm Sunday: C
Williamson, M.	Procession of Palms [SATB] (Josef Weinberger Ltd.)

Passion

[See also settings of Psalm 22]

Anonymous	O Mighty Lord Christ [SATB] (RS 163)
Bach, J.S.	Here Lies He Now [SATB] (OEA 25)
Gibbons, O.	Jesu, Grant Me This I Pray [SATB] (Banks Music Pub. YS 1000)

Gumpeltzhaimer, A.	We Sing the Praise of Him Who Died [SATB] (CH1 48)
Ingegneri, M.A.	Darkness Had Fallen There [SATB] (RS 39) Holy Thursday: B
Leighton, K.	Alone to Sacrifice Thou Goest, Lord [SATB] (AC1 13)
Morley, T.	Lamb Most Holy [SATB] (RS 48)
Mozart, W.A.	Jesu, Word of God Incarnate [SATB] (OEA 29)
Palestrina, G.P.	We Adore Thee [SATB] (RS 67) Holy Thursday: A
Pergolesi, G.B.	Mother, Bowed with Grief Appalling [SA] (AC2 76)
Petrich, R.T.	Ah, Holy Jesus [SATB] (AC4 180) {Herzliebster Jesu}
Praetorius, M.	We Sing the Praise of Him Who Died [SATB] (WHD 48)
Tye, C.	Behold the Savior of Mankind [SATB] (FMB 54) Holy Thursday: C
Viadana, L.	We Adore Thee, O Lord Christ [SATB] (OEA 33)
Victoria, T.L.	Surely He Bore Our Sorrows [SATB] (RS 155)
Willan, H.	The Responsory for Passiontide [SA] (WP2 32)

Patriotism

| Holst, G. | I Vow to Thee, My Country [U] (Curwen 71632) |
| Vaughan Williams, R. | Let Us Now Praise Famous Men [HB 530] |

Pentecost

Attwood, T.	Come, Holy Ghost [SATB] (CAB 66; Novello 29 0223 00)
Bach, J.S.	All People At This Hour [SATB] (OEA 78)
	Now Do We Pray God, the Holy Ghost [SATB] (BC1 12) {Nun bitten wir}
	Come, Holy Ghost, God and Lord [SATB] (BC2 7) {Komm, heiliger Geist}

Bender, J.   Creator Spirit, By Whose Aid [SATB]
                              (CH2 78) {All Ehr und Lob}
Bissell, K.   O Holy Spirit [SA] (OC 40)
Charpentier, M.-A.   O Come, Creator Spirit, Come [U] (MS2
                              72)
Des Prez, J.   Come, O Creator Spirit, Come [SATB]
                              (FMB 68)
Distler, H.   We Now Implore the Holy Ghost [SSA]
                              (MS2 70) {Nun bitten wir}
                              Come, Holy Ghost, Creator Blest [SATB]
                              (Concordia 98-2360) {Komm, Gott
                              Schöpfer} Pentecost: B
Drischner, M.   O Holy Spirit, Enter In [U] (MJ 22) {Wie
                              schön leuchtet}
                              O Spirit of Life, O Spirit of God [U] (MJ
                              16) {O Jesulein süss}
                              O Holy Spirit, Grant Us Grace [U] (MJ 6)
                              {Aus tiefer Not II}
Franck, M.   Father, Thy Holy Spirit Send [SATB]
                              (E.C.Schirmer 1687)
Gibbons, O.   Song 44 [SATB] (AC1 46)
                              Holy Ghost, With Light Divine [SATB]
                              (WHD 9) {Song 13}
Harris, W.H.   Come Down, O Love Divine [SATB]
                              (Novello 19423) {North Petherton}
Hurford, P.   Litany to the Holy Spirit [U] (AC2 98)
Ley, H.G.,arr.   Come, Thou Holy Spirit, Come [SATB]
                              (CAB 73)
Monteverdi, C.   Come, O Creator Spirit, Come [SAB] (GB
                              72)
Noble, T.T.   Come, O Creator Spirit, Come [SATB]
                              (CAB 70)
Palestrina, G.P.   Come, Thou Holy Spirit, Come [SATB
                              SATB] (OEA 80)
                              Come, Holy Ghost, Our Souls Inspire
                              [SATB] (PCB 53)
Ridout, A.   A Pure River of Water of Life [SATB]
                              (AC4 63)
Rorem, N.   Today the Holy Spirit Appeared [SATB]
                              (Boosey & Hawkes 6447)

Schalk, C.	O Holy Spirit, Enter In [SB] (CR1 9) {Wie schön leuchtet}
	Come, Holy Ghost, Our Souls Inspire [SAB] (CR3 28) {Veni creator spiritus}
Schein, J.H.	Come, Holy Ghost, God and Lord [SAB] (MS3 87) {Komm, heiliger Geist}
Tallis, T.	O Lord, Give Thy Holy Spirit [SATB] (E.C.Schirmer 1718)
T.Davie, C.	Come, Holy Ghost, the Maker [SATB] (Oxford University Press A98)
Victoria, T.L.	And When the Day of Pentecost Was Yet Come [SSATB] (RS 118)
Wagner, G.G.	O Holy Spirit, Enter In [SATB] (CH1 64)
Willan, H.	Come, Souls, Behold Today [U] (CS 45) {Kommt, Seelen, diesen Tag}
	Holy Spirit, Hear Us [SA] (WP1 46) {Gute Bäume bringen}
	The Spirit of the Lord [SATB] (SMB 78; Concordia 98-1013) Pentecost: C
Wolff, S.D.	Come, Holy Spirit, Come [SS] (MS1 75)

Presentation

Bramma, H.	God Is Light [SATB] (Roger Dean HRD 246)
Eccard/Davis	When to the Temple Mary Went [SA] (GH 91)
Schalk, C.	In Peace and Joy I Now Depart [SB] (CR2 11) {Mit Fried und Freud}

St. Peter

| Britten, B. | Hymn to St. Peter [SATB] (Boosey & Hawkes) |
| Gibbons, O. | Almighty God, Who By Thy Son [SAATB] (Oxford TCM 37) |

Thanksgiving

| Argento, D. | A Thanksgiving to God [SATB] (Boosey & Hawkes 6026) |

Bach, J.S.	Now Thank We All Our God [SATB] (BC2 13) {Nun danket}
	Now Thank We All Our God [SATB] (Cantata 79) (Novello 29 0494 02) {Nun danket}
Bach/Carlton	Now Thank We All Our God [SATB] (Theodore Presser 312-41338)
Bullock, E.,arr.	Give Laud Unto the Lord [SATB] (OEA 64)
Coleman, H.	Ye Servants of God [SATB] (OEA 108) {Paderborn}
Cope, C.	Pleasure It Is [SB] (OEA 88)
Davis, K.K.	Let All Things Now Living [SATB] (E.C.Schirmer 1770) {The Ash Grove}
	Let All Things Now Living [U w/d] (E.C.Schirmer 1819) {The Ash Grove}
	Prayer of Thanksgiving [SATB] (E.C.Schirmer 1040) {Kremser}
Decius/Davis	To God on High Be Thanks and Praise [SA] (GH 82)
Gilbert, N.	Let All the World [U, 2-part or 3-part] (OEA 119)
Kremser/Davis	We Gather Together [SA] (GH 88) {Kremser}
Mendelssohn, F.	Thanks Be to God [SATB] ("Elijah") (G.Schirmer 3742)
Pachelbel, J.	Now Thank We All Our God [SATB] (Concordia 98-1944) {Nun danket}
Rachmaninov/Davis	Triumph! Thanksgiving [SA] (GH 84)
Roff, J.	A Song of Thanksgiving [SATB] (CH1 19)
Willan, H.	Sing to the Lord of Harvest [SA] (CS 6) {Wie lieblich ist der Maien}
	Sing to the Lord of Harvest [SATB] (CH1 26; PCB 19) {Wie lieblich ist der Maien} Thanksgiving: B
	Sing to the Lord of Harvest [SATB] (Concordia 98-2013) {Wie lieblich ist der Maien} Thanksgiving: C

Willan, H.	We Praise Thee, O God [U] (WP1 7) Now Thank We All Our God [SATB] (C.F.Peters 6588) {Nun danket}
Wolff, S.D.	Come, You Thankful People, Come [SATB, Cong.] (Concordia 98-2636) {St. George}

Transfiguration

Böbel, K.	Down From the Mount of Glory [SATB] (SG 43) {Ich freu mich in dem Herren}
Wood, C.	O Wondrous Type! O Vision Fair! [SATB] (SG 42) {Deo gracias}

Trinity

	[*See also* Isaiah 6]
Bach, J.S.	All Glory Be to God on High [SATB] (BC1 1) {Allein Gott in der Höh sei Ehr}
Bender, J.	Holy, Holy, Holy [U] (MS2 73)
Bissell, K.	Holy, Holy, Holy [SSA] (OC 39)
Bunjes, P.G.	Holy, Holy, Holy [U] (PCB 60) Alleluia to the Triune Majesty [SATB] (CH1 66) {Hyfrydol}
Crüger, J.	Father Most Holy [SATB] (CH1 68)
Dering, R.	Two Seraphim [SS] (AC2 6)
Franck, J.W.	Break Forth in Praise to God [SATB] (CH2 82)
Leighton, K.	A Hymn to the Trinity [SSATB] (AC4 67)
Oldroyd, G.	Ye Watchers and Ye Holy Ones [SB or SATB] (OEA 84) {Lasst uns erfreuen}
Palestrina/Davis	Glory to God [SA] (GH 27)
Reger, M.	We Bless the Father and the Son and the Holy Ghost [SATB] (SMB 85)
Sateren, L.B.	Praise We God the Father's Name [SATB] (PCB 17)
Schubert, F.	Holy, Holy, Holy [SATB] (CAB 154)
Stainer, J.	I Saw the Lord [SATB SATB] (Novello)
Tchaikovsky, P.I.	Holy, Holy, Holy [SATB] (CAB 155; E.C.Schirmer 1779)

Tchaikovsky, P.I.	Hymn to the Trinity [SATB] (Novello 29 0236 02)
Turner, C.K.	O Trinity, Most Blessed Light [SATB] (AC1 159)
Vulpius, M.	We All Believe in One True God [SATB] (PCB 62)
Willan, H.	Bless We the Father, the Son, and the Holy Ghost [SA] (WP2 50)
	Father, We Praise Thee [SATB] (C.F.Peters 6125) {Christe sanctorum} Trinity: C
	Glory to the Father Give [SSA] (WP1 48) {Gott sei dank}
	Holy, Holy, Holy Is the Lord of Hosts [SSA] (WP1 50)
	Holy, Holy, Holy [U] (MS1 78)
	O Trinity of Blessed Light [SATB] (C.F.Peters 6252) {St. Venantius}
Wolff, S.D.	I Bind Unto Myself Today [SATB, Cong.] (Concordia 98-2373) {St. Patrick's Breastplate}

Unity

Schalk, C.	In Adam We Have All Been One [SB] (CR2 26) {The Saints' Delight}

Wedding

Bach/Davis	O Father, All Creating [SA] (GH 58)
Davies, H. W.	Blessed Are the Pure in Heart [SATB] (CAB 17)
	God Be in My Head [SATB] (CAB 114)
Finzi, G.	My Lovely One [SATB] (Boosey & Hawkes)
Rutter, J.	God Be in My Head [SATB] (Oxford University Press 94.326)
Walton, W.	Set Me as a Seal [SATB] (AC4 82)

Index of Hymn Tunes

V. APPENDICES

Organ Works Cited

(Other than chorale preludes; numbers in the second column indicate approximate timings; works suitable as postludes are marked PST)

Alain, J.	5:00		Deux Chorales (Herelle P2342) 11 Sep: C Dorien (2:00) Phrygien (3:00)
			Trois Pièces (Leduc 19744) 11 Sep: C
	6:30		Variations sur un thème de Clément Janequin
	3:30		Le Jardin suspendu
	4:30	PST	Litanies
			Variations sur Lucis Creator (Leduc 20184)
Arne, T.	15:00		Organ Concerto in G Minor (English Organ Music, Hinrichsen 293:15) Epiphany 6: B
Araujo, F.	5:30		Tiento (HOR 6:30, G. Schirmer) 12 Jun: A
Bach, C.P.E.	19:30		Sonata V (Harmonia: Preludium and Six Sonatas: 34) Epiphany 5: C
	14:00		Sonata VI (Harmonia: Preludium and Six Sonatas: 44) 12 Jun: B

Bach, J.S.	5:00	PST	Allabreve in D Major, BWV 589 (BA 5057: 114) 13 Nov: C
	5:00	PST	Canzona in D Minor, BWV 588 (BA 5057: 118) Epiphany 6: A
	4:00	PST	Concerto in C Major, BWV 595 (BA 5051: 65) 13 Nov: A
	20:00		Concerto in C Major, BWV 594 (BA 5051: 30) 23 Oct: A
	11:00		Concerto in D Minor, BWV 596 (BA 5051: 3) 13 Nov: A
	8:00		Concerto in G Major, BWV 592 (BA 5051: 56) Easter 7: C
	12:00		Concerto in A Minor, BWV 593 (BA 5051: 16) 13 Nov: C
	3:00	PST	Fantasia in C Major, BWV 570 (BA 5025: 16) 13 Nov: C
	9:00		Fantasia in G Major, BWV 572 (BA 5057: 130) Thanksgiving: C
	4:00	PST	Fantasia in B Minor, BWV 563 (BA 5025: 68) Epiphany 8: A
	13:00		Fantasia and Fugue in C Minor, BWV 537 (BA 5028: 47) Epiphany 9: A
	11:30		Fantasia and Fugue in G Minor, BWV 535 (BA 5028: 167) Epiphany 7: C

Bach, J.S.	7:00		Fugue in C Minor on a Theme of Legrenzi, BWV 574 (BA 5025: 19) Lent 3: C
	4:00	PST	Fugue in C Minor, BWV 575 (BA 5025: 26) 23 Oct: C
	4:30	PST	Fugue in G Major, BWV 577 (Jig)
	4:00	PST	Fugue in G Minor, BWV 578 (BA 5025: 55) 18 Sep: C
	5:00	PST	Fugue in B Minor on a theme of Corelli, BWV 579 (BA 5025: 71) Epiphany 4: A
	14:00		Passacaglia and Fugue in C Minor, BWV 582 (BA 5057: 98) 20 Nov: B
	13:30		Pastorale in F Major, BWV 590 (BA 5057: 122) Advent 2: C
	7:00		Prelude and Fugue in C Major, BWV 531 (BA 5028: 3) 28 Aug: A
	7:00		Prelude and Fugue in C Major, BWV 545 (BA 5028: 10) 29 May: A
	11:30		Prelude and Fugue in C Major, BWV 547 (BA 5028: 20) 23 Oct: A
	12:00		Prelude and Fugue in C Minor, BWV 546 (BA 5028: 35) Epiphany 6: A

Bach, J.S.   7:30   Prelude and Fugue in C Minor,
                              BWV 549 (BA 5028: 30)
                              Transfiguration: C

                  13:00   Prelude and Fugue in D Major,
                              BWV 532 (BA 5028: 58) 19 Jun:
                              A

                  7:30   Prelude and Fugue in D Minor,
                              BWV 539 (BA 5028: 70) 10 Jul:
                              A

                  12:00   Prelude and Fugue in E Major,
                              BWV 566 (BA 5025: 40) 31 Jul:
                              A

                  7:00   Prelude and Fugue in E Minor,
                              BWV 533 (Cathedral) (BA 5028:
                              90) 2 Oct: B

                  15:00   Prelude and Fugue in E Minor,
                              BWV 548 (Wedge) (BA 5028: 94)
                              23 Oct: A

                  17:00   Prelude and Fugue in E Flat
                              Major, BWV 552 (BA 5033: 2)
                              Trinity: A

                  8:00   Prelude and Fugue in F minor,
                              BWV 534 (BA 5028: 130) 29
                              May: C

                  8:00   Prelude and Fugue in G Major,
                              BWV 550 (BA 5028: 138) 28
                              Aug: A

                  8:00   Prelude and Fugue in G Major,
                              BWV 541 (BA 5028: 146) Lent 3:
                              B

Bach, J.S.   8:00   Prelude and Fugue in G Minor,
                               BWV 535 (BA 5028: 157) 17 Jul:
                               B

               7:00   Prelude and Fugue in A Major,
                               BWV 536 (BA 5028: 180) Easter
                               5: A

               11:00   Prelude and Fugue in A Minor,
                               BWV 543 (BA 5028: 186)
                               Epiphany 8: C

               5:00   PST   Prelude and Fugue in A Minor,
                               BWV 569 (BA 5025: 59) Lent 3:
                               A

               6:00   Prelude and Fugue in A Minor,
                               BWV 551 (BA 5025: 63) Easter
                               5: C

               12:30   Prelude and Fugue in B Minor,
                               BWV 544 (BA 5028: 198) 29
                               May: B

               16:00   Sonata I in E Flat Major, BWV
                               525 (BA 5057: 2) Epiphany 4: A

               14:00   Sonata II in C Minor, BWV 526
                               (BA 5057: 14) 18 Sep: A

               16:00   Sonata III in D Minor, BWV 527
                               (BA 5057: 28) Epiphany 4: B

               10:00   Sonata IV in E Minor, BWV 528
                               (BA 5057: 44) 18 Sep: B

               16:00   Sonata V in C Major, BWV 529
                               (BA 5057: 56) 18 Sep: C

Bach, J.S.	18:00		Sonata VI in G Major, BWV 530 (BA 5057: 76) Epiphany 4: C
	14:00		Toccata, Adagio and Fugue in C Major, BWV 564 (BA 5025: 3) Easter: B
	9:00		Toccata and Fugue in D Minor, BWV 565 (BA 5025: 31) Easter: C
	13:00		Toccata and Fugue (Dorian) in D Minor, BWV 538 (BA 5028: 76) Epiphany 4: C
	15:00		Toccata and Fugue in F Major, BWV 540 (BA 5028: 112) Easter 2: A
	5:00		Trio in D Minor, BWV 583 (BA 5057: 94) 18 Sep: B
Bach, W.F.	2:00	PST	Fugue in C Minor (Peters 8010a: 7) Epiphany 5: A
	6:00		Fugue in C Minor (Kalmus 3110: 15) 17 Jul: B
	3:00		Fugue in Eb Major (Peters 8010a: 14) Epiphany 25: A
	2:00	PST	Fugue in E Minor (Peters 8010a: 17) 19 Jun: A
	4:00		Fugue in F Major (Kalmus 3110: 23) 17 Jul: B
	2:00	PST	Fugue in F Minor (Peters 8010a: 22) 10 Jul: A

Bach, W.F.	5:00		Fugue in A Minor "Alla Capella" (Kalmus 3110: 29) Easter 3: C
	2:30	PST	Fugue in Bb Major (Peters 8010a: 28) 6 Nov: C
	4:00	PST	Fugue in Bb Major (Kalmus 3110: 33) 12 Jun: B
Balbastre, C.	17:00		First Suite of Noels, Second Suite of Noels (selections) (Kalmus 3116, 3117) Advent 1: A
Bales, G.			Petite Suite II: Intermezzo (Berandol 1403)
Bissell, K.			Two Preludes for Organ (Waterloo)
Blow, J.	2:00		Voluntary in A Major (Novello, Early Organ Music, Book 2: 8) 26 Jun: A
	4:00		Echo Voluntary in G Major (Novello, Early Organ Music, Book 2: 12) 4 Sep: A
Böhm, G.	5:00		Prelude and Fugue in C Major (B&H 8087: 5) Epiphany 5: A
	5:30		Prelude in D Minor (B&H 8087: 10) 6 Nov: A
	3:00		Prelude and Fugue in A Minor (B&H 8087: 16) 6 Nov: A
Boëllmann, L.	4:00	PST	Suite Gothique: Toccata (G.Schirmer LB1763) 13 Nov: B

Boely, A.P.F.	15:00		Album of Noels (selections) (Kalmus 9781) Advent 4: B
Boyce, W.	3:30	PST	Voluntary I (Three 18th Century Voluntaries; Oxford 375321 9) Epiphany 6: B
Brahms, J.	9:00		Prelude and Fugue in G Minor (Peters 6333a) Lent 3: C
	5:30		Prelude and Fugue in Ab Minor (Peters 6333a: 22) Easter 5: C
	5:00		Chorale Prelude and Fugue on "O Traurigkeit, o Herzeleid" (Peters 6333a: 28) Good Friday: B
Britten, B.	6:00		Prelude and Fugue on a Theme of Vittoria (Boosey & Hawkes 17194)
Bruckner, A.	2:00	PST	Postlude in D Minor (Orgelwerke: Doblinger DM 364: 6) 24 Jul: A
	3:00	PST	Prelude and Fugue in C Minor (Orgelwerke: Doblinger DM 364: 10) 23 Oct: A
Bruhns, N.	10:00		Prelude in E Minor (Peters 4855: 11) Easter 2: B
	5:00		Prelude in E Minor (Peters 4855: 20) Epiphany 21: B
	10:00		Prelude in G Major (Peters 4855: 1) Epiphany 5: A
	5:00	PST	Prelude and Fugue in G Minor (Peters 4855: 35) Easter 2:B

Buxtehude, D.	5:30		Canzona in C Major (B&H 6662: 158) Epiphany 6: C
	4:00		Canzona in D Minor (B&H 6662: 164) Epiphany 8: C
	3:30	PST	Canzona in G Major (B&H 6662: 170) 4 Jun: A
	2:30	PST	Canzonetta in E Minor (B&H 6662: 168) 4 Jun: C
	2:30	PST	Canzonetta in G Major (B&H 6662: 174) Epiphany 2: B
	2:30	PST	Canzonetta in G Major (B&H 6662: 176) 19 Jun: B
	7:00		Chaconne in C Minor (B&H 6662: 123) 14 Aug: C
	5:30		Chaconne in E Minor (B&H 6662: 129) 4 Sep: B
	3:00	PST	Fugue in C Major (Jig) (B&H 6662: 180) 14 Aug: C
	3:00	PST	Fugue in G Major (B&H 6662: 184) Epiphany 5: C
	3:30	PST	Fugue in Bb Major (B&H 6662: 186) Epiphany 6: C
	6:00		Passacaglia in D Minor (B&H 6662: 134) Epiphany 2: B
	5:30		Prelude in C Major (B&H 6661: 1) 12 Jun: C

Buxtehude, D.	3:00		Prelude in C Major (B&H 6661: 11) Epiphany 6: C
	6:00		Prelude in D Major (B&H 6661: 15) 31 Jul: C
	5:30		Prelude in D Minor (B&H 6661: 20) 31 Jul: C
	6:30		Prelude in E Major (B&H 6661: 25) 3 Jul: C
	5:00		Prelude in E Minor (B&H 6661: 40) 3 Jul: C
	3:00	PST	Prelude in F Major (B&H 6661: 45) Epiphany 8: C
	5:00		Prelude in G Major (B&H 6662: 139) 12 Jun: C
	7:00		Prelude in G Minor (B&H 6662: 144) 24 Jul: B
	4:00		Prelude in A Minor (B&H 6661: 90) 4 Jun: C
	4:30		Prelude in A Minor (B&H 6662: 119) 3 Jul: C
	5:00		Prelude and Fugue in D Major (B&H 6661: 15) 4 Sep: B
	5:00		Prelude and Fugue in D Minor (B&H 6661: 20) Trinity: C
	6:00		Prelude and Fugue in E Major (B&H 6661: 25) 14 Aug: A

Buxtehude, D.	8:00	Prelude and Fugue in E Minor (B&H 6661: 31) 4 Jun: A
	4:30	Prelude and Fugue in E Minor (B&H 6661: 40) 3 Jul: A
	6:30	Prelude and Fugue in F Major (B&H 6661: 48) 7 Aug: A
	8:00	Prelude and Fugue in F# Minor (B&H 6661: 55) 14 Aug: C
	3:00	Prelude and Fugue in G Major (B&H 6661: 62) 4 Sep: B
	7:30	Prelude and Fugue in G Minor (B&H 6661:65) Epiphany 6: C
	7:30	Prelude and Fugue in G Minor (B&H 6661: 72) Epiphany 2: B
	7:00	Prelude and Fugue in G Minor (B&H 6661: 80) 19 Jun: B
	5:30	Prelude and Fugue in A Major (B&H 6661: 86) 4 Jun: C
	6:00	Prelude and Fugue in A Minor (B&H 6661: 90) 16 Oct: A
	6:00	Prelude in A Minor (B&H 6661: 94) 16 Oct: B
	5:00	Prelude, Fugue and Chaconne in C Major (B&H 6661: 6) 4 Jun: A
	7:00	Toccata in D Minor (B&H 6662: 99) 24 Jul: B

Buxtehude, D.	8:00		Toccata in F Major (B&H 6662: 106) 19 Jun: B
	2:30	PST	Toccata in G Major (B&H 6662: 152) 24 Jul: B
	5:30		Toccata in G Major (B&H 6662: 154) 4 Jun: C
	5:00		Toccata and Fugue in F Major (B&H 6662: 114) 3 Jul: A
Cabanilles, J.			Pasacalles de I° Tono (Müller 2676SM)
	2:30		Tiento (G.Schirmer 1666: 37) 7 Aug: A
	4:00		Tiento 5° tono (G.Schirmer 1666: 43) 12 Jun: A
	2:00		Tiento de falsas (G.Schirmer 1666: 40) 12 Jun: A
Cabena, Barrie			Sonata Festiva (Jaymar)
			Sonata for Manuals Only (Jaymar)
	9:00		Sonata Giojoso (Waterloo)
Cabezon, A.	2:00		Christmas Carol (G.Schirmer 1666: 3) Christmas: B
			Diferencias sobre el Canto del Caballero (HOR I,5)
	5:00		Tiento del Quinto Tono (Four Tientos: Kalmus 4477: 1) 12 Jun: A

Cabezon, A.	3:00	PST	Tiento del Quinto Tono transportado (Kalmus 4477: 5)
	4:00		Tiento del Segundo Tono (Kalmus 4477: 8) 26 Jun: C
	3:00	PST	Tiento del Octavo Tono (Kalmus 4477: 11) 20 Nov: B
	3:00	PST	Variations on the Milanese Galliard (G.Schirmer 1666: 6) 16 Oct: B
Carvalho, J.	5:00		Allegro (Silva Iberica: Schott 2415: 22) 7 Aug: A
Cernohorsky, B.			Fugue in D (A Century of Czech Music; Fitzsimmons B55)
			Fugue in A (Fitzsimmons B55)
Charpentier, M.	19:00		Noels (Concordia 979-5404) Advent 1: B
Clérambault, L.N.	15:00		Suite du 1er ton (Kalmus 3308 or Schola Cantorum) 30 Oct: A
	17:00		Suite du 2me ton (Kalmus 3308 or Schola Cantorum) All Saints: B
Couperin, F.	20:30		Messe des Paroisses (selections) (Kalmus 3314) 11 Sep: B
	15:00		Messe pour les Convents (selections) (Kalmus 3315) 11 Sep: A
Dandrieu, J.F.	16:30		Noëls (Schola Cantorum S5463P or Kalmus 3366) Advent 1: C

Daquin, L.	60:00	Noëls (Faber Music Limited) Advent 3:A, Advent 3: B, Advent 3: C
De Grigny, N.	23:00	Premier Livre d'orgue (selections) (Kalmus 4247 or Schola Cantorum 5212) Epiphany 3: A
Du Mage, P.	18:30	Livre d'orgue (Kalmus 4143) 16 Oct: C
Dupré, M.	15:00	Five Antiphons (Fifteen Pieces for Organ, Op.18; H.W.Gray) 2 Oct: A
	5:30	Cortège et Litanie, Op.19, No.2 (Leduc 16850) 2 Oct: A
	PST	"Gloria" from Ave Maris Stella (Fifteen Pieces for Organ, Op.18, H.W. Gray) Christmas 1:C
		Le Tombeau de Titelouze
	10:00	Prelude and Fugue in G Minor (Alphonse Leduc 16.405) 23 Sep: C
Duruflé, M.		Prelude, Adagio et Fugue sur Veni Creator (Durand 12016)
Eberlin, J.	5:30	Toccata and Fugue in G Minor (Novello: Early Organ Music, Book 2: 17) 10 Jul: A
Franck, C.	13:00	Chorale No.1 (Durand, Oeuvres complètes, Vol.4) Easter 4: B
	17:00	Chorale No.2 (Durand, Oeuvres complètes, Vol. 4) Easter 7: A

Franck, C.	12:30		Chorale No.3 (Durand, Oeuvres complètes, Vol. 4) Easter 2: C
	5:00		Five Noels from l'Organiste (Concordia 99-5552) Christmas: A
	9:00		Pastorale (Durand & Cie) Epiphany 2: C
Frescobaldi, G.	2:30		Missa della Apostoli: Toccata per l'Elevazione (BA 2205: 42) Epiphany 5: B
	2:00		Missa della Madonna: Canzona dopo l'Epistola (BA 2205: 53) Epiphany 5: B
	5:00	PST	Toccata Sesta (Kalmus 3453 or BA 2203: 20) Epiphany 5: B
Froberger, J.J.			Capriccio in F Major (Coppenrath)
			Fantasia sopra Ut,Re,Mi,Fa,So,La (Coppenrath)
			Toccata VIII (Coppenrath)
			Toccata IX (Coppenrath)
Gabrieli, A.	2:30		Canzon Francese on "Martin Menoit" (BA 1782: 14) 26 Jun: B
	2:30		Canzon Francese on "Orsus au Loup" (BA 1782: 21) Easter 4: C
	2:00		Canzon Francese on "Pour ung Plaisir" (BA 1782: 27) Epiphany 2: C

Gabrieli, A.	4:30	PST	Ricercar on "Martin Menoit" (BA 1782: 17) 26 Jun: B
	4:00	PST	Ricercar on "Orsus au Loup" (BA 1782: 24) Easter 4: C
	3:30	PST	Ricercar on "Pour ung Plaisir" (BA 1782: 29) Epiphany 2: C
Gibbons, O.	6:00		A Fancy for Double Orgaine (Hinrichsen 1583A)
Gigout, E.		PST	Toccata (Marks) 10 Jul: B
Greene, M.	4:00		Voluntary No. 8 in C Minor (Three 18th Century Voluntaries; Oxford 375321 9) 16 Jun: A
	2:30		Voluntary No. 13 (Novello: Early Organ Music, Volume 2: 1) 26 Jun: A
Handel, G.F.	6:30		Suite for a Musical Clock (Flammer) 26 Jun: A
	2:30		Voluntary 1 (Twelve Voluntaries and Fugues, Concordia 97-5840, p.5) Epiphany 9: C
	3:00		Voluntary 2 (p.8)
	3:30		Voluntary 3 (p.12)
	3:30	PST	Voluntary 4 (p.17) Easter 2: C
	2:00		Voluntary 5 (p.21) 3 Jul: B
	2:30		Voluntary 6 (p.23) Easter 6: C
	3:00		Voluntary 7 (p.27) 31 Jul: C

Handel, G.F.	3:00	PST	Voluntary 8 (p.31) Easter 5: C
	3:00	PST	Voluntary 9 (p.35) 29 May: C
	2:00	PST	Voluntary 10 (p.39) 31 Jul: B
	3:00	PST	Voluntary 11 (p.43) 19 Jun: C
	3:00	PST	Voluntary 12 (p.48) 10 Jul: C
Haydn, F.J.	9:00		The Musical Clocks (H.W. Gray)
Healey, D.			Three Preludes on French Hymn Tunes (Novello 19408)
Hindemith, P.	17:00		Sonata I (Schott 2557) 6 Nov: B
	11:30		Sonata II (Schott 2558) 6 Nov: C
			Sonata III (Schott 3736)
Honegger, A.			Two Pieces (Chester 3026)
Ibert, J.			Trois Pièces (Heugel 27.663)
Krebs, J.L.			Fantasia à giusto italiano (Peters 8122)
	7:00		Prélude in F# (Peters 4179) Epiphany 3: C
Langlais, J.			Neuf Pièces (Bornemann 5337)
	3:00	PST	Organ Book: Pasticcio (Elkan-Vogel) Epiphany 5: B
			Poèmes Evangéliques (Philippo 2359)

Langlais, J.		PST	Postlude I (McLaughlin & Reilly 1798) 25 Sep: C
		PST	Postlude II (McLaughlin & Reilly 1798) 11 Sep: A
	16:00		Suite Médiévale (Salabert RL12360) 13 Nov: B
Le Bègue, N.	24:00		First Book of Noels (Kalmus 4156) Advent 2: A
	1:30		Elevation in G Major (Kalmus 4156: 236) 10 Jul: B
	2:00		Elevation in G Major (Kalmus 4156: 244) 13 Nov: B
	1:30		Elevation in G Minor (Kalmus 4156: 238) Epiphany 2: C
	1:30		Elevation in A Major (Kalmus 4156: 241) 29 May: C
	1:30		Elevation in Bb Major (Kalmus 4156: 242) 24 Jul: B
	1:30		Première Elevation (Kalmus 4156: 25) Epiphany 2: C
Lidon, J.	4:00		Sonata de I° tono (Schott 4218: 28) 7 Aug: C
Liszt, F.	15:00		Prelude and Fugue on B-A-C-H (Boosey & Hawkes) Epiphany 9: B
Lübeck, V.	6:30		Prelude in C Major (B&H 6673: 6) 30 Oct: A

Lübeck, V.	9:30		Prelude in D Minor (B&H 6673: 16) Easter 3: C
	5:30		Prelude in E Major (B&H 6673: 24) Easter 6: C
	3:30	PST	Prelude in F Major (B&H 6673: 30) Epiphany 7: C
	5:30		Prelude in G Major (B&H 6673: 34) Transfiguration: C
	7:30		Prelude in G Minor (B&H 6673: 40) 10 Jul: B
	5:00		Prelude and Fugue in C Minor (B&H 6673: 12) Epiphany 1: C
	5:30		Prelude and Fugue in E Major (B&H 6673: 24) Epiphany 7: C
	3:30		Prelude and Fugue in F Major (B&H 6673: 30) 13 Nov: A
	5:30		Prelude and Fugue in G Major (B&H 6673: 34) Lent 2: C
Marcello, B.		PST	Psalm 19 (PO 9:8) Easter 7: C
Martini, G.B.	3:00		All'Elevatione (Italian Organ Music of the 18th Century; Flammer 5085: 17) Epiphany 5: B
Martini, G.B.	5:00		Theme and Variations (Graveyard Gems, St. Mary's Press) 19 Jun: B
Mendelssohn, F.	8:00		Prelude and Fugue in C Minor (G.Schirmer 976: 96) 25 Sep: B

Mendelssohn, F.	8:30	Prelude and Fugue in D Minor (G.Schirmer 976: 117) Epiphany 3: B
		Two Pieces (Novello)
	15:30	Sonata I (G.Schirmer 976: 1) Lent 5: C
	10:00	Sonata III (G.Schirmer 976: 33) Lent 5: A
	15:30	Sonata VI (G.Schirmer 976: 76) Easter 7: B
Messiaen, O.	4:00	Le Banquet Céleste (Leduc 22893) Epiphany 5: B
		La Nativité du Seigneur (4 vols., Leduc 19.268)
Milford, R.		Pastorale Dance: "On Christmas Night" (Oxford)
Milhaud, D.		Pastorale (H.W.Gray)
		Petite Suite (Max Eschig [Paris])
Morel, F.		Prière (Berandol 1421)
Mozart, W.A.	12:00	Adagio, Allegro (und Adagio) (Drei Stücke für Orgel, Bärenreiter Ausgabe 1868, p.6) Easter 2: B
		Fantasie (p.18)
	6:30	Andante (p.36)

Muffat, G.	12:00		Passacaglia in G Minor (C.F.Peters 6020: 66) 20 Nov: A
	5:30		Toccata No.3 in A Minor (Peters 6020: 9)
	6:00		Toccata No. 11 in C Minor (C.F.Peters 6020: 53) Thanksgiving: A
Mulet, H.		PST	Carillon-Sortie (Schola Cantorum or Marks) Easter 7: A
			Esquisses Byzantines (Leduc 16202)
Pachelbel, J.	7:00		Ciacona in D Major (BA 6444:6)
	6:00		Ciacona in D Minor (BA 238: 46) 25 Sep: B
	6:30		Ciacona in F Minor (BA 238: 54) Pentecost: A
	2:00		Fantasia (BA 238: 12) 10 Jul: A
	2:00		Fantasia in D Minor (BA 6444: 17) 19 Jun: B
	2:00		Fantasia in Eb Major (BA 6444: 19) Epiphany 4: C
	2:30	PST	Fugue in C Major (BA 6444: 21) Transfiguration: C
		PST	Fugue in C Major (BA 6444: 24) Easter 3: C
	2:00	PST	Fugue in C Major (BA 238: 37) 31 Jul: A

Pachelbel, J.	2:00	PST	Fugue in C Minor (BA 5494: 34) Epiphany 4: A
		PST	Fugue in E Minor (BA 6444: 28) 12 Jun: C
		PST	Fugue in G Major (BA 6444: 26) Easter 6: C
	2:30	PST	Fugue in G Minor (BA 5492: 31) 6 Nov: B
	2:30	PST	Fugue in A Minor (BA 5494: 26) Epiphany 4: C
		PST	Fugue in B Minor (BA 6444: 30) 17 Jul: C
	2:00		Prelude and Fugue in E Minor (BA 5494: 3) 3 Jul: A
	3:00	PST	Toccata in C Major (BA 238: 14) Epiphany 7: B
	1:30		Toccata in C Major (BA 6444: 4) Epiphany 6: C
	2:00	PST	Toccata in C Minor (BA 238: 24) 7 Aug: A
	2:00	PST	Toccata in G Minor (BA 5494: 14) 3 Jul: A
	2:00	PST	Toccata in G Minor (BA 5494: 16) 18 Sep: A
	2:00	PST	Toccata and Fugue in Bb Major (BA 5494: 5) Epiphany 8: A

Pasquini, B.	2:00	PST	Partite sopra la Aria della Folia da Espagna (Schott 4215: 17) 7 Aug: C
Persichetti, V.			Chorale Prelude: Drop, drop slow tears (Elkan-Vogel)
Pescetti, G.B.			Sonata in C Minor (Oxford)
Pinkham, D.			A Prophecy for Organ (Schirmer ECS 2135)
Preston, S.			Alleluyas (Modern Organ Music; Oxford 375141 0)
Purcell, H.	1:30		Verse in F Major (Novello: Organ Works: 2) [Now thought to be by Le Bègue] 26 Jun: A
	5:30		Voluntary for Double Organ (Novello: Organ Works: 7) 21 Aug: A
	1:30		Voluntary in C Major (Novello: Organ Works: 3) 4 Sep: C
	4:00		Voluntary in D Minor (Novello: Organ Works: 4) Epiphany 9: C
	3:00		Voluntary in G Major (Novello: Organ Works: 13) Epiphany 6: B
	3:00		Voluntary on Doxology (Novello: Organ Works: 16) Thanksgiving: A
Raison, A.	9:00		Noels (Selections) (Various Compositions for Organ; Kalmus) Christmas 1: A

Reger, M.	Choralvorspiele, Op.135a (Peters 3980)
3:30	Intermezzo, Op.80, No.10 (Peters 3064b) Lent 1: B
	Pastorale, Op.59, No.2 (Peters 3008a)
16:00	Six Trios, Op.47 (Kalmus 9096) 10 Jul: C
	Toccata and Fugue in D Major (Peters 3008G)
Reubke, J.	Allegro (Fugue) (Oxford)
Rheinberger, J.	Sonata No. 3 in G Major (Kalmus)
	Sonata No. 7 in F Minor (Kalmus)
2:00	Trio No. 1 (Ten Trios, Op.49, Kalmus 3794) 12 Jun: B
2:00	Trio No. 2, 17 Jul: B
2:00	Trio No. 3, 6 Nov: B
2:00	Trio No. 4, Epiphany 5: C
2:00	Trio No. 5, Epiphany 8: C
2:00	Trio No. 6, Transfiguration: C
2:00	Trio No. 7, Easter 3: C
2:00	Trio No. 8, Easter 5: C

Rheinberger, J.	2:00		Trio No. 9, Easter 7: C
	2:00		Trio No. 10, 4 Jun: C
Robinson, J.			Voluntary in A (Novello EOM Book I)
Saint-Saëns, C.			Prelude and Fugue in C Major, Op.109, No.3 (Kalmus KO9970: 51)
	7:30		Prelude and Fugue in E Flat Major, Op.99, No.3 (Kalmus KO9970: 22) Epiphany 3: C
			Prelude and Fugue in B Major, Op.99, No.2 (Kalmus K09970) 12 June: C
Scheidt, S.			Cantico Sacro (Peters 11435)
			Hymnus de Adventus Domini (Peters 4393b)
Schroeder, H.	6:30		12 Organ Carols (Selections) (Concordia 97-5017) Christmas 1: C
Schumann, R.		PST	Six Fugues on BACH, Op.60, No.3 (Peters 2382: 22) Epiphany 9: B
Sessions, R.			Three Chorale Preludes (Marks 124)
Soler, A.			Sonata de Clarines (Müller WM 2236SM)

Stanley, J.	4:00		Voluntary in E Minor (Three Eighteenth-Century Voluntaries; Oxford) 4 Sep: C
	9:00		Voluntary in C Major (Hinrichsen 1033: 5) 3 Jul: B
		PST	Voluntary in D Major (Hinrichsen 1034: 25) Epiphany 9: C
	3:30		Voluntary in D Minor (Hinrichsen 1033: 12) Epiphany 9: C
	7:00		Voluntary in D Minor (Hinrichsen 1034: 20) 31 Jul: B
	4:00		Voluntary in E Minor (Hinrichsen 1033: 21) 19 Jun: C
	3:30	PST	Voluntary in E Minor (Hinrichsen 1034: 38) 3 Jul: B
	4:00	PST	Voluntary in E Minor (Hinrichsen 1035: 29) 31 Jul: B
	4:00		Voluntary in F Major (Hinrichsen 1035: 25) 4 Sep: A
	3:30	PST	Voluntary in G Major (Hinrichsen 1035: 38) 4 Sep: C
	4:30	PST	Voluntary in G Major (Hinrichsen 1033: 16) 4 Sep: A
	6:00		Voluntary in G Minor (Hinrichsen 1034: 41) Epiphany 9: C
	5:00		Voluntary in A Major (Hinrichsen 1035: 5) 4 Sep: C

Stanley, J.	5:30	Voluntary in A Minor (Hinrichsen 1034: 8) 3 Jul: B
	6:00	Voluntary in A Minor (Hinrichsen 1036: 33) 4 Sep: A
Sweelinck, J.P.	9:00	Chromatic Fantasy (Peters 4645a: 1) Lent 5: B
	4:00	Echo Fantasy (Dorian) (Peters 4645a: 34) 6 Nov: C
	3:30	Echo Fantasy (Aeolian) (Peters 4645a: 38) 5 Jun: B
	9:30	Fantasia B-A-C-H (Aeolian) (Peters 4645a: 8) Epiphany 8: A
		Mein junges Leben hat ein End (Peters 4645a: 52)
		Unter der Linden Grüne (Peters 4645a: 72)
Telemann, G.P.		Concerto per la Chiesa (Novello EOM 16)
		Sonata für Zwei Klaviere und Pedal (BA 3582)
Titelouze, J.	6:00	Ave Maris Stella (Kalmus 4139: 40) Epiphany 2: C
	7:00	Pange Lingua (Kalmus 4139: 26) 10 Jul: B
	6:00	Veni Creator (Kalmus 4139: 18) 29 May: C

Tunder, F.	3:30	Prelude in G Minor (Four Preludes, Organum, Vol.6, Fr. Kistner & C.F.W. Siegel, p.3) 26 Jun C
	4:00	Prelude in F Major (p.7) 26 Jun: C
	5:00	Prelude in G Minor (p.11) 26 Jun: C
	4:00	Prelude in G Minor (p.15) 26 Jun: C
Turner, R.		Six Voluntaries (Berandol 1423) 16 Oct: A
	2:00	Prelude
	2:30	Chorale
Valente, A.	1:30	La Romanesca (Schott 4215: 4) 7 Aug: C
Valeri, G.	5:00	Sonata No. 6 (Italian Organ: Flammer 5085: 8) Easter 7: C
	7:30	Sonata No. 8 (Italian Organ; Flammer 5085: 10) 27 Jun: B
Vierne, L.	3:30	Préambule (24 Pièces en style libre, Op.31, Vol.1, Durand 8973: 1) Epiphany 2: C
Walond, W.	5:00	Voluntary No. 2 in G Major (Hinrichsen 1770b: 1) 4 Sep: C
	7:00	Voluntary No. 4 in D Major (Hinrichsen 1770b: 6) 24 Jul: B
	8:30	Voluntary No. 6 in D Minor (Hinrichsen 1770b: 17) 21 Aug: A

Walther, J.G.	6:00		Concerto del Sigr.Albinoni (BA 1920: 5) Epiphany 8: A
	8:30		Concerto del Sigr.Meck (BA 1920: 17) Epiphany 8: B
	3:00	PST	Concerto del Sigr.Torelli in D Minor (BA 1920: 52) 30 Oct: A
	7:30		Concerto del Sigr.Torelli in A Minor (BA 1920: 40) 30 Oct: A
Widor, C.M.	5:00	PST	Toccata from Symphony No.5 (Kalmus 4033) 30 Oct: A
Willan, H.			A Fugal Trilogy (Oxford)
		PST	Finale Jubilante (Organ Music of Canada, Berandol, Volume 1, p.21)
Wuensch, G.			Toccata Piccola (Avant S9)
Yepes	3:00		Cançao (Schott 4215: 8) 7 Aug: C
Zachau, F.W.	4:00		Fugue (Three Fugues, Organum Vol.16, Fr. Kistner & C.F.W. Siegel, p.1) 17 Jul: C
	3:00		Prelude and Fugue (p.4) 17 Jul: C
	6:00		Fantasie (p.6) 17 Jul: C

Choral Works Cited

Bach, J.S.

Willan, H.

About the Compiler

ARTHUR WENK (A.B., Amherst College; M.A., Ph.D., Cornell University; M.S., University of Pittsburgh) is Director, Ministry of Music at Aurora United Church, Senior Mathematics Teacher at St. Andrew's College (Aurora, Ontario) and Director of the Toronto Camerata. He has taught at the University of Pittsburgh, Indiana University, and Université Laval (Québec). He has published numerous books and articles on the works of Claude Debussy, music history, generative grammars, and the relationships among the arts. His bibliography, *Analyses of 19th- and 20th-Century Music: 1940-1985*, won the Music Library Association Vincent Duckles Award for the best book-length bibliography of 1989. He has served as organist/choirmaster at Trinity Cathedral (Anglican) in Québec City and has founded and directed *a cappella* chamber choirs in Boston, Pittsburgh, and Québec City.